Praise for
The Answer Is Always Yes

A Booklist Top 10 First Novel of the Year

"Swings with experimental flare . . . The protagonist and prose recall the Richard Fariña/Tom Robbins school of writing. . . . A pyrotechnic debut."

—*Kirkus Reviews*

"From the smoke and mirrors of the New York club scene emerges Magic Matt, the Jay Gatsby of his generation. This painfully unpopular young man's fierce determination to reinvent himself as the hippest kid at NYU is, by turns, darkly comic and profoundly tragic. *The Answer Is Always Yes* is a stellar coming-of-age novel with a nifty, sinister postmodern twist. And it's a terrific read, an eloquent page-turner. How's that for some kind of wonderful?"

—Binnie Kirshenbaum, author of *An Almost Perfect Moment*
and *A Disturbance in One Place*

"Packed with poetry and humor, this dazzlingly written first novel unearths the sorrow behind that strange American sickness, the pursuit of cool. Like the city they eulogize, Ferrell's sentences teem with beauty and ambition— you want to linger at every turn."

—Eric Puchner, author of *Music Through the Floor*

"Ferrell is a good writer who understands hipster anxiety and the aspirations that New York manufactures with every generation."

—*Time Out*

"A stylized and exuberantly written debut novel . . . fabulous."

—*Publishers Weekly*

THE ANSWER IS
ALWAYS YES

Monica Ferrell

dial press trade paperbacks

2009 Dial Press Trade Paperback Edition

Published in the United States by Dial Press Trade Paperbacks, an
imprint of The Random House Publishing Group, a division of
Random House, Inc., New York.

DIAL PRESS and DIAL PRESS TRADE PAPERBACKS are registered
trademarks of Random House, Inc., and the colophon is a trademark
of Random House, Inc.

Originally published in hardcover in the United States by The Dial
Press, an imprint of The Random House Publishing Group, a division
of Random House, Inc., in 2008.

Words and Music of "Psycho Killer" by David Byrne, Christopher
Frantz and Tina Weymouth, copyright © 1976 (Renewed) by WB
Music Corp. (ASCAP) and Index Music, Inc. (ASCAP). All Rights
Administered by Alfred Publishing, Inc. All Rights Reserved.
Used by Permission.

Library of Congress Cataloging-in-Publication Data
Ferrell, Monica.
The answer is always yes / Monica Ferrell.
p. cm.
ISBN 978-0-385-33930-8 (trade pbk.) — 978-0-440-33774-4 (ebook)
1. Nightclubs —New York (State)—New York—Fiction. 2. Self-realization—Fiction.
3. College students—Fiction. 4. Rave culture—Fiction. I. Title.
PS3606.E7535A57 2008
813'.6—dc22   2008006627

Printed in the United States of America

www.dialpress.com

BVG   9 8 7 6 5 4 3 2 1

Cover art and design: Will Staehle

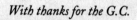

With thanks for the G.C.

THE ANSWER IS
ALWAYS YES

I began research on the story of Matthew Acciaccatura late in the summer of 1996, a few months after the media's extensive coverage of his rise and fall: a lifetime ago, it seems to me now. My project has been to shape the events surrounding him and the people connected with him in the period from September 1995 through April 1996 into a fictional recreation. Early on in my investigations, I became aware of another researcher talking to the same sources, walking the same trails around New York University and those night-clubs where the traces of our common subject were still to be found. I was curious about Hans Mannheim, a German sociologist and recent transplant to New York who apparently wanted to use Acciaccatura as the focus of a case study in his work on the socialization of misfits. Silently I applauded his zeal; I looked forward to reading a scholarly treatment of the subject that was en-grossing me; sometimes I half-expected to run into him, and even kept an eye out for the figure our shared sources described, a quiet man in his early thirties, of medium height, with fair hair, blue eyes, and a self-effacing demeanor—but our paths never crossed. It was not until Dr. Mannheim's arrest and arraign-ment for the killing of Terry Ford in April of 1997 that I finally reached out to him.

His response to that brief note sent to his detainment facility on Rikers Island has been extraordinary. In addition to parting generously with his time and copious data—including original interview cassettes and transcripts, photographs, and diverse material evidence—Dr. Mannheim, when given my completed manuscript for a final review, surprised me again with the insertion of numerous revelatory glosses and addenda. There seems to me no righter way to tell his remarkable piece of this story than to include these notes here in exactly the form in which he produced them.

M.F.

ONE

1.

The bedeviling notion that his new roommates would be in any position to mock him was instantly dispelled when Matt pushed open the door of Room 403. There at the end of a dim corridor, two figures stood silhouetted against a bright white wall: one large and broad-chested, his crossed arms fanning open now for a grand fool's wave, the other lumpish, painfully hunched, even from this distance visibly a noncontender. Matt moved closer, tennis sneakers smacking on the waxed wooden floor, eyes adjusting from the fluorescence of the dorm's outer hall. The big guy was actually wearing—dear God!—that purple freebie WELCOME NYU CLASS OF 1999 T-shirt they were giving away downstairs, a pair of khakis, puffy running sneakers, and a sublimely cheerful hick's grin. The smaller one, idol-still, was dressed in a brown button-down that hung over graying black jeans, his feet encased in orthopedicky black shoes, his pale head protruding like a mushroom. From the vector of his glasses, he seemed to be staring at the back of the first guy's head, an embarrassing, dreamy smile on his soft lips.

For a moment—ah, blessed moment, like hanging upside down on a swing while the whole blue-sky world spins, dizzyingly far below—Matt's stomach somersaulted, and everything warm and kind in him went gushing toward these two strangers. To think that as late as an hour ago, skimming above the steel-blue Hudson on the George Washington Bridge, he'd still been earnestly praying for a reprieve from this Dwight Smeethman of Somewhere, Minnesota and Joshua Cohn of Brooklyn, that some miracle could blind them from whatever chink there might be in his untried social armor. Please! *These* two? How innocent, helpless, like puppies trying to lick your hand from the gurney, where in minutes someone would come put them to sleep—or at least so the big hick seemed, waving manically, irrepressibly happy. Well. Clearly, fate was throwing the first pitch here underhand, a giant, innocuous softball. Shifting the cardboard box pressed to his chest and surreptitiously wiping a hand free of clamminess for his practiced high five, Matt stepped up.

Then, without warning, a series of small accidents happened.

Really, Matt had timed it expertly—just at the right moment raising his hand to meet that of the sandy-haired guy lunging forward—yet what he came crashing down on was the kid's forearm. A short struggle ensued as Matt's hand darted about, wildly seeking to strike palm. "Whoa," said the guy, rueful. "It's okay, buddy—just trying to shake your hand." The guy looked over to the right: no! Here were *four* other guys, two standing, two sitting in wooden chairs pulled from desks, shades of sly amusement on their faces.

Now Matt dropped the box. Now he gasped. Now the box was cracking, bits of his notes' yellow legal paper showing through the tape. "Oh my God," he said, "I'm so sorry." Instantly, he knew: saying this was precisely as stupid as that time in fourth-grade science when he had clapped his hands ecstatically on seeing the green of a seedling peeking from his Dixie cup and gasped, *Oh my goodness,* so that Mrs. Markham the teacher, ashamed for him, had actually had to look away from those rows of kids clapping, mock-gasping, *Oh my goodness!* all over the room.

"It's okay, buddy!" The guy had slapped a broad, reassuring hand to Matt's back. "It's your room—you can put that anywhere!" He laughed convivially at Matt, at the four kids gathered together, at the powder-pale kid standing still by the back wall. "So, welcome, Matthew! It's excellent to meet you finally, face to face!"

"Thanks. You too, I mean. Totally excellent. Oh, um, but, actually, it's Matt."

"Right on!" The guy gave Matt a diplomatic grin. *Okay, if you say so.* "Well, I'm Dwight. So, guys, this is my roomie *Matt;* Matt, I want you to meet some guys from down the hall, Ken, Dan, Ben, and—ah!" Dwight broke off, skipping the fourth. "What am I thinking! Before we go any further," with a steady pressure on his shoulder, Dwight wheeled Matt around, "our other roommate, Josh!" Dwight flourished with his free hand—*voilà!*

How-style, the pale kid by the back wall lifted an arm furred with tiny black hairs, then awkwardly thrust it down. " 'Lo." He flushed, glancing quickly at Dwight.

Somehow—was it Josh's reverential look? the way Dwight casually looped an arm about Matt's neck and dragged him this way and that over the room, to the open door of a single bedroom and then by a double, waving over windows and desks and speaking so confidently, so *fait accompli* of the necessity of drawing lots? who can say from what several flowers the honey of an intimation is made, but at any rate—Matt understood.

They thought yours truly their inferior! I mean, how funny! Mr. Freebie T-shirt on the one hand, and here—Dork City, this overgrown pastry of a Josh! Quite, quite droll. The hand thing was a dreadful mix-up, of course, and the box, but—please! I mean, merely let them scan his clothing, exactly in accordance with the styles he'd espied and copied down from life. These were real vintage gray fine-wale cords from the secondhand section at Urban Outfitters. This was a hipster T from Screaming Mimi's. These were *Adidas*. Or maybe they didn't know enough about sneakers to comprehend?

"What do you think, Matt?" Dwight was beaming at him.

"Hmm? Sorry, what was that?"

"It's all right." Dwight granted him a tired, knowing smile. "Buddy. You must be exhausted from your long drive."

"No, no—oh." Matt caught himself before bringing up New Jersey. "I'm fine." He nodded vociferously at the four visitors. "Go ahead. What were you asking me?"

"What you thought of the pad," Dwight replied.

Pad. This meant an apartment, doubtless here their suite. Okay. Now what he needed was something killer to shoot back. Just a little something. To say, hey, who's cool? Me, not you. "The pad? I mean, it's . . ." He smirked for time. "Well . . ."

"It's pretty great, wouldn't you say?" Dwight cued him like a kindly teacher.

Matt looked over at the four guys, nearly permitting himself an eyebrow raise. But didn't anyone notice how high-handed Dwight was being? *Great.* He could do vastly better than that anyway. There must be something for this exigency in his slang glossary. Let's see now. "As for me," he patted back a faux yawn, peeking through slitted eyes, "I'd say it's *the bomb.*"

But the guys did not seem impressed. Hard to tell for sure, since Matt's view was obscured, but the Asian kid—Ken?—clearly laugh-coughed, and Ben, a short, stubby guy, seemed to exchange a look with Dwight; he may have snorted, unless that was just his chair's scraping on the floor. What? *The bomb* was a perfectly good term. Hadn't it just appeared in an interview with some rap star? Maybe it was a little too advanced for them, streetwise, slick; these four were excessively white-bread for such urban lingo. Dwight, meanwhile, had a wide euphoric smile veneered over his face, as if Matt were perhaps a dolphin that had just docilely flipped for him in the air. *Neat trick!*

"I like it." Josh glanced protectively at Dwight. "I think our suite's pretty great."

Dwight began rubbing Josh's shoulder like a masseur. "Oh, so does Matt. That's all he meant. Isn't it?" Dwight winked at Matt. Suddenly, he let his hand go still on Josh's shoulder, then flashed him, Matt, and all four of the guests a grin. It was a beautiful grin: a masterful grin. A grin that said, *Let's you and me slip off the shackles of the world, my friend, and ride away on motorcycles into the distant California night.* Yet it was also somehow a grin that said, *We're making real progress on drinking-water wells in sub-Saharan Africa—we're going to beat this whole world-poverty-injustice thing!* In all the times Matt had rehearsed the thousand-kilowatt smile called Confident back home in Teaneck, he had never quite mustered up that luster or, for that matter, lost his resemblance to a slightly daft vampire. "Dudes!" Dwight announced, overwhelmed by surprise and epiphany. "This is going to be one fantastic year!"

At Dwight's invitation, the visitors began chattering about their trips: Dan, a wiry type in a navy Izod and clean blue jeans, had ridden in from LA on the same plane as Cameron Diaz; Ben, the short guy, had packed while *completely hung-over* from a *humungous* going-away party he and three of his friends had thrown, which led into a discussion of graduation parties. Matt recalled the way he had celebrated his own graduation: a noontide trip to Charlie Brown's, during which his mother sniffed at his sticking to the smorgasbord salad bar (as ever unable to appreciate the need for that dietary regimen practiced since the reception of his acceptance letter), followed by, at home, in the backyard, a well-tended bonfire of high school things—AP Chem notes, SAT prep books, and, most deliciously of all, materials from the college counseling office, such as the form where Mr. Blaine had penned a list of distant second-tier schools. Did they really think they could ship him off to "special" places like Reed College? *We think you will do best in a smaller environment, where uniqueness is treasured and your distinctive gifts will not get lost*... Those appalling naysayers.

They were getting up, the visitors. They were stretching, preparing to leave. Missed your chance! "Ah, g'bye," Matt croaked out, hastily shooting up from the desk as they started to walk past. "Catch you later." He gave the first one, Ben, a sprightly wink.

Oh. No.

Ben did not smile. Instead, his face twisted up like some sort of badly manufactured Cabbage Patch Kid. His head jolted back in disgust or astonishment, his ugly squat mouth dropping open. "Catch you later," the guy repeated, gruff, not without perhaps a taint of irony. He was a few paces past when his voice returned, borne up from the echoey corridor. "Did you see that?"

"Ssh."

"He winked at me."

"Ssh."

"I'm telling you, the kid—"

The door slammed shut, blotting them out.

Matt squeezed his eyes closed. He had chosen precisely the wrong one. It was Short-Boy-Something-to-Prove: Matt knew that type. Like Jake Garbaccio, who, in order to make everyone on the school bus forget how easily his name lent itself to Jake Garbage-io, spent the whole of to-and-fro-school transports in sixth and seventh grade inventing new tortures for you.

Dwight coughed. "So! Guys."

Matt flashed open his eyes to see Dwight posing cross-armed.

"I'm going to join those kids for lunch in a minute, which by the way you guys are totally, totally welcome to. I want that to be completely clear: you guys are my homies. Okay? It's all good. Right, buddy?" Dwight extended a hand low: Josh gazed and then fondly batted at it. "Right on. But should we just go ahead and get this whole picking-lots thing out of the way?" Dwight found a slip of paper and began writing out lots, with Josh looking eagerly over a shoulder. "Bro, ready for your date with destiny?" He stretched out a palm to Matt.

Please send me a sign. Just so I can survive. Please.

—But it was *D* for *Double* when he unfolded the slip.

"Oh, bummer," said a mournful Dwight. He shook his head when Josh unfolded a *D* as well. "Sorry, man." Dwight put his hands on his hips and sighed. "All right. So that's settled. Anyone up for lunch?"

"I've got to go unpack my car," Matt muttered. "See you."

He swept out the hall door, pushing blindly through kids and parents and bags until he found the bathroom, the stall door slamming behind him and, with a wicked twist, safely barred. But what's wrong with you? Getting all rapt in reminiscence like that. You need to open your mouth at the critical juncture. You need to go through the motions! Keep your eyes on the prize here—do you expect another shot at a *vita nuova* is likely to come knocking at your door? "I told you," he whispered aloud, hands on his naked knees. "You have to. I told you. Come on."

What kind of a creature *was* this Dwight? Matt was shaking his head, a grim, tight-lipped smile on his lips. Thoroughly annoying, that's what, full of himself, fulsome. But really: focus. Not a veritable jock, though Dwight's appearance and movements did tend in that direction; too sharp, on his toes for that. Nice, even nicey-nice, cheesily touchy-feely and inclusive. And yet—liked, apparently. How had he managed to pick up those four guys, get invited to lunch, direct their conversation like a leader? Like their *president*, for Chrissakes, striding about broad-chested, generously looking everyone in the eye, a student-government type. Hand-shaking! And winking—*he* gets to wink! Yet liked nonetheless, Dwight. Josh seemed practically in love. A strange new species indeed. Are you jealous, sir? No, of course not, sir, don't be absurd.

Leaving the bathroom to make for his car, Matt felt his mood tilt like a feather toward upper air: why, here in the halls, outside the dorm—hoisting navy trunks, crate after crate, a lavender velvet couch riding regally through blue heaven, all manner of stereos, standing lamps, potted plants—were scores and scores! It was absolute folly to zero in on one encounter with four random kids, or to overconcern himself with two dolt roommates, when here were dizzying, limitless other friend-possibilities. The hall meeting? The Ice Cream Bash for the entire freshman class at nine this evening? Simply, when all this unloading was through, he would return, shower, gel, and slip into the first of his crafted outfits: a fresh page, a starting-over.

Preparation was finished, now. He had done his part to an utmost of which he could be proud: via cottage cheese and beets, sit-ups in his room and long walks in the nature preserve listening on headphones to the whole of the *Morte d'Arthur* read by Derek Jacobi, he had whittled away no less than twenty-seven pounds of flab. Now the dun-colored sweats and hideous whale-sized turtlenecks in which he had lumbered through the halls of Tenafly High lay bagged up, shoved in sepia attic light beside boxes of all the old favorite books—the real French *Maldoror*, the underlined Gibbon, the Nietzsche scrapbook, the handmade map of Napoleon's progress across Europe, all too risky to bring to school yet too sentimentally precious to leave open to his mother's reach in his room. And wasn't the new wardrobe a meticulously chosen thing resplendent with his devotion? Numberless were the hours he had given this summer to sartorial surveillance, sketching hairstyles and the cut of jean and sideslung bags at Washington Square Park on his thrice-weekly field trips to the city, poring, in the Astor Place Barnes & Noble, over British magazines where lean, malevolent types slouched with skateboards. And then the hours of stretching his money until, in the smelly vintage-clothes boutiques of the East Village or down at the Salvation

Army, under flickering fluorescent panels and in flimsy cheap mirrors, the look came together into a semblance of cool. And further hours, week after week, riding subways and buses eavesdropping so that later, at the drafting table, he might crack open his ripe memory in the crafting of possible normal-kid conversations. Then practicing, in his bedroom fervently chanting, *What's up, Catch you later, How's it going,* to a Radio Shack recorder—and cringing on playback, and standing up and sitting down, and trying to sing first in case that helped open the mouth muscles. There in the well of his bathroom mirror he had made the pout of Aloof, the arched eyebrow of Intrigued, various species of grin till they verily trembled in readiness beneath the surface of his skin.

Matt shut the car door with a happy bang. What now could obstruct him—from friends! Real life, finally! He wasn't totally incognizant of what that might be like. There was, after all, Max Sanders in third grade: for almost a month they had walked to the comic-book store and chewed Jolly Ranchers and sailed paper boats in the ditch behind school, before Max defected to the dorks and refused even to wave him a hello; there was Ramin Parhiscar, the Persian boy who had befriended him for the whole joyous year of fifth grade. Before Ramin's dad was transferred to Ohio, they had done science experiments with a chemistry set in the Parhiscars' fusty basement, watched television, pretended to be ninjas, and occasionally walked down to the reservoir, where Matt watched his friend toss pebbles and talked about those strange metaphysical enigmas, like how did you know God existed? though Ramin was always more interested in aliens. There was the gifted camp in southern Jersey in the summer after ninth—there he had managed, somehow, to make himself plausible to no less than seven other kids and slip into their group; he had written cheerful, witty letters on the most varied subjects for two more years until one April, Chip, the very last corresponder, turned silent.

That wasn't *so* long ago. He might still have the aura of friendability. A certain facility, flexibility with the tongue, saying credible things. And now there was his cartonful of slang vocabulary and sketched-out conversation notes, the little black address book in which were copied the listings of hip-seeming restaurants, clubs, bars from *The Village Voice,*

Time Out, Paper, down to little dollar-sign signifiers and asterisks in short-hand of cash- and coolness-level. Now there were these two suitcases brim-filled with vintage cords, dark denim, snapfront cowboy shirts, and pastel guayaberas; there was a white box with that pièce-de-résistance on which he'd staked the lion's share of his summer earnings, a pair of black calf-high, two-hundred-dollar 8th-Street-bought Italian leather boots. Ready as he'd ever be to accede to the Promised Land.

And as this certainty scattered sparks in his upper body, the scalding New York that was all around took him up, enchantingly. It seemed like scenery that might be pulled down as soon as he should blink, turn: café, deli, record store, boutique with mannequins staring glassily out at the maroon tenements iced with pigeon shit across the way—*New York, New York!* Matt yelped inwardly, gleeful, squeezing warm cardboard to his chest.

But when he had dragged the last of his things upstairs and was standing by his new desk, panting, sweaty, rubbing his throbbing red hands together, the buoyant outdoor mood ended abruptly, with a knock at the door. Since Josh was absorbed in manipulating a tiny speaker beside his computer monitor and Dwight nowhere to be seen, Matt walked down the corridor to answer this. There on the threshold a smiling African-American man in a cornflower-blue button-down shirt leaned toward Matt, enveloping him with a distinctly alcoholic aftershave. In a baritone, whiskey-mellow voice, this figure introduced himself as Dirk, their RA. And then, as if it were a matter of mere pleasantry, he added that the first hall group meeting would commence *in five—remember*?

"Christ." Matt flashed down to the bare skin of his left wrist. Could it actually be almost two in the afternoon? Lord, he would have to keep better track of time if he really wanted to stop wearing a watch. Now what was there to do? No time to shower. No time to go over his notes. And this—this sweaty shirt, these dirty pants—no time to find that suite of clothes identified as *Outfit (Casual) #1*?

"Are you all right?" Dirk's astonishing green eyes twinkled.

"Totally," Matt promised, waving goodbye as Dirk and his aftershave moved on to Room 404. He croaked out the news to Josh (Josh was now adjusting, at a glacier's pace, the brightness dial on his monitor, his eyes drawn in to the screen's blue glow) and tooled down the hallway to the bathroom. Thankfully, this was empty: Matt splashed some water on his face, wet a paper towel and scooped out his underarms, ran trembling fingers through his hair, which in patches was sweat-stained to brown. It's going to be great. You're going to be great. Hmm—I'd even say *the bomb*. Oh, you kidder, you. Listen: you must never try that one again. Hear me? Do you hear? I'm talking to you. I'm listening.

Then he was walking down the hall to the common lounge.

First, he saw architecture. Here were a series of dismal oblong orange couches, their fabric pilled and worn, facing, at the end of a plush acid-green carpet, a black television squatting on a low rolling cart. Then he saw people, but merely as spatial entities, seventeen or so large boulders: it was in this still-imperfect phase of perception that he nearly plopped down beside Ben, that evil troll, but caught himself in time, doubled back to wedge on the floor between a tall, abstracted guy and a frizzy-haired blond girl whose strangely yellow-tipped fingers roved almost obscenely in the fuzzy carpet's nether regions. Once Dirk began droning on about ID cards, computer labs, stuff any idiot with a manual would know, Matt began covertly sussing out the selection.

There were two jocks: the guy to his left, in head-to-toe unmarked navy-and-gray sweats, and a ponytailed girl opposite in a ripply purple tracksuit, both staring up at Dirk like calm cows. Out. There were two preps in short-sleeved madras shirts lounging tanned and languid next to Dwight on a couch. Negative. There was one of those skinny Asian prepubescent-ish girls, still wearing her hair shapeless, pinned up on either side with faux-pearl-encrusted barrettes, no doubt a cellist or violinist or anyway school orchestra geek. Sorry. The real jackpot appeared to be two girls on the opposite side of the room. One was dressed mod, similar in vibe to Matt's general wardrobe, her narrow torso enclosed in a white collarless jacket and long side-folded legs in ivory trousers, her hazel eyes blackly raccoon-ringed, her flaxen hair straight and shoulder length; medium-pretty. The other, leaning back on her solid hands, was chubbier, mopped by a blunt cut of green-rimmed platinum hair, and dressed kind of futuristically in cargo pants and a net shirt. Periodically she would mutter something to the mod girl, something rude-sounding and monosyllable, while the two blatantly rolled their eyes.

Matt could feel himself growing warm. It was as if there were ovens in his fingertips and a balloon tugging upward, giant, uncontainable, in his chest. In a moment, by the end of this meeting, by this afternoon maybe, he might have these girls as friends. They could be rolling their eyes together as a threesome and smoking cigarettes and stomping around the dorm, finding others for the gang—the runaway success of a gang, the gang everyone would gawk at when it passed. How stylish, how urban, out-and-out *it* these two were (and the blonde really quite pretty if you looked at her right)! Oh, to meet a Tenafly kid in the city with these girls by his side! *What's your name again?* he would sneer on a street corner to Rob Peterson or Rande Wilks, jockishly stupefied by his manifest thin, hip presence, *You look vaguely familiar,* while these two laughed along, the blonde with a proprietarily girlfriendish finger linked through one of his belt loops.

"Whew!" Dirk was grinning genially. "That's a lot of information for you to digest! But don't worry: you can find all of it in your student manual and you can always—always!—come talk to me. I'm right down the hall."

The room regarded him dubiously.

"Now it's on to our real business! Why doesn't everyone say his or her name, where you're from, and something interesting about yourself. All right? I'll start. I'm Dirk, I'm Three-L. I mean, heh," he sniggered, "that's third-year law school to you. I'm from Atlanta, Georgia, and, let's see—I play the banjo in a bluegrass band."

Dwight leaned forward on the couch. "What's your band called?"

What on earth? Matt riveted his eyes to the carpet's waving sea of acid green.

"What's it called? The Sweet Morning Stars." Dirk beamed at Dwight. "You a bluegrass fan?"

Dwight smiled modestly at the room. "Been known to play a little washboard on occasion."

Oh my *God*. The poor fool! Full-on hari-kari. —But oddly: was no one noticing? Not even cargo-pant girl rolled her eyes.

"Fantastic! We'll have to jam sometime. So! Why don't you start?" Dirk nodded at a pretty girl with an oval face on the couch to his right.

"I'm Malena Jacobs," she said. Metal buttons on her mauve cardigan glinted, businesslike. "I live in Berlin."

"Berlin as in Berlin, *Germany*?" Dirk politely bugged his eyes.

"Yes," she affirmed. Her serious mouth was pursed. "My dad's a diplomat."

Something interesting. Let's see now. Well, for starters—hmm. No reading. *NO MENTIONING BOOKS:* that was one of the new Rules.

"I'm Carly Hale," an ice-blonde with a nose that tapered to a pointy tip was saying, or shrieking, in a squeaky soprano. "I live on Park Avenue—"

"—So right here in New York!" interpolated Dirk, his jaw set rigid but still unimpeachably good-natured. "We'll be fine with just the city, folks."

"Okay. So I'm from New York, but I went to school in New Hampshire—with him and him." Her chin picked out the two guys in the madras shirts; actually, they looked related to her somehow: their fair hair, their loose, easy limbs. "And I sail."

"You sail?"

"Boats," she replied, exasperated. A sinister little smile came over her lips.

Dwight expatiated on his Habitat for Humanity work, the rewarding fun of student government *(aha! bullseye)*, and his plan to try for an a cappella singing group (this was *three* things, but Dirk didn't stop him); a girl named Mary with a floating bob of black wavy hair and a strange collarless button-front tunic said in mellifluous British tones that she was from Alexandria, Egypt, and had never before visited America; Josh spoke rather impressively about his internship in international news at *The New York Times;* a predictable burnout in actual tie-dye and high-top Converse, Thomas Riggles of Newton, Massachussetts, announced with uncontainable glee that he had followed Phish on tour that summer; Heather Thorndike, the mod girl, tossed her long flaxen hair and sneered that she had spent the summer as a fashion assistant (going to shows, you know, parties, that sort of thing) at *Sassy* magazine while Sara Carter, the cargo-pant girl, had been touring with her band; and just as things got down to the wire, the frizzy-haired girl beside Matt jerked up from the carpet to announce that she, Elaina Kazides from Scottsdale, Arizona, was one of a team of inventors for a new computer language currently being packaged for release in 1997—thereby throwing him off entirely.

Dirk was nodding at him.

"That's very interesting," Matt said. "Wow."

"Yes, it is," Dirk agreed. "Now what about yourself? I'm sure you've done something just as interesting. You see, everyone, that's what I think you'll find here at NYU. Your entering class is gonna have concert pianists, Westinghouse scientists, champion golfers; I know for a fact there is a champion ballroom-dancing duo right in this dorm—yup! anyone here like ballroom dancing? They're going to practice in the dance studio in our basement, all spectators welcome. Anyway, trust me when I say you won't believe the richness and diversity of your peers. So. I'm getting carried away here. What interesting thing do *you* have to tell us?"

Jesus Christ, did the guy have to put it that way? "I'm from New Jersey," he said. "I mean, ah, first, I'm Matt."

In hindsight, in the God's-eye of retrospection—where everything recurs eternally, like the figures on a carousel over and again spooling by with their ghastly frozen, lacquered, bestial smiles—there would always be this feeling of fumbling through the matériel of his life up to now: his mother, behind the register at A&P, wearing her cheerful smile and plastic purple-triangle earrings; the dilapidated front of their house, with its peeling gray paint and broken, slanted gutters, probably the shittiest of anyone at Tenafly High; his Math Counts! medals and Bergen County Debate Tournament trophies lined up on the tops of bookshelves in his blue bedroom; the rotting hammock supposedly hung by his father, making it at least fifteen years old and magically alluring, suspended between oaks in the tiny backyard; himself red-apron-clad, cooking lasagna, his specialty, when his mother, tired from a bad shift, needed to soak in Calgon, put her feet up; the nature preserve, its overgrown paths with flapping markers about the tree trunks red, yellow, blue. And over and again, however many times he reviewed this common room scene, implacable Memory, that cruelest of faculties, would always at the appointed moment whomp him on the back so he coughed out finally: "I like to take long walks in the woods."

Matt kept his gaze locked on Dirk and a dazed half smile plastered on his lips despite the chasming moment yawning open, the circle of faces trained on him turned prismatic, cubist, by peripheral vision. *Don't.* Don't what? Start weeping, screaming, foaming?

"Great." Dirk nodded at the jock to Matt's left. "Uh—next?"

Another opportunity shot out of the sky. When the meeting concluded, Matt rose with the others. He watched Heather Thorndike and Sara Carter slip out, Josh get caught up in a group talking incomprehensible sports, and Dwight, cross-armed, fresh-faced, discharge expansive laughs at the preppy guys and Carly Hale. He watched his own hand dip into a ceramic bowl for pretzels to stuff into a dry mouth. How encircled we are, isolated as if by magic unicorn-horn powder, squeezed into a parallel, airless dimension, unobserved. But come on. Couldn't *long walks* be parlayed as sensitive-boy, a wild Rimbaud? A gaffe, yes, but as serious as that? Perhaps they were simply too bland. Just look whom he was dealing with here—a handful of jocks, preps, goody-goodies!

Matt brushed himself clean of crumbs, heavy-lidded his eyes, and strode out to the hall.

Now. Now would he find them, the real ones, by going back and forth in the dorm, by walking up and down in it. Two at a time he took the steps to the fifth floor, eyes shorn of innocence and reverie. Ordinary sorts wearing baseball hats passed by in a cloud of sulky intransigence. A girl with a long chestnut braid and Life Saver–colored knee-highs (on someone else maybe cool but not with her large glasses, her faux Keds) turned from a corkboard to give him a probing look—directly he bent to the water fountain. Close call! Looking studiously at the wall, he scurried past. Floor Six. A number of doors here were open; Matt slowed, digging a hand around in his pocket as if distracted by searching. Framed in one door, girls sitting cross-legged on the floor beside a bed done up in lace and pink satin were chatting animatedly, a buzzing circlet of boring feminine energy, saccharine. *Oh, quit,* came a Southern soprano.

Silly. Suddenly in a burst of merriment the voice trilled, *That just is not the way the bond market reacts!* Well! Really quite advanced for their age, no? Matt passed three pallid, malnourished male hippies and one plump hippie girl in a raggedy dress hacky-sacking, awkwardly jerked by invisible strings. More stairs. Oh, he would find *Them,* all right. Merely, a touch of patience. Probably they were more selective with their presence; they wouldn't be seen hovering about, desperate.

On the seventh floor a water-gun battle was in progress; the eighth was oddly deserted, and, ugh, rather stinky: what was that rancid *scent?* Matt bounded all the way to floor eleven, bending by a fountain to wash out the taste.

When he stood up, a being of utter cool was striding past.

In one bulb-shattering flash, the kid exploded on the brain's film. A thin-lapeled black blazer worn, cheeky, over lowslung jeans, jeans with that magical stiffness along the edges never-to-be-found in the stores Matt had seen. Beneath the blazer, a battered Sex Pistols T-shirt, ripped at the collar, where a slim sash-tie was looped, to drape along an enviably scrawny lean chest. *Boom, boom, boom* went his boots along the waxed hallway as—his lips knotted up in a pernicious smirk, his bold blue eyes grazing the top of Matt's head, his black hair marvelously bed-headed, waving unkempt tendrils in the air—the stranger passed by, and with a rude leap took the first couple of stairs downward. "Babe, I'm not waiting for you," he warned, not bothering to turn.

And now a second body appeared, a towering girl in a red mod jacket and black miniskirt, shoving her feet into gold sandals. She was blond and ponytailed and oval-faced and model-gorgeous, a version manyfold cooler than Heather Thorndike from the meeting, blooms of rose on her creamy cheeks, her brow marble-smooth, a pair of wide-set topaz eyes. "You asshole," she drawled in a low, husky voice, and brushed past Matt as if he were part of the wall.

Matt hung over the railing of the stairwell to watch their heads sinking down the flights, first the guy's, impetuously shooting forward without once looking back, then the girl's, her cord of angel hair swinging behind like a last sympathetic tassel of the whole beautiful mirage.

When they vanished, Matt rushed over to the window that looked onto the courtyard: where the two figures soon reappeared, walking over to a little group of bodies draped around some concrete benches.

Well, you have to go down now; that's obvious. Oh, is it? he's in a hurry: look, he isn't even sitting; besides, what are you going to do? This isn't a museum where you join the rear of a tour. *What's up?* that's what, walk down these stairs and say it to them.

Whirling through the stairwell's turnings, Matt thudded down flights, nine, seven, six, until he was standing before the glass door looking onto an empty courtyard.

At four-thirty Matt slipped out of Third Avenue North, sped home—the plan without a hitch, his unsuspecting mother already two miles away on her shift—he parked the car, left the keys near the fridge with a red scrawled crayon note, and was speeding back via bus by seven. One might have felt guilty to ditch her so; though she had not exactly been looking forward to helping move him into school—indeed had seized each opportunity that came her way to knock all things touching his scholarship to NYU—she had at least planned on it. In the dim kitchen before he'd jetted this morning, the pencil-printed letters of his clumsy excuse had fallen against one another so awkwardly: *Sorry, Mom, just found out, freshman orientation at nine-thirty* and *didn't want to wake you,* the sentimental bushwa of *you need your rest* and *I'll call as soon as possible.* Yet what else could he have done? Bring her with him to school? That was no way to honor the single chance granted after black years. Simply, his mother was the magic ingredient for social doom: mix and watch all contents sink to the bottom. Well. He was doing a marvelous job of that all by his lonesome. Come on, now, sir: the time was not for the dissipations of despair but action.

How brilliantly promising was the sky as he rose on the escalator out of the subway at Astor Place—blue-black, a comic-book ink spread out lavishly, drowning all stars: though wasn't New York always so starless? Walking back to the dorm he lit a cigarette, just as he'd practiced all summer: instantly his mind was singing with nicotine. Then, on the strength of this, in an I-can-do-anything spirit, he decided, approaching

Third North with a quarter hour to spare, to set a certain thing right. After all, authority figures, though of no social importance themselves, could nonetheless skew the reception of a persona through all manner of cue, from the dubious intonation they lent your name to that singularly damning thing, their empathetic glances in your direction. Not if he could help it! He gave Dirk's door a neat rap.

"Hello, Matthew! Matthew, come in!" Dirk seemed genuinely delighted to see him. He ushered Matt toward two leather armchairs grouped on either side of a slim mahogany end table. "Good of you to stop by!"

Jeez—did Dirk think he was trying to brown-nose? "It's Matt." He creaked into the near armchair.

Dirk's peremptory hand executed a quick pencil note. "So, have you looked into the hiking trails on offer around here? You know," he delivered of himself a sage, raspy jaw-scratch, "I believe there're even some in the city; I might have some literature if you—"

"Um, actually, actually that's exactly why I came over," Matt pointed out, sighing perhaps a tad bombastic. "I just wanted to clear up—I feel like I gave you a wrong impression. Of me. What I said today. It was just really . . . inaccurate, you know."

Dirk's wide grin didn't budge. Then he nodded, still vaguely smiling. "Okay. Why don't you tell me again what you said today?"

"I mean, right down in the lounge. When I was all, like, *I like to take long walks alone.* Like, I just didn't want you to think: whoa, weird, ax murderer!" A jaded chortle.

But Dirk's grin seemed to tighten, to grow entrenched. "Actually, I didn't know you meant alone—"

"Or with friends," said Matt. "I like it both ways. I just meant it sounded, I don't know. I mean, there's lots of other more normal things I like to do. Even interesting things. I don't know why I said that one." Stop talking. "It just popped out. I could have said something else." Please stop talking. "That's all I wanted to say."

"Matthew, I'm really glad you came in this evening—which, by the way, I hope you're planning on going to the Bash?" Dirk checked his watch and looked over at Matt. "Good. You know, Matthew, starting school is a difficult thing. I hope you realize that. You're leaving home, you're coming all this way—"

"I'm from New Jersey," Matt interrupted. "Teaneck? Just across the George Washington Bridge? It's really close, it's practically New York."

"That's nice." Dirk showed his teeth like a toothpaste commercial. "Not too far from your mama's cooking!" Indeed, as long as Matt was near the frozen aisle of a supermarket, he could never be very far from his mama's cooking. "But, you know, the thing I realized when I left Atlanta is that home isn't a place that you can measure by miles. It's a *feeling*. A feeling of security. A safety zone. And the truth is, when you come to school, you lose that. Hang on a second." Dirk pushed up from the armchair and walked to a dark-wood armoire, which he opened. He retrieved a slim yellow piece of paper and returned. "Everyone goes through this. It's just a fact that for some people, the transition is more difficult than for others. You know? Nothing to be ashamed of. Here, take a look at this." Dirk pushed the yellow sheet on the table toward Matt.

HOMESICK?[1]

The Wellness Center of NYU welcomes all first-years to a special two weeks of Anxiety Counseling . . .

"Oh no," mumbled Matt, pushing the paper back. "This isn't me."

"It's nothing to be ashamed of." Dirk's startling green eyes were sun-lightened seas of pure empathy.

---

[1] No! This is an entirely, and one may say dangerously, short-sighted judgement to draw! Please pardon me my explosion, but I have been moved beyond the ability of keeping silent when I consider the many tragedies, large and small, which may be averted by better systems of diagnosis and aid. The tender youth arriving at university emerges into a disorienting kingdom, an event which for many is the first „earth-quake" in their psycho-social development. (I see again that Hans who some thirteen years ago appeared at the Freie Universität in Berlin clutching one valise and his passport, which had just been rifled by the East and then the West German border-guards on his train from München—terrified, with his heart in his mouth! However, such reminiscence takes us beside from the point.) I praise the American university for equipping dormitory facilities with watch-men over the spirits of new students, but at present we must say the wards' training is not adequate to these matters, a lack which may result in innumerable catastrophes.

"No, no," he said. He was getting up now, grabbing his courier bag. "It just, it isn't me. I mean, ha, I'm not homesick in the least."

"Matthew..." Dirk was following him to the door. "As your RA— would you, could you just take the information? I have a responsibility here. Could—"

"Okay," he said. Whatever would make this end. He already had the door open. He was one foot into the hallway.

"Great. Thank you. I appreciate that. And by the way—oh hey, Dwight!"

Somewhere between releasing the doorframe he had been gripping with one hand and trying to stabilize the loop of his courier bag as he turned, Matt let go of the little yellow piece of paper, which tilted weightless in the air and touched down, one side, then the other, and skidded to a stop by Dwight's feet. The giant block letters of *HOMESICK?* faced up.

"That's mine," said Matt, snatching it up.

Dwight traded a look with Dirk. "Okay." He tapped an orange Frisbee against his leg. "Um, heading back to the room?"

"Yes," croaked Matt.

"Be there in a sec, man, just returning this."

It was not a disaster. It was not a disaster. Merely a mix-up, with Dirk—and easily explainable to Dwight. Later, he would try to cajole Dwight into a good chuckle over it: *Ho, administrative paranoia!* he could say. Back in the bedroom, Matt scanned for a place to put the paper; Josh might find it in the trashcan; he slipped it in his courier bag; get rid of it outdoors later. Not to let this incident rattle his concentration. The Bash near Washington Square Park was the culmination of his day: it was *designed* as a mixer, a way to meet freshmen; it would therefore singularly, by necessity, afford the chances he had either failed to spot or squandered, even in great numbers. He must be unruffled.

Suddenly, in a burst of sportiveness—just as Matt had donned *Outfit (Party) #1* (a pale blue guayabera, acid-green slacks, and his irresistible new boots)—Dwight popped up at the double room. In a striped button-down, halfway preppy and halfway loud, he leaned against the doorframe to inquire if Matt was ready. "Let me get it," offered Dwight, jabbing the light switch with his elbow so the suite sank to darkness, then led the way out, elaborately holding open the hall door. In the plaza outside the dorm, Dwight shot up an arm, barking *yo* to guys who barked back; "Frisbee kids," he explained apologetically. When they had cleared the environs of the dorm, Dwight began to whistle. Abruptly he stopped and turned a face radiating contrition and sympathy on Matt. "Called my parents today. You know, I can't believe I won't see them for four whole months." Voice almost cracking with priceless sadness.

Matt gazed at sweet-faced Dwight out of louvered eyes. So, that was the way it was going to go down, was it? A clever one, a slippery one. A maestro, in his own hick way. Taking advantage of this opportunity to firm up the hierarchy of underling and lord: why, bravo, applause was in order! "Listen, Dwight." Matt tried to even his voice, to iron it offhand. "I know what you're trying to do, and I appreciate it. However, I am not, contrary to whatever Master Dirk Proctor may believe, in any way homesick."

"Hey buddy, I didn't say you were homesick! I was just—"

"That's all right," Matt interrupted, showing Dwight a knowing smile. "You're very, ah, *kind*." An ironic torque on *kind*. "Your point is taken!" he said, quavery, though managing to quell a violent *Let's skip the charade!* "Okay?" He opened his hands wide.

"I hear you, buddy. I hear you." Dwight thoughtfully ran a hand through his clean sandy hair, unpersuaded, clearly. Then he scratched his nose. "Well, all right! Let's rip this party up!" He swung his arms in wide circles, clapping his hands.

The barbarous vapors of charred hot dog hovered above Washington Square Park; now the perimeter of the "Bash" was dimly visible in a brick courtyard, crowds of white T-shirts circulating like slow moths.

"Hey, it's Caleb! Hey, buddy!" called Dwight.

Caleb Houghton, one of the two preps with Carly Hale in the hall meeting, had changed into a blue blazer with gold buttons. Looking like a cross between Kermit the Frog and someone from an L.L. Bean catalog, he swiveled his elongated neck, nodded politely at Dwight, and waited for them to catch up.

"I'll find you guys later," promised breathless prevaricating Matt. Then he dashed into the orbit of swirling bodies.[2]

Showtime. He should scan the crowd first. Keep an eye peeled for that supercool duo and their crew of before. He should just make a circuit, purposeful, aloof, and map out the promising. Only then should he move to a first strike.

A fatal twenty minutes clicked away as he circled, ducked under arms, squeezed through crevices: fatal, for his nerves got jangled through sheer suspense. So once he finally zeroed in on a girl hanging to a line of hipsters—here at last the bootcut dark denim, the vintage shirts similar to his own look—his fortitude faltered when, after meeting his eye, she giggled toward another girl. He darted quickly off; three whole minutes ran their course before he realized: come on, now. Probably she'd laughed at an unrelated joke? Not to be rattled—that, that was the key.

There were gorgeous clouds of cool-kid smoke by a back left corner group, and he, too, slipped one out and lit up, nonchalantly as you please, and with a perfect bored *flâneur* face grazed their margin. This time Matt tried male: a tall guy in goth black, leather pants, studded belt, daubs of black under somewhat woeful eyes. He was slightly detached, draping his tremendous hulk along the metal railing.

---

[2] This very „orbit" I spotted from the fifth-floor window of a nearby office complex, seeking momentary release from that mind-numbing psychology department reception where Lisanne, then my wife, and I first met her new, abominable colleagues. There can be no error: deep in my memory is etched this day when Lisanne and I entered what would be the lodgings for our New York year at 108 E. 18th Street, a sunlit studio in a brown building on a peaceful street. After minor cleaning of the flat and of ourselves, we hurried to this first of her professional obligations, in fine spirits if justly tired. Perhaps what most astonishes me of this recollection is the notion that one individual in the throng below (Matthew) and one individual in the room where I stood (do not imagine that I will enshrine his memory here, that jet-haired Casanova in his foppish linen suit and bogus cinema-idol smile) would prove so momentous to the directions of my life, even though the evening was then experienced by me as no more than the witnessing of a routine exchange of academic courtesies, soon to be muted in oblivion.

"What's up?" Matt squinted and blew out a stream of smoke.

The guy shrugged and waved a lethargic hand in front of his face, which for one bad moment meant *Get lost* instead of implying *Yuk, smoke.* Matt half-giggled at his own skittishness and mumbled a *sorry.* Amicably, then, he twisted so his smoke floated aside and asked where the guy was from (his veins froze a little to hear *Jersey,* as if he might be discovered, but next it was *Holmdel,* South J, too far), and was still gearing up toward references to *Steppenwolf* and *A Clockwork Orange,* which he knew to be shareable teenage talking points, when his ship felt the first pinprick of the iceberg.

"Freshman?" said the guy. "Oh, I don't go here. I'm just waiting for some friends. They went to hit on those girls over there." He pointed to three other kids, also dressed in black but scruffier, messier, so that the townie B&T provenance was unmistakable, who were making two budding slatterns laugh in a way that required constant smoothing of their loose, greasy ringlets. "You can see the party from the street."

"Oh." As there was nothing else: "Actually, um, I have to go find the bathroom."

Matt made his way through a considerably thinner crowd; at the sidewalk, groups of four or five kids departed, yelling, *Wait up!* or *Where's Chris?* or unintelligible plans. Across the courtyard stood Dwight absorbed in a universe of preps, Caleb, Carly, others. Ice cream entered Matt's mind. Let there be ice cream, sir, just this once, to boost our morale. All right, then: just this once. Shy as a bride, he slunk up to the folding tables holding punch bowls with paper cups floating in cool water, all strawberry, the singularly inedible strawberry. Whatever. He picked up a soggy cup and balsa stick, sat on a low pediment, and dug in.

Then something unaccountable happened: whoever in heaven was playing merciless tetherball with Matt's heart, perhaps weary of a sudden, left off for a spell. For now, when least expected, while he sat gorging on the chess-pawn-shaped pediment, a plumpish boy[3] with soft brown eyes drew to his side and growled, "*What* a selection."

---

[3] This is Jason, our chief collaborator! He deserves a special gratitude: Matthew's former university, once having examined my credentials, placed me in communication with his

"Indeed. Would you believe all they have left is strawberry?"

"Not the *ice cream*!" the boy snorted. "I'm talking about the, er, Ice Cream *Bash*." He plopped down on the curb. His dark jeans flipped up at the cuffs; his hair, raked into spikes, was brown but for a bleached streak purplish under the lights.

"Oh. Well, yes—of course, that," Matt spat out. "Ugh."

"The people are just so..." The plump cheeks scrunched up in distaste. "So fucking preppy! I thought I came here to avoid that shit. NYU—hello! It's like fucking Scarsdale all over again." He smiled. "I'm from Scarsdale. Jason. Hey."

"Hey. Matt." Matt made a waving gesture, which he was able quickly to turn into wiping his pants. "So, you were saying?"

"The baseball haaats! The J. *Crew*." Jason rolled his eyes. "And for another thing, there's not, or at least *I* haven't met that many kids who are like, you know..." He cocked his head and gazed coquettishly into nowhere, sliding out a Newport. *"On the bus."* He winked at Matt, conspiratorial.

What? Matt cycled through slang, lighting a smoke to buy time. A way of saying with-it? *Branché,* as the French say? "Tell me about it"— deep exhale—"there's *nobody* here on the bus."

"It's like, where are they?"

"Exactly. I mean, they have to be here..."

"...but I don't see them."

"It's like—" Matt shaded his eyes, miming scanning the crowd. "Come in, Houston, Houston, come in."

Jason giggled, a genial hiccup, like the Pillsbury Doughboy. "Yes!" He adjusted his ample ass on the curb. "I might join QU, I don't know. Are you going to?"

And for anyone who has spent painstaking summer days poring over

---

closest companion, the young homosexual Jason Kirsch. From the start, this spectacularly cooperative Jason Kirsch was also the closest of companions for my research; it was his words, along with certain photographs and supplementary materials he provided, which formed its incipient ground. Hello, Jason! I wish you very well!

the veriest crannies of the manual, that meant: Queer Union, the gay and lesbian student group.

"But—how am I *gay*?!" Matt gasped.

"What? *On the bus,* hello?" Jason mimed crowd-looking with his fat dove hand. "What was all that about? Who were *you* looking for, girl?"

A long moment while Matt stared at Jason's chipmunk cheeks as the boy drummed his fingernails on a denim-covered knee. "Someone nice," he heard himself say. He cleared his throat. "Sorry. It was a . . . misconstruction. I thought we were still on the whole loathing-preppies thing." He looked down into his cup, where the strawberry ice cream lay melted into bland waves.

"*Well,*" remarked Jason at last. "Don't worry, you have." Matt looked up to find Jason smiling. "Found someone nice." He gave a neat pat to Matt's shoulder. "Hmm. Are you going to eat that?" He took the cup and shoveled pink ooze into his mouth, crumpled the paper and set it by his foot in the gutter, then turned back to face Matt. Suddenly he cackled, folded his arms, and laid his head on his knees.

"What?" But the curve of Jason's back just shook, evidently with laughter. "What's so funny here? What? *What!* Spill it, bucko!"

Jason actually fell over on his side now, sprawled along the curb, face scrunched up like a newborn's. Finally he could breathe. "Spill it, bucko? Who are you, crazy boy?" He dabbed at his eyes. "Sorry, I totally don't mean to bust your balls, but, um, it's just: are you sure? I guess I never saw a straight boy wear boots like those."

His Special *New* Boots that had cost the best part of his summer earnings trucking groceries, watering plants, all manner of shit work for—"What's wrong with my boots?"

"*No-thing,* nothing's *wrong* with your boots." Jason smoothed his spiky hair. "They just scream West Village Fag, that's all!" He snorted, laughing and flailing his hand on the curb. "Sorry to bruise your um, fashion sense." He dabbed at his eyes with a knuckle. "Oh dear. Oh dear." He cleared his throat primly. "If it's any consolation, I happen to like West Village Fags *very much.*"

By the time maintenance wraiths slid from the shadows to lift plastic tablecloths around softened ice creams and stained napkins, Jason had smoked four more Newports, sketched his life story in awful übersubur-ban Scarsdale, gossiped about a dining hall scene, and generally involved himself as Matt's first college friend. As they walked to the dorm on a cushion of the night's thick smells, rotting garbage, rank whiffs of orchid and gardenia wafting out the windows of restaurants tinkling with glass-ware and silver, Jason bobbed beside, a miniature dynamo. He talked rapid-fire, on and on, and if he stopped for a second it wasn't shut-off time exactly, since something palpable pulsed from him through the dark muggy air: goodwill? Geniality? Warmheartedness? He gave you the benefit of the doubt: he seemed just waiting for you to say something he could love.

They parted on the fourth floor—Jason was two up—and when Matt put his key in the lock, he felt he might just manage it. In the darkened room patterned by the salmon-pink lights of the courtyard, he folded his slacks tenderly, he stood the notorious boots on his wardrobe's floor, he pressed his head awkwardly down on the pillow: Jason Kirsch, dinner-time downstairs in the dining hall tomorrow.

EXCURSUS BY DR. HANS MANNHEIM

Here, if it may be permitted, I wish to interrupt in order to make some elaboration—yet first I should issue a warm greeting to all readers, from your fellow pedestrian on this march in the footsteps of Matthew Acciaccatura! Yes, is not reading so like a pilgrimage: one applies feet to the well-worn steps already trodden by the character, the protagonist, in this case the, if we may arrogate this word to one so young and largely self-concerned, hero? So it appears to me as my body rests in a squeaky armchair of cheery aquamarine vinyl at the rear of this library, which, though smelling as it does of the debris from books, and small as it is with only two large tables and a spread of bright modern chairs, dissolves utterly from my perception as I turn these pages so that instead I run, leap, and tiptoe among these early exploits of Matthew all through the streets of Manhattan.

My friends, I did not wish to suspend your own voyages in this survey of one of the most fascinating youths of our time. How could I? Yet I must. Although I have been cooperative in a paramount degree with my research, turning over all documentary aids and providing detailed explanatory summaries to the author of the present text, it is inevitable, is it not, that between the account produced and my understanding some substance should escape. For after all, not only am I steeped, stupendously, perhaps beyond the call of reason, in varied material qualities impossible to communicate (the precise soft gold slant of light in an afternoon schoolroom, let us say, or again the mixed pepper-bleach scent of a dormitory toilet), but in the case of Matthew there is sensitive information which I by training and experience can best interpret. Should I then hold my tongue out of politeness? No, I do not think so. As to questions of right—as in, do I have the right of interruption?—I shove these aside. Do we not all wish for the richest portrayal of Matthew possible? There can be no „mine" and „yours" in this matter. And therefore I unloose the chain from my tongue so it may race about like a jubilant dog.

However, in fact it may not race too jubilantly, for what I have here to transmit is of a dark and melancholy nature. One bitter pill, my friends, and then all will be as before, merry young bodies playing social games on warm evenings. Here it is:

Until the moment you have so recently witnessed, Matthew Acciaccatura has never truly enjoyed the bliss of friendship.

What a solitary march across desolate waste territory equals that life without companionship, without some other brought as near to one as any blood relation through the magic of this specifically human thing called friendship! Never enjoyed? What can this mean? That throughout childhood, when children play with hoops and swings and scamper over rock piles and dig tunnels to Australia and consume cups of apple nectar, there was never a single „buddy" for Matthew? Precisely. How can this be possible in our progressive world? you ask. A fine question: merely allow me to open my dossiers and notes and I shall present for you the background history of this tragic person.

Nestled in the Bergen County, some half-hour journey if free of traffic from New York City, lie two adjoining towns, Teaneck and Tenafly. Here was Matthew Acciaccatura, an only child, raised by his mother (age thirty-six at the time of the events described, of high school education, a checkout cashier at the Teaneck supermarket A&P) and for a time his father (first name lost to me by a malignant inkblot,[4] divorced when the subject was three, profound traumatic loss) in a two-story abode (closely resembling a hunters' cabin, with its loose-fitting slats, now an ancient quail's egg grey but pregnant with signs of having once been robin's egg blue)[5] in Teaneck, though due I believe to a zoning irregularity he was educated proximally in Tenafly.

Renting a compact auto one autumn day from the firm of Hertz, I visited both towns; indeed, I witnessed the very birthplace of our subject (Englewood Hospital). Sampling local fare, I consumed one ice cream at Häagen-Dazs and one grape soda (subject's childhood favourite) at Toni's Slice A Pizza II; wishing to take in also the area's recreational amusements, I attended a film at the Tenafly Cinema on Claremont Avenue and watched through a window women covered in Latex attempt a sullen style of aerobics at Karen's Fitness Connection. Here is what I have found. Demographically, both towns are almost exclusively white, with an unusual degree of affluence; many of the women who crowded in costly autos to the Tenafly High School at the close of classes wore fur coats, golden ornaments, and that stiff hairstyle peculiar to the upper-class matron. If in Teaneck there exists at least some proletariat (of which Matthew and his mother fell to the

---

[4] At this time, I wish to voice an intense gratitude to Mr. Wayne Phipps and the staff of the Office of the Warden for extending to me the benefit of my notes. (Those parties who take a special interest in the back-story, so to say, of field research may wish to know that „my notes" consist of 1) five A5 ring-bound square-lined notebooks; 2) three air-sealed plastic boxes, intended for kitchen use, in this case sheltering photographs and diverse other materials (ticket halves, serviettes, maps, a wire-fastened bag of earth from Teaneck); 3) a paper carton including my recorder and upwards of thirty cassettes, all of which are labelled and logged with counter cues for ready examination; and many other objects, great and small.)

[5] A serene but unobliging Vietnamese family now occupies this home. How my heart beat as, in the costume of a natural-gas meter-person (purchased Goodwill) I wrote down a string of meaningless numbers, then proceeded to survey its rooms on the pretext of a suspected leak! I am afraid my momentary terror has obscured partially the memory of those settings of our subject's childhood.

lower end) to rub jowls with the *Lumpenbourgeoisie*, Tenafly is more extreme; I excerpt to you from promotional real estate materials: *Make no mistake—Tenafly is among the most elite communities in our country. Nationally distinguished for its superior school system, Tenafly is a haven for discerning families who wish to educate their children in a public school setting without compromising on their standards of prestigious achievement. With its quaint, small-town charm—combined with the convenience of its proximity to New York City—Tenafly has long been a byword for the ultimate in suburbia among the most affluent of buyers.* It amazes me when people say this country is a mobile, effectively classless society.

Readers, hear me. In this *superior school system which does not compromise on the standards of prestigious achievement* of a town representing *the ultimate in suburbia for the most affluent,* young Matthew Acciaccatura suffered actual atrocities. The juvenile homosexual Jason Kirsch has provided me stories, and I have interviewed those members of the staff courageous enough to disobey the „publicity ban" placed by the headmaster of the Tenafly school.[6] Yes, I know you wish to say, *Es wird nicht so heiss gegessen wie es gekocht wird,* it is not nearly so hot in the eating as it is cooked up to be. We have all suffered certain unpleasantnesses in our school years. Who has not been tied to a tree in the play-yard? Who has not been tripped when coming forward to the slate? Who has not had his undergarments stolen and hooked to a flagpole? Who has not been called by some roguish label, such as „Hans Hook-Penis"? Should my mother have had the habit of pressing me to her on my return from school and thereby inhaled that unmistakable salty aroma of tears, I am certain she would have many times discovered my splotches of facial red were not due to the cold I cursed but rather to such quirks and whims of my boyhood colleagues. These youthful games, they may feel painful at first, but eventually they will scab to fond memories; at the least, they must serve as key pathmarks in our process of socialization.

However, in Matthew's case the gay times passed beyond bounds.

---

[6] Thank you, my dear brave M and S. Your kindness shall never go forgotten.

So you may credit me, I shall append some examples. In no special order, thus: the incident when Matthew was locked in a supplies cage in the gymnasium on the last afternoon before spring leave (fortunately, a custodian discovered him towards evening); the incident when Matthew's yearbook photograph was taken and, pasted above the caption SHE SUCKS IT GOOD, copied and affixed about school; the incident when his ninth-grade science experiment, an innovative hygrometer, was stolen from his hands and, during an evil game of toss-ball, smashed on the sidewalk before it could reach the library, all its costly mercury rolling off in tiny toxic balls; the incident in his eleventh grade when a way was found of squirting urine through the vents of his locker, so that when he returned in the morning he found his notebooks and textbooks wet, stained (two weeks before final examinations; he could do no more than apply disinfectant to the pages); the incident when word was spread about campus that he possessed lice, so thoroughly that even the nurse, deluded, slight-brained, summoned him to the office and insisted on herself verifying; truly, so many many incidents, and so much daily hatred, the little and constant humiliations which even insolent children many years younger than he or arrogant teachers (whom we may imagine were threatened by their brilliant pupil) felt easy inflicting on him, without any second regard.

Can you still shake your heads and say *no*? Yet let me remind you I am in possession of facts, which derive from interviews, which are recorded on minuscule cassettes and annotated on small pieces of paper. Now perhaps you will sigh, so it has happened, we believe: but why? He must have deserved it. There must be something wrong with this Matthew.

Let us consider. What may be wrong? Do you recall certain small ones from your own school days, who were inserted in rubbish bins or had their books seized and transported willy-nilly, kept away in a most cruel fashion? So now please can you explain: why did this occur? Were they too slender, too round, too clumsy, too stupid, too clever, did they possess a laugh like the cry of a horse, or perhaps favoured a revolting variety of sandwich, or perhaps wore a wool sweater of an unusual colour Mother had knitted? Ah. If this is what you mean by „deserve," as in „Matthew deserved it," yes, why not?! He *was* different, of this we know. We have ample facts at our disposal: that he was poor in physical education; that he finished the textbook for all of first grade by mid-October (and an edition for second grade a pair of months later), that he was in a different socioeconomic stratum from the other children with their doctor and lawyer papas and mamas (indeed, after the age of three, he possessed no papa at all); that he preferred activities such as reading all the day indoors while other boys are out constructing tree forts and shooting off false pistols. In the photographs captioned *First, Second,* and *Third Grades* I have seen, framed on a wall of the library at Tenafly Elementary (he is absent from the class play-field round-up thereafter), Matthew presents neither an attractive nor confident appearance: he wears corduroys and unmodish leather shoes (this while his peers are in jeans and trainers) and gazes up like a well-greased dumpling. Yes, awkward, strange, even physically grotesque (before his spectacular loss of weight)—but was this a *deserving*? If you are a feeling person, I beg you: imagine what effect the total lack of any companion may have, when a boy has not a single other to confess the hot, trembling emotions brimming from his youthful soul. And as if this condition were not sufficient, please add that sequence of humiliations we have discussed, suppose an atmosphere of perpetual terror—now, who among you will fail to meet with stirrings of outrage and sympathy in his breast?

Do I over-speak? *Not a single other to confess, etc.,* the skeptics query? I am not unaware of a certain boy named Max Sanders, or a certain other boy named Ramin Parhiscar, or a certain summer institute for intelligent children. We may strike Max Sanders instantly; after two happy weeks together, this heartless youth's betrayal must have rendered more woe than he ever did joy for our hero. As for Ramin Parhiscar, who can argue that a nine-months' incident at the age of ten counts for friendship? And may you not be as disappointed as I to learn that Tucker „Chip" Williams, now an engineering student at Case Western University and considered by Matthew the closest of his former summer „friends," could not recall the boy (not even when mailed a colour reproduction of three photographs) and perplexingly, one might say maddeningly, maintained neither to have written nor received so much as a single postal card from our hero. Can this be friendship?

Since I do not anticipate disturbing your peace again at such length, perhaps I should take this moment to tell you some few words about my credentials and research methods, which until now I have only glanced upon and which may therefore create some doubts in your minds. I am a sociologist; since a certain fateful evening in May 1987, when I turned round my auto on the Ku'damm, recovered the distance back to the Freie Universität of Berlin, and pushed a note of resignation beneath the locked door of the Philology Department office, I have followed one goal: the study of the socialization of children. First at the FU, then at the Humboldt-Universität where I pursued my mentor, the esteemed Herr Prof. Arne Blum, back in those heady early days of reunification, I have devoted myself to Microsociology, specializing in particular on what I term the „lonely-child," that one excluded entirely from the normal network of juvenile social relations. Now is not the time to introduce to you the urgent necessity of my work, which, as is my hope, will go some way to illuminate and thence, should my recommendations be put in practise, to alleviate the sufferings of the extreme pariah. (A matter of consequence to all, not merely the pariah: it is in this way we may eliminate the occurrence of those school shootings, those detonations of home-made explosives that disaffected lonely-children inflict upon peers/teachers, which tragedies continue to be wrongly credited to so great a variety of actually impotent sources.) Having completed my Habilitationschrift in 1994, I began a one-year lectureship at my alma mater and would have performed a second such term had I not then moved to America at the ultimatum of my wife, who lives now in Seattle where she has been able to guile her way into an associate professorship and is not important to us today.

Here in your country, I experienced certain financial pressures. Well, let us be frank each with the other, confining ourselves to the strictly professional: the linen paper I sent in a large variety of applications were unable to excite any institution into an interview, nor could they obtain a minor research purse. I was at the point of making a call to my father in München of that sort no adult wishes even once in a life (so to say, the soliciting of funds), when the generous actions of Herr Prof. Blum prevailed—in short order I was installed in an administrative position at the MPS Section on Collective Behavior and Social Movements. As this limb of the MPS is nascent, never did there occur much mail in my shiny rolling cart to deliver, and thus I enjoyed an unforeseen benefit: many hours to devote to contemplative research. What happy days of exploration and discovery these were! In the warmth of a premature spring, about the hour of five, I would emerge from my office to walk some blocks and sit on a bench in the Washington Square Park, where I watched children of all ages at games and battles until long after dark. Who knows how long I might have gone on in this way had not our electrifying subject entered my life?

Yet I believe we do not choose our tasks. The world is full of accidents—accidents or happenings: who can truly distinguish between these? Was it accident I should meet with this lovable boy instantly before his name showered the newspapers, I, the right one, exactly the man enabled to understand him? No, I can not take that pessimists' view. Although I may not discuss how my path came to cross so definitively with Matthew's,[7] I disclose that one private experience allowed me (and my scholarship in alienation had prepared me for) a matchless aperture onto the heart of this adorable boy—whom the media, concerned primarily with the economic benefits granted by titillation and fantasy, seemed to be doing their uppermost to slur. Thus did I pronounce: Hans, you are one who comprehends something greater of this tragic boy. Hans, now is the moment to enter the field. Hans, whichever danger or pain may await you, whichever risks you may run alongside, this solitary youth must be restored to true reputation.

---

[7] Regretfully, all indications of my experience of this youth must remain behind veil until such time as my disclosures may not have an adverse effect upon a jury.

Such momentous pronouncements for myself these have revealed themselves to be! Swiftly, after first shooting off a postal card to Herr Prof. Blum heralding my project, I leapt into the phase of data-gathering. I have already mentioned my exchange with Matthew's former university, that presentation of my credentials which led to my being connected with the young homosexual Jason Kirsch. Further, in order to better understand Matthew's plight, I sought out the key sites and, wherever possible, went under the identical experiences that had proved so disastrous for him: I visited the night-clubs, cafés, dining halls, classrooms, and even surveilled the dormitories where Matthew had once been, in order to certify the accuracy of my comprehension of the social workings of the university sphere. What joyful hours these were, dressed in my filched custodian's uniform, pushing a broom along the luminous hallway right into knowledge! I may have resembled the extinct sabre-tooth tiger with my pasted-on moustache, but the ruse functioned: no one[8] gave me a second glance as I glided along the gleaming rubber floor, drawing nearer to some undergraduate conversation, some flustered girl or boy caught in the foehn of social drama. I tell you, it is intoxicating to observe how like kittens or puppies in their naïve savagery they deal out snubs and jokes and even delicate shoves—all of this in preparing to be *adult*, which is to say caught in the exquisite net of human relations. Yet it was not all joy: when I listened to their laughter rising ghostlike out of sight in the stairwell or, equally mesmerizing, spotted through a window a bundle of children exchanging amiable punches, I felt something. I hardly know how to describe this feeling. I felt Matthew's absence, so much I seemed almost to be moving in a cloud of his absence. But it was not the absence you may think of, his final disappearance from a bright stage. No, the one whom I felt a lack of was more this early Matthew, the Matthew of September, October, November, when he was not a part of the games, was unseen, an outsider with his nose up at the glass, watching, just as I was.

---

[8] Or so in the time I believed. Later, I came to regret the notice these forays had drawn to me.

2.

School began on the fifth of September. And its inception marked the beginning of a gray period Matt occasionally referred to as *hell*, which was to say the infernally perpetual iteration of the same disappointing day.

Morning after morning he woke in the haze of Josh's sweat stench, unsealed the hall door and marched the seven squeaking steps to the bathroom, where, under the sink or shower's marvelous water, he tried to wash off the particles of nightmares—which were these very days, blown up and reconfigured. Then he pivoted on a heel and walked back down the hallway, fashioned from a mysterious bouncy rubber and tinted nauseating purple and mint, where if there were kids, lingering by the water fountain, dangling plastic baskets of Pert and Zest, brushing crusts of sleep from their eyes, he felt his heart surge hungrily forward at the bars of its cage—but they scraped pitiless glances over him a moment, then were past.

What should he have done? Wave? Approach at eight A.M., with nothing to say?

Back in the room he flung his legs through a pair of pants, in the oyster-colored light that the courtyard window threw, while Josh's insistent snore rapped against his ear until, dressed, he grabbed his courier bag, shoved it full of notebooks, and bolted into a fresh heartsickening day. In the stairwell a feeling belled up in the gut like vertigo, while he stood staring down at girls and guys in jeans and T-shirts who skipped along, swapping chitchat or in-jokes—just pursuing them with pathetic stick-ing eyes. Next came the dining hall, that vast savanna where zebras and lions and giraffes, distanced in their social groups, grazed at tables upon bagels and mugs of coffee, immersed in their own sphere unless some earthshattering laughter or terrifying ding of spoons on bowls called them to some loser who's dropped his tray in a spectacular clatter of plas-tic and Cap'n Crunch. There Matt trembled, clutching his rhomboid tray, his fear skyrocketing out like a flare set off into the sky; pacing the aisles, he sought some kind eye among these faces, skirting the preps' table where Carly and Caleb might be seen glittering and rich and angu-lar, skirting the table of jocks, huge statues draped in fleece, skirting the goody-goodies in button-downs who hailed from Iowa or Indiana and were smilingly, irrepressibly Christian, skirting even the dorks, because even they had barriers, passwords one couldn't begin to know, video games and computer-code jokes, till at the end of the gigantic hall, spot-ting no one who would reliably welcome him, he slipped into the side room, that annex where the other isolatoes sat spaced over twelve picnic benches, facing unpaged textbooks, spooning untasted food into their mouths.

And when he exited into a crisp new autumn day, when, on time again, he zipped through morning New York, febrile with its sick elec-tricity all charged up overnight, then passed by the triumphantly arched park and landed at Meyer Hall: what did he find there?

Droves of kids disappearing behind doors. Thousands of black spiral binders flipping open; thousands of ballpoint pens uncapping, echoing a gunshot ricochet.

Now, let's not get hasty, he'd said at the conclusion of week one. Not even when he got his federal work-study assignment: assisting in the M&O office, that is, Maintenance & Operations, that is, *janitorial* labor, in Hayden Hall. Couldn't it be worse? Like those poor kids backstage at the dining hall—who had to pick your plates off the trays and wipe gloved hands over your leftover food and mush it in the bin; through the open kitchen door you could always see their pale faces straining, bodies obscured by the revolting aprons and buff uniforms. And hadn't he made friends, even excellent friends, with Jason? Dinnertime that second

evening had turned into lunch the next day, which turned into an afternoon of chatter in Jason's room two flights above Matt's. Time dissolved
with Jason, its littlest nanospheres scattered into the recesses of the day.
Slouched at a table, combing fork tines through spuds, or lolled back on
his bed, picking at a nappy sock, Jason was a penguin-shaped firecracker,
delivering definite opinions on everything from Audrey Hepburn to arm
hair, interspersed with scattershot laughter and offhanded quirks that
made Matt think. A first chum—even together a team, *The Goy and The
Gay,* as Jason had nicknamed them—isn't that a solid start?

Yet as "classes began" and "people settled down"—all those famous
stages he was purportedly awaiting—no one, not one acquaintance
more. What was a boy to do? Sometimes, if Josh was out at the *Washington Square News* office and Dwight off with his preppy friends, Matt
would sit by the door listening to conversations in the hall, just to get an
inside track on how the back-and-forth tennis match of banter began.
But it was maddening; the vital moments were either blurred or body-
language cues like hand slaps, God knows what. He'd thought for a time
the key was to expand the range of contact-chances; well, sir, he did that:
he remained ruminant and slow in the classroom after lecture, he
borrowed pens and grinned, he stood blindly before the corkboards of
Meyer Hall overflowing with notices about psych experiments and fan-
tastical summers abroad, he even traipsed out to the water fountain once
per class, in case some friendly-seeming kid would be doing something,
anything approachable on the benches there.[9]

Not that he hadn't *seen* promising friend possibilities. There was that
magically cool kid from the eleventh floor of Third North, who always
wore ripped Ts under the same pinched black blazer and stepped jauntily
in boots like Matt's own, smirking, alternative, cool. His name was Scott

---

[9] Yes! I recognize this hallway vividly, as my former wife taught in 214 Meyer and I therefore walked these same footprints amid the swirling of children many times to collect her
from the seminar room, or simply to sit on a bench outside with my back to the wall,
knowing that behind it she was inspiring thirteen youthful minds with her bright, smiling, lying face.

Belfast, and the crew spotted through the window back on the first day had instantly snapped tight about him and his royal consort, that Amazonian, Julie-Christie-faced, six-foot-tall girl, who habitually tucked her jeans into knee-high boots and blond hair into a messy chignon; those two were always moistly, openmouthed smooching—dashing, romantic figures from an Antonioni movie. Matt regularly had the usual daydreams, that he and Scott Belfast would be thrown together somehow, in a classroom, in the bathroom, and Matt would say something scintillatingly witty and Scott Belfast would crack up and by the end of it, *Hey* (a discerning eye cast now over Matt's clothes), *why not come to our table for lunch?* where he would meet Lady Liza Andrewes and the rest of the cool-kid gang, And They Lived Happily Ever After. But such an opportunity, like those antecedents fantasized in high school, never presented itself, though he had gone in search of it. He had roved Eleventh Floor, nonchalant, reading bulletin boards. He had offered the Scott Belfast hanger-on Sheila Meeks, a short girl with a mop of dyed-black hair, a light in the forecourt of Third North; she had clapped a hand about the fluttering lighter flame, grunted *Thank you,* and turned before he could open his mouth. What anyway could he have said? *What's up?*—whatever he may have inscribed in his notes—so far was shaping up to be not much of an icebreaker. In point of fact, the only people who ever offered real openings to Matt were helpless losers themselves: like Jillian Lawrence from Fifth Floor, also a veteran of Math Counts!, the Bergen County interschool league, who once, while her strange fleshy lips foamed saliva at the corners, asked him down for dinner. Jeez! And Carel, the Czech physics genius from his floor, wished perhaps to make a study break? so often that it was becoming somewhat awkward until the advent of Jan, miraculous *other* Czech physics genius from Third North (what are the chances? Thank you, Lord), put a stop to that.

New York, in this context, was brutal. Gorgeous white pampered dogs loping territorially along the sidewalk of lower Fifth Avenue exerted more power, more financial, social clout than he did. There were tiny children in gingham, who could probably not say more than a handful of words, who were nevertheless more real than he was, in the eyes of the black nannies they dragged about, imperiously ordering, or in the glittering eyes of doormen encased in their carapaces of wool and brass. SoHo, the West Village, even Chelsea—Bond Street, Grove, the sink of Prince where people in capelets, futuristic sunglasses, and clean shaves spilled out of restaurants and stores, streaming straight ahead without stepping aside: he was gum under shoe; no, he was less than that. The stores were filled with things he couldn't afford, the groceries massed piles of food he couldn't eat, and the baseline experience of walking on the streets was blown candy wrappers and the noise of car doors slamming, taxi after taxi gathering its passengers, rich businessmen with briefcases where gold locks glistened, a group of Russian or Swedish tourists lovely and leggy and laughing, dragging their Prada shopping bags in after them, ladies crushing out half-finished cigarettes under pump toes before getting in and slamming their doors, slamming door after door in the hotel of his mind where he wandered each of the carpeted hallways in solitude and midnight.

"Aren't you worried?" he asked Jason one afternoon. He was lying on his back on Jason's bed; Jason was on the soiled putty couch, smoking, illegally, by an open window. It had been the usual sort of day. After Moral Reasoning lecture, he had "done errands" (fingering notebooks in the stationery store, lingering by the magazine stand in CVS with a tube of toothpaste), then made his way to Jason's single, where they had listened to Morrissey and scrutinized the freshman facebook, as they always did. That dark tome, with its thousands of black-and-white squares like pieces in a vast, inscrutable game, could never be exhausted—there was something narcotic about it; drinking in those pictures, hour opened into hour like black flowers. He and Jason had invented categories: there were *normalcies,* to nab Harding's word, fresh out of ordinary lives in bland Midwestern states; *lost* international students, looking blown off-course already in these before-school photos; *artsos; politicos; sailors*—rich, preppy, good-looking dauphins and dauphines, who lounged moneyed and easy gazing off yachts into their prospects of forever-summer—and their uneasily related subset the *brokers,* always fresh-washed semi-men who in actual suit jackets paged at lunch through universes of stock stats, their minds wholly trained on that blank shut book, that air-colored fiction called *The Future.* Almost every day Matt and Jason exchanged some bit of news that bore out the destinies inhering in these two-inch seed crystals. Today it was Jason's turn: he'd spotted Anna Waters, a textbook sailor if ever there were one, after weeks of uneasily hanging with her normalcy roommates, at last walking icily side by side with Carly Hale.

"Worried?" asked Jason. "What for?"

Matt turned to his side. He propped his head up and gazed at Jason, unwashed on the couch in dirty socks and a graying T-shirt. "Did you even go to class today?"

"Me? Of course I did. I wouldn't miss Professor Reynolds for anything." Jason made the "hot" sound, a noise between rolling Spanish *r*s and a cat purring. "Clark," he whispered breathily, "as I like to think of him."

Matt fell back on the bed. "Worried. It's October, October fifth, for Christ's *sake*."

"So what? For holy Mary's sake, whom you must know I pray to every day?"

"Sorry. And we don't have any other friends. When are *we* going to hook up with our crew?" He scrambled up and flopped forward on his stomach, propping his jaw with both palms. "What are our pictures supposed to mean?"

"Ohh, baby." Jason's warm brown eyes sent rays of fellow-feeling into Matt. "I'm sorry. But—and do *not* take this badly—my picture says *Bashful Little Fag*. Or at least that's what I tried to make it say. And I do have, um, Stan and Jorge. From QU."

"Swell." Matt dropped his face into the maroon bedspread and linked his fingers on the back of his head. "Thank you" came out muffled.

"Maybe you should join QU. Your boots alone . . ."

"That joke is so agèd," replied Matt, hunching up onto his elbows, "it's decaying. Like your splendid stinking bedspread."

"Now, now," said Jason. "Now, now. Here, have a chocolate." He held out a box of Russell Stover.

Matt reached for a turtle. One hundred calories, most like. No slice of bread this dinner. "Listen. It's over. People are already beginning to tidy up, turn the sign to *closed*. Even dorks have friends now. Do you know Philip, that midget with the dragonfly laugh? I'm serious, it's like the buzzing of their wings. Anyway—I saw him at breakfast with friends. Literally making Spock fingers. And Dwight—the other day, at the salad bar, he picks up a bowl, meets this kid: right off he's jawing in that we're-two-like-minded-guys way he does, and by the end of the line, presto. Invited to a party."

"Dwight's good." Jason took a chocolate from the box and chewed. "He's very, very smooth. He can do it. What about his friends? Is there even one you might—"

Matt shook his head. He'd met them, mostly, tagging along to a couple of parties. Both times, after an hour of sipping a sweet, terrible drink by a potted plant watching the ballets of hello and chitchat, he had been forced to slip down the stairs toward home. The first night, a guy named Walker and another named Taylor had sidled up, *noblesse oblige*, and Walker inquired, "So you're Dwight's roommate? Where are you from?" He tried putting them off the scent with "just outside of the city," but next they had to know where he'd gone to school. And after that, Taylor merely folded a cocktail napkin to his thin lips, his eyes picking over the room beyond Matt's shoulder; a sheepish Walker dug deeper into his khaki pockets as he wondered aloud: "Oh, somehow I thought you were up with Scudder at Groton." Some illustrious academy—that's what they'd expected! It was all like something out of *The Sun Also Rises:* And where did you prep, old chap? "Walker," Taylor jutted his chin toward a group by the drinks table, "do you see who's here." A tall collegial type *actually wearing* a yellow ascot lifted a tumbler at them; murmuring beautiful *excuse me*s, the pair hurried off. For the rest of that evening and at the next shindig, if any of that crowd glanced Matt's way, they might nod, might say "Timothy" or "Andrew" and offer a stolid hand, but mostly they stared through, as if he were some glass panel jerked out and leaned against the wall.

"Welcome to Scarsdale," agreed Jason. "I know that type. Fully. What about Josh? Could you make nice with him?"

"I would like to. I've tried." Well, he *had,* asking what classes Josh was choosing or how his day went, but the kid always responded with grunts, tantamount to rudeness. Yet Josh certainly was smart, had a magisterial knowledge of current events and a dry, acerbic wit that came out, in the conversations in the room or hall Matt was party to, as little sniper hits with the kids he knew. Which appeared to be legion. Matt sighed. "You wouldn't believe how many people he already knows from New York. Besides, he's never here. He eats his meals in Hillel, and every weekend, starting Friday afternoon—vanished. Home to Brooklyn." And how could someone intelligent as Josh like Dwight, that fatuous cretin? Of course, if Matt entered, Josh didn't even tilt his vision from his computer screen to return a handful of pained monosyllables—yet instantly he shot from his chair, was clinging to the single's door, laughing puppy-ishly when Dwight waltzed in. *Don't fall for it,* he wanted to shake Josh and say, *you're better than that.* But the blank-eyed stare Josh would give Matt when he passed by eviscerated such altruism.[10]

"God, Dwight." Matt let his hands fall to the bed. "He makes me actually nauseated. You know? Just seeing his big, fat face. Just hearing that voice—all husky, as if he's *so* sincere—ugh, it just makes me want to gag. Pass me that box again. Please." He lifted out a white-chocolate square. Alas, no glass of milk this evening. Maybe he wouldn't even be hungry. He really did feel stomach-sick.

"You know who he reminds me of? Bill Clinton. The scratchy voice? So *earnest;* even the way he looks at you . . . That boy has it down. Mm, I'm kind of nauseous too. Nauseated. Whatev'." Jason tossed the box to the couch so the chocolates jumped. "Let's go down to din."

Matt checked his watch. "It's only five forty-five! It's so empty now. It's kind of sad."

Jason stared at him. "The dining hall's open. I'm hungry. Let's go."

"Fine," huffed Matt. And thudded down two flights to change his sweaty shirt.

---

[10] Since a fair mind is the rudiment of any good investigation, and as Herr Prof. Blum always informed me, *Jedes Ding hat seine zwei Seiten,* each thing has its two sides, I contacted these two heartless youths by phone and mail and electronic mail and brief, unobtrusive personal visits. They have not only refused interviews to assist my restoring the good name of their former roommate, but Joshua has even attempted to suggest that he had never lived with Matthew, which any simpleton with a 1995–1996 NYU Students' Directory can tell you is utter falsehood.

Dear God: no, not *now*. Dwight was home; through the open single door Matt could hear that smooth operator rapping on the cordless from all the way down in the double, where he rummaged through the wardrobe for something clean. "You're too kind," Dwight was saying. A gentle *thunk-thunk* indicated he was playing catch with his ridiculous springy ball against the wall. "That's very nice of you to say. And listen, hey, I had no idea you lived so close. No, no, I didn't. You should come in sometime, have lunch around here, see the place. Yeah, whenever you can. Don't be silly—that would be great. We would totally love that. All right. Don't believe me! All right, well, if you get a free day sometime. All right. And you know what? Matt just came in, I just heard him. Okay, we'll talk again. Have a great evening..." Dwight's sprightly steps crossed the common room—one of Dwight's friends wanted to talk to *him*? Matt felt a caffeine rush shoot up and illuminate his brain, incandescent electric hot—then Dwight was in the doorway extending the cordless and a toothy smile. "Your mother."

Matt grabbed the phone. "Mom?!" He smiled grimly at Dwight and shut the double's door.

Her nasal voice came over the line. "What a nice boy that roommate of yours is. He's so polite. Dwight, it's Dwight, right?"[11]

Matt coughed and turned away from the door, squeezing himself to the far end by the window in case Dwight could still hear. "Yes, it's Dwight." Infallible. Her instinct for needling was unerring. In the five-odd weeks since school's start, her interest in all things NYU had been tepid, to say the least. Having gamely accepted being left behind (when he'd called the day after, she noted only that the move must have been "real hot"), she contented herself on his biweekly calls with the passing of tidbits about Hollywood movies or what Tenafly High moms had lately picked up a jug of milk at the market (luckily rare, as Food Emporium in Fort Lee was where their schmancier groceries habitually hailed from). But in moments on the phone with Dwight—bingo! She knew!

---

[11] She would not speak with me. Repeatedly I tried; repeatedly she cut the telephone line. So it went, at least once a week, for two months, until the afternoon she threatened to call on me the police. In retrospect I see this was perhaps only an idle threat.

"I thought so. So polite. He just invited me to lunch."

"What did you say?" Please God let her not have said anything about the A&P!

"I said I couldn't, I said I was busy!" Her voice went shrilly high. She laughed; something distasteful in that laugh, a girlish flutter he didn't recognize. It was almost: *flirtatious.* Jesus. Imagine her showing up— Dwight would dismiss her 180 pounds on sight as a frowzy-headed grocery bag blown to his doorstep from white-trash land.

"...political science." She was polishing off something he'd missed. "What's *your* major?"

"Um, I don't know yet, Mom. We—we don't have to decide until the end of sophomore year."

"Huh," she said. Satisfied; confirmed. *I thought so. Failure.* "Well, could you do political science?"

"Of course I could," he snapped. "But I won't."

"Why not? It sounds very—"

"Because I *hate* it."

"—very intaresting. Okay, Matt, what's the matter? You hungry? You always get so cranky when you get hungry."

"I'm sorry, Mom. Actually: uh, that *is* it. See, I was just going down to dinner."

"Oh! You shoulda just said so. Go, go! Make sure to get plenty of good meat. All I wanted to tell you anyway is that I saw on TV there's a humungous sale going on at Macy's and I know you don't have any pajamas. I know you think those little shorts are enough—"

"Ma!" He slept in boxers and a T-shirt. "Mom, I'm fine!"

"You could at least get a robe..."

"Mom, I have a robe. Don't worry about it! But thank you. I'm fine. Okay? I better go. I'm meeting a guy for dinner. A friend."

A silence on the line. His mother knew his friend situation. Though the topic had never crossed her lips. "Okay," she said, her voice strangely indeterminate of feeling, "you better hurry up then. G'bye."

He felt himself flush. A little Rubicon had been crossed here. After all these years of wondering why she didn't try to help, or console, or at least admit it: what sort of freak he was. At worst she had been deliberately turning a blind eye, at best it was embarrassment. Why had he avoided telling her about Jason—except to forestall a vulnerable, open moment? Well, here. There had been no congratulations. In fact, she had practically raced off the line. A lightness was in his brain, a feeling of blood rushing everywhere unobstructed in his body. He was loosed from something, some long, rotting almost umbilical line. Here at school, out of her reach, he was a new sort of person; she didn't know him anymore, didn't even have that on him. He skipped out, dropped the phone on its cradle, and zoomed into the hallway, down the flights of stairs to the lobby.

"*There* you are." Jason sprang up from the wooden bench. "Oh, much cleaner."

"Sorry," he said, grinning contentedly down at the shirt he'd neglected to change. "My mother called and wouldn't let me get off the phone."

At the food stations, he drizzled full-fat dressing over his salad in celebration and at the last minute snatched a peanut-butter cream pie. Over dinner he found himself uncommonly gregarious—*on*, as if skateboarding through universes of words, snazzy. And when near the end Jason waved to Stan just entering the conveyor-belt line, Matt wondered aloud, "You know, you might be onto something. With QU." Wasn't that Jason's gold mine for new friends? How could we have underestimated this avenue?

"You wanna join QU?" Jason lifted out a green Jell-O cube.

Matt happily banged the cool Formica table. "I mean, *activities*. I mean, duh! That's the way to do it!"

Activities. When he got back from dinner—the suite becalmed, empty of Dwight and Josh—he crept into the common room. Trembling, he flipped through the student handbook, the buzz of the fluorescent light like the noise of his own lasery excitement. There were, oh my God, dozens and dozens of clubs. And all this time he'd thought of joining a club as mainly ornamental, a kind of extra, what one did after firmly settling into a social position. Here he was taking laborious water-fountain trips in Meyer Hall, smoking hopefully outside the dorm: when how

much more abundant, how much more prolonged were the contact
opportunities these offered. He leaned back on a chair and raked his
eyes over the list. Plum Blossom Wushu Society—whatever is that? such
a beautiful name! Ah, tomorrow he could winnow this tremendous
register down to two or three suitables. Quite true; he shook his head in
disbelief he had failed to consider it all properly until just now.

That night, capitulating to the precipitous tail-off of his pie's sugar rush,
Matt went to bed shamefully early. And thus, having rested already, after
Josh roused him at four—when Josh's sleep cycle reverberated the double with its loudest, battering-ram snores—Matt was wakeful enough,
even once the room quieted, to hear another noise.

A girl was crying. Through the fire door, its light wood letting
through the sound.

There were five girls living next door. Obviously it was not Carly
Hale, who had probably not lost a tear from the glacier of herself in all of
her eighteen years; there was Sara Carter, who Matt knew for a fact lived
on the far side of the suite by that window shade she had painted orange,
visible from the street; Marcia Brandton was definitely out, as Matt had
witnessed her leaving Third North with an overnight bag and a mantle
of impenetrable hauteur; then Jennifer Liu—but, so happy, such the
decent nice-nice type, plus, with her shrill pipsqueak? it just didn't sound
right.

Mary: the Egyptian girl, with the floating dark hair, Mary, who always looked as if she'd just eaten a poisonous mushroom. What a quiet
girl! Had he ever heard her speak? Only the eyes, behind pearly-rose-
rimmed glasses, were expressive: calm, implacable, but somehow definitely sensitive, soft and rich in their deep velvety blackness. What did
he know about her? Her mother was an architect, he had heard someone
say. She was middle height, with an innocuous slender figure; she wore
long cotton collarless shirts over shapeless tan pants, no-brand sneakers;
she had a very erect posture and moved gracefully, placing one foot in
front of the other quite straight. Had he ever even seen her eating in the
dining hall? Maybe not with anyone and not alone, not at all. Now and

then, though, she could be spotted in the common lounge, with furred slippers and sheaves of crisp blue airmail paper on which she transcribed line after line in a steady hand.

She was still weeping. A water clock, self-enclosed, neither speeding nor slowing.

He understood. He recognized this kind of desolation, the pure blackviolet bloom opening to enclose you with its Venus flytrap mouth. *You're not alone,* he could get up and whisper, *it will get better*—but these cheerful platitudes, they never would have helped him; he could not just unload them on her. Still, he felt linked with her, invisibly, firmly: as if the two of them were two green shoots tied together through the fire door.

Forty-eight hours later it happened again. He woke up, heard her. And often from that night on, he listened. Ever a light sleeper, he hardly needed to try: some hollowed-out time, he would flash awake, fold his arms behind-head, and, sure enough, if Josh stopped snoring, the noise would float in, ghostlike, unbodied. There might come a few small coughs, or little breath-catch gasps, but otherwise Mary kept up an un-interrupted weeping. Eventually the sound would diminish, not as if she'd stopped, exactly, simply grown quieter or faced away from the door. Then he'd shut his eyes and without trouble plummet into slumber.

In the days, he watched her. He watched her padding gravely along the hall to the bathroom with her toiletries in a wicker basket. He watched her methodically chewing corn chips while she read the con-tents of the bulletin board. He watched her bending to take a drink from the fountain—first she took off her big glasses and then, with the same hand, cupped the curly fringe away from her forehead in a way that made her round olive face almost beautiful. What else could he do? Every-thing that happened between them at night happened without her knowledge. And in the hallway, under the fluorescence of day, it all seemed as distant as something in another country, another life.

3.

Activities: that was the new watchword. Over lunch in the dining-hall annex, Matt narrowed down the list (Brazilian Capoeira? the Ayn Rand Group?) to two possibilities. First, Parliamentary Debate. Here at least he would find a footing easily: after all, in high school he had placed quite decently in a couple of Bergen County–wide tournaments. Perverse, not to mention tragic too: though lost at leisurely chitchat with his so-called peers, nonetheless before a judge and armed with a topic, he could whip his words expertly into utterance, there where the wheels of logic were all that mattered.

Yet when he opened the door to Meyer Hall 504 at five-fifteen on October 9, saw a splenetic red-faced guy finish declaiming about biodiesel at the podium and a girl in loafers preparatorily smirking before rows of hawkeyed notetakers...Well. *This* again? All that vacant rhetoric left a sour taste. Patiently, Matt sat through the charade—"And *he* expects us to believe," the girl might say, with a derisive jerk of her head, dragging giant piles of xeroxes to her aid, from which she read strings of numbers and words, and once even, "If you believe that, I have a couple of bridges to sell you"—feeling his fingers tingle with shame for the red-faced guy busily scribbling notes, until finally the professor warbled, "Time!" Then Matt bolted from the room. No, debate was not the best spot for finding friends; just a bunch of sharks swimming round in an auditorium.

Rather, his other choice was perfect: nothing competitive, something

calm and celebratory, common-cause: the Asian Cultural Union. *To pro-*
mote the understanding and appreciation of the cultures and histories of
Asians and Asian-Americans, the register said. Doesn't that sound nice?
Summer afternoons after Mrs. Nakamura paid him for cutting her grass
and buying groceries, while he took green tea in her lemon-yellow silk-
covered living room shaded by scarlet maples, she'd explain about the
prints framed on her walls and show him the work of Hokusai and
Hiroshige.[12] Dazed with those serious, ethereal things, in the heady first
week of class he had flirted with a beautifully sibilant but alas too work-
intensive and difficult section of Beginning Japanese. Yes, the ACU.
Wouldn't they have screenings, symposia, fascinating trips to museums?
Just imagine: a room filled with paintings, with pleasant conversation,
and you're in a corner speaking of brushstroke to a little group interested
in that stuff too!

So Wednesday afternoon Matt shook off a leaden gray day passing
through a glass double door in the Asian Pacific American Institute and
walked down a bland institutional hallway to stand in an acid-green
sweater and trim navy Dickies—*Outfit (Casual) #5*—before the receptionist, a tiny Japanese girl dwarfed by an enormous steel desk. On the
wall above her was a glossy picture of Mount Fuji, rich and grassy, where
impossible fluffed clouds hovered in a serene blue sky.

He cleared his throat, put hands to his sides, and bowed from the
waist in the neat style Mrs. Nakamura had taught. *"Konichiwa,"* trilling
the *wa* so it hung pleasantly in the air, work it, let's work it out baby,
"watashi no namae wa Matt Acciaccatura-*san desu."* Or—maybe she
wasn't Japanese; her mouth had popped ajar into puzzled-look. "Ah, good
evening. My name is Matt Acciaccatura, and I'm interested in joining—"

---

[12] Mrs. Nakamura: a most agreeable woman! A widow of fifty with the damp skin of a
young girl. What a happy hour we passed, in this very sitting room, sipping such tea,
swapping anecdotes about her young pupil, she what she remembered and I what I had
gathered. (It was in this way, to my misfortune, that I chanced to let fall from my mouth
the eventual trajectory of Matthew, of which, living under a stone, perhaps, she had
heard nothing. However, I am fairly certain I managed to unsay all I said by cleverly simu-
lating translation errors. We parted on cheerful terms.)

"Ssssh!"

Through two pinned-open doors to the right of the girl's desk, Matt saw a long auditorium aisle at the end of which a speaker on a stage was gripping the podium, seeking out the noisemaker beyond the lights, while mere feet away rows of kids twisted in their seats, shooting angry glares directly at him.

"Oh!" he squeaked, jerking toward the doors—and knocking over a cupful of pens with his courier bag, swinging wide. The pens clinked on the floor and began to roll, the blasted cheap Bics! "Oh! Oh, I'm so horribly sorry. Wait, I'll..." He was on his knees now, scrabbling on the floor under the giant desk.

Scurrying down from her side of it, the receptionist giggled. But nice. She had sparks in her black eyes and was astoundingly thin, a scaffolding of bones over which a gold tarpaulin of skin was tautly, glisteningly stretched. Two rudderlike collarbones peeked out from the neckhole of her pink sweater, which widened as she propped herself up and brushed her fountaining sprays of silver earrings. *"Hei,"* she whispered breathily, "Matt Acciaccatura-*san*." Giggled again; what a pretty tinkle. "I think you can see, the meeting's already started. Anyway, go take a seat. I'll get this." She reached for the pens in his hand and warmly smiled. The left earring stretched as she reached; now Matt could see one of its strands had hooked inside the loose weave of the sweater's high neck.

"Hold it! May I touch you for a moment?"

"What?!" Her jaw fell, more surprised-pleased than aghast.

"Just..." Deftly he managed to unhook the silver link. "There. You don't want to, you know—pull on the lobe, disastrous, happened to my mother once, went all the way through..."

"Oh." Craning down at the sweater. "Thanks." She flashed back to him and winked. "Now give me the pens. I've got this."

"Righto." He released them into her nimble grasp, accidentally touching the slender fingers. Now he slunk off to secret his offending body inside the auditorium—but moments after he slid his butt into the empty back row, the audience erupted in applause, started speeding toward the doors. Had he mixed up the time? Out in the hall, while some groups were heading down the walkway to the outside, others appeared to be staying, or rather turning left into another, smaller room: behind their bodies Matt spotted folding tables laden with refreshments. Why, a little reception! Excellent, he was ready.

He strode to a table and filled a plastic cup with soda water.

"Oof!" A short, stumpy Korean girl had accidentally collapsed her broad heft into him; holding up her hands as if to keep him at bay, she crept backward away. "Doh!"

"*Je*sus, Katherine, you're such a klutz." Two other Korean girls materialized.

"It's okay," he declared, generous. He slouched toward them.

The tallest one, likely the leader, scrutinized his sweater. "Are you in the ACU?"

"Yeah," he snapped, in the vocal style Aloof. "Well, this is my first meeting."

"Oh, you're a *fresh*man," the first girl said, manically scooping chips in dip.

"What'd you think of the speaker?" whined the middle girl, singsongy.

"Um." He could frame this as badass. "Whatever." He shrugged. "I missed most of it . . ." Then crown it with a snicker, for the truly arch and cool effect.

"Oh, wait, wait." Holding up her red paws, the evil dwarf revealed a mouthful of dip and broken chips. "You're not that guy who—" She cackled ecstatically. "You totally are! That guy who like came in the back and started all—*Konichiwaaaa!*"

"No." The eyes of the tall girl filled with disbelief.

"Sorry," he mumbled. Was that loserish? His accent was actually pretty good back there.

"Hey, is that Issey?" The middle girl tipped her head across the room.

"Issey!" Tall Girl waved to a kid with an expert shag. "Bye," she murmured to Matt.

"*Konichiwaaa . . .*" sang the dwarf under her breath, brushing crumbs from her shirt.

So. A boy shows up a little late. A boy talks a little too loudly, okay, in Japanese—they probably hadn't even noticed the pens thing. Brilliant!

Konichiwa—sayonara! Already the crowd was thinning; scanty groups clung to columns in the center like filings around magnets. Couples were shaking on their coats, shouldering bags, and bobbing along like merry rowboats toward the door. Wait a second, was he the only white person here? Ah, jeez. How had he missed that? Certainly white faces had passed by in the auditorium, but this event was evidently a private party. How crazily must he stand out: *what's the white boy doing here?* God. If he moved too quickly now, he would cry, it would just come out, water from a crushed sponge. He gazed off into space, feigning to read the signs on the wall opposite.

"Hold it," said a pert voice, "you have broccoli on your cheek." Then a small hand had brushed his cheek with one deft gesture. "Gone," a tiny girl before him asserted definitely, "Matt-*san.*" It was the girl from the receptionist desk, standing a whole half foot below him in a pink sweater dress and knee-high black leather boots. Her hair was cut asymmetrically, nearly to the shoulder on the right while the left side bounced at the length of the silver earrings' sprays. A mischievous smile crimped her lips, moistly covered now in some kind of gloss. "I forgot to ask for permission! But maybe you don't mind. It's Sophie," she added.[13]

---

[13] Is it not amazing what insignificant minutiae Eros makes use of? In my own case, a simple mix-up: I had purchased a ticket to hear the always thought-provoking Herr Prof. Fritz Memling from Darmstadt talk on new approaches to the mind-body problem as applied to small-group organization but had mistaken the date. So I was sitting in my small wooden seat staring confusedly at the stage where a little woman shaped like a vulture had just trotted to the podium, under a banner that read: Dr. Patrizia Moretti, when Lisanne arrived with her ticket for the identical seat. *Entschuldigung,* she said—you could tell immediately that she was French, and then I noticed that I knew or rather recognized her from the department—and by the time we had untied the whole situation, we were laughing so fiercely that the silly usher asked us to leave. He was a narrow youth with a tremendous number of blemishes and a voice so very high and nasal, his attempts to sound authoritative were only making us laugh harder: I felt some tug on my arm and turned to see Lisanne in tears, tears of hysteria, and then she was dragging my arm up the aisle, waving her hand in front of her nostrils and mouth as if her laughter were something she were inhaling. So together we ran, away from Dr. Patrizia Moretti

Quite all right, he said, or thought he said. He was smiling and the room was filled with blurring volumes of water. She was complimenting his Japanese accent. With a curled finger she was calling him over to a wall with something, a rectangle something, a piece of paper, a train time-table, a calendar, God-knows-what-it-was, a schedule of ACU events, he was blowing bubbles through his mouth, *Uh-huh, thank you,* grinning, inane, and, just because there was nothing else to say, he wagged a finger toward the Isamu Noguchi Sculpture Garden poster and noted how that museum was hard to get to but really lovely. She narrowed her eyes at him. *I* love *him,* she claimed accusingly. And for the whole long instant while she stood staring, barely a foot away, before she tossed her hair and asked, *When did you go?,* breaking the spell—her sentence had dissolved to reform as what it was not: fine wires of her love for *him* snapping tight through his veins.

Why should a girl by the name of Sophie Yamamoto come brush the broccoli from his cheek? And why, further, should she ask him back to her place for something to eat? These and all other questions Matt put into the hands of fate, as he trailed by her side through the just-rained, gleaming streets. It was too much to keep up with her speedy boots to worry about his own body moving aptly, too much to take in all her swerving banter to worry much what he was saying back. By his side crossing between taxis before traffic lights went green, darting across the wide double river of Houston Street—where she turned back at the median to check for him with an open, crooked smile—she was lovely and as perfectly unbelievable as the Tooth Fairy, and as they talked tiny

---

standing spotlit on the stage, and out the doors, past the tables of the antiquated book-sellers, into the free, fresh air of a summer day. Then I bought her a mint ice cream from that stand which used to be just two hundred metres down, and opposite the big gate on Unter den Linden—which was really more like gelato, the style where they pour the mint sauce on afterward, because she leaked it on me, on a grey sweater, brand-new, which my father had just given for my birthday and when I saw her eyes go wide as she dabbed with her napkin and expressed that she would take it away for cleaning, I loved her, already.

explosions of her mirth twirled through the conversation like fireflies, and as they walked he could almost see her bones churning like gears, she was nearly translucent and he was in love.

Sophie, a sophomore, second floor on Sullivan Street, next to a Japanese restaurant whose owners gave her leftovers because they liked her. This much he received, tossed back and forth in his mind while sitting at her kitchen table, nibbling on a seaweed snack unwrapped from its cellophane. Graceful, she slid around the room with plastic containers of gyoza and soba, heating things. Sophie's whole studio was a tender spot of bright light, something radiant and overfilled in his chest. Every detail was perfect—the furniture: two antique lamps with fringed turquoise shades glowed white and warm here on the sill above the kitchenette's studded vintage table; a set of nesting tables in gentle burnished gold, too fragile-looking to bear any weight, delicately balanced on their long arched legs before the open threshold to a bedroom made up in white and brilliant green; on the walls were small framed prints of color gradations like Josef Albers or Klee, on the refrigerator two pinned pastel postcard paintings of the Annunciation. There Mary, infinitely calm, her narrow hands pressed together, her body, washed in pinks and light blue, sat slack in a purity of patience—while he sat just as slack, watching Sophie glide in the kitchen, her body reedlike, swaying, an animation in the fingers and lips that reminded him of mice, some unreachably intelligent, trembling creature.

"Beautiful." Oh God! Backpedal, backpedal, sir. You can't just *say* that out loud to a girl. "I mean, ah," he coughed, scanning for what to mean instead of *you, oh, you.* "The Filippo Lippi painting." He gestured defiantly past her toward the postcards on the fridge, as if sheer confidence would lead her astray. "You know how they got that glimmery gold effect? They put an underlayer of gilt and took a sharp tool—"

"Punching." She unveiled her lopsided smile. "I know. Poked through the paint. My class took a trip to the Met last year. It's so gorgeous in person. *Glimmery gold,*" she repeated. "I like that." From the sink, she glanced back at him, leaning one skinny arm on the silver rim and cocking her head, hair flopping. "Hmm. I'm surprised you know that technique. I just heard about it here in my major intro course."

"Yeah." He grinned, sheepish. "I guess I just like all that stuff. Vasari, you know, all those guys." Matt stuffed more seaweed snack into his mouth. He had just mentioned a book, for heaven's sake, broken one of the fundamental Rules. But, "Vasari," she murmured, setting down two red lacquered bowls and turning back to the sink, "I love Vasari." Maybe all bets were off here? "Punching," he went on. "Such a crazy concept."

She traipsed to the table and for one horribly painful hot instant poked his shoulder with a chopstick, then winked. "Consider yourself punched." She handed him the pair. "Here you are."

Here he was indeed. Ah, how he managed to sit *here* without screaming he'd never know, spilling out of himself some chit and chat on this and that; it was a hop-step from Lippi's cropping to perspective in Hiroshige, the views of Edo and his very, very favorite with the ghostly courtesan behind a screen—hers too! *(No. Yes. That's so amazing!)* How he managed to nod and laugh and at the same time twist noodles round the chopsticks, ease these properly to his mouth—impossible, hurrah, it was eye-hand coordination and singular, God-given luck. And she was eating it up! She suddenly *ugh*ed and threw her head back so he could see inside the dark country of her nostrils.

"I know," she sat up to say, her eyes rolling, "it's not fair that all those Japanese kids take Beginning. They're fluent to begin with and just do it for the easy A." The slim sandbar of her brow sped into angry rills: how would they feel if you touched them? Soft and warm or smooth and cool or papery light? "It's just so stupid."

"Yeah," sighed he, his lungs too furred up with something to speak. "Yeah." His body was lightning-rod-oscillant, beyond control. Soon he might visibly shake. "Um, do you mind if I use the, um . . ."

"Right in there." She pointed into shadows past the bedroom's threshold. "Just take a left."

Wobbly, he pressed himself up from the table and managed to make it into the dim white and rich-green bedroom area without event. There were plastic circles attached to the large wall at the bed's head, large pastel blue and white circles, harmonious, serene. There was a calm white couch along the right wall beneath three windows, where pastel blue pillows sewn with abstract patterns of silver glinted in the streetlights' orange glow. This place was a paradise, so strange, operating parallel to the real world, to NYU, as if suddenly and without warning he had stumbled into a cave or enchanted cove, peaceful and filled with jewels. He turned left into the bathroom, switched on the light, and stared at his face in the mirror, gripping and ungripping his hands on the counter edge for steadiness. Did he look cute? He twisted his head around, trying to find a decent angle. His cheekbones looked nice, actually: jutting. His eyes . . . a little toadish. But perhaps she liked that. Big and blue; perhaps the eyes were a plus. He checked his teeth: nothing. He flushed, ran water in the sink, and slicked down stray hair, trying to work the longest ends over the tops of his big ears.

Exiting the bathroom, he shrieked. There to the right of the couch, shadowed in that opposite corner he hadn't looked into before was a— a—"Oh my God," he said. "It's just one of those, those . . ."

"Ha!" he heard her yelp. "So you met Susie. My dressmaker's dummy."

The bulb of a head gazed at him from atop a rigid body.

"Sorry." He slipped back into his seat and stared down at the table.

"Don't worry about it. It even happens to me sometimes." She put a hand over his—*electric*, oh my sweet Jesus—and when he looked up she was grinning. "Anyway, isn't it nice to be frightened sometimes?"

"Ha, I don't think so."

"You don't? I love it. Not all the time, of course, but a little, you know, jolt." She retrieved her palm; Matt felt it go away like a magnet, still drawing on him. "What's your biggest fear?"

His brain was washed. Simply: slate-clean. Staring at the curve of her hands on the table—little soft live seahorses—it was impossible that outside the black windowpanes a world existed. . . . Think, sir. He had to give her something, not sound like an idiot. He closed his eyes. And, instantly, a vision—screaming, scores of kids racing toward him lying on his back in the grass—everyone ten years old, irrational and tiny, coming to leap on him as if he were a quarterback tackled to earth, their soft bodies falling and, all light pushed out, continuing to fall...He shuddered, opened his eyes.

She was staring, her lips pursed to the side. "You looked like you were wishing. You were breathing so deeply. Like you were about to blow out birthday candles or something. So." She leaned back, her foot tapping air. "What you got for me?"

"Oh, we don't need to get into that. Truly."

"What? After all you made me wait? You've got a good one, I can tell."

He smiled; his heart beat obedient as the wings of some naive bird nestled in her palm. Their eyes caught, and stayed, the golden air flypapering their gaze—then her eyes sparked impish, and she let out one of her tinkling iridescent laughs.

Somehow he didn't get lost going back home, though he wasn't even trying to find his way. Pulled into the circuit of the moon, the path seemed to tug gently, towing him by invisible cords through the washed streets—it must have rained again; no, it was still raining, just misting, seeding his face with mites of wet. At this hour on a weeknight, the streets were cool and vacant. Only now and again a taxi passed, skimming along the surface of the rainwater, the four white digits of its license number glowing through the moist dark air.

Dizzy, he lunged up the stairwell to slowly creak open his bedroom door: where the Imperturbable One wheezed with tranquil regularity. That settled it; Matt could hardly still himself down to sleep now, anyway. He slipped into the common room and turned the futon chair to face out the window into the courtyard. From the soft hushed room with all its lights off, all Dwightness and Joshness smoothed out into ineffectualness by the benevolent fingers of Lady Night, he stared out into the window's square, which somehow contained everything in the world, pulsing. Green-finned shrubs and bare wooden benches drifted in the salmon-pink clouds of sodium lanterns. Still too far, that fresh dark—he threw open the window and sniffed up huge nosefuls of wet breeze.

She had shown him a picture book of a ruined city and paintings by some Russian, all squares of black or white on white till he felt a little bell at his center ringing a silver excitement. She had spoken of near-death events and déjà vu, had even gotten him to swap earliest childhood memories: the aqua ruffled carpet where at age two he thrilled to see for the first time that he could read; she, at three, back in Kyoto, the city she called home till seven years ago, had placed a stone in her grandfather's rock garden—somehow just right for her, practical yet graceful at once. *Sophie*. Can you possibly—like—like—like—*me?* She was an apricot in a white bowl and the bowl too, she was water, rain and the rare emptied chill of something all blissfully spent. Delirious, my God! Yes, You're behind this, aren't You? Mm, don't think we don't know.

A shout boiled up from the courtyard. Two incomprehensible syllables, yelled by a few male voices. Then a scratch, bump from the other side of the wall—"What?" came a pouty shout. Carly Hale, so unnervingly near to him! He held his breath.

Outside, the guys drowned in guffaws. Then, "Carly—Carly—!" belted out.

"What?!" she shrieked. The petulant ice queen.

"Car-ly!" Someone struggled into the radius of lantern light. Dwight's friend Taylor. "Come out here, Carly!" He fell again in toward the building: drunk, from the sound of it.

"Carly!" they all called, clapping. "Carly—Carly, we love you!" someone shouted, then another and another.

"Shut—up!" Carly cheerfully screeched. A happy smack of metal; probably shut her window. The syncopated echoes dropped to murmurs, then silence. Gone inside.

He closed his window, quietly so Carly couldn't hear. Then he crept around the futon and the desk chairs and the rough folds in the natty carpet. Why, of course. As if they could spy from some watchtower when someone floated free above their domineering: they came, crushed out your spot of contentment. Just like that. Like snapping their fingers. The sound of those voices—horn notes from the king's hunting crew, aristocratic laughter as they plow through the brush, flushing you and your small heart out, in a hurried frightened flight like a horde of ungainly fowl. What other person not of *Them* would have liberty to barge around, so publicly shout—to flirt in the open, unashamed, and so late, at nearly midnight for Chrissakes, waking everyone and damn-it-all who hears?

A feeling of doom roosted on his heart, like a black bird, pressing, forceful, down. And yet, as he slid into his bed, tossing in the waves of Josh's snores, the bird raised its sleek jet head: it was she. *Sophie.*

4.

It was like waking up on Christmas morning. It was like having slept right to the afterlife. All you needed to do was get out of bed and dress and you would find yourself in the beautiful new world. His body's whole texture had changed: he was sinuous, lizardy; squirming in the sheets, all his tendons felt limber and stretched.

Had it happened? To him? A girl, and such a rare foal too, a sand-colored fantasyland of black sparkling eyes and pink grinning mouth always winging lightly away on some new bit of banter or another quick, urgent firefly laugh. Ah, he was a fool! *This* girl, to have picked him up—like a dropped piece of paper she uncrumpled to read what was written there? Was she playing with him, a sadist, or in the pocket of some group of insanely cruel ones?

No: something incontrovertible had happened in their lamplit gaze, in the minutes turning over rapidly, excitingly like dice; there was something in the murmury treble of her voice, in her tremble when he'd kissed her on the cheek and that indrawn breath, yes, that was it, her scissoring inward like an accordion, with the half gasp it emitted—and what had pressed her, what had squeezed her if it were not the vise of This Same Thing—

Dear God: I am in love. He poked his feet out the bedspread and wiggled as he told them too, for we are in love, and you, and you.

Josh padded into the room and snuffled in his direction.

"Hey," greeted Matt, feeling liberal.

Josh found a tissue, blew profitably, and waddled back out.

I am in love. He unsheathed himself from the bed. He wanted to taste Cheerios in love, to unfold a newspaper in love, to wash his face with splashes of lovely water in love! He pinched his cheeks in the wardrobe mirror. Stop grinning, you idiot. Already 10:05—if he rushed, he could dash up to Jason's before Moral Reasoning.

"Hullo." Jason finally opened the door two flights up, grumpy and fuddled with sleep. "This better be good." He shuffled to the couch, blinked at the milky light. Jason's room had a musty, cloistered odor; so far Matt had noted parts cumin and socks.

"You will not guess what happened to me last night." Matt threw down his bag.

"Let me try," Jason rasped, pushing open the window and lighting a Newport. Exhaling meditatively, he crinkled one eye. "You shat yourself at dinner."

"Similar, yes, if by that you mean the occurrence of something totally impossible. Try again." Matt stood, arms straight out at the sides—his best pinstripe pants and crisp button-down: to let this red-letter day shine out!—as if Jason could read the news there.

"I know, I know." Jason cleared his throat. "You hooked up with Carly Hale." Roman candles of laughter going off.

"Yes! You're *very* warm." Matt sat down on the bed opposite and put both hands on Jason's knees. "I met a girl. A girl who likes me!"

"What?" Jason stubbed out the fresh cig, leaning forward keenly. *"How?"*

"I know!" He grinned. "It's crazy. Jason. Jason. She is fabulous."

"Hmm. I don't see what she's doing with you, then," Jason sniffed.

"I know!" crowed Matt, jumping up again. "My question exactly!"

"Well, spit it out. Is she cute, pretty, beautiful, or sexy?"

Matt pictured four cartoon sections of red meat, each quadrant cursived with one of those words. "Ugh! Please don't sully her with your loose talk!"

"Don't get all uppity on my ass." Jason bent to light another cigarette.

"Listen to him. What do you know from girls, anyway? Have you ever even kissed a girl, *Matt*?"

"Yes, I have. But thank you ever so for that moving show of support."

"Where? On the cheek?"

"On the lips, I'll have you know." He most certainly had kissed Becky Lee, twice, when he was thirteen, at gifted camp in southern Jersey.

"Oh, how about that! Mazel tov." Jason smooched two grand Edith Piaf kisses in the air. Then he grinned evilly. "With tongue?"

"Yes, with tongue. Satisfied? Once. All right?" Matt picked his bag up.

"Calm down, I'm just asking. Wait, don't go."

"I have Moral Reasoning lecture." Matt headed toward the door.

"Wait! Are you going to see her again?" Jason padded up behind him.

"Tonight." Matt turned back at the open door and clung to its edge, flushed with joy, facing Jason breathing heavily in his mauve T-shirt and gray sweatpants. "Tonight. We're going to the movies."

"Tonight? Oh my God, that's serious. That's now! Listen, I'm sorry. You just come back here after your three o'clock—we'll whip you in shape."

"Shape?"

"Yes, shape. For your *date*! Ugh, go on, just trust me!"

Matt bounded down the steps, bag swinging, extended to his full height and imperious, on a mission, into the brilliant sparkling chill of an autumn morning bordered with changing trees, and paper scraps and desiccated leaves skimming along the streets in the crisp breeze. The kiss with Becky Lee should count for quite a bit. He knew what it was like to be close to a girl, to feel the palpitations in your hand as you clasped that mysterious other having no idea what, if anything, it thought. Sophie's hand, of course, would be different from Becky Lee's; she was more swanlike and small, breakable; he would have to treasure it gently in his palm. What he most remembered of the kiss at gifted camp was that it was very soft. And there was no clear definite end to it. It was like biting into a marshmallow in the dark, when you don't know if you've finished it or have more still to go. First closemouthed under a streetlight in the parking lot, where he'd stood on the curb for her; later they did it with tongue, behind the bushes. And that was the one he'd replayed. He had followed her movements, their tongues going round about like those northern anchovy once seen in an aquarium—silvery thousands in a cylinder tank circling each other without stopping or slowing, a vision both calming and electric.

He had been drawing the same undirected matting of lines for the last five minutes while the professor kept yammering about Freud, Freud and Vienna, Freud and primal scene, Freud and blah blah blah. He turned the page. And started zigzagging a fresh matting. Becky Lee, that queen of evil. Of course, as history knows, she had to dump his dork self the following day, sitting next to Patrick Martin right from breakfast and never bothering to speak to him again—even though they shared the same algebra section and had to study at the same table day after day for that final week of camp! He didn't think it was his kiss that drove her screaming off, though it wasn't any glowing accolade; you couldn't ex-actly be sure any of what he'd done was right. Funny, you do see pictures of sex in the movies, etc., so you know what you're supposed to do there, at least sort of, but what went on in the unpictured dark of people's mouths to make them good kissers? Were men supposed to make dart-ing motions inside the woman's circular swirl?[14] Did you move your tongue the whole time?[15] Whatever it was, he could learn. He didn't feel a priori unsexual, per se. The trick would just be hiding from Sophie that nearly no girl had looked at him twice. And also retaining her mysteri-ous interest, however one accomplished that.

All day, everything he did—trudging through kids fanning across Meyer into fluttering classroom doors, veering near-collisions in the cafeteria—she stayed inside him, or rather the idea of her, hiddenly with him like a card kept in his breast pocket, a wafer under his tongue. Then to call her whole image out: that sent thrills, over and again, like touching an outlet just for the joy of being shocked! Amazing how quickly a girl could turn a person to crazy. He had never imagined it would be so, though Dante and all talked it to death. The feeling with

---

[14] No.

[15] Yes.

Becky Lee had mostly been fright. She was pretty, there was a sexual sense, but she was a closed object, one of a number of pinballs ricocheting in the social sphere. *Getting this girl would make us more popular,* he remembered thinking. And that was also what he'd thought in high school. No doubt every loser has those fantasies where Alexa Stern, lab partner extraordinaire and nicest popular girl in your grade, suddenly sees there is more to you than commonly supposed. She looks up above the putrid frog mess between you somehow instantly filled with admiration for your delicate surgeon's hands; she invites you back to her house to work on the lab report, where you unveil your knowledge of Rimbaud, of van Gogh; the snow is falling as you walk out and her mother locks the door, saying, *Wow, that Matt really is a gentleman;* Alexa bashfully, quietly concedes this. Then falls for you deeper, harder, *Stop it, guys,* she says in the hall after you pass and the crew hoots, *He's actually really cool.* And in fact *that's* the priceless moment—the silence descending on those guys as they glance around all insecure in the strange new universe. The vision tapers to flashes next: you're going out, doing what everybody else has done for years, eating cheese fries at the Tenafly Diner, lingering under the marquee saying, *What should we see?* and then you buy her a soda, she gives you a ride in her Rover, there you are shutting the—

Things always break down somewhere in a fantasy. It was *impossible* that he should find himself casually getting out of a Range Rover and shutting the door. That athletic, red-blooded, expensive vehicle; he'd probably trip on the step-down shelf and break his little finger.

All of those girls—unattainable, pretty, even glamorous with their fresh-brushed hair, opulent jeans, and squishy sweaters—he had secretly felt them unworthy. There was a tinge of revenge in his visions: they would be sorry when he came into his own, would see how he overpassed them the way a rocket zipping toward a distant galaxy passes the orbiting moon. Even in his imaginings of the new him, girls had fit only to a limited degree, a shadowy she-thing by his side when "the crowd" was hanging out, some creature petulant and bored complaining together with him, who nevertheless always stayed a frightening stranger.

But with Sophie: all day the memory of her light hand on his forearm; her light hand fell and fell again on his forearm like a feather he could still feel.

"Now," said Jason, "do you have any idea how much experience she has?"

It was 3:45. The excitement had solidified in his veins to metal, making it difficult to move or speak. Matt found himself sinking down, head buried in bed pillow.

"Well," Jason sighed, "can we assume she's not a freak-o like you?"

"Where is this coming from?" Matt pushed himself up, incensed. "You've been nothing but Mr. Meany-Face since I told you."

"Mr. Meany-Face? There's the crazy boy I know and love." Jason's face looked actually sort of ashen. A rueful smile curled the corners of his lips. "I'm sorry. Would it help if I told you I was a little bit jealous?"

"Jealous?"

"A tiny bit. Stop blowing it out of proportion."

Dear God—did he mean . . . ? Was this the undercurrent of their so lifesaving companionship? "But, Jason. How do I put this. Ah, recall with me, if you will, the moment on the first day, when I said I was not in fact on the, the, as you say, 'bus' . . ."

"Oh Lordy my." Jason smirked up at the ceiling. "Not of Sophie, you retard, I don't want to get in your pants. Jealous of you. I want some action too."

"Oh," said Matt. "Well, I'm sure you'll find someone."

"I know that." Jason began taking objects out of a plastic bag and putting them on the trunk that served for a coffee table: paper towels, Windex, a juice glass, two hand-sized mirrors. "It's just, I'm ready now. I just came out now, at school, you know. Told my parents, like, August. Well, I told my mom, *she* told my dad. My high school friends, no idea, none. We used to play spin-the-bottle, you know. I had a girlfriend too. Yup. Sandy. Tenth grade. What a stupid time. I wish I'd never done any of it."

Jason was gazing off into space, above the potted plants by the door.

And Matt stretched out a hand to Jason's shoulder. No words to address that sort of thing, the things people like them brought along—carried as if in locked cabinets across huge spaces of time, perhaps always. Still, as the heat vents clicked on and began releasing a steady stream of warm dry air into the room, his body did not seem to care about the limits of communication. His body was sending something like the heat toward Jason, a warm radiant river from his chest. So say something here: you must let Jason know.

"I'm sorry," Matt heaved out finally.

"I know." Jason turned to look at him. His eyes were serious and open, depths and depths of brown chocolate. "Thank you." He tightened his lips. "Anyway!" he called in a bright voice, patting Matt's knee. "You! Let's go!"

It took all of two hours and the virtue of two mirrors before Matt was pronounced fit to date. He exchanged his shirt for a black version (pink "way too faggy" for Jason), they forked through queasifying spanakopita in the dining hall, and then Jason tapped his arm, wished him luck.

In forty minutes he was on a sticky pay phone to Jason.

"Jason!" he croaked. "Jason! The tickets are sold out!"

"What?"

"*The Nights of Cabiria*—it's sold *out*!"

"I thought you were supposed to pick them up 'in advance'?!"

"It is," he panted, almost tearing. "I thought it was in advance."

"Oh, dear. Thursday, Fellini, Film Forum."

"What do I do? I've tried everything! I've spoken to the manager! I've got my name on a wait-list!"

Jason cleared his throat. "Pray?"

He ran up and down the line of ticketholders, begging everyone to scalp him their seats. "Just two tickets 'r all I need, just two tickets, *please?* . . . Thank you anyway." His vision was blurring, he was about to cry, he was all humbled over and speaking by now to people's torsos. And then, at the very end of the line, after, trembling, he gave his plea, he heard a gasp, followed by a startled spurt of laughter, and looked up: it was she. *Sophie*.

She put a finger to her lips. Dragged him inside the glass doors, mimed for him to take off his jacket, took off hers, straightened her hair, *ahem*-ed. Marched across the red-carpeted lobby to beside the front of the line, where an exhausted-looking ticket-taker stood ripping. "We're back," she said, smiling. "Oh—sorry, it was the other guy we talked to here, who got our tickets before. Anyway, thank you both!"

And just like that—it was that Bonnie and Clyde—they shuttled inside.

5.

A movie. Black-and-white figures flickering on the sibilant screen. Then a midnight stroll, an arm-in-arm. A glass of Lillet in a tiny dark French bar she pulled you to in the tilted SoHo streets off Sixth, smoking cigarettes, facing out the window onto a sidewalk with hydrant and mailbox, a sidewalk as real as they make them. But then the whole thing teetering to flight... the whole thing a hot-air balloon ripped from the silk of your heart, pistoned by lung-breath—a kiss, groping through silt after silvery fish, then the smoothness of those shoulders, two dazzling live stones in your palms—

She drank not hot chocolates but hot vanillas from the corner store. She danced to Britpop, manically shaking her black hair. She wore a white sleeveless T-shirt to bed. She peeled lemons and popped them in her mouth in sections. She liked to be kissed on the tip of her nose. She carried melon candies in the pocket of her purse. She loved, but was terrible at, crosswords. She smelled like orange blossoms in the crick of her neck. She only wrote in a deep-blue pen. She had tadpole-smooth skin between her small tight fingers. She woke every day at eight A.M. She could *never* properly say the word *eleven*. She drew cats in the margins of her notebooks. She kept a miniature tea set in a box under her bed. She was always in the mood for it to snow.

Splendor in the evening when she exited showered, dressed in a blue-and-white-checked robe, clean down to the soles of her straight feet, a turbaned goddess with a wayward smile and darting eyes who hitched up the window to light a cigarette; radiance in the morning who leapt from their yet unsexed bed to make small kettle and stove noises kitchenward—fluffing up a pillow to watch her scampering movements, he suffered actual craving in the arms to catch her nimble body, craving in the lips to ferret out the sleek, delicious crevices of her neck—until, fists on hips, she stomped back grinning to the bed and said, *I know you're awake, you lazy boy!*

She hung hats on her walls, felt hats with feathery reachers right out of the '20s with their half net veils. She had a trunkful of beaded and sequined things, ropes of fake topazes and pearls, embroidered purses and a coin-keep made of metal mesh whose openwork hold tinkled when shook. She had a collection of Venice masks, porcelain-skinned mysterious demi-faces with gouged eyes and jeweled beauty marks nesting in a velvet-topped box in the kitchen closet; she had an aviary of fake birds perching on real branches high to the left above the bed, brilliant pinks, barbarous yellow, emerald green—like a Joseph Cornell box released into air, peering down with their solemn gazes. She listened to Lady Day, Betty Carter, and Arvo Pärt; she knew all of Duran Duran by heart. She had liked Matchbox cars and cap guns as a tomboy; she could still skip stones and showed him so at a pond in Central Park.

They went everywhere. Godard, fruitsellers in Chinatown, crêpes on Hudson, gorgeous autumny exploratory voyages along Bedford, Barrow, and Commerce Streets. Often they went with Jason, who became friends with Sophie so quickly it was imperceptible—a glance, an ionic charge jumping from one to the next. Indeed, after a week of dodging and diffidence, Jason had at last agreed to meet and within the space of ten minutes, would you believe it, was giggling away on Sophie's white couch. It pleased those two to tease him, tenderly, attentively, in a way actually that bestowed the sensation of being cherished. God knows why they still liked him, when more and more of the rope of him pulled out and was perceptible to the naked eye: his fascination with Napoleon, with Huysmans and the *flâneurs* of Paris, or "In the Wee Small Hours of the Morning" as sung by a young Frank Sinatra. Somehow they liked him still, and still; together they even seemed to like him more.

It was Jason who found out Sophie's talent. Sure, the clothes she wore ought to have been a giveaway, like the cloche hat and pearl-crusted gloves that bordered a minimalist leather jacket, or the high-necked pirate-Parisian blouse nipped at the wasp waist with a metal-studded biker belt, worn over skinny jeans and white go-go boots. Yet Matt hadn't understood what it all tallied to, not even with dummy Susie staring from the corner, until Jason, with his usual bullheadedness, followed up the trail of a reference Sophie dropped to her handiwork. Then Jason made her, though she picked skittishly at her string of pearls, show the gauzy blouses and dresses she herself had designed and sewn with a desk that now at a touch—huzzah!—opened to reveal a Victorian machine. Taking down a box from the kitchen closet, she brought it to the bed, lifted out crepe-paper snakes and finally streams of multicolored silk and netting, and deposited them on the lap of Jason, where he sat on the couch. "Um, another dress," she mumbled, veiled in hair, rooting, tossing, "and this—can be worn as a top, I guess . . ."

"These are amazing," Jason said quietly, after an awe-filled hush of holding up and examining, his lap still covered with blue and beige-lined rose. "You know you have a gift."

After that she hung one on the wall, her favorite made frock, an orange sheath dress lined in light-blue tulle. She wanted to be a designer— *there*, it was out.

And so they shopped. At the baby designers' in the East Village, at vintage stores in arcane city nooks, at sample sales in faceless warehouses so shushed-up, so word-of-mouth, they seemed like stage sets or underground political meetings thrown up overnight to be taken down secretly the morrow. It was a pleasure to watch her in force. Plunging into a pile of old clothes, she emerged minutes later with a purse, an A-line skirt, like a deep-sea diver returning with pearls. She liked to find him deals, and what with a faux-fur-ruffed parka, two tiny-collared silk shirts that invisibly buttoned, plus a man-bracelet, leather, buckled—nothing over thirty bucks!—soon he was looking better than hitherto suspected possible.[16] What he'd never considered she taught: she pulled at seams to test

---

[16] During this identical period Lisanne and I were engaged in a similar enterprise; in hopes of propping up her success in the classroom, we expended much of our meager

their strength, showed where a shirt's shoulders should be, wondered did he know his torso was short? his legs long? that he might go low-waisted, to lengthen up above? Beige turned his skin green, see? While the snapfront cowboy shirts, alas, puckered awfully on his narrow chest, dissembling man-breasts, the guayaberas were far too busy with their frills for his frame, and the flatfront pants went too high: but at least, she conceded, they showed off his cute butt. (*Cute?* He twisted in the mirror to peek.) Gradually, thanks to her cues, he seemed to be shearing off a suffocant, ill-fitting cocoon.

One breezy afternoon smelling of fresh roasting nuts from the side-walk vendors, they were window-watching along the steel-girt streets of SoHo, among the elegant dogs, the Italian tourists, and the pine-straight models, when she, without word or pause, opened a door and slipped in.

It was an imposing palace of plate glass and laser-bright space: LOLO ZED, letters against the glass said. Metal rods hovered magically in air, suspending hangers where—azure, watermelon, lemon-yellow, magnolia-pink—numinous wraps and dresses floated vaporous and radiant as Sophie's, yet hovering here in the dozens they seemed to inhabit their own lifeworld, like the flora and fauna of a fabulous planet.

Sophie's heels were clicking down to the lower floor; he caught up to her in a circular room: more racks, and at one end a mysterious ground-to-ceiling thing of billowing blue material. With dilated eyes and a little *o*-mouth, Sophie stepped in to check out the tremulous blue ovum. It was a kind of inflated dressing room, unskeletal, delicate as parachute silk so it kept rippling and shifting, as if in infinite response to an invisi-ble, heavenly sigh.

---

means on suit jackets and silk blouses. However, our shopping expeditions offered none of the joyful exploits Matthew and Sophie experienced: there may be nothing more dispirit-ing than passing under the fluorescent beams of „discount" shops amidst squalling babies, the racket of cheap hangers being scraped mechanically along metal racks, and large-bodied women who wander like ghosts along the black-painted walls, their arms loaded with ugly clothes dripping colour-coded tickets, all the while keeping a pleasant smile in readiness for when your well-loved wife should leap from the dressing room horribly trans-formed into some grinning Margaret Thatcher, missing only the rigid hair and pearls.

Abruptly, all of a sudden: "Let's go," she breathed, her small fists gripping his wrists.

He followed her up the stairs, past a reptile-eyed manager immobile at a slick desk, past a security guard standing still as a carved jade soldier, past the glass front into November dusk: where under the streetlight of the corner she had stopped, was crying without a sound.

It took some time to unpack that one with her, to understand her feeling about a beauty there that went beyond speech, a beauty absolute and no longer human, which she knew illuminated her life yet would be always out of reach—a paradigm along the lines, it sounded, of Dante's celestial rose, or Plato's unbodiable good, so that in the end he revealed to her how at times he had felt something like that too. And they wound up talking till it was light, unpetaling that million-petaled question of what marvelous energy absorbed and circulated through the universe, and when it was light she leaned over from cross-legged on the bed and kissed him. And when she kissed him he put his hands atop her shoulders and she put her hands on his back and when their clothes were off she guided him in for the first time toward a core of all that mystery.[17]

That was what they did together, opening, unraveling like mummies. Well, no. *She* wasn't a mummy; there was nothing willful about her wrapping or grotesque about what it swathed. *Her* "embarrassing" stories meant days of squirming over English in eighth grade as a New American or being so tone deaf that she was always assigned the triangle in Orchestra and even Chorus. Big, excuse his French, whoop. But whatever she had, she did tell him. She told him about Japan; about her mother, who studied depression in a lab at U Chicago through mazes and mice and dissecting their pea-sized brains; about her father, a consultant who in the evening made elaborate dollhouses, sitting with a cigar and saw slippered at the kitchen table; about her little brother the

---

[17] Which is to say: Matthew loses his sexual virginity. In case some one may be led by such delicate discretion to miss this important developmental step.

Sega game-player; she told him about a speedboat accident, a psychic experience seeing ghosts, her kiddie crush on Johnny Depp from *21 Jump Street*. And every story was like a square-inch window into her, where he could see right through blood or muscle to history, fear, irrational passion for certain things—why watermelons, why eight A.M., why Josephine Baker? why turquoise, why Grand Marnier, why the Sienese Annunciations on her refrigerator?—so that the more and more she showed him, she assembled herself as real in his presence: a separate universe like him membraned by the cellophane of skin.

In their violet-lighted pillow talk and lengthy dusktime walks, he took Recent Modern History of Sophie too. He learned how pre-Sophie used to hang around the Art Institute in Chicago and there met a boy who plucked her budding rose (a huge relief, Matt considered, for he certainly could use the teaching). And lucky for Matt, last year after Sophie had formed inseparable friends with a freshman roommate and stayed bound in that girl's group, her boyfriend began courting Sophie, so that a fall-out shattered all at year-end. Indeed, she had been so lonely so far this year, she had even sent off a transfer application to Berkeley— *Withdraw it!* he croaked; *don't worry, I'll never get in out of state*—and thank God for that: how would she ever have bothered with him if she'd had an active group of friends? Oh, it was fated and strange for her at just this vulnerable time to find him. They replayed First Day over and over, both as nostalgia and running joke; he'd come up to her by the sink, kiss her cheek, say, "You have broccoli on your cheek," and she might smack him back and say the same. Once they had a whole pillow fight saying, *You have broccoli—here—and here—and here!*

And she hailed from a place with a beautiful name: Lake Forest, just right. She was the silver locus of the lake; he would be happy, gratified, to be the forest about her—

But could not. There was a blockage, a granite ocean in his veins.

Yes, indeed there was a thing not even Sophie's fingers could reach.

All by itself, the dorm was sufficient to do him in. Tonight it was worse than usual. A Friday. Sophie was off with a cousin down from

Vermont, too family-blabbermouth for his tag-along; Jason in Scarsdale
for a bris early tomorrow morning. It was Friday night, after dinner,
nine, just the time when the banging began, the doors in the hall, everyone shrieking, half drunk already. You could hear them: there: and there;
there must be a party on this floor. He could try to show up? but what if
it wasn't a party-party, what would he do? *Thought I heard music, thought
I heard noise?* Safer to stay here. Yes, stay, and, like a pig in its pen, circle
the suite; then, having taken green tea, lie alone here all dressed atop the
bedspread in the pose of corpse, arms at his sides. Melodramatic, sir.
Think so? Yes, sir. But—

Bang bang bang went the door.

Matt gasped and sat up on the bed.

"Dwight, we know you're in there!" "Dwight, we can see your fucking
light!" "Come on out, dude!"

Jesus motherfucking Christ, my God. They were—

Metal: the door was opening . . .

He jumped down and crawled under the bed. The trunk was at the
foot; he should be hidden.

Booted heavy steps echoed in the suite's corridor. "Where are ya,
man?" They entered his room—Matt held his breath. " 'Snot here. It was
the Rat's light."

"Is he here? Ask him where Dwight—"

"Nah. He's not here."

"Impossible." That was Taylor's voice, Matt knew it by its acid-tinged
high pitch. "The Rat doesn't have a life."

"He's probably whacking off in the bathroom."

" 'I ruv you, Rat, I ruv you.' "

"Shut up, faggot. 'Sget out of here."

Waigh waigh wauuugh, sang out Taylor, a faux-Chinesey jingle. There
was pounding on the walls of the corridor, the noise of the hall door
swinging shut behind, then the ringing of their heels on the rubber floor
outside, and, diminishing, away.

Matt crawled out from under the bed. He was trembling; he could
hardly manage to pick a dustbunny from his tongue. What was that all
about? The Rat? *I ruv you, Rat*—and that tune—what on God's green

earth? Sophie? So this was what he got for introducing her to Dwight outside Meyer? When she had sweetly shaken, shaken so sweetly Dwight's overweening paw, and even granted him afterward: *Well, he seems nice.* Mocking her—for being Asian? Those WASP giblets of racist garbage!

Matt punched the air, sharp jabs through an endlessly giving atmosphere. Those fucking prepsters! All these weeks those lords and ladies had gone luxuriating about campus as if it were their own pleasure garden, conferred on them as part of God's feudal, hierarchic law. Oh sure, they weren't anything but the same old preps as at Tenafly, not special or cool per se. Yet the rest of us just till away their fields and, *Dominus, Domina,* look up to and worship them; *O grant me an audience; invite me to your party; grace with kind eye my imitative attire.* And he himself had done this too: like a startled hare he had fled beneath the bed. Alone on a Friday night? That would not have gone down without a sneer from them. So it was still riding his veins, his fear, curled up in the body like a sleeping disease. How did they manage it? And why Dwight? Who wasn't from some posh boarding school—no, nothing but a hick from bumblefuck! Why had they taken a shine to that slab of mediocrity?

Somewhere out there, in some bar, in someone's dorm room, perhaps on this very hall, perhaps next door, perhaps in the room directly above his head right now, Dwight was laughing. Dwight was crinkling his brows together and Being Serious while he listened to someone like God. He was spinning his solid bulk around to introduce two people with that air of refined, good-natured politeness he affected. Dwight was meeting new people, he was going further and further and further in.

Matt walked down the corridor into the common room. The floor seemed to be tilting slightly, a sea deck, the ceiling to be lowering. Dizzy. But let him lay eyes on the Dwightness, the bizarre black magic that had caught such hordes in its enchantment. He crossed the threshold into Dwight's single.

Wow. How it mesmerized: a scene of naive normality. Regard the way the calendar is tacked to a corkboard, with actual dates marked on it, acknowledged, owned. And a *pennant;* unselfconsciously flagged against the wall! Mustn't that feel liberating? To say, hey, I care about such and such, nail it up there in plain sight. He shivered just thinking of the knowingness into his life his mother would have had if he'd done that at home. Ha, hardly; he was not so simple or unkind as to expose, say, his cherished Nietzsche to her critical eye—rather easier anyway when what you had to stick up was *Boston Red Sox*; *Me & Rich at Yellowstone.* And look at that proper laundry basket! *Exactly* the thing— where did people learn this stuff? With those normal white athletic socks, as if laid there by casual accident. And a leather-bound appointment book—right on the desk, for anyone to see. Totally brazen, unashamed. *Game. Concert.* Some illegible *Dinner.*

Dwight was the Real Deal. It almost brought tears.

Matt shook his head to clear it and fumbled out into the common room. He leaned his elbows on his desk. There was no place to steady his body, thwanging like a rubber band, plucked. Why? Why could he not simply be happy? He had the best girl in the world, the slimmest lissome orchid, liking him, unbelievably. He had a best friend with whom he could be sane and honest, and even have *fun* to boot. He had escaped Tenafly and Teaneck, and, really, if you thought of it, NYU was puppet-show compared with the daily, physical grinding down of high school. Yes, that danger was past: he had driven away from the street, gone sailing off like Ulysses; now nothing would trick him back.

But *Waigh waigh wauuugh—I ruv you, Rat*—with a singsong, at a whim, nonetheless, They could still barge right in....

Dear God, how to get out of this maudlin mess? His mind, powerless in the brain cage, harbored thoughts that scrabbled around like birds trying to find their way out of a glass house.

Well, it was Friday night. A night for smashing.

He strode across the common room, pocketed his smokes, smoothed his hair, and sallied out the main door. Downstairs was vacant for a change; everyone must already be where they had meant to go; he skimmed along the hall's surface, a diamond gliding along incomparable featureless glass. Outside it was black-eyed November, bottomless as only New York. He fired up a cigarette: the smoke bit like the icy air into his nose. In a hurry; why was he in a hurry? Ah yes: as always, speeding to some terrible conclusion.

Now it was the opera of the cosmopolis! A delivery boy shot past on a bicycle. On Second Avenue a great alien street-cleaning apparatus ponderously coasted alongside glistening puddles of green. Mimes, pall-bearers, a gaggle of gelled, statuesque men in black tie waited to disappear inside the mouth of a limousine. At Lafayette he fought through a clutch of punks, running cleanly across the long intersection where shattered glass stained the island and crunched underfoot, glass, glass, gorgeous shattered glass! The sounds of skateboards died out in the darkness toward Astor Place. He walked faster, though calmer now. The air somehow sweetened near Fifth, where he loped past the watchful eyes of doormen, potted plants in windows and ridiculous permed dogs pissing in the manicured beeches. How almost-fun this was! *New York, New York! It's a wonderful town! The Bronx is up and the Battery's down!* He swung north on Seventh, skirting four ambulances clinging softly to the curb like dirigibles. *New York, New York!* He was a tuning fork at play in the forces humming beneath the crossroads of the city. On 13th Street a streetlight buzzed off-on, off-on, maddeningly; on 14th, a man silhouetted in a high window stood with hands propped flat at the glass as if under some celestial arrest.

Now the broad cobblestoned spaces of the Meatpacking District fanned out before him, a stream of stones with gullies and tricky eddies. In incandescent halls, wax-faced men shifted dials on machines whose fingers lifted bricks of red cellophaned flesh. He shivered. It was quieter, colder here by the Hudson. He didn't know these streets, blundered along the cobblestones until the tangle resolved into the West Side Highway.

Cars shooting by like luminous bullets.

He raced dangerously to the median, waited, and raced to the far side. Nobody was watching behind; he headed north, slipped through a gate in the wire-mesh fence.

The river spread itself. Crenellated with light, a moving army. What was there to do now but watch, watch this liquid black hole draining slowly into the future. And it was from that bank, from that far side, that he had stood and stared, from the Englewood Boat Basin by his battered car, out bus windows along the snaking circuit of Boulevard East, and imagined—that it would be different? Here: right where I'm standing!

He turned to face the whole illuminated swathe of the city, the turbid water lapping at his back. Strangely clearheaded and sane, as if here by the river he had siphoned out all the rillets of bile through his mind's eye. He strode north a ways before hustling over the highway toward a fresh cross street. Even before attaining the block's edge he could make out some commotion farther on—odd: in this boondocks neighborhood of shuttered warehouses?—bodies, dark-dressed, silver, gold, packed tightly together, beneath a raised platform before two silver doors.

It was a nightclub, evidently. It was dozens and dozens of people decked out in feather boas, flashing cufflinks, fur giving off a wild static, their teeth shining as they plied with encouraging grins and nods their mates in this line hemmed by red velvet ropes. Like an inspector, Matt clasped hands behind his back, lollygagging as he slipped along the far side of the street. How they hoisted their purses, ran hands through hair already faultless, how they flicked peremptory ash onto the concrete! Such polished and clicking shoes: so much confidence to be heard in their tattoo! And what was it like to be merry like that, to have the inner wherewithal to freely join this grand urban orchestra?

You might as well ask what it was to be Dwight: to be normal. Oh, who needed the lot of this blasted race!

6.

But when at 9:13 Matt woke to a sky of pewter rain poking through the bedside window, tiny pellets streaming to the bricked courtyard washed from salmon to brilliant gleaming red...he was abashed. *What is your problem?* Dashing around bellyaching, sulking hither and yon about New York? Blinking at the gray light as the rain lobbed its glutinous freight against the windowpanes, he padded out to the common room. And there discerned what he hadn't when he'd beelined right to bed last night: three rapid flash-flashes on the answering machine's mailbox number three. *Sophie.* From 10:23—home, but couldn't find her keys...could she possibly sleep over? At 10:47—just trying again, in case, my super, can't reach him: a weary, aggrieved sigh before the click. And finally, 12:01, in a tight voice—not to worry, she had managed to get inside; g'night.

He snatched up the cordless and ran back to his room. "I'm so sorry," he blurted to her muted *Hello.*

"Matt?" A skittish laugh. "Wh-what happened?"

And here, though he might have said any number of things—*I was taking a walk; I was in the midst of a depressive episode; Sophie, I was rapt in senseless anguish*—he contented himself with a simple "I just got your messages." Still redolent of the truth.

"Oh." Disappointed, though. "Did you—not hear the phone?" she wanted to know.

"N-no." Which, strictly speaking, was even also true. "Can I make it up to you? How awful. Sophie. I'm so sorry. Please?"

"Matt!" Now her voice had relaxed. "Hey. It's not your fault."

Right, of course. Though nonetheless, guilt, you know, a curious creature…and he flung over the line dozens more words gutted of meaning until she not only yielded to brunch (his treat) at Freddy's on Prince Street but requested *The Originality of the Avant-Garde and Other Modernist Myths* from Bobst Library—if you really are feeling suddenly so chivalrous!

Chivalrous? Not exactly. What he felt as he slapped down the hall to the bathroom for the morning douse was more in the vein of mortification. Last night, while he'd moped round the city, he had left his lady to freeze, locked from her home. Yet the wrong done was more than that. Giving Sophie up as someone who couldn't understand, maybe did not even deserve to hear what he was feeling. Why? Just because she hadn't been forced down the same loser trail of tears in her childhood? Well, don't you want to have a single true person-to-person connection ever? Here you are at school, the new life! This is precisely the opening you've begged for: you will simply have to chance it.

By the time Matt thudded past the security desk, out the front door into the newly dry-eyed day, where gleaming yellow taxicabs, slick, swooshed up, making that pleasing slurry sound on the wet streets, he had cut himself a fair shake. Let yesterday close on its maudlin contents, all. Fine. But from now on: with Sophie, full disclosure.

When Matt veered left from Washington Square Park into the library, Mary Fawzi was standing by the circulation desk. Above a stack of three dark books she proffered her ID card to the student checker. So Matt lingered, fumbling with his wallet, wiping his feet repeatedly upon the sodden entrance mats, as her books were passed over the magnetic machine—and when she cradled these under an arm, then turned toward the exit, he placed himself in her way.

"Hello." He slipped her an amiable smile. Precisely the same height as he was. Had they ever stood face to face together? "Mary."

"Yes." Bewildered: her sloe eyes dilated further behind thick lenses. "Matthew."

"Matt." He coughed, polite, dropping his gaze to the books under her arm. *Fixed Stars and Irregular Planets,* the spine of the top one read. Science? Might have guessed.

"Oh—I'm sorry." A slim index finger pushed her glasses up by the nosepiece.

Ah, Mary: not the nosepiece! "No—it doesn't matter. Whatever. How are you?"

"Fine." Even in a word, that admixed British flashed out like tinfoil from her voice. He wouldn't be able to replicate her tone, the breathy *i* of *Fine*. "And yourself?"

"Good! You know. I woke up early. Saturday. Good day for . . . a little studying." Now, that's just blather, sir. Surely even you can hear that? But he patted his courier bag as if to underscore their common ground.

"Yes," she said again. Her posture was conspicuously erect, the thin olive neck keeping her round face rigidly high amid the heavy black waves. Too erect, too definite; a normal kid would be shifting her weight here, slouching ironically. She needed a good talking-to tutorial, this helpless, fendless thing. "I have some reading as well."

And they stared at each other. All righty, then. Ho-hum. *What weather we're having?* What did you have in mind for this little confab, hmm? At last he heard his voice make a fuzzy laugh, and hers a giggle, very thin, like a glass vial breaking. "Well." He surrendered, stretching an arm out in you-may-pass. "I guess I'd better let you read."

"Yes." She shifted her books. Then all at once grinned, wide, cheeky. Really? One might have expected something more feminine. "Though there is hardly any hurry. There is always more reading. Isn't there?" she asked, suddenly curious, probing his gaze intently. Perhaps he hesitated too long before nodding earnestly, saying, *Oh, always.* Because she began to look away, and by the time she added, "I suppose that's why we are here. Of course," she seemed to be talking to herself. "Goodbye," she said, formally, almost curtly, her eyes grown already closed and opaque before she passed.

As she walked by, the cuff of her pink collarless shirt brushed his bare wrist. Soft foreign cotton. A touchable whisper on his skin. Mary. Queer bird! Not the most adroit of tête-à-têtes, though it was nice to hear her laugh and speak, instead of just weeping. He marched up the central stairs. A good deed done there, however ineptly. Next time we'll try to work up some surefire topic before we open contact with her.

It was either this incident, with its sense of doing right by all and sundry, or the feeling that the previous evening was bile under a bridge, drained far away. Or it was simply *faute de* dinner: but while he searched Art History for Rosalind Krauss, his thoughts revolved gratifyingly toward the nigh repast. Walking from the library into an afternoon changed all to crisp blue, he lit a cigarette, the spark of flame licking up from his lighter eager, tame as a dog. Now it was on to eating fresh scrambled eggs someone's generous hands tended. And what else, what better could there be, than his dining companion, Sophie, *she!*

Across the walkway on a park bench sat Mary. Her back toward him, but since she was diagonal and far, her profile was clearly visible. An expressionless face. A dilapidated yellowed paperback. With her left hand, she rolled something between her fingers, then threw it to the ground. Bread; some pigeons investigated. Faintly her lips rubbed each other, as if smoothing out ChapStick.

It is possible. That's what he should say to her. *It is possible.* Not merely have a friendly check-in with her: *that,* truly, was the news he bore, what she needed to hear, what she would understand in the right way. For wasn't it staggering, the current rate of change: just two months ago if you had told him he would have a Sophie and a Jason—

A red leaf above Mary had detached from its tree; now it went turning over and over itself with its five flame fingers splayed out, rapidly training around like a lutzing ice-skater, and landed flat across the crease of her book. She jolted up: to fix the providing sky with a painfully unironical, guileless smile.

Faugh. Matt lifted his peacoat collar against the wind and stomped on. *It is possible*—who could say such stupid things.

Sophie was waiting by the door of Freddy's in a dark-green velvet skinny blazer, white frilly blouse, and tight jeans, her black stocking socks tucked into white high-heeled pumps. She shifted a Lucite-handled frame bag as he noosed her waist: so small, all of her felt holdable in one palm. The waiter signed them into a table by the back wall, underneath a mammoth mirror that reflected golden autumn light.

"Hello, stranger," she trilled. The mirrored gold gave her whole skin glow.

"Hello, strangerette." He winked.

"Ah—where's my kiss?"

He leaned over the table and pecked her cold lips. Thinking: *Sorry. Not again this madness from me.*

"Oh," he said, settling down again on the banquette. Because, sandwiched between a table of well-heeled Euro-tourists and a trio of men clinking flutes of mimosas, sat Scott Belfast and his lady in the far corner, directly opposite. Scott Belfast was slouched in his chair, scowling, hands jammed into his jacket pockets; Liza Andrewes was stretching her model-sized arms, mouth open to disgorge a lioness yawn.

"What?" Sophie squirmed around in her seat. She groaned. "Ah. *Those* two."

So he was in a place the cool kids had chosen! Perhaps Scott Belfast would see. With Sophie. Sharp-dressed: though maybe her frilly blouse looked a little deranged? Matt felt his face grow hard-edged, and his eyes sag heavy, bored, worldly. A leaden torpor draped about his lips. Unassailable. Cool.[18] "Do you know them?"

"He's in my Renaissance Art class. Unbelievably annoying. He thinks he's so smart. Mm, how about pancakes and eggs—split?"

---

[18] It is at such moments that one may feel disappointed in, perhaps even unsympathetic toward, our hero. Has he not so recently concluded a hysteric episode concerning the organizations of social hegemony, and has he not further disavowed his foolish behavior? We may well think, Matthew, why can you not be satisfied with the love of one woman—and with a best friend too! Between Sophie and Jason, is it not a life satisfying enough for you? Why do you always seek the elusive chimera of „cool"?

But to take this view, my friends, would be to underestimate the force of desires and sufferings long-ingrained in the lonely-child's psychology, which like the roots of pernicious weeds retain their hold even when they are by the conscious rejected. And indeed, oh my youthful confederate, so it is for us all, we are guided by currents of our subconscious over which we have no power. The only difference between us and yourself in these matters is that your experience was simply *Erlebnis* for you, while it is now *Erkenntnis* for us, so to say it was only what you lived through, not what you recognized; then you did not apprehend or know, as we know in seeing all of your errors made plain. Now that we are helpless to intervene.

"Sure. You pick the eggs." He tapped his front teeth. Even here that prodigy stood out. The world seemed to move around him, to gather about the scene of Scott Belfast black-dressed, pouty, and languorous, twisted now so that one imperial arm hung over the silver back of his chair. The droop of his fingers down; a flash of fine-boned wrist as he inclined two lazy fingers toward Liza Andrewes's upcurved lips.

"My God," marveled Sophie, after giving the order and the folded menus back to the waiter. "Stop staring."

His cheeks took fire. "I'm not staring," he mumbled. Examining his hands' mottled backs.

Sophie twisted to check them a second. "What's the big deal any-way?"

"Don't you think he's pretty cool? He's so, I don't know. Rock-star. Very charismatic, I mean. Just watch him."

Sophie snorted. "I have watched him, in seminar. No rock star. Not charismatic either. Trust me. A fucking idiot: he talks on and on in this really irritating nasal voice."

"He talks in class?" Truly? Wasn't that a Rule—Never Participate in Class?

"Oh my God, yes. The other day—"

Matt nudged her denimed knee. *"They're coming over here,"* he hissed.

"What?" She leaned in eagerly.

"They're—"

"Yo," Scott Belfast told Sophie. He gripped the silver bar on the top of her chair.

"Hel-lo, Scott. How are you?" A startled smile splashed over her lips.

"This is Sophie; this is Liza." Scott snapped his jaw back and forth.

Liza offered a hand to Sophie, amber-and-red bangles clanging on her long white arm. "Pleased to meet you." A drawl of honey-dripping syllables. "What's up?"

"Hi, Scott," added Matt.

Scott's eyes rested upon Matt, or rather Matt's outlines, shadowy, vague. "Uh . . ."

"I'm on the fourth floor. Of Third North. Your dorm." Please some-one stop me.

"This is Matt," inserted Sophie smartly.

"Matt, yo," said Scott Belfast. Liza Andrewes was staring the other way, adjusting her tawny mane. "Well." Scott gently banged the back of Sophie's chair, a wide band on his middle finger clinking faintly. "I guess I'll see you Tuesday." He rolled his eyes at Sophie and pursed his lips to one side: *Isn't it such a nightmare?*

"Tuesday," she chimed. Frozen smile.

Matt recovered his breath as he followed with his gaze Scott Belfast swaying through the crowd, those swooping side-to-side movements like some kind of eloquent music: and could *he* ever manage to imitate that, that perfect *sashay?* Outside, through the plate-glass window, Scott Belfast drew Liza Andrewes gruffly toward him; she lifted the lapels up on her dove-gray big-buttoned captain's coat and—very melancholy-nineteenth-century-heroine with her lowered eyes and the splay of that fantastic mane upon the wintry wool—leaned her angelic head some inches down onto his cheek: before they strode off, invisible cameras clicking.

"Now I feel really bad." Sophie was glaring at Matt open-eyed, mouth still frozen in an agonized smile. Finally she *arrgh*ed and hit the table with her right palm. "That was so mean of me. I *hate* talking shit about people."

"I should say so." He smiled evilly. "The guy seems to like you."

"I know." She shook her head side to side, mournful-slow. "What I was *going* to say was that the other day he asked if I wanted to study for the midterm together."

Matt's lungs seized up, squashed by an iron vise. "He was hitting on you?"

"No, no, stupid. I mean, probably not. I don't know. But anyway, I had to invent this excuse. I'm sure it was totally transparent. I just didn't expect—oh *fuuuck*." She thwapped morosely at the table again. "Nooooo. I think I told him I was working the Chan Library desk to*day*."

"Uh-oh," he sang-said. "Whoops." But he couldn't help grinning. His Sophiekins had dissed Scott Belfast! The Lord works in mysterious ways. "Well, if he's such *a fucking idiot* he won't remember, eh?"

And then the waiter set down two five-pound platters, steaming and smelling of maple syrup and fresh baking—in other words, of a pure, transcendent heaven.

Matt was measuring the pancakes' breadth with his knife—three pancakes, you could each have one and split the third, but a slice down the middle of the stack was right, equal shares of fruit topping and this globular red sauce—when he looked up: she was holding one muffin of eggs Florentine aloft, watching his knifework intently.

"You're so weird." Her eyes were serious, scrutinizing his face as if she could spy in it meanings shifting beneath the surface.

"Oh!" How had he let it show? What would a normal boy have done here? "I just want to be fair. Wanted to make sure you, also, had . . . were given . . ."

"I know." Suddenly her lopsided smile: it was a fruit cracking open, to show fine rows of pomegranate seeds lined up inside. "I mean I like it. Go on. Please do."

7.

And then it was Jason's birthday, the last Friday before Thanksgiving break. They were going to celebrate. "I don't want a party-party," Jason had yawned, "just drinks with you and Sophie and maybe Stan and Jorge from QU."

How very Jason! How faux naïf! As if they could possibly muster enough for a party—not in any universe where *party* meant more than, say, seven.

Matt landed on Jason's doorstep smack at ten A.M. with a set of streamers and Mylar balloons to rouse him into a *Happy Birthday!* He skipped Expressive Cultures section for lunch so the birthday boy would be spared the eating-alone today. He actually ran (disguised by his hood; not-running was a Rule) at three to help Jason with his packages. And passed the afternoon in Jason's room smoking, playing records, opining as Jason concocted an evening outfit—dissuading him from a tight black T-shirt (not mentioning the reason, the prominent gut) in favor of a mustard-yellow red-striped number (excellent for Jason's washed-out color), thanks to what his lady had learned him. Finally, he choked down an embarrassingly early bowl of Cajun Seafood Gumbo in the dining hall, walked Jason back to Main for his Stats quiz, cheerily bellowed *Good luck!*, then dashed home, dressed himself, and headed for Sophie's.

She opened the door smoking, her thin fingers no bigger than the white cigarette, wearing an electric-blue loose silk tunic over black denim—so tight, for a moment it seemed if he reached over and thwanged the waist rim he could rubber-band her off to Russia. "Hmm" was what she said, before she waved him into the kitchen, putting out the cigarette in her orange-and-green spacecraft ashtray.

"What's wrong with it?" he wailed as she ran her fingers over his clothes, making little adjustments.

"Nothing, I'm just . . . *there*," she decided, stepping back.

He rushed to the bathroom mirror. *Quel* masterstroke—it did look much better. His collar was lifted over the sweater's neckband, an extra button undone, the bottom of his shirt untucked from the waist, and the cuffs of his pants folded in so that they cropped neatly against his boots.

"You have a magic touch." He turned, reaching for her silky blue waist. "It's like a laying-on of hands . . ."

She clucked, making a wry face as she slipped a pack of Ultra Lights into her beaded purse. "Huh!" she gasped. "Go, go! It's eight twenty-six, go!"

As they clicked down the black-and-white tiled flights, Matt ran as always he loved to do his hand along the banister's serpentine unbroken curve. Outing in style! Not even a dive bar, the real McCoy, thank you, confirmed by a look in his old black book. *Swank* was penned next to this name, plus three neat asterisks. God, how long ago the summer notetaking was: already that handwriting felt remote as the script of some dead culture, Linear A, Babylonian. So innocent, ignorant then, copying places hardly knowing where Mercer or Greene Street were. The only one they'd tried thus far, Match on Spring, had turned out to be men in suits, blank-faced women, a crass too-old New York devoid of magic. And the big NYU bars seemed to be more suitable for raucous groups of seven, eight, ten—once he had peered through the window of Shea's on MacDougal, where, in dismal blue fluorescence, baseball-cap guys poured each other plastic cupfuls from beer pitchers.

Sophie squirmed her hand into his jacket pocket and linked. "You're trembling! What the hell?"

"Well. I just want him to have fun! To look back and say, eighteen. My eighteenth birthday left nothing to be desired."

"What?" She *tsk*ed. "Don't be stupid. He'll have fun. You know Jason.

He'll drink himself silly and get all messy and lovey and slurry." She squeezed his hand.

True. Like the night Jason had force-fed them Malibu till he dragged them into a toxic-breathed hug on Sophie's white couch. How beautiful Sophie had looked under the lamplight then; with that Asian blushing gene, she went sex-crimson on drink, a gorgeous red dripping throughout her skin. Matt kissed her glossy head.

Down on Sullivan, a dashing man in a slender suit leapt from a taxi, loping away with his tottering date along Prince. Well, we are out too, just like you, and you! Matt patted his pocket for cigarettes. Yes; everything in readiness. Matthew Acciaccatura is on the town! He felt like Frank Sinatra or Fred Astaire, some glamorous man in top hat and tails who would be swinging along the lampposts of the street.

"This is it." Sophie had gripped a door handle in both tiny fists and flung it open.

Thunderous house music burst out. Matt cloaked his features in Indifferent as the bouncer ran a flashlight over their fake IDs, but even this flimsy laminate thing, bought preparatory over the summer from one of those 42nd Street joints near Port Authority, did the trick. Then he entered after Sophie, already threading the throng. He mimicked her, exaggerating the pliancy of his body as it wound around people without giving them so much as a look, aloof. Glances strayed over him like searchlights as he pushed and strained, while Sophie's small form kept going into the crowd, vanishing among those who scissored across her path, then reappearing for a second; gone. At last he caught up to her under a dangling rooster sac of glowing red lanterns: where Jason was seated at a table crowded with faces and a haze of blue smoke.

"Hey!" Jason jumped up to dole hugs and moist kisses. "Sophie, Matt, this is Stan, Jorge, Tom . . . Sophie, you—look—*fabulous*. I love this." Jason plucked at her ripply tunic. "Didn't I tell you?" He winked at the guys. "Did you make this too?"

Sophie's eyes went wide with alarm. "Um, no." She recovered enough to murmur *Hello* nicely at the three of them, who chorused back, Tom raising his hand. "Pay no attention to him. He's full of lies."

Jason began to cackle. "Oh, Sophie, ever modest. Fine. Have it your way. Sit down, sit down you two." He flapped his hands and fell giggling backward into a chair. "Omigod! You see how *moved* I am by your presence? Ha! Sit down!"

"Are you Jason's roommate?" Jorge yelled over a robotic techno beat.

"Ugh, *no*!" Jason shrieked from down the table, where he was busy spilling Stan's drink. "I told you, I have a single. I did the whole"—he twirled his finger next to his head—"*loco* thing on the housing form." Jason's face beamed red and sweaty. "But *practically* we are, right, Matt?"

The waitress had materialized at his elbow. Waitress? Demigod with turquoise china-doll eyes. Every part of her white skin shone, as if the sculptor who had made her had loved rubbing his hands over that exquisite marble, its fluted tendons and smooth continents of breast. "What would you like," she drawled, heavy-lidded, monotone. Her eye zones glittered, covered with a gouache of dark sparkle.

"Can I have a cosmo?" Sophie expelled a puff of smoke.

Matt coughed. "Uh, I'll have—the same."

"*Yes!*" Jason pounded the table. "*More* cosmos—they make *great* cosmos here. I'll have another too." Jason sagely nodded his head.

"*Ja*-son," chided Sophie. "Don't you want to make it to nineteen?"

Jason laughed so hard small tears appeared in the corners of his eyes. "Oh dear."

"That's Jason for you." Stan offered a convivial smirk to the group and patted the birthday boy on his arm.

"Right," said Matt, pointing at Stan with his cigarette, just to say something. What did these people know about Jason? Strange to think that Jason had been living a parallel life with them, going to QU dances, to a couple of clubs on Sunday, gay night. Jason was putting his head down on Stan's shoulder. *Don't be a Gary,* he was saying, slurring. Stan snorted. *How dare you?* he kidded back. Some kind of in-joke.

The waitress glided back with their drinks and Matt drew out a wad of cash, forfending Stan, who made a move to treat Jason—"I've got it," Matt declared importantly, dealing out a twenty for all three. *My* best friend, thank you!

"It's nineteen." The waitress stared down at the twenty. "His is Stoli." Pointing accusingly at Jason.

"Ahm," said Sophie, "hang on a sec…" She opened her purse and handed a couple of singles to the waitress, who sighed and slid off.

"You tip them a buck on *each*?" hissed Matt into Sophie's ear. "Up front?"

"Yup." She smiled and squeezed his hand.

Matt tried his drink. At first it tasted cotton candyish, but then there were sparking threads of lightning so that the afterfeeling was of scorching wires fanned through his tongue. He sipped, took a gulp. Instantly—looseness, swells of joy moving through him. So quickly, like coffee, it massaged the brain, lifted, stretched it… Someone was rubbing his mind clean with a wet eraser. He smiled at Jorge beside him. It was the moment for the book of his tongue to open. Yes, you can. "So, Jorge," he murmured, making each word punchy, meaningful. "Have you been here before?"

"Mm-hm, once. But *she*," Jorge threw his eyes at Stan, "got sick in the men's room."

Matt felt the words *How dreadful!* coming to the fore of his tongue and stomped them out. "Crazy," he supplied instead. "What happened?"

Somehow they were dancing. They were lifting their hands, shaking them in the strobe lights, he was moving his feet and no one was peering through the darkness to see, he was torquing his torso, bending his knees like the dancers on MTV. Now he was walking down the shaking gangplank to the bathroom. A flash of the waitress's face, grimly slipping him a cosmo. A joint Stan passed to him: this was narcotics, sir, marijuana, at last, like a real boy, drawing on it, counting to hold the smoke in as they told him; two blooming petri dishes for lungs.[19] His pack of cigarettes whitely empty, crumpling in his palm. Pink-haired girl approached

----

[19] Our hero's first criminal act. (I dismiss as a youthful prank his and Sophie's attendance at the film for which they did not purchase tickets.) (As well as the immature consumption of alcohol.) (For are not this nation's laws on that point so excessive as almost to provoke rule-breaking? Your legal age is not only five years higher than that of Germany, it is the highest of all the world.)

him, asked for a light, then as the record changed said, *Madonna!* and *Wanna dance?* but he said, *I can't, I can't,* and waved her off joyfully. He was powwowing with Stan and Jason about how filthy Jason's single was—*You don't even want to know what I found there one time,* Matt laughed, shaking his head—when suddenly Sophie, who was dancing with Tom, reached out and grabbed his hand and they were all up together again, on the dance floor, where everyone was covered in war paint that the blue and red lights threw, they were lumbering through the darkness of a foreign jungle, just battling through, it was the last night on earth.

I can't seem to face up to the facts Was he was moving a mouth *I'm tense and nervous and I can't relax* Not him, but the other, was the other him *I can't sleep because my bed's on fire—*

"DON'T TOUCH ME I'M A REAL LIVE WIRE!" he shrieked.

"Oh my God!" Jason yelled, "I *love* this song!"

"I love *you guys!*" Matt screamed, holding Sophie's and Jason's hands.

Psycho killer . . . better run run runrun run runrun . . .

That acute insistent high-pitched tone was not a garbage truck reversing, but—Matt slammed the alarm and fell back on the bed. Good; Sophie undisturbed. And: Jason? Passed out on the couch; when had they gone to sleep? But, oh. Oh dear, fully dressed.

So this was *la vie nocturne* . . . sticky. Smoky—ugh, his throat. Some C-section had butchered the gullet. Jesus Christ, he had smoked an entire pack. *Before* coming back; then Jason's Newports. And marijuana—who knew what that did to your throat, scarred lungs. His whole mouth was a roomful of wool, the tongue a burrowing moth . . .

Ugh: and A Whole Day of shift before him.

Saturday was his day for the M&O office in Hayden Hall, the big dorm on the west side of the park. So far, this had turned out not-awful. Naturally a cushy situation like Sophie's, reception at the A/P/A Institute and the Chan Library of Fine Arts, would have been preferable. But NYU contracted out their real "custodial" services, the cleaning and vacuuming of hallways and common rooms, leaving him largely paper-pushing in the office, with only the occasional demeaning refill of paper towels in the upstairs bathroom or disbursing of toilet paper to kids who knocked when no one was around. Frankly, it was rather pleasant. The windowless room where nothing that went on in the rest of the world invaded. And: janitors. Hadn't they always been the nicest of all throughout his years of school? Ernie, who discovered him in the locker junior year. And Julio, who helped pick up the pieces of that ceramic jug he made in fourth grade. Maynard, who would punch his shoulder and say he was going to grow big muscles—what a nice thing to do, out of the blue. Everything about them was likable: their calming navy uniforms, neatly hung up in the office; their gentle camaraderie, men being kind and playful; and the honesty of their work, the real cleanness of everything about them, including the sweat on their white undershirts at the end of a hard-earned day.[20]

He was going to be incredibly late. He seemed to have set the alarm for 10:07 instead of 7:10, wildly optimistic anyway. No way he was making his eight hours. He put on boots—oh dear, upside down, the room—and kissed Sophie's blanketed toes goodbye.

She kicked him. "I'm still mad at you."

He grabbed her foot. "What?"

"Mad. I'm still very mad at you." Her black eyes were afire.

"For what?"

Her arms lifted and dropped wide on the bed. "Ugghgggh! For what? Don't you even remember? Flirting? Dancing with that girl Sarah? That punk chick with the pink hair? And the waitress?"

"I danced with the waitress?"

"Flirted with her. Jesus Christ. Talking to her about acting, her auditions, some Stravinksy shit—"

---

[20] In the Hayden Hall office, a small wooden chamber impregnated with that scent of deep pipe-smoke which recalls very old railway waiting rooms, I discovered one custodial labourer who not only remembered Matthew but even expressed a liking of the boy. And I must now take this moment to mention a profound debt of gratitude: the extra uniform donated to the cause by this same kind spirit, whose name I am sure I should not mention here, which enabled, in comfort, my hours of surveillance at Third North. *Gracias.*

"Stravinsky?"

"Stanis-somebody, I don't know."

"Shut up. Shut up. Shut up," intoned Jason.

"Jason. *My* apartment here."

Jason propelled himself up with one hand. His hair was sticking out everywhere. "Oh. Okay." He rubbed his eyes. "Hello."

"Ask Jason. Wasn't Matt flirting with the waitress?"

Jason nodded and yawned. "Yup. When I came over, you were all going on about some God stuff. You guys were like in the corner for like twenty minutes."

Matt slumped onto an edge of the bed. "Really? Was she talking back to me?"

Sophie thwacked her pillow and arranged it behind her, sitting up. "She was totally into it. *Do you think so? Do you really mean that?* I thought she was going to cry at one point. I kept trying to talk to you guys—"

"You even flirted with Tom. Who was supposed to be for me. Hello? My birthday. You don't even play on my team."

"I'm sure I wasn't *flirting*. I don't even know how to flirt." He rubbed the comforter over Sophie's legs. "Right, my sweetest sweet one? How could I possibly?"

"I really don't feel well. Oh my God." Sophie laid both palms on her face. "Um, Maaatt? Do you think you could go make some toast? Burned toast, burn it. And there's some gelatin in the pantry. Mix some with water. Like a—a spoon with a cup."

"Poor Sophie," Jason called. "Should I open the windows for some air?"

The feeling Matt had manning the toaster, watching the copper-brown blacken, go slowly dark like a piece of paper sipped by fire, was certainly evil. His little ladykins was audibly moaning in agony. But he had flirted, convincingly it seemed, with that gorgeous modelly waitress! What on earth had he said? He remembered scraps. *The thing about New York,* her strangely opaque turquoise eyes tilted down at the floor, *city of strangers*—something so agonized in her fixed stare, lit intermittently by a strobe, that he: maybe replied back with Vico's *Scienza nuova*, modern-city-cum-jungle notion? Ooh. Wouldn't have guessed that would go over terribly well. Yet there had been a sort of clear-air calm in the dark-ish vacuum of that back corner, two souls meeting out of any context whatsoever—there you could let go the ropes on your tongue so its sail billowed out. Well! Who would have thunk it. He'd like to try that again. Might need a bit of liquor in his system, of course, or maybe pot, and smokes to allow for distracting hand gestures: keeping the manic rest of the body occupied while a genie crept out of the lamp of your mouth.

He stirred up the gelatin: it hovered, a small gray cloud in a cup. Coming, my damsel in distress!

It was quiet at Hayden Hall, eerie-quiet. On the third floor the fluores-cent beam flickered as he slipped his key into the office door. He sat down behind the desk, folded his hands behind his head, and leaned back in the chair, which obligingly tilted.

Perhaps the world might not be so bad.

Perhaps there was something heretofore invisible in him that could in the future open again. This morning, over toast, they had looked at him differently, Sophie and Jason. As if he had just won a Nobel Prize, of which they were carefully not speaking. They must have been shocked last night, badly shocked. That waitress was about five thousand degrees cooler than any of the three of them: he had done something impossible, scaled a Mount Everest on tiptoes—only to descend, forgetting just about everything. He gazed at his hands. Small and red-patched from cold, dorkily knuckled, the hands of a meticulous knob. Weren't they?

8.

School emptied. One by one kids double-locked their doors, dressed in their warmest winter coats, and made the air around Washington Square echo with the rolling of luggage wheels along pavement, on their way home for Thanksgiving break. Even those kids who lived far away seemed either to have flown off or found someone to stay with. Wednesday, when bathroom stalls swung open emptily, when the cafeteria conveyor belt snaked a circuit with just his own ketchup-splattered plate, Matt could no longer put it off.

He trudged out with his bag and plunked down on the A train to Port Authority.

His car filled with strangers. A Latina girl kept checking her reflection in the blackened windowpane. Outside, a woman in a red suit ran along the platform—but the train drew away before her; she threw down her suitcase, cursed euphorically. Oh, if he could stay, just ride around with these people on the train! He could gate-crash the Thanksgiving luncheon at the international students' center, putting on some foreign accent. And how like an inverse of his kiddie fantasy, that idea: to run off on a steamer for parts unknown. Where, after a day of hard work and human brotherhood, say digging sewage canals in Africa, if someone passed the wine gourd and inquired, *And where ees home forr you, Friend Matt?* he might laugh, rueful, shake his head, hardly recall. *Now, let's see. There was a little town . . . it started with a T . . .*

But Port Authority presented no escape. Inexorable as ever, with its

Christmas music piped in, its dazzling megalopoli of magazines under blazing, stagey lights, the changeless destinations blaring out over the loudspeaker. He was heading home.

Merely to endure: that was the task. Merely to lie still and let it wash over him, a stone beneath poisonous flow, these five days.

His mother was waiting at the bus stop. Under the streetlight, at night, the silver Camry seemed like a shark, idling by the curb in wait for him. Inside, the car's overhead light was on—there she was bent, looking at something—slathering her dirty-blond ringlets, the masses of her shoulders in the orange uniform, with a fiery color. He lifted his bag higher, made his mouth and eyes perky, and unclenched the door handle.

"Matt!" she squealed. "Get in, get in, you're going to catch a cold." Waving spasmodically. Then her arm drew him inside a cloud of White Rain hairspray and meat-smell: he kissed her cheek, squeezed the canvas-stiff tunic. Something crinkled between them; when he pulled away she shoved a pile of envelopes toward his hands. Self-congratulatory, she smiled as she cast the rearview a worldly glance and began warily guiding the car into the vacant street. "I know how particular you are about your mail."

Evidently she had forgotten about his having forwarded all post to NYU: this little pile consisted of several implorations he use a drycleaning service in Bergenfield, cleverly printed as to appear in a personal, cursive hand, and one belated invitation to subscribe to National Geographic's kiddie *World* magazine. But who could interrupt her obvious pleasure? What kind of monster would do that? She was trying; that was a fetching surprise. "Thanks, Mom!" he said, or shouted, expending a touch too much effort there. And in the instant before he clicked off the overhead light, he saw the slivers of her blue eyes bulge with delight.

Maybe that's all it took? Not be smart-ass, moody, not try to show her up, just cheerful, loving. That wasn't overmuch to ask a son. So when she boasted, "I'm taking all tomorrow and Friday off," shoving open the front door and wiping her feet on the smudged blue rug, he murmured, "That's excellent!" and gave a little laugh. Or when, "I told Fred—you remember Fred Meese?—I said to Fred," she went on, fumbling in the closet, kicking off white faux Reeboks without undoing the Velcroed high-tops, self-importantly careless as a rich matron with alligator pumps, "I said, 'My son's coming home from *col*lege, so I hope you've got some other...'"—he joyfully reached for a hanger, nodding. Was she actually proud of him? The extra punch put into *col*lege, the patent significance of a son's visit?

Suddenly, she whirled on him. "What is that?" Reaching, cross. "That *jacket*?"

He clung at it protectively. "It's not real, if you mean... I mean, this is fake fur round the hood." His beautiful parka that Sophie had picked!

She was patting the hood's fur ruff, lifting and setting down her hand, mesmerized and disgusted as if what she touched might be herbage from some other planet. "It was expensive?"

Not even a question, just a statement of failure with a little uptick at the end. "Oh no. I mean, it's used."

She snatched her hand away. "Oh, Matt." She shook her head, giving him a disappointed look. Now she marched airily past him and into the kitchen. "I don't know why you buy that stuff." Sound of the sink running. "What if someone died in it?"

Someone's going to die in it, if you don't leave me alone. No, stop overreacting, you. "Mom, I got it in the kids' section." He walked over to the kitchen and leaned in the doorframe. "I don't think anyone's died in it." He extended an arm, then casually and as though happily let it drop, as if this were all just a little joke of hers, inoffensive chitchat.

She held up a finger as she drained a giant tumbler of water, then set it down, wiping her mouth with the back of her hand. "I wouldn't be so sure." But she shifted her weight and gave him a consoling, maternal look. "Well." She reached to ruffle his hair. "Next time you'll know." Then she drew back her hand, as if revolted though gleefully so. "What do you have in there?" She turned the tap, began washing her hands. "Ugh!"

"It's just gel, Mom." He reached up, gently patted. "Just trying to look...neat."

"Neat!" she hooted. Now, what was so funny about *neat*? So worthy of her clucking and shaking her head as she bustled around the kitchen?

You're right, Ma, gel is disgusting, vintage clothes are disgusting, you're always right about everything, happy Thanksgiving! Yet see how her hands—on the refrigerator handle, slicing carrots, white and knuckled red, oddly youthful—kept looking just like his own. This is your *mother* here. Come on, now. Incalculable reserves of patience are yours: if you only tap them you can stand anything.

But she knew the way to get to him, to expertly work the levers on the switchboard of his nerves. She knew how to make the seconds of a minute bend and distend like faces in funhouse mirrors, till he was slogging through a dinner of infinite length, a dinner of galactic magnitude. First—*You're going to get yourself sick!*—she shipped him up to his room for those ghastly fox-faced slippers presented for the sixth-grade Christmas, which somehow, demonically, seemed to keep up with his own growth. She played deaf when he said, *That's enough, Ma, I can't, I can't eat any more,* heaping his plate with sodden macaroni cedillas, remarking only with a stony-eyed stare that he looked emaciated, for Chrissakes. And for someone absent, for someone many hundreds of miles away in the wilds of Minnesota, Dwight might as well have been sitting there in the empty chair given how often he came up: *how did Dwight's Halloween concert turn out? oh, you didn't go?* Raising her eyebrow as if Matt's absence signified a want of bravery rather than interest.

And yet. Everything negative was leavened by the lighthearted air with which she filled him with bits of this-and-that, seemingly saved up for his visit: how Sarah-Lu, his hick cousin in West Virginia, had delivered herself of a boy babe, mother and child doing swell; how Emmalouise, his mother's coworker and best friend, had given her a key chain that, if you clapped, shrieked till you found it—and here in fact the marvelous thing was: right in her breast pocket! "Do you want it?" she asked, cradling it with both hands, in awe as always of gizmos. "I know you're good about your keys, but I thought maybe you could use it at school." And wasn't it cute of her to say? At last she ran out of novelties, remarking, "What else," to herself as she looked around the dining area. Suddenly, "Hey, Matt!" she blurted, her face shining guilelessly above the cream-stained plate. "Guess what I haven't done in a long time?"

And when the solution she had in mind to this question turned out to be *Play Upwords,* that humble board-game with stackable Scrabble-like letter tiles, when she giddily clapped her hands and snatched away their plates, then stomped upstairs to find the old set, when he was left washing dishes by the sink with lemon-scented Palmolive and waves of warm water, all he could feel was a dull chill in his chest that might be guilt. Upwords, to play Upwords with her son: what she wants. And you, you heartless prodigal, dreading this visit—paranoid, that's what you are, forever assuming she means to knock you![21] Just give her a chance, try talking as sons talk to moms.

Ensconced on the couch, with soft xylophone tones pealing from the ancient radio (her favorite, Lite FM), he made the word *juggle* and then, as if offhand, while he jotted down his score, began to tell her about Sophie.

Ping ping ping chimed the gay radio xylophones in the long moment after he fell silent and before, cheeks smoldering, he looked up.

She wasn't smiling, exactly. Though her lips were parted so the upper left-of-center snaggletooth showed. "You have a friend," she mused dully, though transforming the term sexless, chaste. Then she recovered enough to give her tumbleweed hair a reassuring pat. "Wonderful. And she's Japanese, how intaresting." She took a sip of Crystal Light, then raised it toward him for a second, as if having just thought of something. "Did I ever tell you I had an Oriental roommate at the Shore?" Brightly.

Bullseye. There was a rigidity in his chest and a strange pressure

---

[21] Now, why is it that Matthew's mother could not even once speak out on the subject of her son?!! As a result, we may never know the answers to many mysteries concerning their relationship: a situation, it now strikes me, that queerly mimics the uncertainty experienced by Matthew. And by so many other children, I wager. For I confess, I know a similar uncertainty in my bond with my father; often in the past I have wished to inquire if he has always intended to make me feel as one embarrassment to him, if his sharp remarks are as scornful as they appear or merely loving jokes that express a fatherly concern with an eldest son, who has made certain wasteful mistakes with his life? However, now I shall wish to delay any inquiries until he has perhaps been so generous as to help defray whatever sum my legal expenses eventually tally to.

around his temples that prevented him from being able to properly see, think. The Shore.[22] Was it time for that, then? If his mother hadn't spent ten weeks as a waitress in a boardinghouse on the New Jersey Shore, she might actually have had to take on the task of communication, instead of being able to resort to these ready-to-hand stories, all those wacky shenanigans cycling through her discourse with such regularity they resembled cut-paper shapes on a magic lantern, spooling continually across the walls of his life. And *Oriental*. Should he even bother to correct?

But she had something better up her sleeve. "I talked to your roommate Dwight's girlfriend, you know? She answered the phone when I called, you know, it was a while ago. Allison. What's her last name?"

"Carleton," snarled Matt. That trifling nana. That poster child of blond blah, unbeautiful but echt sailor, who had taken up with, or rather been taken in by, Dwight these last weeks. Difficult to say precisely how long such dupery had gone on: Matt had become aware of Allison only by degrees, first as a stolid bulk of good nature following Dwight with shining eyes while he talked volubly at the prepster table, before the indubitable conclusion set in when she and her corn-silk clews began adorning the suite. In the pair of early-morning conversations they'd labored through,

---

[22] Our homosexual friend Jason possesses a most interesting theory. (For, Jason, it will not be wrong to say we are friends?) Now, what is Matthew's birthdate? 22 June 1977. And what is the gestation period of the normal human baby? Nine months. And when did Matthew's mother labour at the boardinghouse? Upon her graduation from high school. And how old was she when Matthew was born? If you will visit my early „Excursus," you will find that Ms. Acciaccatura was thirty-six years of age when Matthew was eighteen. So, although it is purely a speculation, Jason has it as follows: Robin, then Falwell, graduates from high school, works at a boardinghouse at the New Jersey Shore, meets Matthew's father, engenders a child in the weeks after Labour Day, weds, the hasty marriage falls to pieces in part due to the arrival of infant Matthew, and the mother blames Matthew passively thence on for having doused the rosy promise of her life, etc., etc. Jason is the solitary author of this hypothesis, which he indicated was never suggested by Matthew. Is it not a riveting theory? Lacking Robin Acciaccatura's cooperation, it must remain so. (Unless a Mr. Acciaccatura will see this??!!! Great God, why did I never think of this? Hello, Mr. Acciaccatura! Please write to me!)

Allison mostly stared at Matt, an indulgent demi-smile on her lips, as if he might be a low hurdle her horse needed to jump.

"*Carle*ton. That's a nice name. What a nice girl. Did you know, she's from that place in Connecticut that Emmalouise's husband was from, you know—Da, oh, what is . . ."

Perfect, why not? Now on to old Emmalouise. A Southern belle who had briefly enjoyed a flush of beauty around the age of nineteen and, on her incipient Me Decade travels across America the Beautiful, met, then over the course of twenty-four hours married, a man above her station in Vegas. Flush dissolving by the age of twenty-three, her marriage dissolved too: and she was summoned from the world's higher stages to abide in Teaneck, New Jersey. When not on shift at the A&P, she docked her intimidating weight on his mother's couch or on her own boudoirlike love seat, where she was surrounded by nineteen-, twenty-, and twenty-one-year-old Emmalouises peeping coquettishly, even somewhat saltily, out of a set of heavy gilt scalloped-edge frames. Resting her diminutive feet, choked in white pleather sneakers, on a footstool, she could spend hours dusting herself with scores of cheese puffs, as if carefully restoring to her fingers the artificial color they had leached during the day.[23]

"Darien." His mother had found it at last. "What a nice girl that Allison is.[24] And she plays tennis, did you know that?"

"You know, Sophie makes clothes. She's really, really talented. I've seen—"

"What do you mean, she makes clothes? She has to make her own clothes?"

"No, she doesn't. But she—"

----

[23] Perhaps the least useful interview in all my months of research.

[24] At the time of my inquiries, Allison Carleton was in India for the year observing the Samarkand tiger and taking those photographs which have been printed in the official school newspaper (*Washington Square News*) of local residents with exceptionally gleaming white teeth.

"Used clothes. Homemade clothes. I don't see what's wrong with your old clothes anyway," she muttered, craning over the board.

Matt stared at the sliding glass door dead ahead. There in the reflection was the lamp, the couch, a largish woman holding back her hair in one hand as she gazed down, and a young man sitting rigidly gazing out engulfed by the roiling swirls of red and orange hues bounced from the lamplight and carpet. I'm going crazy. God, just one cigarette, one drink and a cigarette and everything she would say could wash over him like a steamship on the surface of where he lay, fathoms down, breathing water.

"Fried," she declared.

Eh?

"I made *fried*," she announced, rolling her eyes at him. "Here, gimme that." Snatching the score sheet from his side.

"Wow," he said, "that's weird. I think I was just starting to fall asleep. Maybe we should finish this tomorrow?" He stood and faux-yawned into a fist.

"Absolutely!" A bashful smile fluttered to her face. "I've got you right where I want you!"

Which was funny because ever since he'd reached the age of reason she couldn't manage to beat him at a thing. "Good night," he breathed, heaving himself balefully about her chest.

By early Friday he needed escape. Just a couple of hours. To tool out of the house and car-wise rove the streets: get *out*. Enough already, my God, let this cup pass from me. He made the move after breakfast. He had swallowed her bacon, a thing both repulsive and lovely, still pinkish, sticky. Then he raced upstairs and grabbed two big garbage bags of outsize old clothes on the excellent excuse of Salvation Army.

She frowned. "They're open today?"

"I called," he devised.

"Well," she said reluctantly. Staring at the bags: they were *perfectly good clothes*. "All right."

The car wheels screeched as he spun from the curb. He ate up the familiar roads speeding toward Englewood. And when he entered the store, plopped the bags by the counter, nodding at the glum woman who went back instantly to her crossword—a surge of sheer relief poured through him, so much that he was drawn perhaps to buy his Sophie a something? He walked over to the wall where scuffed purses hung above rows of books and records.

That's where he saw Gene Kim. Going over a crate of battered vinyl.

Gene Kim was wearing a black overcoat and blue-and-red striped cap, from which strands of black hair extended: Gene Kim, whom Matt had seen stalking the hallways of Tenafly as an alternative god, black-dressed and always hanging out with Julie Raffel, the beautiful redhead star of school plays, whose giant breasts were famous. Gene's reedy body swayed as he pivoted to look Matt over. "Hey man. I know you. Right? But where?"

"We went to Tenafly together," revealed Matt—stupidly. Better if Gene didn't remember! One year, tenth grade to be exact, before Gene Kim transferred to private.

"Wow." Gene Kim proferred a hand for Matt to shake. "Crazy. Your face is familiar . . . but I can't say that I remember . . ."[25]

"Whatever," said Matt hurriedly. Please don't.

"Look at what I got here." Gene Kim lifted up a few records placed crossways on the crate. "Serge Gainsbourg. The Velvets. Lenny Lavventura."

"Cool," asserted Matt, checking over Gene's shoulder with the air of a connoisseur.

Gene let out a little-boy smile. "These are gonna go over great. I spin records." He twirled his fingers as if stirring an invisible drink.

"Oh." Matt nodded vaguely. "Right on."

---

[25] The genial Kim (a bad pun, sorry: it is my weakness, or better to say one of them) demonstrated equal absent-mindedness when approached for aid in my researches. A most unhappy loss, as he could have provided a welcome outsider's viewpoint on a critical incident.

"I mean," now Gene's long fingers tapped dismissively over the face of the records, "I just DJ kid stuff. But it's such a *trip!*" he bent closer to assure Matt, shaking his head in friendly wonderment. Suddenly Gene looked at Matt intently. "Hey man, where do you go to school?"

"New York. NYU."

"That's *awesome.*" Gene's eyes widened. "What's hot in New York right now? What're the good clubs?"

Matt knew this one easy. The black letters in *Time Out* font appeared before his eyes. "Well, Spin City. Decadence. There's Robot Parade, but it's kind of over." He patted back a false yawn. "You know?"

"Oh man, arrgh!" Gene stamped one green Adidas. "I wanna go! You're so lucky," he wailed. "I'm up at Wesleyan; there's so nowhere to go out." Then Gene stopped stock-still. He cocked his head. Black strands unfolded over the lapel of his overcoat. "Wait a second. Listen." He grabbed his stack of records tightly and leaned over. "What are you doing tonight?"

The air in the store seemed to have turned to softest snow, light friable pieces of white. Behind, Matt could hear hangers scratched along a rack. The cash register drawer banged shut. So, the world was going on: though Gene Kim, standing, breathing, one foot away, had maybe just asked him to hang out. "Um." Not to seem desperate. "Why?"

"I gotta hear what the New York DJs are spinning. I'm only here till Sunday. Listen, I'm totally serious. Tonight. My girlfriend's down from school with me."

"My girlfriend's in New York," he barked, inappropriate.

"So we'll go? Like tonight, really?" Matt must have nodded, because Gene was scribbling down his phone number on the back of a pink receipt. "Call me. Like, we'll go at ten or something." He handed the slip to Matt. " 'Kay?"

"Yeah," said Matt, folding the paper into his pants pocket. He started to edge off. He was going to fall down: his knees were water-wobbly.

"Hey, wait a second," shouted Gene from behind.

Here we go.

—But the kid was grinning when Matt turned. "Hey man, what's your name?"

"Matt," he said. "It's Matt." No last name. Less recognition chance.

"Right on, Matt. I'm Gene. Cool." Gene nodded; Matt began wending away again. "I'm counting on you!" Over his right shoulder, Matt caught a glimpse of Gene pointing at him. "Good club! Good music!"

Then the silver-blue steering wheel was rotating cleanly in his hands, the Camry speeding Matt neatly away. Impossible. *I'm counting on you.* That thrusting finger.

"Hi, Mom," he called on walking in and, grabbing the cordless, marched straight up the stairs to his room.

"Wait a second, wait a second." His mother pounded from the kitchen to stand at the foot of the stairs, hands on hips. "I made you some lunch."

"Uh, in a minute, Ma, gotta make a phone call..." He shut the door, effectively blocking out her riposte. Pressed *Talk,* but clicked the phone off, put it on the trim bed, and banged his head against the wall twice. Once more. Then he sat, stomped delirious feet, and called Jason in Scarsdale. Perhaps that club spotted by the river his horrible night of errant wandering, right near the West Side Highway? It looked the requisite level of cool and impressively large, all those varieties of well-dressed bodies waiting behind the red ropes. He could surely ferret out its name by a cross-check with his little black address book. Oh, let's just put our heads together on this with Jason. Who at least *has* darkened the doorstep of a nightclub, unlike yours truly?

"So let me get this straight," Jason sighed. "You want me to come down to the city for some club tonight."

"Bingo, Jason, that's right."

"And what club is that?"

"Any club. That's the point. A good club. Someplace really cool. It's your call."

"But why do I have to come?"

"Be-*cause,*" he hissed. "Just because. You and Sophie both." As if he would survive otherwise. And how weird would that look? Like he couldn't rustle up even a couple of friends? "It'll be fun," he crooned. "I'll pay your cover."

"You know, I hate to say it, but tonight, it just isn't that good for me. My cousins are up from Baltimore, my whole family is going to be here—"

"Jason?" He felt like he was going to break the phone. It would crack in his hand. "Jason, this is, this is . . . ah, how do I . . . This is The Thing, okay. Like this is, this is It." What was he saying? "This is, you know . . . if we, um. Like, if you wanted to, ever . . ."

"*Okay*. Enough already. Okay. Who's your daddy?"

"What?"

"Say it, say, 'You're my daddy.' "

What?

"It's an *expression*, you doof."

"Like 'Daddy-o'?"

"Yes, like Daddy-o. Unbelievable. All right, Daddy-o, I'll call you in an hour."

"Thank you," he said, hoarse. "Thank you."

"Lordy. This kid better be worth it. Bye."

Matt pushed from the bed. Walked into the hall, opened the attic-stair door. Up there he pulled a string; below a bare bulb, he found the cardboard box with tenth-grade things, closed his hands on the glossy smoothness of a yearbook cover. There: Gene Kim, joking, with bolo tie. That picture had been famous. Girls had giggled over it; the more daring and favored surrounded a live Gene on a landing in the library, busily scribbling with special colored pens. Matt always left early on yearbook days. This year's edition featured Mrs. Walters, the librarian; she had kindly reached for his book, silent since she stuttered terribly, and in her fine grownup writing penned, *Have a nice summer, Steven!*

Pah. *Steven*.

9.

At 11:44 by the blue LCD of the dashboard clock, Gene's low sporty car turned left onto the block of that club Matt had suggested and Jason had concurred upon: Cinema.[26]

Matt leaned over Sophie's lap in the backseat to peer out her window. Again the pavement was littered with people. They were walking toward the river, in their studded belts, Mohawk hair, shiny rubber vests, the nakedness of somewhat hairy chests, biker caps, glittering silver platform shoes. In their leopard coats and Gucci six-inch heels, expensive Versace-style suits, a black cocktail dress with a triple strand of pearls. In mirror-paned sunglasses, blocking the phosphorescent streetlights that cast rays on the pockmarked and shattered-glass-covered sidewalk, turning it to the surface of the moon.

And there near the end of the block, on a dais with stairs to either side, seven huge black men in dark jackets watched over two women with clipboards standing at ground level by the head of a velvet rope: against which the hundreds pressed, impossibly dense.

---

[26] Here we are! Some fanfare is in order, is it not? For it is this identical night-club with which so much of our investigation is concerned. Now I am surmounted by a wave of nostalgic impressions—leaving aside my initial visitation of the site, I estimate that between September 1996–April 1997, when my work was prematurely snipped by the approach of policemen, I attended Cinema three nights/week, which thus became for me as a „second home."

"Whoa," said Gene, "I think we found it."

"No kidding," murmured Brenda, Gene's girl, from the passenger seat; Sophie, to Matt's right, merely gave his hand a cold squeeze.

Suits, ravers, preppies, trendies, goths, homeboys: every single type he knew from life was surging here against the rope, while a brace of beautiful tall models stepped out of a cab and scissored on their ridiculously long legs through the silver doors, first nodding to one of the clipboard girls. These two girls looked fierce, both on stilettos, screaming something Matt couldn't hear through the window. As he watched, one of the clipboard girls waved in five suits, while the other girl pointed two homeboys away.

Did it just depend on which of these girls you got? Or pure arithmetic, a matter of the club's numerical capacity? What was the idea behind the clipboard? At the river, the car veered left and circled back toward a pay lot. They all unfolded out of the low seats. Brenda, pretty and towering but unexpectedly blah of dress—black mock-turtleneck sweater, jeans, and clumsy mauve boots—paused to *ooh* over Sophie's jacket, a stiff white high-necked vintage thing that went down to her calves, tailored to fit even her tiny shoulders. Like some sort of Second Empire lieutenant: Sophie had, it was true, outdone herself; when Gene gave her a respectful nod, Matt's small petty heart brimmed over with pride. Then, in the brisk wind careering off from the Hudson, they managed with difficulty to light four cigarettes and in silence walked back, Gene and Matt with their arms about the freezing girls, to join the rear of the line. Coughing to hide triumphant-smile, he scanned the far side of the street where he had sulked along: could a mere two weeks be all it took? First Jason's birthday—then to return to stand behind these identical ropes here with *Gene Kim*!

Now forty minutes of heartless slowness passed. Luckily, through the hydraulics of crowd flow, early on Matt got shoved ahead of Gene, squeezed between a gangly youth in a white chinchilla jacket staring blankly out in space and a ravaged woman with acid-washed jeans and crow's-feet who kept screeching, "C'mon, man, I wanna *dance*!" After all, here was no place to employ the conversational topics he'd thought up (*Wesleyan, the new Aphex Twin EP*, and whatnot, which anyway had to last the night), and one can only wink or grin eagerly for so long: and it took forty whole minutes—of strange smells, leather and cigarettes and sickly perfumes opening and shutting about him like carnivorous plants—before Matt could step up to the plate.

Then it was make or break, do or die.

"Step aside," spat out the clipboard girl in emerald silk, clicking open the side rope for him. "Over twenty-one."

"But we *are* over twenty-one!" Matt rooted madly for his fake ID.

Yawning, the girl put a scarlet-nailed hand on her slender waist, hitching the dress up slightly. She scowled at him. "Are you going to stand there and argue with me?"

One of the bouncers eyed him menacingly. "Step aside, sir."

"What's the problem?" came Gene's affable voice. "Just here to have some fun."

Gene Kim stepping up to the head of the ropes—his cheeks lit by the spotlights above the dais beyond, his lower lip pouting coyly, with two strands of hair protruding from the striped cap as if artfully placed there by the same stylist as a pop star like Beck's—was precisely the same unanimously adored Gene Kim of the jazz-rock concert in tenth grade, plucking a bass, bending toward the microphone to *woo-woo* along backup on "Jumpin' Jack Flash." There was an ache in Matt's throat where the words *What's the problem?* should have come from, with that honey-and-salt texture, smooth yet gritty, universal and yet selective, directed here at the girl with the clipboard pressed to her brilliant dress.

The clipboard girl gave Gene a wry smile. She turned to half-glance at the bouncer. Then she swayed back to face them, her red hair swinging. "You're all four together?" And she unhooked the rope.

Burning, inward, down, Matt took the rear as the four of them passed the granite-faced doormen, paid twenty bucks apiece at a row of ticket windows, traversed a corridor with black walls and purplish light, and emptied into a large room. An *enormous* room. He couldn't see the end of it, except a shininess far in the darkness that might be wall. Beats from the surrounding speakers pounded into his chest as he scanned the scene: girls in halters waving cigarettes, guidos in black keeping a hand on their pockets while scoping out the ladies, Chelsea boys in wife-beaters hoisting bottles of water, wrinkled women with Texas blond hair sipping white wine out of plastic cups near balding men in crumpled linen jackets. Gene and Brenda decided to wait there by the bar while Matt and Sophie voyaged to the coat-check, the meeting point with Jason et al. Who hopefully would have gotten in? But Jason had been here before, purportedly, and anyway there were enough not-especially-cool sorts here to inspire optimism on that score. So, what had we done wrong out there, exactly?

The coat-check turned out to be no closet but an entire room the size of most bars. In the center, a huge apparatus with ten separate circles of coats wheeled round in orbits.

Jason snagged Sophie in a hug. "Hey!" he chirruped. Thanksgiving had evidently agreed with him: his face gleamed a touch oily, and beneath a bold printed maroon shirt his belly seemed to have buttressed itself comfortably. "Glad to see you. You're late!"

"You're alone!" gasped Matt. "What the hell happened?"

"Well," Jason waved a cigarette, *"nobody* could come. Tom is sick—he wanted to tell you he wished he could come. I think he has a *crush* on you!" Jason pinched an arm.

"And?!"

"Oy, listen, it's Thanksgiving, remember? People go *home*. And they don't all live in *Jer*-sey." But Jason's warm brown eyes searched his. "Sorry," he mumbled.

Sophie squeezed Matt's hand. "Hey, it's okay. It's going to be okay. Just tell him that your friends, they're all away for Thanksgiving. You didn't realize they were going away. It's o-*kay*. That's totally understandable, totally normal."

So Sophie and Jason had wonderfully intuited. Okay. Wasn't this plausible? By this point, a couple of extra little deceptions was hardly much to scruple over.

This music was low, nefarious, a current's undertow. With Sophie leading, he was wafted on its tide from the coatroom through shadows and blinking lights back to the circular bar: where Gene and Brenda were somehow not waiting. Matt circled the spot. Glasses were raised, eyes raked over him; now and then a darting blur of bodies picked up and sped forward like a school of fish he had sent into motion. No Gene, no Brenda, tall and unmistakable. Sophie went to make a pass—*she* was careful, precise; surely *she* would find them. But she returned shaking a troubled head.

"Maybe they went to the bathroom?" Jason offered.

Matt led the troupe through a hall lined by plaster arms holding torches where ravers sucked lollipops and fiddled with pastel backpacks, upstairs to a steamy bathroom where skinny wrecks with indigo under-eye bags were laughing, ghastly, leaning half out of the stalls. Were those maybe junkies, real-live addicts? A man clasping a girl tightly by the hand led her toward a stall, beside which three men, one in clown makeup, stood together, giggling.

Negative.

Now they tried a small blue-tiled bar, coiling between bodies, shaken by the strange stuttered sounds of the mechanized music. A man in shades and five stunning models, a new set from the ones before, cheered champagne flutes. Nope. They powered through the whole floor, sweeping the observation deck above the lower hall; into a Turkish pavilion with gauze curtains, where people at marble tables reclined on round oversize bolsters; through a fin de siècle cabaret where a drag queen slowly danced atop a red-lit stage; on and on, a Chinese opium den; a savanna, Astroturfed, with couches shaped like zebras and giraffes; last, a room made of glass. Here were glass cube tables, glass benches, go-go dancers in glass cylinders, and, at the center, a fountain spouting what looked like liquid glass. Past this, they hit a set of stairs going down.

"That *has* to be everything." Jason lit a cigarette, rested his hand on the railing. "Maybe we should go back to the bar? I bet we just missed them; maybe they went and came back."

Matt blinked, long. *We have to find them* had turned into *Where are they?* which had turned finally into silence. You're being foolish: he could feel this, like the time he'd cried in the car, fifth grade, when his mother refused to drive him for a slice of pizza. Sheer frustration. Sheer withholding of the world. "Fine," he said, hoarse. But in the opium den he had spotted something, a recess, a shadowy niche. "You both go down. I'll just be super quick."

Back in the den, he slipped into that space he'd seen. Leading from it was a corridor spectrally lit by blue fluorescent panels. Past homeboys blowing cannabis in his face, past a girl crying into her glass while her boyfriend murmured insistent words at her, he broke out into a vacant section. After another hundred yards, the hall ended at brick wall.

To his left, a black drag queen in a white wig and silver leather dress towered above him behind a red velvet rope. "List only," she snapped when he made a motion.

"What?"

"Guest list only." Sighing, she leaned a bare shoulder against the wall.

"Oh, I see. Well, I just need to see if my friends are in there. I'll just be a sec—"

"I'm sorry, I can't let you in here! This room is VIP, Guest List *Only*!" She glowered down at him.

Bitch! They had to be in there. The only place left in the club! And a special place—naturally, Gene Kim would have been drawn here. And now what if we don't show up? How would that look? *I couldn't get in?* For the second time tonight? Matt stared blandly at the drag queen, biding his time, the hounds of his mind loosed and racing out toward fleeting ideas. Just insisting was obviously making her very angry. He would have to perform his approach in a subtler, more flattering fashion. That was the way, really, Gene had handled the clipboard chick. Not to argue: not a matter of pressing one's rights. But to establish a rapport. He backed respectfully away when two trim men approached and she—see, something about their knowingness, conspiratorial as they pecked her cheek giving rise, yes, there, to her gregarious, shy almost-blush—undid the rope, clicking it shut after them seamlessly. Then Matt stepped up to the spot.

He pursed his lips coyly. He coughed. And he reached into the voice-box for that noise Gene Kim had made out at the ropes. "What's the problem?" He looked straight in her brown eyes. "Just here to have some fun." Oh, it was good: it was almost husky!

She raised one coffee-colored eyebrow. Cocked her head, bewildered. "What?"

"I said." Languorous, he laid his upper torso against the threshold frame, holding out a just-between-us smile on the tips of his teeth toward her. "What's the problem?"

Before she could reply: "Coco!" a voice rapped out from behind.

The drag queen whipped around to a fortyish man in an elegant black suit. For a long moment it seemed as if something was wrong with one of his eyes, as if he had a glass eye or an involuntary ocular seizure, but when the twitch was over Matt could tell the man had simply winked. His mammoth eyes were hazel-green and vaguely horrifying, almost protruding from the curve of his tanned, leathered face, and his body was wise-guy square. The most appealing thing about him was the suit, narrow-lapeled, all floaty panels, as though by one of those Japanese designers whom Sophie admired. " 'Sall right." The man nodded at him. "Kid's a friend of mine."[27]

As if the world had said, *I'll see your buck and raise you a hundred.* As if the man had remarked, *This boy is my long-lost son.* So 2 + 2 = 5 totally absurd, Matt found himself saying "Exactly!" and admitting a knowing laugh. How long had that man been standing there?

Coco unclicked the rope and shook her head softly. "Why didn't you just say so?" she whined.

Matt followed the man into a dark room. A deep pinkish-red crystal bloom in the middle of the ceiling emitted a low glow over a little dance floor, and there were dim fixtures on the walls above banquettes behind the ten or so black tables around which small groups were quietly gathered.

Small, clubhouse-small, and extremely calm in comparison to the

---

[27] It pains me that I can provide no first-hand account of this exchange. Of the three persons present, one has gone beyond the reach of my call, another, discovered to be working for a night-club in Tel Aviv, no longer remembers, and the last refuses interview on the grounds of potential adverse publicity. Perhaps someday when the long shadow of government no longer hangs over this affair, when the barking dogs of the media have definitively run on in their heedless quest of the next prey, I may speak with this remarkable individual and obtain his version.

rest of the club. A tiny, rather tame bar stood against a wall, where just a couple of people were standing by while a bartender in a white button-down shirt poured drinks from a metal shaker.

The man was studying Matt, his protuberant hazel eyes groping like octopus suckers. "So how ya been?"

"Fine," croaked Matt. "About the same. You know."

"C'mon." Now the man was moving smoothly toward the bar, skirting the dance floor. "What are you drinking?" He eased his elbows onto the black mica counter.

What does one drink? Well, it certainly was the most popular option at Jason's birthday party. "Cosmo," Matt coughed, "please." While the man ordered, Matt turned aside, scanning. Too dark in here to tell for certain, but there seemed no girl tall enough for Brenda acccompanied by a slim black-shirted guy.

People say that in those watersheds, the Marc Antony meeting Cleopatra in the streets of Ephesus moments in a life, you feel something strange, a hackle of hair rising up from the nape, someone walking over your grave. But when this man swiveled back from the bar, passing Matt a V-shaped glass through the reddish light and taking a healthy swig from his own fresh bottle of water, even when he winked again and said, "Looking for your friends?" Matt felt nothing, except a nagging fear of being discovered. "Gowan! Take a good long look, I don't mind," he announced.

Matt peered at the bodies flickering in and out of the strobish atmosphere.

"Satisfied?" Now a grotesque girlish smile played over the man's lips. "Listen, kid, between Coco and me we've probably heard every line a million times." Leaning back on the counter, he screwed up his eyes toward a spot on the ceiling. "*I'm just looking for my friends.* Ah, ah," he commanded, holding up a hand to shut Matt up, "I don't need your apologies." Suddenly: "What's your name, kid?" Tilting his head back, he peered down at Matt with a pompous, evaluative air.

"Matthew Acciaccatura," he managed to say. "Thank you for the drink."

"Pleasure to meet you." The man lifted his water bottle as if in cheers.

"I'm Vic Spector." He looked at Matt for any sign of effect. "And this is my club."

Matt sucked in his breath so fast he lost a bit of cosmo; dabbed with a bar napkin.

But Vic Spector was gazing impassively into the crowd. "Do you know why I asked you to come in here tonight?" he mused thoughtfully. He spun on Matt. "Do you know why I'm even *talking* to you right now?" His shoulders fluttered disgustedly.

Matt shook his head.

Vic stared back into the crowd as if toward a sunset, a grand sentimental moment. "Because you got something, kid. You've got a very, very rare quality." Vic took a meditative sip. "Man, every time I find one, it gives me chills." Capping the bottle, he shivered showily, his blazer's ends shaking like a marionette's limbs. He shot Matt a canny glance, then made a discarding gesture with one hand, where a prominent, square silver ring glinted. "I love it. As many years as I've been in this business . . . 'cause that's why I'm here. To see what I see. What you don't even—" Now he drew himself up to gaze at Matt proudly. "All right, kid, you wanna know? You wanna know what you got?" Wary, Vic checked over his shoulders before leaning in to half-whisper, "The fire in the belly. You're *hungry!*" Vic glared at Matt rather voraciously himself.

Righto. Matt could feel his mouth idling in a dazed deer-in-headlight smile.

"You see all these people?" Vic waved a magician's hand toward the crowd. "They're out here having fun. They're drinking, sitting with friends, flirting, showing off, networking, whatever. Their desires are *lateral.*" Vic made a flattening, horizontal gesture with his free hand. "While your desires are vertical." He pumped the hand up and down, a little elevator. Then he screwed his eyes onto Matt, hard. "Why did you really come here tonight?" he asked accusingly.

"I was looking for my friends," Matt murmured, chastened. Was this the part where everything turned nasty? A signal from Vic—then Coco, the bouncers . . .

"No, you weren't." Vic slammed the water bottle down on the bar. "Why did you come to my club?"

Why *was* he here? Gene Kim? Was that an answer? Once in my life, just once to impress—you have no idea the stress I'm under here! Not playtime for me. Yet maybe the man did in some shape understand. I mean, was that part of what he'd meant? With his *lateral, vertical* business? "Wh-why does anybody come to a club?"

Vic bellowed, "See, see, you can't even say it." Tilting his head to the side, he leveled a tender gaze at Matt. "I been in this business a long time," sadly, he examined his hands, "I know what I'm talking about." Then Vic stood up tall. He began jabbing his finger toward Matt. "You're going to have to admit what it is you really want if you're gonna rise to the top here. Because it's not about just *having fun*. You gotta keep your eye on the ball." Vic pointed meaningfully to his own temples. Above, all around, the song shifted to a spectacularly apposite "Hungry Like the Wolf." "What is this piece of shit music—" Vic muttered under his breath. Lunging over, he snarled at the bartender, *I told him already* and *Duran Duran* and other words Matt couldn't catch. The bartender nodded politely, wiped his hands on a towel, and walked off. At the far edge of the counter he beckoned to a woman with a round silver tray, said something in her ear. She nodded too before scooting off into the crowd. When Matt turned back, Vic had a generous, lordly smile ready for him. "When it's your club..." explained Vic, sniffing. "Declan is a *ter*rible DJ. Anyway, listen." He was rocking back and forth on his feet, heel-toe, heel-toe. "I see something in you you don't even see yet. There's so much raw potential. And I can take all that and shape you into a pro-moter. I am the one who can make you a star. Here." He shot Matt a shy, vulnerable glance as he plucked something from his breast pocket and thrust it out. "What you do is you take this home, you call me on Monday, we'll set up a meeting.... Do you even *know* what a promoter is?" He cackled, incredulous. *"Ohhhh,"* he bit his lip, "it's a real pleasure to meet you, Matthew. A real, real pleasure. We're really going to make this work. Kid, I'm gonna teach you *everything*! I am gonna Make You *Fabulous*." He winked. "Trust me."

Matt accepted the glossy black card. VIC SPECTOR, DIRECTOR shone out in glowing white capitals. There was a strange crackling sound. Vic ripped a black box off his belt, shoving it up to his mouth. "Go for Vic," he shouted into the walkie-talkie, then pressed it vehemently against his ear. "No, no, don't *you* do *any*thing—I'm on my way." And he dashed from the room without another glance.

Matt brushed the black sheen of the card with his thumb. The print didn't disappear, like reflections in a stream. *White lines . . . going through my mind . . .* sang the music, above, behind. White lines: these stamped-out capitals on the obsidian black, running left to right, into the future. Lazily he opened his wallet, tucked the card behind his driver's license. Over his shoulder, the bartender was clearing away Vic's bottle. "I'm all done," Matt said, nodding at his glass. There are witnesses, you see: a real scene: a real bottle, card, and you're not crazy in the least.

He walked to the ropes, nodding absently at Coco, down the narrow corridor, into the opium den.

"Matt!" Sophie was tugging at his arm. "*There* you are. I've been looking for you forever. Listen: we found Gene!"

What was it that pulsed in him then, as a sportive roil of fake smoke absorbed his torso, momentarily blocking out Sophie from clear view— was it merely an effect of the music, which suddenly sped up its beats from wild, virtual drums? Was it the hot-pink fingers of that cosmo just finished, starting to play scales with his veins, tightening those strings toward impossible heights? Or could it be no such admixed thing but purely the first mad flush of happiness, a happiness beyond reason, the happiness of the insane? For all the drawbridges of his mind were down now, letting thoughts in-out over the dangerous moats of normal logic . . . oh, there were birdsongs, banners, egrets flapping through the brain's dark. And when the veil of smoke between them was rent: "That's wonderful," he breathed, drawing Sophie into a squeeze that whirled her through air to set her laughing, smoothing her hair back, on those little booted feet.

TWO

1.

For years Matt, flipping through the pages of one of his favorite picture books, the battered hardcover *A History of the World in Full, Living Color*, would hover over the illustration of Henry IV, Holy Roman Emperor. Henry was a small figure with a matted beard, pale blue eyes, and a badly-watercolored fur coat, kneeling in a field where drifts of snow massed everywhere before a castle with a closed door. The castle was Canossa, high in the Apeninnes. The year was Our Lord One Thousand Seventy-seven; January, to be precise. Inside the castle was one Pope Gregory VII. Over the last twelve months, in an escalating struggle over the reins of empire, Henry had made a series of mistakes, of botched bluffs and ill-judged gambles. Now the German nobles, their bonds of allegiance annulled by Henry's papal excommunication, were primed to meet at Augsburg, where they would almost certainly elect a new ruler. And thus did the desperate king dare one last rash coup. Thus did he ride up wintry mountain paths to kneel for three days begging clemency in this rimed field: three days, seeking deliverance with his pale blue eyes fixed on the pope's barred portal.

Matt would loll back on the bed, and, pressing the whispery pages of the book to his chest, float out toward distant Henry. What could it have been like? When, first by an inch, then by feet—revealing a stone foyer coruscating with red and gold torchglow—finally the door opened, and the pope called him in?

When the door opened. When a blockish, paunchy man in a

thin-lapeled Japanese suit beckoned, so you got up off your knees, dusted off, and stumbled toward a pulsing rose-colored light.

Not until Matt bid adieu to Gene and Brenda (last-minute deciding to "crash in the city"), not until he had led Sophie and Jason seven windy blocks to the Empire Diner on Tenth Avenue, and they were installed in a booth, just beginning to tuck into cheese fries and whatnot, in Matt's case an egg cream, did he begin. He licked sea froth from his straw, placed it on his napkin. He gazed out at them, calm and sane. "You're never going to believe this."

They didn't.

"Whatchutalkinbout, Willis," said Jason, a cheese fry dangling from his mouth.

"Matt," said Sophie, putting a hand on one of Matt's, glancing worriedly at Jason. "That's impossible," she hissed.

Matt told the story backward, forward, and sideways, like a room to walk around in, touching the sides of walls and jumping on the floor to feel solidity and depth. "I can't believe it myself," he kept saying. To what questions they shot him he gave convincingly exact answers: he even made use of the salt and pepper shakers (himself and Vic) and the sticky bottle of Heinz (Coco) to mime where all parties had been positioned at the start of their fateful meeting. Finally Matt dug out the glossy black business card and placed it on the table between their water glasses.

"Wow," breathed Jason, looking on awed, almost crestfallen. Then: "Holy motherfucking God." He turned away, hand in the air. "I'm so getting a milkshake."

Sophie gazed at Matt appraisingly. She pushed her peppermint tea forward, folded her arms across her chest. "I guess he does look kind of cute tonight."

"He does! That shirt—if someone didn't know better, you might take him for—" Jason broke off to order a pistachio-vanilla milkshake, while Sophie mused, *I got him that shirt* . . .

"What? If someone didn't know better?" Matt demanded to know.

"They might mistake you for, you know." Jason dropped his Newport pack on the table. "Some kind of—man about town?"

"Thanks, Jason." Matt shook his head soulfully. "What an excellent vizier you'd make. You tell it to me straight."

"Listen, I'm not trying to be obnoxious." Jason glanced defensively at Sophie. "It's just . . . realistic. Look, you guys, like Sophie said, you almost didn't get in there tonight. I mean the *front* door, forget about VIP. And now they want you to be a promoter? There's obviously a, you know, some kind of disconnect. Call me loco, but I guess it's just that hungry stuff you were saying—"

"I'll help you with your outfit," Sophie declared. "I'll do your outfit, I mean. For your meeting. If you want me to."

"Thank you." He smiled at her. "My lady rideth to the rescue."

"Aww. There you go!" Jason insisted. "I'll help too! I know somebody who, like, DJs small parties—his dad's with my dad's hospital. I'll ask him all about the whole promoting thing when I go back to Scarsdale. Yay, you guys! Come on!" He reached out his hands enthusiastically toward them.

They all clasped.

"What should we say? Eureka? Olé?" Matt suggested.

"Olé!" Jason fell back in the vinyl banquette, emitting a flatulent boom.

They all banged their hands once on the table, shouted *Olé!*, and threw them in the air.

"Wait," said Matt. "And me? What do I do?"

"Oy." Jason rolled his eyes at Sophie. "How about you just try to not obsess? That should keep you busy."

That night, after Matt and Sophie waved goodbye to Jason making off for Scarsdale in a regal beige Mercedes, they kissed and rubbed naked on the bed, and when the lights were off and they were tucked inside the sheets yawning toward sleep, he placed her small cool hands on his face, let her rove there like a blind girl over the face of a mild, charmed lion. "Are you impressed?" he whispered toward her.

"Ugh." Her hands sank down. "Don't say such stupid things.

Besides." She fluffed up her pillow. "I thought you were supposed to try not to think about it."

"Roger. So . . . how about: what did you think of Gene and Brenda?"

"I thought he was a phony. And she was boring. Next question."

That his lady could reject Gene Kim thrilled, a rich chord played on the harp of his heart. "All the girls in my school thought he was the coolest cat's-meow." He kissed the frail shells of her fingernails, heaved a sigh of pleasure.

She retrieved her hand. "Cool, schmool." She had picked this tic up from Jason. *Late, schmate. Tired, schmired.* "Why do you give such a crap about what's cool?"

"Okay," he sighed, flopping over onto his other side. "Good night, then."

"Don't be a prick." She rubbed his middle.

Her hand on his waist was a burning weight. How simple it was for everyone else! Have friends, don't have friends—cool, schmool—what's the difference, but a momentary inconvenience? Well, Sophie and Jason had utterly missed the point: this much was clear. He reached down to her hand. Useless to say, but he might as well try. "If you had been me until now," he began in a tight voice, "you'd understand."

"Maybe." She snuffled her nose into the crick of his neck, scooted her other arm under his waist, and squeezed. "I just don't want you to be sad. Me and Jason think you're the cat's-meow no matter what Vic Spector says."

"Thank you." He bent his head back toward her shoulder. So what if they weren't capable of comprehending? He would just have to keep that disability in mind. They didn't mean not to get it. "Um." He traced a spiral on her thigh. "Would now be a bad time to mention it's *Jason and I*?"

"Yes," she said, biting his neck.

Soon, it took hardly ten minutes, her breath distended into sleep-tide: but he couldn't fall into it. Before his watchful eye, the ceiling was successively denuded of layers of paint until from the brown-and-pink of darkness-and-streetlight it became a fabulous wintry Wedgwood blue—and finally absolute China white, a blank and frigid field larded with hoards of featureless, endlessly soft snow—

2.

Monday morning arrived at last—10:20: well and good, he had actually overslept; even Josh was out of bed and vanished. Right now Professor Mason would be waving chalk around a blackboard, scratching *Tokugawa, divine right of kings* in spindly yellow script, but today there would be one more seat unfilled in the auditorium, one triangle desk still folded where yours truly usually sat. For today was the day of the Day.

With a practiced hand—*en garde!*—Matt drew out the stack of cards from under his pillow, placed there both to hide from Josh and as if sleeping on them might help him memorize. It wasn't so very much, merely some definitions and answers, just whatever info Jason had returned on the train with yesterday regarding the profession of *promoter*, plus whatever snippets of persona they three had devised *chez* Sophie last night. AGE: 23. After all, he had best be legal. PROVENANCE: New York City. Colorful as it was, *New Jersey* presented grave image difficulties. GUEST LIST: Why, your assiduous promoter's register of invitees. COMP: *Complimentary admission* for those happy guests let in gratis on the promoter's say-so. REDUCED: *Reduced admission;* please, this is easy. ROPES: Barrier of entry to the common creep; he.

Matt jumped from bed into the autumn day that wanted him.

When he phoned, a bored man refused to pass him to Vic (lucky, for Matt's voice cracked and quavered most uncoolly), instead simply informing him that the meeting would be at three. Four hours off! A dilatory Matt killed the minutes with a stroll, an extended breakfast and reverie session, thumbing sightless through a student paper, till finally it was time to make his way to Sophie's. And there on the green eiderdown she had laid his outfit—so thoughtful, his lady, she had even ironed out the hanger marks of the collarless charcoal Helmut Lang button-down, along the waistband of the black Costume National pants. At 2:22 he was staring at a boy in her bathroom mirror, checking each last molar for stray bits of cereal, for stray bits of *him* leaking through . . . and precisely twenty minutes later, his shaking fingers were pressing green bills on the cabbie by the curb before Cinema. The white dais was still here, and the double silver doors shining in the bright sun, but now it all looked bare and simple, a little abandoned temple here by the river. Matt trotted up, tugged on the rightmost door.

He entered a bare and spacious purple-carpeted lobby, which a model-like man in a newspaper-boy cap was crossing. Both hands wrapped about a stack of cards, the man paused, tipped his olive-skinned face to one side. "Are you here to see Vic?" He blinked limpid horse eyes when Matt nodded. "This way. I'm Adrian."

Matt followed swaying Adrian down a set of stairs lined in black felt, through a room edged by silver tables and chairs stacked in piles and smelling faintly of vomit and Lysol, into a low-ceilinged tunnel, up a stairwell ending at a door—

Into a large corridor. When the door clicked shut behind, it dissolved into a mirrored wall. "Over here," droned Adrian, already climbing a pediment to another, unremarkable white door. Inside—a conventional office: desks; computers. Phones, the underhum of conversation. "You can have a seat here." Adrian waved to a black leather couch before, snuffling, he glided off, disappearing behind a white wall.

"Sorry, Xavier, this time of year is crazy, you should know that," Vic's voice announced from behind the wall. "Besides, I—to be honest, I don't really see what we have to talk about."

"What do you *mean*?"

"It's nothing personal, I love you, I was *thrilled* to take you on again after all these years, but the numbers just aren't there. Miranda, show him his numbers."

"I've already *seen* my numbers!"

"Xavier. Thursdays just haven't been holding their own. Let's be honest: you're not performing. Andrew is furious with you, livid, did you know that? Omigod, whoaaaa. Look, between you and me, he wanted me to *fire* you. 'Get that lazy cunt out of my room, please, Vic, I don't want him involved with my party': that's exactly what he said to me. I—I—hadda talk him down. So you should really *thank* me, all right? Is this the thanks I get?"

"Two hundred?! That—"

"Is the best I can do. Miranda, is my three o'clock here?"

"Yes," chirped a girl.

"So, Xavier..." Steps rang out on the wooden floor until a handsome African-American man with shaved head and well-defined pecs beneath a green knit shirt appeared with Vic. Again Vic was wearing a black suit, hands jangling around in its bulging pockets; there was something raccoonish about the way he moved, irregular and shrewd: darting, twitches. "Maybe take a few weeks, you know, cool off, think about what we talked about today. All right? All right."

A stricken Xavier shook his head, but he and his built shoulders passed with admirable grace out the hall door. Jeez. Adrian, Xavier: did you have to be modelesque to work here?

"Mat*ty.*" Vic whirled at him as soon as the door had closed behind Xavier. "Right on time. C'mon, c'mon, step into my office. Miranda," Vic paused by one of the doors to shout, "I don't wanna be disturbed for *any*-one, you got that? C'mon in, Matt."

Step in. To the open door.

"I'm *so* sorry you had to sit through that..." Vic's eyes were two giant pools of commiseration, as he waved Matt into an ordinary office; ordinary desk, an ordinary phone, a corkboard overflowing with photos: Vic, with vaguely oily people and what appeared to be a macaw. "Have a seat." Vic sat down heavily, tucking in his suit's stray lapels over his stomach. "It's a sad story, really. Xavier is the *greatest*," he sighed, flicking a thick black fountain pen absently. Finally he shrugged. "Well. So... thanks for coming by. I hope it didn't interfere with any of your classes."

"Excuse me?"

"Heh heh heh." Vic slapped the desk with the flat of his hand. "Don't tell me, don't tell me you don't even *remember* when you got class. What are you, a freshman?"

So much for being twenty-three. "Is it that obvious?" Matt murmured, with a brave smile.

"Obvious! The kid asks 'is it obvious'!" Vic looked around incredulously at an unseeable audience. "Are you *serious*? Listen, kid." He hunched in close. "Prob'ly anyone could tell you that. And me—when you've been in the business as long as I have, you just, you *know* these things. That's your *business*: to know things. You just—you just pick up on them, see?" His meaty hands lifted and flipped, as if to show himself unarmed. "See, when you meet somebody, all right, there's all kindsa signals they're sending out; they have *no idea* but they're projec*t*ing themselves all the time..." He grinned and crossed his legs. "Sounds complicated but it's really, it's really very simple. Now you, you know, you're just starting out, so one of the easiest things you could go by is *shoes*. Shoes tell you everything you need to know about a person. You look at someone's shoes—bam! You got 'em. You know immediately, they're a homeboy, a rocker, a suit, a Euro, whether they're just a mook, a guido, whatever..." The pen tapped two quick impatient raps on the desk. "All of it—it's all in there."[28]

"I see. Right, sure." Perhaps his Special Boots were giving GAY GAY GAY. Matt uncrossed his legs and tucked the boots discreetly beneath his chair.

Stagily, Vic mimed wiping his brow in relief. "Whew!" He glanced

---

[28] How interesting. Perhaps now I possess a further understanding of that occasion in which Lisanne told me she wished me in future to avoid approaching her office in my black-and-yellow tennis trainers; they did, it is true, bear the markings of their reliable use. At the time I only laughed in an indulgent fashion and pulled on her nose affectionately, *With a good will, my little young-hare!* (do you say this in English? is there perhaps a better translation for *meine Häsechen*?); making a small note in my mind of an I *must not* but remaining ignorant in regard to why, I considered it as other of her nonsense-commands (*Do not walk naked in the apartment, Do not speak of your yoga practise to my colleagues,* and so forth).

under the desk, bugged his eyes, and let out an abrupt burp of a laugh. "Because they really are wannabe. They're throwing off your whole look. Here you are doing like deconstruction Ann Demeulemeester or maybe that's Lang, and you've got the boots of some B&T mook who comes in off the subway and buys the first thing he spots on Eighth Street. Am I right? Ugh, don't apologize—" Vic *tsk*ed dismissively, gave a contemptuous toss of his head. "Here, look, I'll show you." His right shoe exploded on a pile of papers atop the desk. "See this? I had it made for me, bespoke, in Japan. Look at the heel—and the fineness of the leather—go ahead and touch it, there you go; I mean, if you think you can get that at Barneys, you're out of your head!" His hazel eyes blazed, defiant.

"Very nice." Matt smiled politely. "The leather is excellent."

Vic dropped the shoe unceremoniously to the floor. "Ha! Ha ha!" He fell backward in the chair. "I love it, I love it! Oh, you got a lot to learn, kid, it's gonna be very exciting watching you *grow* here. *Verrrry* exciting. A kid like you—ah! The possibilities are endless! I can tell just from *looking,* you're a natural. You see," Vic's head swiveled robotically over his shoulder and back, as if checking to make sure no one was listening, "not everybody has what it takes to be a *promoter*." Hush-hush; apparently a *promoter* was some species of covert agent. "It's a very complicated business, it's an *important* business. Only people who are gifted in *very* special ways are cut out for it." He began rocking his hands in waves, soothingly, like a magician or hypnotist. "Takes a lot of brainpower, takes a lot of skill. It's about—you know what it's about?" Vic leaned over the desk toward Matt, crushing the papers below his elbows, with a starry late-night look as if he might be about to propose. "You gotta just look at somebody, and"—he snapped his fingers, scornful—"*talk* to them *in their language*. That's the secret. You follow me? What's the secret?"

"Talk to them in their language," Matt fired back.

Vic was caressing his own hands, rubbing them together in a reassuring manner. "Good, good. You see... you're like, a promoter is this little pivot, between all these worlds. You got me? Now I've got an analogy for you, college boy. Just for you. Picture a circle." Vic inscribed a circle on the back of an envelope with the fat sleek pen. "And now imagine—what is this, the radius, right—so you've got all these radiuses." Vic made a number of strokes. "And this, this center here, it's, *what?* Think. What is it—what's so special about it?"

"Equidistant? I mean, it's in the middle, exactly?"

"Nah. Of *course* it's in the middle, that's why it's 'center,' genius. Now I want you to think. Is it a part of this radius?"

Matt nodded.

"And that one?"

"Yes."

"And what about this one? And this one? Okay! So you see, all these radiuses—they *think* this *center*point is one of *them*. But they got it wrong, every time. The center belongs to nobody. It just seems like it does—it talks to everyone else, in their language." He threw down the pen. "See? That's you, that's promoting in a nutshell. What's amazing is how few people can do it. You think I can ask Adrian," Vic shuddered, "or Charlton, or any of those other rocket scientists I have working in my office? They're either too stupid or too busy getting their rocks off, they don't have their eye on the bottom line. I need talent who can think: about our bottom line. That's where their minds have to be. But Adrian, every week the idiot drinks up his own tickets—I don't think he's given a single one out! Ever! That's why he's always gonna stay an errand boy. Or take Xavier. *He's* a promoter, and he used to be not bad. But his numbers are going down. Why? Here I am, I need him out there nabbing fashion queens from Desmond at B Bar, I need him poaching from Rob and Larry's Sunday tea dances, I need him picking off suits from Maximillian's downtown, and where the *hell* are the queer ravers from Save the Robots or a place like that?" Vic jabbed his index figure definitively at the center dot in the circle. "I want all the gays from him, you follow me? But every Thursday night, there you go, there's Xavier sitting at a table having *fun* with his own fifteen friends. Well, so much for him!" Vic snapped, fisting up the envelope, with a ferocious belly laugh tossing it into the trashcan. "Right?"

"Absolutely." Matt made his face aghast at Xavier's insensitivity. *The nerve!*

"Okay, kid. I think we understand each other. Am I right? *Talk to them in their language.* And listen—it's about energy!" Vic threw himself back in his chair, as though repulsed by an invisible force field. "You gotta be electric, a live wire! You gotta be *hungry,* that's the key; first time I saw you I noticed, I said this kid is *hungry.*" He looked right and left for applause. "Am I right? You *want* it."

"I do."

"Fabulous." Vic grinned. For the first time in the meeting, he seemed calm. He traced the desk with a finger, as if softly rubbing the embers out of a post-sex cigarette. "Listen, kid, you think I don't know you. *Quiet,*" he nearly cooed, one hand executing a pacifying, downward clamping gesture to forestall Matt from interrupting. "But what you don't understand—is, I do. I know what you want, and I know why. And that is what I am here for. The reason I am on this planet. I help very special people achieve their potential. Okay? I see things. And I see you." He squinched up his eye as if peering through a scope.

"I—"

"Ah, ah, ah"—Vic waved his hand dismissively—"I don't need your thanks, all right? That's the *last thing* I need. I'll be, it'll be thanks enough when I see you creaming along. Oh my God, you're gonna be *amazing.*" He slapped both palms on the desk. "Well, it's a done deal. I personally am very satisfied. You satisfied?"

Matt nodded. "Perfectly."

"So let's put you on, you'll be doing Fridays in the Red Room, the party's Down Below, I think that's really the right scene for your crowd, young but it's edgy and hip, you know, very downtown, so Friday you'll meet Marshall, it's his room, I'm sure you two will get along." He rapped his nails on the desk. "Perfect, so we'll have Miranda give you mebbe two hundred invites for Down Below, she'll set up a voicemail box for you, when you go out she'll walk you through everything, and—oh! I almost forgot! You're not ready to start!"

No fucking kidding! What happened to *I'm gonna teach you everything, kid?!*

"We gotta come up with your *name* for the business cards. Let's see now, Matt, Matté—"

"My name?"

"Your *club* name. I mean, *some* people use their real names, but I wouldn't advise it, I reeeally wouldn't. Oh God, people'll never let you alone. You know? So let's see now. Matt, we've got Matty-Matt, Mattias, Mattel... You know your name is very hard, you know, not easy at *all* for this, at *all*." He glowered at Matt, suddenly suspicious, as if Matt were engineering this on purpose. "Matt. Matt. I know—Matthilda. Matthilda; it'll be great! No no, everyone'll think you're a queen, there's already two in that room, we want a little straight crowd mixing in there Friday... This is where it gets difficult, you know, this is where it takes," manically tapping at his blotter with the stubby pen, "a lotta skill. Matt. Matt. Oh: I've got it, I've got it! Oh it's fabulous. Fabulous. Magic—Matt. Isn't it incredible? Magic Matt! Isn't it *fabulous*?"

"Fabulous," he heard himself say.

"All right." Vic grabbed the phone, jabbed a few numbers, checked his nails. "Hello?" he barked into the phone. "Brett? Well, get him. *Yes*, it's Vic." Vic seemed to have forgotten him so thoroughly that Matt was up from the chair and halfway out the door before Vic's eyes lit on him again. "Wait a second, wait a second, c'm'ere." Vic threw a heavy black wallet onto the desk, began jamming his fingers around in it. Scornfully he tossed one, two, three, and then, after an infinitesimal pause, a fourth hundred-dollar bill onto the desk. He slapped down the wallet, snatched the bills up in his fist so that they crackled. "Here. Go buy yourself a decent pair of shoes. I *told* you, kid, don't thank me." He was waving Matt off. "Consider it a signing bonus," Vic yelled as Matt inched through the door, the crackly bills burning in his right hand. "Oh, nothing." Vic curled into the phone. "New promoter. Friday. That's *riight*, Brett. You better watch your crowd. Heh heh. Well, you never know!"

3.

Outside, the street wavered. Everything was fluctuating haze above the perfect firmness of these postcard invites clutched in his hand like a deckful of magic carpets. New York loved him: how could he ever have doubted it? Dark buildings leaned over his shoulders dreamily like maenads, red-lipped and flaming. Chill breeze off the river burrowed amorously in his collar, clutching at his nape, his chest. And all things were coated now, absolutely drunk with heavy orange late-afternoon autumn light—he, alone, went wading through bronze butterscotch walls. Oh impossible day! Was that really a building shining in the sun? Was that really a sky, that torn rag of cobalt? And—cars? How I love you, cars! He stretched out his hand toward the placid downtown stream of traffic. He touched his face, marble-cold from the breeze. Who are you stranger, you strange, strange boy? And what have you done with the *me*?

It just did not compute. Even after, courting pneumonia, walking the thirtyish blocks to Sophie's, nothing, nothing was clear but the presence of club invite cards in his hand, the four bills burning in his breast pocket along with Vic's business card, newly emblazoned with a signature: which meant Matt must have passed this test. Astonishing, since he had said merely a handful of words, and almost all of these parroted. But Vic Spector—it seemed he had extracted whatever information he needed here. As if Vic's huge eyes did all the probing and discovering while the continuous stream of talk he discharged was really just to keep the specimen etherized, calm. Though you couldn't tell what that needed information might be. *I know what you want, and I know why.* And yet, it was true—if there was ever somebody who was "hungry," who would throw himself with total zeal toward learning and working for success here, who could keep an eye on a bottom line at all times, was that somebody not yours truly? Even Miranda's tour, when lovely brunette Miranda with her conservative striped skirt and listening gray eyes had taken him over the club, saying what sorts inhabited which rooms, rockers in the Opium Den, the fashion crowd in the Champagne Lounge, while the mere plebes of *street* were consigned behind this nasty black curtain to an unremarkable large dance floor—wasn't all that classifying very like his facebook rituals with Jason, when over little black-and-white pictures they would call out *sailors, losts, normalcies?* This he could do. This categorizing he was prepared for, from the earliest days, from sitting in Ms. Benowitz's second grade compiling elaborate hierarchical charts—like some Paracelsus, like some medieval alchemist dreaming the ladderway up to gold. Who else was better equipped, mentally at least? His little black book, with the bars and restaurants all copied out, all categorized: o secret weapon in hiding, now will I wield you! And Dwight? Matt shivered, slotting the key to the lock of Sophie's building: Ah, Dwight? How you like me now?

Thudding up the shaking tiled stairs to her door, opening—instantly she rose from the kitchen table, swishing a cataract of black hair over his frozen cheek bent in for the fragmentary kiss. "How did it go?" she breathed. Then he set down the invites on the kitchen table: and she screamed, and he.

Twenty minutes later Jason fell into the room with a bottle of champagne and a pack of paper cups around which assorted cartoon Smurfs were repeating *Happy Birthday.* He dropped on his knees at Matt's feet. *"My hero."*

"You may rise, my knight." Grinning, Matt rapped his knuckles lightly on Jason's skull.

Now Jason was up, sweating, patting his pockets for a smoke, and squeezing Matt's shoulder all at once. "This is so fucking crazy. Cinema. Motherfucking Cinema. This is so fucking *cra*-zy! We are so set for life!"

he shrieked. He flopped on the third kitchen chair and began fanning himself with a plump hand.

It was impossible to explain. Yet Matt tried, yammering about the labyrinthine passageways, about Vic, practically a troglodyte in his elegant suit with these obscenely mammoth eyes that walked all over one like octopus pods. Odd, no—everyone else who worked there was rather fantastic-looking. "Down, boy," he counseled Jason, already bouncing salivarily in his chair.

"Well, it doesn't seem weird to me." Jason airily waved a cigarette. "That man is the money. Capital. He doesn't need to be a pretty boy. He hires them. That's what he's got you for."

Sophie cocked her head, staring at him; Jason stole glances between puffs on his Newport. Not entirely friendly. More as if Matt, a known quantity, had suddenly metamorphosed into someone else, a stranger they were trying to get to know. "Oops," Matt floundered, abashed more than flattered. "What a blunder *that* is for them, then, eh? Can I steal one?" Deflecting; deferentially, he waved a Newport in the air. He pressed the lever of Sophie's new table lighter: once, twice, three times, an obedient orange flame shot out from the torch of the pewter Diana arrested in mid-stride, her metal toga daringly aslant. Their look: it was like that time post-Jason's birthday, after he had chatted up the gorgeous model waitress and they had treated him with kid gloves, a kind of sad perplexity and reverence. He inhaled. Instantly he cracked a smile, remembering. "But wait. Vic Spector only wants me for my mind. He said so. That I could keep an eye on the bottom line. That I could be strategic and not have fun. *That's* why he hired me." He nodded deeply, triumphantly.

"Ha," Jason snorted. "Got you pegged already. Matt knows exactly how to be paranoid and not have fun." He smiled weakly at Sophie.

"But what do you do? Actually?" Sophie's brow was creased.

"It's knotty." Matt put his fingers tip to tip like a Patton. After the room tour, Miranda had walked them back to the main office and sat them in swivel chairs before a desk, handed him a clipboard with handwritten lists attached. Different promoters handled each of the different scenes. You wrote out names of people you invited, some totally "comped," some to pay reduced admission, in this case ten bucks, half the general cover. For each comped person you received two dollars, for each reduced, five. On the lists Miranda paged through for him, there were circled fractions, comp over reduced, 13/45, 26/78; one list, with XAVIER in red caps at the top, boasted a dismal 7/14. Then Miranda counted out two hundred postcards, apparently "invites" to Down Below, the event every Friday run by Marshall in the downstairs Red Room: the glossy front bore a picture of a pale man with long stringy hair dressed in a Catholic-schoolgirl kilt, holding a mannequin dressed exactly the same. MEET YOUR DOUBLE IN THE RED ROOM THIS FRIDAY NIGHT, the caption read in white Goth print. These were to be marked with his initials and distributed to whomsoever he chose over the next four days. Some should be passed to cool-looking people on the street, others at bars and clubs, up to his discretion; anyone who brought one in on Friday automatically paid reduced. At the end of the night, the ropes girls would tally all those with his initials, write the number on his list. A check would be cut. Simple.

"Simple?" echoed Sophie, wrinkling her nose. "Sounds like a lot of work to me. Though I guess you do get paid more than work-study. If you had five over fifteen, that would be . . . eighty-five dollars. Which is pretty good, I guess. Though you do have to go out all the time, spend money, and you probably need a lot of new clothes, so—"

"Sophie. This is not a . . . a *money* thing. Don't you know what this means? Don't either of you know what's happened? Here, let me show you something." He emptied his breast pocket onto the table.

"Where did you get all that money from?" Sophie gaped as if it were stolen.

"It's my signing bonus. It's for new shoes. Shoes are very important." Matt leaned back, sighing. "They tell you everything about a person. You know?"

Sophie arched an eyebrow, tilted her head to the chair back. "Mm."

Jason peeked under the table. "Ha! Let me guess. West Village Fag? Is that what Vic Spector said? Did Matt ever tell you the story of how we first met?" He spun excitedly to Sophie.

"But *this* is what I'm talking about." Now Matt held up the business card Miranda had retrieved from Vic at the end of their info session. *TREAT THE BEARER LIKE ROYALTY,* Vic had scrawled on the back side, along with a messy ballpoint *VS.*

"Holy shit," said Jason, chastened.

"Huh," said Sophie. She turned the card over, over again in her fingers. "Huh."

"With that card," Matt tapped the filter of a fresh smoke on the table, "supposedly I can get into any nightclub or bar in New York. For free. The VIP." He lit and grinned, a maverick, daredevil grin. "*Now* do you see what I mean? My brother and sister," balancing the cigarette in the ashtray, he held out his hands for theirs, "we have been lifted to a higher ground. To a higher mode of being. No longer shall we," he squeezed, gazing ecstatically back and forth between Jason smiling giddily and Sophie rolling her eyes, but now coquettish-coy, "be mere plebeians in this city, in this school! And he who was lost has now been found. And he who was last shall now be first. Do you read me? Musketeers?" He stared into the black almonds of Sophie's eyes and then into Jason's melted M&Ms. "Right? One for all and all for one. Are you with me?"

"Okay," said Sophie, at last blushing happily. "Right."

"I'm in!" whooped Jason. "Are you crazy? Of course! Hot boys, here I come!"

"Good," breathed Matt. "And now," he knocked their clasped hands against the table, "what did we say last time?"

"Wasn't it Olé?" Sophie wondered.

"I say mazel tov!" shouted Jason. Then he gasped. "Motherfucker! I forgot the champagne!" He jumped up from the table.

"You have broken the sacred ring!" called Matt dolefully.

"Shut up and get the cups, bitch!" shrieked Jason, as the foam dribbled over his fingers into the sink. "L'chaim!"

What he had was four days. Less by the morning: eighty-four hours, 5,040 minutes. Over a bowl of milky coffee at Sophie's, while she padded back and forth getting progressively dressed, he marked the cards' white underbellies with a special pen of hers, a sparkly silver gel: *MM* for Magic Matt. When Sophie finally pronounced herself ready, he tackled her to the bed and let her go again, oh, shining pink balloon, off to class, and then he was alone in the apartment: and just as suddenly was he finished with the stack. Time.

For two hours he circled aimlessly through the streets, discounting this one and that one, too old, too young, too fat, potentially violent, potentially homeless, probably non-English-speaking, and just too downright scarifying for a first trial. A pissy rain started to fall. In the bagel café at Father Demo Square he sat on a stool by the plate glass, watching the pigeons scatter and collect again like bits of trash. Stage fright. But what if he tried to write something out? He found a napkin clean of cream cheese and rubbed his pen against the white. Now what? Hello? Greetings? Ugh, my kingdom for a word, just one, just to crack wide the glacier of initiatory ice. Ciao? Ciao bella? Come come now, Matthew, you're Magic now. What do you say?

What is cool?

What is inarguable, perfect cool?

He closed his eyes. Mick Jagger on a London street, young, raffish, his gawky ass swaying side to side, devil-may-care. James Dean, loose and delinquent, leaning against a hot rod on a suburban street in California, all black and luminous moon-color. Flapper girls in beaded wigs and men with pomaded hair in tuxes dancing with clicking heels to ragtime tunes, the Charleston with long black-clad arms swaying. *Hey bearcat.* Hmm? Oh: slang, flapper words, yes, from that paperback picked up at a yard sale, years ago; how did it go? *Hey, baby vamp. Don't be ridic. Getting tight.* The white mouths of the bodies were opening and saying words from the bibliorum of his brain—an androgyne voice, a mind-voice—*Bee's knees, Enchanté—*

He flashed open his eyes to the napkin and began writing.

Hey, baby vamp. How would you like to fox up a darby party at a joint called Cinema? Milk for the kitten—slipping the invite. Bam! It would do for the present; now for a male version. *Hey, cowboy.* Oh dear no. *Flyboy* was an aviator, though it sounded kind of distorted hip-hop. Matt tapped his teeth. *How would you like to hoof it at . . . a little speakeasy . . . razzle-dazzle, this invite lets you.* Yes: perhaps for the men, put the emphasis on power, what this will enable, rather than flattery. Well. We have a general idea here, enough to get the ball rolling.

He swept up his sesame seeds, swept himself out into the misting rain. Keeping keen barker-eyes peeled—come on, step right up, ladies, gents, to the Magic Show!

Not two blocks away, he saw:

A girl in tall boots, stamping beneath the broken-down marquee of the Waverly Theatre. An overcoat, retro; she had to be nineteen, twenty. Blond hair, streaked pink in front: she blew it, cruelly, up from her eyes. Maddeningly perfect in all aspects of age, dress, manner—and waiting, no less! Stationary! Ready! Now. Slip out a flat black card from your pocket pack: go speak as if you were made to loop this voice track.

She raised her shoulders, quizzical, as he stepped forward holding the card out before him as a sort of shield. "Hey, baby vamp," he heard himself whine. "How would you like—a fox like yourself—to come to my little shindy this Friday night?" Could have been worse. She sniffed, noncommittal, wiped her nose, staring at the card, straining to read the writing upside down. "At Cinema," he urged. "Um, have this card, kitten, I don't bite." Nice extra! He yawn-grinned, gazed at her from beneath slitted eyelids.

"Thanks," she said. She reached for the card, flipped to scan the back. "Maybe. Thank you." She nodded at him, dull and peaceful.

"Ciao," he sighed, lifting, lucky improvise, two fingers in wave as he wafted past.

He wafted himself all the way down the next block before pumping his arms wildly in the chill wind. One!

Now he lifted the collar on his peacoat against this nuzzling fog, a private detective in the scummy *quais* of Paris; he let his feet wander, take him where they would. They took him, print by print, eastward to MacDougal, to a trendy Asian guy with horn-rimmed glasses and dark denim locking a Vespa to a parking meter. *Hey, stranger,* Matt began, a hopefully un-gay smile plastered to his lips. *Got a mo'?* The guy held his helmet, took the card, said, *Thanks, man, cool:* Matt floated south down the street, inwardly doing flips in the half-pipe of his heart. Next he hit a doe-eyed dear coming out of the Dean & DeLuca on Broadway with two steaming cappuccinos: the shameless hussy waist-pushed her purse forward as a gesture of *in there* and piped up, *Two please—do you mind?* A harder sell were two gay men in matching olive-green galoshes, who actually laughed when he said the word *Cinema,* but then—at the end— my, my: couldn't stop themselves from wanting it. *Why not?* said one to the shrugging other. *It could be a good time.*

—Then out of nowhere, cojones[29] bestowed by God-knows-what, as they reached, Matt snatched back the card into air. "What do we say?" he sneered. "Mother may I?"

"Please?" they both begged.

"Candy for you and you." He dealt, generous, and sauntered off.

Unbelievable! At Tompkins Square Park he walked right into a hornet's nest of three punk girls with their massive, scabbed, mean-eyed dog: *they* took it. Two Rastafarians on a nearby bench, though insisting in lovely lilted Caribbean English, *We got our own par-ty Friday nights,* took it anyway and saluted, one mumbling, *Cinema,* as the other started singing the word in a reggae descant and he was walking backward several feet to salute too and answer their big, brilliant smiles—*everyone, everywhere,* they took it! Even fashionistas, in the spare steel runnels of SoHo—they scowled, looked jaded down, but they took it. Even scary grunge-style guys in hoodies at record stores in the East Village put down their vinyl and took it. Even—Mayday, how can you think of walking up so close and—skaters! Skaters at the Astor Cube held still their boards in one rough gloved hand, coughed gruffly, and took it! A magic amulet, the word: merely to say *Cinema*—and no longer *nerd* but arbiter of social state! This was like being made impervious to fire; he stuck his hand again and again in the flames to test his power.

---

[29] Misspelling? This word is not in my available dictionary. Cojoin, cojudge.

Riding an escalator groundward at Barneys Downtown, where he'd been to piss posh, he mused, he probed. Yes, the invite protected from social fallout, but under its umbrella there was an undeniable something he was doing right. He was strategic, there was that, in his approach to the runway of their faces: after long years of sitting on rocks by the reservoir mulling things like why exactly did the cool kids tolerate Jeremy Reese, one couldn't help but immediately see—this one is leader, this a sycophantish vizier, this a bitter quasi-refusé who will bite any hand that nears. Now how to manipulate the spiel felt fairly instinctual. For a leader, appeal to that we-are-men-and-women-of-the-world quality (perhaps starting by skimming a condescending eye about your humble surrounds); for a number two, stoke the lapdoggish desire of pleasing a better (emphasis on exclusivity, the currency of Cinema's name: what— you mean to say you haven't *heard* of this place?!!); if conditions forced a refusé, you aimed for a spirit of defiance, rebellious Guy-Fawkes the-revolution-is-now, and-this-is-step-number-one zeal (*Yo* man—direct address: direct eye contact: show no fear as you bolt right up to the person, tough). Starting school, he'd simply never had the mechanism in which to burn such dormant fuel. Though, true, then he had been looking for friends, a different matter altogether from these sixty-second pragmatic battles. And let us not be overmodest. There was clearly some *je ne sais quoi* to this speech: you could just see it in their faces. Time after time while he watched, their world-weary disaffection dissolved as they got caught off guard, oddly charmed. Well, why the surprise, cat eyes? Master Matt Acciaccatura is not your same old dead fish in the box.

Tired and happy like after a good cry, he walked over to Third North: the suite vacant, thank the Lord. He folded an armload of outfits into a bag to move to Sophie's, at least through his first Cinema this Friday night. How small Third North, how quiet the halls! He felt huge as a grownup in the nursery at naptime: their little corkboards with intramural volleyball sheets, cutout construction paper and photos. They were probably jawing away about some kegger in a dorm room—while he was out joining all New York! *I am gonna Make You Fabulous,* Vic Spector had said. Well, and then he'd come back in this very hallway, rap on their doors, and laugh, laugh shattering glass.

He paused by Mary's door. Dorks moving up in the world, Mary! We'll get there eventually! I'm out there dinging a miraculous stroke for all loserkind! But if only there were something to do for her too. Well, she wouldn't enjoy coming to Cinema. A girl like that: she probably had never taken a drink in her life, and can you imagine her dancing to that music? But what *would* she enjoy? He didn't know thing one about her. He never heard her talking through the fire door, or playing music, or doing anything besides crying and whatever it was that made those soft clinking noises, probably shifting her desk drawers. If only he could just provide hope for her: *your troubles will end, look at me! No one could have imagined mine would cease, and see!* But how empty without some idea of how she could go about it. Maybe there was a good club for girls like her. Nocturnal Weepers Anonymous. Maybe Sophie would have heard of something, some feminine hobby circle. Yes, sometime when he had more leisure, he would finesse this, or try. He would absolutely make a move, ask Sophie's advice, then make his approach.

Right now they had their work cut out for them. At the year's start, he'd received one of those E-Z apply credit cards: now was the time to set his solvency afire. Matt collected Sophie from the Chan Library; hand in hand they walked south along Mercer, while he sipped at her throat and growled snippets of the speech into her slender ear.

She was in hysterics. "That's not what you say!" She put a horrified hand to her mouth. "Oh my God," she murmured. "Who would have thought." Then she grabbed his arm with both hands, drew it near her, and with this tillered him down Spring: toward, at the very first store she chose, a pair of military-futuristic round-toe, calf-high, molded leather boots. $495.

"I think we found your shoes," she whispered, standing awed beside him.

So Tuesday, Wednesday, Thursday, Matt, skipping classes, scoured downtown, hitting marks with invites; late in the afternoon he met Sophie to walk through dressing rooms into impossible outfits, trying everything from glam-rocker shirts to draped Armani wool trousers; then, carrying packages over their arms, they returned to her pad, where he snacked on lightest things like shumai and miso (fasting for a last-minute edge of glamour) while boning up on downtown chitchat. Clippings from *Paper*, Brit mags like *The Face*, *ID*—DJs, hot house tracks, avant-garde designers, the venues of upcoming bands' tours—he arranged in thematic piles on the coffee table, pressing their sundry informations between his mind's tight pages.

Tuesday, Wednesday, Thursday at nineish, she kissed him luck (a big presentation in Ren Art on Friday, she must hit books), and Jason stepped in to aid with what was easily the most nerve-wracking of promoterly tasks: club distribution. The first night, halfway to Space, Matt halted on the sidewalk. "Tell me you brought your fake ID," he implored Jason.

"Yes, yes." Jason dragged him onward by the coat sleeve. "You only told me twelve times."

Leaving the roaring bars and restaurants spread about upper West Broadway, they soon saw a crowd at a glass-fronted club. There was a square of red carpet surrounded by two stanchions, a woman standing scowling between these in a black leather coat with fur collar, and a very large black man in a parka sitting beside her on a stool. Matt pushed his way to the front, holding out Vic's business card before him.

The woman laughed as she turned it over. "Vic. We love Vic here. You tell him Raven said hello. You do that?" She unclipped the rope and let Matt and Jason pass through, then shut it and her face to two pudgy blond girls just then edging up.

"Holy shit," mouthed Jason, walking backward under the blue lights of a narrow corridor toward echoey music.

They beelined to what appeared to be the main bar. "Cosmo, please." Bored.

"Same," noted Jason, equally listless.

Opposite, red velvet banquettes rolled away in strange organic shapes: dotted before these were clear cubes lit inside with white lights. And around such cubes were beautiful people. Beautiful. As if formed out of golden plastic. One woman bent to light a smoke, her hair illuminated by the cube so every strand glowed separately blond, glossy, perfect. Her upper-arm curve looked delicate as an unfleshed bone. And so long—was she six feet tall? Where did they grow these people? Matt sniffed. "Decent crowd."

"Adequate," agreed Jason.

The crowd twisted into new shapes. Now and then a man, or almost always a man, approached to order a drink with utter sangfroid. Just so unutterably cool, these people, and all here together without any exception, like an independent country: Beautifulland.

"Well," Matt said after his cigarette expired. Draining his cosmo. "I'm ready to go home. You?"

"Ha," remarked Jason, grimacing.

"Actually, you know, we have accomplished something very important tonight. We've seen the scene, you know, sussed it out—gained some very valuable information."

"Hello?! How many of those stupid things have you handed out today?"

Matt glared. "Listen. It's harder in here." He checked over his right shoulder. "First of all, you're watching."

Jason snorted. "That's the least of your problems." He dabbed at his mouth with a napkin.

"Thank you," Matt articulated crisply. "Ever candid with me. So— you see. I'm out of my league in this place," he hissed between clenched teeth.

"Matt," Jason rolled his eyes. "Because I love you dearly, I'll tell you this just once. If you go back home right now, I am never going to listen to you complain again about how shitty your life is. Vic Spector hired you for a reason. Now go out there," Jason made a shooing motion toward the far side of the room, "and work your thing. Oh, look." He pawed at Matt's arm. "Behind you. Her?"

A stunning Asian girl in a tube top. With a bill pinned between fore and middle fingers: clearly waiting for the bartender. "Go, go!" hissed Jason. "Before she leaves!"

"Cool your heels, yippiekayay." Matt shut his eyes. We do not know this girl. She does not go to NYU, does not know anyone from Tenafly. Okay? They're all strangers.

He opened his eyes, curved around the men, slid in to her side. "Hey, bearcat."

She pivoted her face on her palm toward him, blinking, inquisitive as a fish.

"I know it isn't any of my beeswax, but how would a lovely mamselle like yourself like to join in a little shivaree at Cinema this Friday night?"

Who knew, sir, what the hell was being piped into the airducts of this city.... Matt walked through bodies back, barely aware of Jason's awe-struck "Were you flirting with her?" as he collapsed against the bar, held on to it for steadiness.

Because she took the invite. That night, every one he approached: they *all* did.

Tuesday, Wednesday, Thursday, Matt, head spinning with pink cosmopolitans and echoing with a whole night's murmurs, threw off his pants and loped into bed with Sophie—all but woke her up, raining golden joy. *This is it, Sophie. This is it.* To think, he had run in circles around Dwight and the preps: why had he given up on real-world cool, the bars and restaurants written in his black book? For these people were the real deal, the cream of the crop of every social caste! And to be not just a spectator but part of it, a mover 'n' shaker in the central secret life of the city of this time—as Scott Fitzgerald to Paris in the '20s, Toulouse-Lautrec at the *fin de siècle*.

How you like me now, Taylor? How do you like your Rat?

The fact was: when he sidled up to spiel, the fashion crowd, the rock chicks at CBGBs, all stopped, then from his, this, lowly, once-dork hand—they took it. The whole maneuver became easy, an abracadabra he did night by day and day by night; he could practically do it in his sleep.

And then, suddenly, of the stack of invites: there were none. Friday at 3:13 P.M. It was a red-dreaded kid with a CCCP army parka and stovepipe pants outside Tower Records who sauntered away with his last

one. Done. Matt leaned upon a parking meter, gazing off down Lafayette
to Houston, where yellow taxis darted toward the Friday evening everyone, every working stiff or schoolkid in New York, was waiting for—that
brief island of life that made it all worthwhile. He was cleaned out. His
pocket was empty. In six or so hours, he would be at Cinema. Done. He
began to walk, mechanical, down the street. Place your bets, gentlemen.
Les jeux sont faits.

4.

Matt halted at Crosby and Prince. There behind plate glass a Christmas display had been set up, a whole moving apparatus where smiling elves shifted silver-wrapped packages into and out of red metal train cars looping beneath a huge Santa on a snow-topped rock. As Matt watched, the train cars snaked slowly in their circuit, now empty, now filled, empty—the elves raising and lowering silver packages with equal pleasure.

Happiness. Matt continued down the cobblestoned street. Wasn't there an expression—as brief as happiness? For a moment, you're filled, brim-filled, with some mysterious gift, which a moment later is cheerfully lifted from your grasp; thus empty on you go from whence you came. And why? Were there so few pleasures in life to go round? Just to deliver one square of happiness that would stick, wasn't that within his power? Almost three hours remained before time to head to Sophie's for showering and dinner...squirting rebellious smoke into the sky, Matt tripped downtown and west, zigzagging till he was by that steel-girdered store where she had once cried: LOLO ZED.

Security opened the door: ah, so that statue does move after all, one wouldn't have guessed it from his stock-still posture on our last time's visit. Matt nodded, coughed in a way he hoped was important, and stepped inside, where the white space spilled out before him like a Grecian bath with columns and light. The radiant sheer dresses and wraps hovered in the air like tropical birds. With one finger, he traced a deep-green silk.

"*Hi,*" confided a sallow man in a thin black suit. The same as before: but this time round, it's up and at 'em, hmm? They really could smell money. "The men's is on this side."

"I know," snapped Matt. "I'm looking for something for my girl-friend."

"Oh, of course . . ." Down the row, the man stayed, straightening wayward sheaths.

So Matt slouched, let everything hang confident and terribly bored. Carefully dissatisfied, he worked his way along the wall; then his heels clicked down the stair into the lower room, where the inflated dressing unit, that beatic mass of blue gauze, trembled as if breathing.

There it was—*Selah*. Shell-pink and threaded with pearlescent beads, shimmering. A camisole like a jellyfish, flecked with tiniest drops of orange-red.

He coasted it to his arms gently, almost afraid it would dissolve, and voyaged up.

"Oh, *this*," the salesman gushed, seizing the hanger from Matt's hand. "It's just *gorgeous*, isn't it?" The man hurried off toward his slick desk, as if afraid Matt would change his mind, and handled the credit card reverently in both hands. "I just *love* it, I've loved it from the moment it came in. You know, Lai uses absolutely the *best* silk. The *best*. The head buyer from Bergdorf's was in here a minute ago, and he just said, 'Lai is a magician with silk,' " the man extended a pen and the slim white slip, " 'she's an absolute *magician*.' "

Matthew Acciaccatura, he scrawled, a little ball of black twine. This spells the end, sir, of that there credit card.[30] But she would love, love, love, and let her have something she could love purely, without feeling it is an imitation, or a warehouse-sale off-size she can alter, or simply not From This Store, which she cannot afford. How easy, happiness! One could simply hand over the object of ultimate desire. No? Mm, there was some Dante business to that effect. A child wants an apple. A boy wants

---

[30] I should conjecture so! When I visited this store, I did not locate a shirt for less than four hundred dollars.

a horse. A man wants money, power, fame. It keeps shape-shifting on you, receding, an elusive ghost, leading you onward: that magical body that promises to answer all your questions, salve all your wounds...

And what did *he* want? Outside he was smiling in the dusk, which laid velvet fingers on his lips and neck. What do you want from this city, from its flaming carnival of lights? What do you even want from *tonight*? So looked for, so labored over?

On that mystery he surfed all the way to Third North.

It was really a simple thing. He was just going to zip inside the dorm and grab his blue velvet jacket with buttons on the shoulders (since there was a faint almost springish note in the breeze this first December evening): but immediately, as soon as he'd entered the elevator hall, Matt felt the teeth of the place close on him. Only four days since he'd been here last . . . but how far a voyage! Away from the infantile, ugly mint-green and purple hall, with its rubber gymnasium floor, from Carly Hale, Caleb Houghton—

Dwight.

Dwight was standing in the hall with three other guys: Taylor, Adam Faire, and some stranger with dark hair and scornful eyes. When the elevator doors—and why, why had he been so lazy as not to take the stairs?—peeled open just before them, and Matt was forced to step out.

"Matthew!" Dwight raised a hand, moving eagerly toward him.

This was a high five. Matt could see it coming. He managed to jam his hand up in the air in time for the slap. Sort of.

"Buddy!" Dwight had placed a soothing palm behind his shoulder. "When was the last time I saw you? Like, before Thanksgiving." An incredulous Dwight whipped his head back and forth like a wet dog's. Suddenly he frowned, as if Matt had been holding out on him. "Where you been? Wow, look at those. That's some pair of boots." He gave a little laugh, glanced over at the guys, who shifted to stare at Matt's futuristic boots. Adam Faire emitted a low whistle. "And you've been shopping—again." Dwight made it sound like an insult, as he eyed the LOLO ZED bag.

"Um." Shut up, you loon. You creep. Get your hand off before I snap it. "It's for my girlfriend."

"Right, right. You introduced me." Dwight moved his hands to his hips and winked assertively, as though recalling he had officially stamped that relationship approval. "Seki—Saki—what's her name again?" His face lit up with sheer multicultural curiosity. "Sorry. I'm not good with . . . names." To the right, Taylor, leaning against the wall, emitted a little cough, discreetly covering his mouth.

Matt stood, the dazed smile burning as if permanently into the cheeks. Should he zing Dwight back with a caustic rejoinder and stride off? But all that came to mind was to leer a sardonic *Something like that.* "Suh—Suh—" he started: then quailed, muttered, "Sophie," and beat down the hallway with an uncertain wave.

Trust Dwight. Trust Dwight to thoroughly shit on your parade. Matt stomped into the room, grabbed the blue velvet jacket hanging innocuously in his wardrobe. Only by dint of luck did he happen to notice the bit of crumpled paper on his bed.

Josh's meticulous handwriting on a torn bit of notebook: *Rick called.*

Rick? Matt sat down on the bed hard, crackling the paper of the bag. There was no known Rick. *Vic?* But he couldn't just call—you rang for me?—if wrong. How like Josh to make this error; a carelessness tantamount to negligence ever characterized his handling of our affairs. And lately he was wending to the worse: forgetting messages from Jason and Sophie, talking agonizing periods on the cordless when Matt expressed the need to make a thirty-second call, even inviting friends over when Matt was in the common room hunched over some bare-minimum studywork at his appointed desk, and, somehow most rankling, turning off the light switch in the bedroom when Matt was dressing, as if he did not register on Josh's Richter scale. And when Dwight made one of his offhand contemptuous remarks at Matt's expense, who rushed in with a sniggering giggle? Matt heaved a sigh, grabbed the bag and jacket, and sallied out to barge through the hall bathroom door. No one. There was no helping it now. He marched up to where Dwight was telling what appeared to be a very humorous anecdote to Taylor & crew, and tapped the hateful shoulder. "Um, where's Josh? Do you have any idea?"

"Josh?" Dwight turned to him a look of lordly composure and kindness. *Why must you be so errant, my prodigal son? Return to the fold and I will welcome you; I will kill the fatted calf as I take you in my great arms.* "I don't know, Matthew," he said softly. Like a psychologist. *And how does that make you feel?* "But it *is* Friday. He may have gone home to Brooklyn for shul." Dwight smiled, as if, despite everything, his good nature was enough to sustain the both of them. "What's up? It looks," Dwight lowered his eyes tactfully, "maybe important."

Ha. He wasn't falling for that considerate act. Matt shook his head. Started walking backward. "But thanks. Have a great night."

Forget them! Just call Vic. Only do it without any of their possible interruption. He thudded up the two flights to Jason's, knocked, waited, even knocked again before entering—unlocked as ever—and thus was totally taken aback by the soft moaning, *oh, oh,* he heard as he neared and the faint rustle of sheets.

A clatter of magazine: Jason and Matt both screamed, Matt clapping his hands over his eyes. "I didn't see anything!" he blurted. Just a blob of skin-colored what-is-that on the bed.

"Don't you ever knock?" Jason shrieked.

"I did knock! Lock your door when you...do that." Matt shouted back. "Will you?" he added, gentler.

"You can open your eyes now. You fuck." Jason was lying supine on the bed in a pair of sweatpants and a stained maroon T-shirt, staring dead at the ceiling.

"May I use your phone?" Matt sang sweetly. "And by the way—um, isn't it almost time for someone to get ready?"

Jason groaned and plodded to the bathroom.

"Vic," Matt tersely, urgently told the receptionist. "Magic Matt."

"Magic, baby, how ya doin'," crackled Vic over the line. "Just so you know, your roommate is, like, from another planet. Whoa."

Thank God! "I know. It's random housing."

"Right. So, Magic, I was calling because your list didn't come through."

The guest list? Wasn't he supposed to bring that with him?

"Oh no, no, I wouldn't advise it. You see—what happens when your people start showing and you're still out vacuuming?"

"Vacuuming." Of course. Whatever that means. "Oh—sorry."

"Fax it right away. Attention Miranda. Ciao."

The line died.

At Jason's desk, under the green halo of a banker's lamp, Matt lifted a page from the printer and wrote out a list: Jason Kirsch; Sophie Yamamoto; Jean-Paul Brisbane, Jason's Scarsdale DJ. Perhaps he *should* really have invited Jason's QU group, though there was no telling how they'd dress or seem. Well: nothing prevented him from just jotting down their names, eh? Six. Absurd. What popular promoter type would have only six friends? How many would, say, Scott Belfast have, a real leader of a clique?

By the time a toweled Jason reentered, Scott Belfast, Liza Andrewes, Myra Washington and that whole posse, plus a fictive few, had been neatly printed up to person twenty-three. Snatching up the page, Matt admonished Jason, *Remember, Sophie's at seven,* then dashed off through wakening streets to the Kinko's by Astor Place.

And once this sheet was fed through the machine, Matt, still panting, but melting already with relief, set off, with the inordinately expensive package on his arm, through the lovely darkness toward Sullivan and Prince. He arrived to find Sophie menstrual, in a funk; sitting on the closed toilet cover with her head in her hands, she didn't look up for a kiss, merely muttered would he *please, please* go buy her some Advil. When *Where should I get it?* was shut down by *Where do you think?,* he left the package on the bed *(What's taking you so long? God, go, please),* having silver-markered a huge *OPEN ME.* But when he returned with a box of ibuprofen and a chocolate rose from the deli by Houston, Sophie was already sitting on the bed; even in the darkness with the bedroom lights off, her eyes showed shining, her cheeks moist. The tissue paper lay unfolded in a pale cumulus beside her, the camisole was cradled in her lap. "You silly boy," she said, breathless. "I *love* it," she whispered. "You're crazy. You are going to be one broke boyfriend." She dragged him onto the bed beside her and they sat in silence, head touching head, her fingers stroking the fabric now and then. "I'm going to wear it tonight...and you are going to wear your black Costume National top. And pants."

"That's the spirit."

"Are you nervous?"

The refrigerator began loudly humming. What he most wanted now was to fall backward onto the soft squares of the quilt and wake up maybe tomorrow, maybe weeks from now, rubbing his eyes like a child who's fallen asleep in storytime and knows that everything that was going to happen, which had been so exciting just before he shut his eyes, has happened anyway without his hearing. *What was it? A happy ending?*

"I have to say," started Sophie, cautious, "well—does all this promoting stuff really seem worth it to you? I mean, look how you've spent your whole week—is it always going to be like this? Like, it's not like the money is so..."

Matt felt something tighten in his chest, just below his throat. When she said such things, it showed how little she understood—then he was cast into outer space again away from her. "You may have to trust me," he said. "I can't explain why it is." He reached up and touched her hair: ah, and just to touch that glossy stream restored the connection, somewhat. What to say? The inexorable otherness—the inner bane—What They Did To Me—a rich history, someday you may come to agree?

"Okay." She was sighing with relief, as if that were enough. "I'm happy to trust you. But it's okay if I'm not so crazy about it?"

"Of course." He wrapped an arm about her waist, kissed her smooth head. Though it did make him bristle a bit: but, of course. She was she. And he was he. And the thing was—the magical thing—she liked him *anyway*.

There was a flurry of banging and doorknob-shaking, then Jason's voice squealing, "Put your clothes back on, kids!" and she was up, wiping her eyes, laughing, holding the door open: now Jason, in black shades and shockingly squeaky-clean—when was the last time he'd actually shaved?—waltzed in, holding a bottle of champagne.

"Let's get this party started!" Jason whooped. "Enough nookie. We'll get some lights on...and you're not even dressed! Or are you going to wear that?" Hand on hip, he scanned Sophie in her sweatpants and little cut-sleeve T-shirt.

"Look." Sophie held up the top. "Matt bought it for me."

"Wowww. Where's mine?" Jason laughed his machine-gun laugh. "Come on, hop to it." He popped the champagne over the sink.

All through dinner of gyoza and soba, Matt unfolded little pieces of the evening's meaning. "We just have to show up. See who's there. I don't think tonight really matters. I mean, I've only had four days total. And Miranda said Vic didn't expect me to meet my numbers—"

"Ssh." Jason poured him another half mug. "We're going to just have fun."

Then suddenly it was 10:13.

"Oh my God." Sophie craned toward the window when the taxi had reached the street and was inching west along a block lined as far back as Eleventh Avenue by a column of bodies packed five deep. "I forgot how insane this place is."

Now Matt was feeding a wad of bills into the driver's palm, and leaping out.

No one in line was smiling. Faces in shades of bored, affronted, worried. Near the front, a girl in a purple mini and silver platform boots was trying to catch the eye of one of the clipboard girls (ah, good: neither one recognizable from his last night here) while rocking back and forth, masticating gum manically. "Fuck!" she moaned, quiet.

"Ready," Matt said beneath his breath and strode forward, vaguely aware of two shadows following behind. He marched straight up to the clipboard girl with short black spiked hair and a roomy hip-slung leather skirt. "Yo. I'm Magic Matt."

Her face was surprisingly serious. Rings of black liner around her brown eyes. "How do I know? Do you have ID?"

"Um . . ." She had swallowed one of his heartbeats.

"I'm just kidding." She grinned, flipping through the pages on her clipboard. "Got your list. Can I cross off any names?" She made two deft lines through *Sophie Yamamoto* and *Jason Kirsch* and snapped out two yellow tickets. "Let me just stamp their hands for the VIP. Red Room, right?" she asked, a small object concealed in her palm. Jason stumbled forward: she pressed it on the back of his hand, then Sophie's. "Yo, do you have Magic Matt's drink tickets?" she called to the other girl.

"You're Magic Matt?" a gravelly voice inquired. Tossing back a white cottony mane, the second girl approached, her almond, maybe half-Asian eyes narrowed in that stare of the most cutting kind of bitch. But then, from the top of her stocking, she blithely drew a stack of little squares. "There you are, man, have a good night. Great to meet you," she pitched over a shoulder at him, moving on.

"Yeah, great to meet you," the first sang dully, turning from the crowd to wave.

So polite! Like being licked by tigers. "Thanks," he replied, making his voice unsurprised. Then, trailing Sophie and Jason, he passed by no less than seven security guards, unblinking in their massed power, and stopped at a short, freckled personage with huge lips, who ripped Jason's and Sophie's tickets. "And . . ." Wide blue eyes trained blankly on Matt.

"I'm Magic Matt," he blurted out. "They didn't give me a—"

Now the clownish face opened up, a soft, giant flower. "Fabulous! I'm Peter Boy. With an *I*. B-O-I." He flopped his hand from the wrist a few times. "Whooee! It's hot in there tonight!" he squealed, giving Matt's arm a needless pinch.

They thudded through a corridor to the left and came out suddenly in a new place, a balcony above a giant dark room: where hundreds of bodies were pouring beneath careening red lights. Metallic house beats pummeled from the air—the noise of eagles beating steel wings. It smelled strongly of fake smoke, mixed with real smoke, alcohol.

"Oh my God." Jason was tugging at his shoulder. "*This is so awesome. I cannot believe we just cut that whole line! I cannot believe we have stamps for the VIP!*"

We have arrived. Matt gripped the railing, scanned the crowd. *Nous sommes arrivés. Siamo arrivati.* He cleared his throat, reached for Sophie's hand, dragged her through the wave on waves of people that fell against them, through the blue-tiled bar, the Turkish pavilion, cabaret, pulling Sophie and behind her Jason toward the basement Red Room.

This time Coco was standing sentry in a canary-yellow silk sari; she even had stuck a comely red dot on the smooth chocolate of her brow.

He was ready for this one. For now it was time to make pax with the great Valkyrie. "Hey, pussycat," he nipped coyly. He threw his body against the doorframe, hopefully nonchalant, flirtatious. "How's the rumpus in there tonight?"

"Oh!" She grinned down at him, a huge conspiratorial grin. "They're okay, I guess." Almost bashful!

"I want you to meet my girlfriend, Sophie"—this was going so well, unbelievably well, please do not fuck this up, please—"and Jason, my favorite friend. This is the fabulous Coco, the keenest queen I know." He tossed his head toward her possessively.

"Hiiii there," Coco cooed down the nearly two feet to Sophie. "She's such a *doll*."

Matt winked his accord. "So: shall we?" He glanced back at Sophie and Jason, both of whose mouths had popped part open with shock.

In the Red Room, a totally different sort of party was happening. The scene was mellower and darker, edgier, slicker. *Your own—Personal—Jesus*, Depeche Mode was crooning. Around the walls the red velvet banquettes were filled with bare skinny arms and noses, dangling hair and earrings. Silver buckets were attached to the black tables; that's right: *Bottle service only*, Miranda had said. One had to purchase a whole exorbitant bottle of Absolut or Skyy to gain the pleasure of a sit-down. In the center, just before the bar, a small wooden dance floor was clustered with languidly swaying forms.

"What was that?" Sophie hissed to Matt.

"That was her—the drag queen! Who I met with Vic. Just trying to butter her up. You know, strategic alliance. *Realpolitik.*" He squeezed her hand. "What did you think?"

Sophie turned away in the direction of the ropes, then back to him again. Her lips were pursed. "I'd say it worked."

"Thanks! Shall I get us some drinks?" He felt for the tickets. "Jason?"

Jason was staring at the room, eyes two round pennies. "Cosmo," he muttered.

By the bar stood the kid from outside St. Mark's Bookshop. And a statuesque girl who worked at Anna Sui, in a red one-piece jumpsuit belted white round her svelte waist; that was a Wednesday hit, if I remember right. And—oh! That gay couple who was so rude! They were *here*! His peeps had come! By eleven, no less! Matt tapped his drink-tickets on the counter, gleeful, and when he slid the squares over to the bartender, it was the same blond clean-cut cornfield sort from last time, he happily gave his name as Magic Matt, new boy in town. "Excellent!" shouted the bartender, flashing a grin that seemed to proclaim *We're all in this together!* as he lifted a bottle.

"Have you seen Vic?" Matt couldn't resist asking. Let him see—let him see!

The man shrugged, raised a charming palm in the air. "You know Vic."

"Right, of course," Matt shouted back. Sure thing. I hear you. Loud and clear. We're on the same frequency. He peered over a shoulder. "What about—Marshall?" Shouldn't he check in or something? It *was* Marshall's party. "Is he around?"

The bartender scowled. "Not anymore." Down the bar he reached for a shaker. "Not Any More," he repeated scornfully, each word timed to a wrench of the metal container.

Whatever that meant. Matt raised a glass in farewell, scurried back to the main area.

And here as the hours slid by, Matt found his hands full with a surprising meet-and-greet. All night, faces flickered toward him, smiling, with names that slipped away; perhaps afraid he would not invite them again, they *wanted to stop by* and vow they were having *such a fabulous time*. Some even inquired about a "hotline," which must be the voicemail box set up for him at the club; but, "I'll have business cards next week," he whined, "apologies." They offered cigarettes, chairs, they nervously introduced him to their friends, with *This is the guy who . . .* and a discreet cocked head. They were trying to get on his good side; they were actually *fearful*. While Sophie danced, elastic, getting into it at last, and Jason bopped along beside her, he was a small red spot scuttling across the floor, infrared, a searchlight, finding faces that bloomed toward him like nightflowers.

So the thing went off: well, even to grand effect. And when they fell out through the doors after four—the street clear and their language unmixed with the music and voices, suddenly unfamiliar—it was almost too ludicrously perfect. "Sophie!" He gripped her arm, almost falling with her into the street. "Jason, look! Snow! The first snow!"

They raised their hands to the sky.

CHRONOLOGICAL GLOSS BY DR. HANS MANNHEIM

Have you wondered at my silence? Have you presumed that I am dozing at my task, reading these pages blindly, without care, since it has been so long a time after I have spoken? That shall never be; do not fear, as you tread the paces of your journey, I stay always beside you, like a mountain guide carrying a ruck-sack packed full with informational supplements for when you might require some emergency shot—you, dear readers, invisible and in the future, unknown to me; I must believe that you exist, that you can hear me through these scratchings of a pencil on the back of a printed page. Why, then, do I break in precisely now? It is only that my heart is moved. Can I be a man of stone? No. Oh, this is not because we approach the happening of the tragic events, though that is also true and saddens me. Merely, I am thrown overboard by memories of how it was at this time, the beautiful city in winter, which perhaps you do not know, which perhaps these pages do not sufficiently make in your minds, all the vital activity of the downtown vicinity, taxis and people stepping forth in the streets and the café where I was accustomed to get a splendid variety of herbal tea; I can almost feel the steam from the handy portable cup so often given me. I think of this 1995, when in the autumn Lisanne and I moved to New York and she began her appointment at NYU. What happy times there were at the very start! I have told you, we had so diminutive a flat, at least compared to our former on the Raumerstrasse (by the calm green quadrangle of Helmholzplatz in Prenzlauer Berg, where on warm evenings the weak click of table-tennis could be heard from our window some nights until dawn). Yet how happy we were with it even so, our tiny igloo on the seventh floor! In those days she had but one suit and three blouses, so I spent many afternoons at the launderette employing special cleaning packets in the wash machine while waiting for a position to rise up, for any college, or research institute, or foundation to answer my expensive stationery with a yes, we are in need of such a man. With great vividness I can recall the night after Lisanne's initiating lecture: we celebrated with a dinner of Japanese cuisine at a restaurant in the East Village so minuscule it contained only four small tables. And we had so much sake that on the return journey I purchased for her one bouquet of flowers and fell down to my knees and said, *Will you marry me?* And she said, *I already have*, and I said, *Then do it again*, and she came and kissed me and said, *I do, I marry you.*

Where has it gone? At this moment when I look up I see: a wooden table on which many have engraved initials into the green paint; a desk at which the librarian rests, shifting constantly so that the metal of his chair grinds at the plastic tiles of this little reading room; higher still, a fluorescent panel, whose white light quivers as if it has just been beaten. And what I hear is: that man's chair; my own breathing; the squeaks of vinyl beneath me. Tomorrow when I return during recreation hour to take my chair once more before this well-worn green table, all will be identical. None of these too-solid objects can open like doors and show me the gay honks of cars, the merry babble of restaurants, the delightful shouts which blurred into one seamless scream each noon from that public school whose number escapes me—it was one and one half blocks distant; I would pause after lunch to listen from our kitchen window—all those delights are vanished, securely locked away from me. But even you have been shut off from this also, in a fashion: even you in New York or such places, cities I have never visited such as, for example, Chicago, or Cincinnati, where there must be also taxis and the dancing lights of restaurants and decorations of reindeers at Christmas. For you have been cut off no less than I from this space in time, 1995, an era of riches, innocence, safety.

Do you remember it? Listen, I have gathered facts to provoke your memory. In 1995, global stocks began their unprecedented and dizzying climb: the U.S. market, dragged by the then-new occurrence of „tech" firm IPOs, improved at the astounding rate of thirty-seven percent. In 1995 *Batman Forever* emerged supreme at the box office; Americans watched Jerry Seinfeld, when not reading *The Celestine Prophecy* and *Men Are from Mars, Women Are from Venus*—complacent, confident books, „super-hero" adventures, obvious reflections of your tremendous wealth and the fresh post-Cold-War stability. It was not until the end of 1995 that the Nobel Peace Prize winner of 1994, Yitzhak Rabin, was assassinated by a hostile Israeli citizen. The Fourth World Conference on Women gathered representatives from 189 nations in Beijing. The Mexican peso became worthless, but as the IMF calmly passed fifty billion dollars over the table, fully half from your opulent country, the world, after scratching its head, merely smiled. Do you remember? Do you remember 1995?

For I cannot forget it. Turn back and back, I would say to the calendar, or perhaps merely stay in July, the month before Lisanne and I packed our possessions in the old flat, when it was so hot in the evening we drank Berliner Weisses and lay on the frayed red quilt, then on in the darkness made love to the African drummers out there in the shadows of our own summer-green and fragrant Helmholzplatz.

5.

In the morning, the light dusting of powder had disappeared. But the parked cars, the black streets were gleaming, as if in mirthful signature of *yes,* just for this, for Matt's trudging, like a veteran returning from battle, back to Third North with a sackful of dirty, smoke-soaked clothes slung over a shoulder. The suite was empty when he waltzed in. Oh, Saturday—right, Josh in Brooklyn; and Dwight? Singing idiots practice? Perhaps. Well, just as well. Though once his role at Cinema was settled to certainty: what a revelation this was going to be! Matt flitted around, making green tea on the hot ring, and was swallowed up in his wardrobe gutting it for a dry-cleaning bundle, when the phone rang.

"Magic, baby." The unmistakable Vic Spector. "How ya doin'?"

"Excellent!" Matt practically shouted. "Ah, how you—doin'?"

Vic loosed a hearty, somewhat ill-spirited bolt of laughter. "A guy like me is always doin' all right."

Note: never ask that.

"Wasn't it fabulous last night?" Vic crackled, back in fine spirits. "The club was *fab-ulous.*" He rattled off a register of last night's star guests, the famous names of two actresses and a musician, one of whom had even been seen "dancing on *tables* in the Champagne Lounge. It was un-believable," Vic decided. He sounded giddy, a little boy. Then he calmed to softer, consoling tones, almost cooing. "I mean, I've known her since she was a *baby,* but Jennifer, she's really grown up, you know."

"Yeah?" Not to seem too nonplussed.

"I'll introduce you next time. If you're still around! Sashaaa," Vic purred off-phone. "What are you doing, Sasha, Mila, come to daddy, look what daddy has: *yeah*. There you go. And your crowd," Vic snapped, suddenly loud, "you did very well for your first night. Let's see now... you did forty-three reduced and three comp. Wait, what?—no, three comp."

"All my friends are out of town!" Matt blurted.

"Oh, I *know*, it's the weekend where *ev'rybody's* out of town..." He didn't sound sarcastic: seemed to buy it, though maybe a touch irritated at being told something he would already know. Vic swerved through a conversation like a drunk driver, reeling up to vertiginous cliffs only to veer heart-stoppingly off. "So. What'd I tell you, kid? Did I tell you? I never make a mistake. I'm incapable. Okay, mebbe once, once in twenty-five years," Matt could hear Vic's smile, "which isn't doing too bad, if you ask me. That's why other clubs are always trying to poach my promoters, they just can't do what I do." A compassionate sigh. "I mean, Sonny—you know Sonny Reich from Satellite? A guy like that would've said, 'What are you doing, Vic, you're going to give this eighteen-year-old no-body with *mook boots* a list to one of your VIPs?' I mean, just imagine the ugly fucking disgusting people you could be bringing in off the street!"

"Oh—" Matt rushed to say. "But—"

"The thing is, they look but they don't see. You have to think cre-atively. You have to look beneath the surface. You can't be superficial; it's *death* to be superficial in this business, I'm telling you. Because we don't live in a flat world. The world is always changing, and if you want to be ready for those changes you have to think, future—how was Declan, was Declan all right last night?"

Declan?

"Or was he still spinning records from, like, 1983?" Vic sniggered.

"Oh." What *had* the music been? "He was... fine," Matt murmured cautiously.

"Aha! So, finally: he listens! He's so dense, you have no idea how dense Declan is, and if he didn't know, like, every fashion person in this town I would've eighty-sixed him months ago. I still might, I mean, his people know Cinema now, they know my ropes girls, they probably'd still use us for parties after the shows...Well. Magic. Come in Monday, we'll get you paid, Miranda'll give you the new invites, and that's it, we'll see you next week. All right? All right." Out: the line was dead.

On the bed, in his underwear, Matt actually clapped to himself with brazen glee.

Monday afternoon, as told, he dropped by the club. Miranda doled out his check, new invites (some kind of witches' sabbath, with a he-witch resembling last week's marionettist), and two boxes of business cards in a white paper bag. Right outside on the sidewalk he drew one out, with shaking fingers. And here, in inconstantly glittering lettering: MAGIC MATT. There could be no doubt; now and forever! I am that.

Two hundred twenty-one dollars was a spectacular amount of money; not, perhaps, in relation to the debtors' hospital-style tab he had racked up this week, but the beginning of fortunes to come. And though its potentially transitory strength was not enough for him to march into M&O and quit, he took Sophie and Jason to Nobu, where Jason taught them how to kamikaze with shots of sake in tall glasses of Sapporo beer, shouting, "Banzai!" And a table of bankers—shirtsleeves rolled, Montblanc pens glinting against tight Holland bond—glanced over from time to time, but with no astonishment at all. *They think we're rich kids. Like Carly and Taylor and Allison.*

He threw himself into the second week, trying to smooth out the kinks into science. Yes, already only the occasional target turned him down, probably more out of shyness than chic—cantering off after at an unnatural speed; but there was something he was beginning to see. Their taking the invite was not his object. They needed to haul their asses up and dress on Friday night, freeze in line with the other plebs, and, last but hardly least, have a good time (how else would he get repeats?). If two hundred invites had fallen from his fingers last week, while only forty-three marks crossed the club's threshold, he must be pulling a roughly twenty-five percent rate. How to improve? How to clinch the sale?

By trial and error, he learned to accost the wittle pweety ones in SoHo not at two but one o'clock, on their way *to* lunch, not back, when they were harried. Only *then* should one circle across to Nolita, where the cool crowd had tumbled out of bed to nurse their morning cappuccinos in retro diners and were under the radiance of the day's first caffeine. A fabulous girl among the smoke-breakers before an office building didn't want to be drawn to a corner for a confidential tête-à-tête but, right on the bold stage of the pavement, be told before beholders she had what it takes. For flattery, there was always that; "What a scarf, I love it; ohhh, my girlfriend so wants a coat like that: Marc Jacobs? He's so the man... I *know*..." I was there—I'm the one—I saw: *I understand you.*

It was on this second Friday in the Red Room that he met Marshall,[31] the supposed party host, who collided with a wet kiss onto his cheek where Matt stood waiting for a cosmo. "Darling," the creature swooned, grotesque, in a cheerleader sweater ripped at the shoulders, thick-flicked eyeliner running down his cheeks, and too-tall stilettos that forced him to totter. Evidently this was the pale-faced figure who on that first party invite had clutched a marionette, on this week's version played the squint-eyed witch in the center of the sabbath. "I'm Marshall, darling, and soooo glad to meet you." Lifting up his neck to gaze down, Marshall batted frightening false eyelashes. Something was wrong with his mouth: the two pillows of his scarlet lips, his whole chin, hardly seemed to move when he spoke.

----

[31] Some readers already may be cognizant that Marshall Demopoulos (alias Mad Marshall or Marshall le Marquis but usually simply Marshall), an addict of heroin and a former celebrity of the nighttime entertainment sphere, vanished in February 1996 within hazy circumstances. My understanding is that, „on the lam" from the authorities for thirteen counts of narcotics- and conspiracy-related charges, he has repatriated to his native Greece.

I am fond of this word *charges*, which contains no kernel of guilt-imputation as does our *Beschuldigung*. I enjoy learning all your American legal idioms. This week I like also *hearsay, felony,* and *deposition.* What mysterious and official sounds they have! Particularly *felony* (our clumsy *schweres Verbrechen*), which seems a beautiful woman's name. (Or is that merely because my sister is named Felicia, called by us Felly?) (She is not beautiful.) (Fortunately she will never read this.) (For why should some one member of our family take interest in Hans?) (However, in this case: Es tut mir leid, Felly. Aber du weist gern, dass du keine Schöne bist.)

Matt threw his weight to one side, winked. *"Enchanté."*

"I told Vickie"—Marshall lurched and clutched at the bar—"I told Vickie I was soooo thrilled about it. It's been so boring here lately." A cackle turned into a cough, which flecked Matt's cheek with tiny gifts of saliva. "You'll spice things up a bit..." he yowled, sounding like a drowning cat.

"Marshall!" A skinny blonde with dark craters for eyes picked at his arm.

"Let go!" he shrieked.

"Marshall, c'mon! I'm trying to help. Jesus, you know he's gonna leave with everything if we don't find him now."

Marshall visibly wavered, as if calculating his need for whatever *everything* was, then shrugged, giving Matt a wan you-know-how-it-is smile, and allowed himself to be pulled unsteadily off by her hand on his arm.

Curiouser and curiouser, Alice. So this was the famous Marshall who ran Down Below in the Red Room. Batting 1.000 in the category of *roommate,* aren't we, just like Third North. At least *this* creature was friendly. But how could such a noxious sump possibly promote? In comparison, the job Matt was doing, giving a pinch to this one and a kiss to that, recognizing or doling out a bit of mystery in *Yes: right: but where did we meet?* as required. No wonder Vic needed him!

And numbers grew; they mushroomed to sixty-three. He was the demiurge tinkering in the large planned garden, the humble hand tending the new life.

"Good night, Magic!" called Peter Boi, flapping a limp hand. "Night, Magic!" said Lacey, the clipboard girl with spiked black hair; "Nice crowd tonight!" Angel, Lacey's cotton-haired confrère, actually bugged her eyes at the number on his list. They were still standing by the stanchions outside, though there was no one now waiting behind the ropes; three-thirtyish and freezing. "Holy shit," moaned Angel in her gravelly drone. "Much better than Marshall," she muttered.

"How did—how did Marshall do?" he couldn't resist asking, unclasping Sophie's hand to edge up beside Peter Boi and the girls.

"God only knows," said Angel, flinging her hair over a shoulder.

"He forgot his list at home," explained Lacey. She stared into space, bit her lip.

"That isn't all." Angel rolled her eyes.

"*Please* don't tell that story again." Lacey shook her head wearily. "I'm sick of it."

The first week he had mostly been holding his breath, and the second was still hazy, a stroboscopic aftereffect—only as the third stretched out new green leaves did *it* begin to reveal itself in earnest. Hello, my name is Matt Acciaccatura; I'm a club promoter; he could say that, it wouldn't be a lie.[32] He could talk to anyone in the street with all the miraculous ease of some fakir walking a gauntlet of live coals. He could traipse into any club or bar simply by flashing his wee 2×4 business card—hopping lines, skipping through ropes, getting free drinks right under the eyes of real VIPs.

Therefore the nature of his situation at NYU began to redden at the edges like a ribald joke. His doppelgänger, Matt the Bland, could exit his suite, meander through a corridor packed with his entire hall group, zip down the crowded stairs, find a seat in the dining hall, eat a plateworth of miserable mash, and bus his tray—all without engendering a single look or "hey." Every time a stray glance passed through his face as if it were nothing other than empty space, Matt had half an inclination to tap one twitching finger on the offender's shoulder and say: "Pardon me, sir. Yes, you. Do you know that in the eyes of the objective world, I am vastly cooler than you? Indeed, you are a mere single-celled organism in comparison with my highly evolved, semidivine state." Ah, at any instant

---

[32] Who has not felt delight in assuming a new identity? I remember when I wed Lisanne telling repeatedly to the mirror *I am the man of the most beautiful woman in the world.* Ha! Let us laugh. Let us laugh loudly so it will not be possible any one misunderstands we do not see the humour, the real hysteria of this black humor.

he could reveal his higher incarnation—like a comic-book hero, Bruce Wayne and Batman, with just a quick-change in the bathroom, superpowers *on!* and...look, world, there's Magic Matt! Oh, you could dig your toes in the moist earth of that identity, it was solid—you could trust in it now!

But as if the lares had heard his crowing, one malevolent djinn decided to ram a stick into his axle's spinning: on Monday afternoon Miranda floated into the lobby with a frown; handing off his goody bag, she declared: "Vic wants to see you in the office."

Matt nearly fell down the felted steps behind her, heading through the room with stacked tables and chairs, the tunnel, up the dim-lit stair, and through the mirror door—

"I've had it with him!" Vic was yelling at a blonde with a tired face. "Are you telling me he's not *back* yet? That's it. Tell him to stay in Paris! I don't have to take this bullshit! Where're my dogs?!" The same elegant Adrian, again in liquid slacks and newspaper-boy cap, passed Vic two powerful leashes attached to a pair of large spectral white dogs with yellow eyes, panting silently, queerly identical and regal but for their big mouths hanging open to reveal pulsing coral-red tongues. "And you can tell him Vic said so. Tell him, 'Vic Spector hates your guts, never show your face in the club again, he'll see you in hell.' All right? All right? All right. C'mon, Matt," Vic ordered between clenched teeth, careening past him to a rear door, "we're taking a walk."

"Nothing to do with you," Vic spat when they were halfway down the block. He was racewalking, but the ghostly dogs were floating ahead without difficulty—noticeably less than Matt. "Just this asshole who works for us. Who *used* to work for us. Until I fired him this morning." He jerked his head violently in at least five directions, then steamed across the street. "It's a tough business. You know? It's really, it's not cut out for everyone." He grunted. "Well. Magic, I'm proud of you, you're doing very well, *very* well, you know. You did, what wassit, sixty, sixty-three reduced this past weekend. So you seem to be, you know you're maintaining your numbers, which is fabulous. Fact, it's a twenty-five percent—do I have my figures right?—it's a twenty-five percent increase, week over week. Which is, you know, it's not incredible, but you should feel all right. All right?" The traffic light shot green; observing a decorous silence they crossed the wide avenue. "You know, the thing I'm concerned about, Matt," Vic picked up again on the far side, "it's not so much your numbers *per se,* it's the *quality* of your crowd. You follow me? See, your crowd is—it's not that your crowd is *bad,* it's not that you have a bad crowd at all, not at all. No no no no no no." Vic had halted while the dogs surrounded an abandoned couch whose stuffing was seeping out through a gash in green chintz; now they turned away, disgusted, and loped on. "Listen, kid, it's like this. I'll tell you a story from my stock-broking days."

"You were a stockbroker?" slipped out, accidentally.

Vic did a double take, looked over his shoulders as if embarrassed for Matt before unseen bystanders. "You didn't *know* that? Oh, I was huge, I was fantastic, I was featured in *Time* magazine. Look it up, *Time,* February what was it, 1977. I've done everything, kid. I was an army brat, moved around so much I lived on every continent by, like, the age of eight. I worked on an oil rig in Alaska, I've been a hippie"—Vic held up his free hand in a stubby peace sign—"I marched on Washington.... You know the Chinese believe, the Chinese believe we each have nine lives. Well, I've been through about seven of those already, in *this* one. I dunno what's next for me—nirvana!" Vic fluttered his eyelashes, miming a coy befuddlement before such celestial mysteries, then let loose a raucous, utterly unmystical guffaw so the whole suit shook. "Someday I'll tell you, I have more stories than anyone you'll ever know. So when I was a stockbroker, one time this guy in the next office comes over and he says, 'Vic, how do you do it? You're always making money, and here I am, I did business school and college—but you...' I mean, I went to college too, for a year though, baseball scholarship, dropped out, uh, that's another story, but I mean, here this guy was asking *me,*" Vic stood up cock-proudly, "how to deal with his stocks! I didn't need business school! I didn't need any *text*books! You know what I told him?" He stopped abruptly on the sidewalk to glare at Matt, which caused the dogs to fix him with their own threatening yellow eyes.

Well, now. Matt shrugged his shoulders. Buy low, sell high?

"Always keep a diversified portfolio," Vic declared meaningfully.

Then, arms out at his sides, gazing up at the blue sky, he marched on in the halo of giftedness that evidently surrounded him. "You get it? And that's—it's exactly the same for a nightclub, at least a club of this caliber. All the parts have to fit together. Everything's in balance. It's like a food chain, an ecosystem. I've got everybody, I've got the models, I've got the gay crowd—I've got the homeboys—we went over this, 'member? See, what I do is I bring all of these different worlds *together* in *one* place, where they can feed off one another. Now, if there's one thing I don't have, or not enough of, not as much as I'd *like*, it's the college kids. Unbelievable, I know. I mean, this town is fulla them, how many colleges we got here, and I *know* they go out every night, they got their parents' money, they just don't come to Cinema." He shrugged. "Prob'ly they think they can't get in, because our door is so tight. And I mean, that's *true*," he cackled, "we run a tight door, I wouldn't have it any other way. But there's, you know, there's gotta be beautiful people at NYU like anywhere else. Right? I mean, let's face it: I have Wall Street guys looking to pick up hot young coeds. I have cutting-edge DJs from Sweden, from England, from Tel Aviv—they want to spin their music for a crowd who can dance to it! I need fresh faces, kids with a little class, to mix with all those freaky-dinks Marshall brings in. And everybody wins. That's the thing. Am I right? So *that's*," he punched Matt's arm for emphasis, "where I want you to come in. Course, I still want you to draw from everywhere, but just, you know, focus on that pool, all the circles you know at NYU. That's what I want you to start bringing me. You got me?"

All the circles I know. Of course, all my wide net of friends. So. Was this going to be snatched away too? Matt nodded fiercely.

Vic had halted at the window display of an expensive-looking menswear store. "Oh, I *love* this place, I *adore* it, isn't that *adorable*?" His finger jabbed at two stuffed dalmatians lounging in a quilted nest. Then his gaze flicked down. "Do you like that, girls? You like that?" The dogs bobbed their heads in friendly unison, twitching their eager paws. "Should we go in? Sasha, Mila? All ri-ight, if *you* say so . . ." A peculiarly kindly note thrummed in his voice, like Santa Claus. He threw open the glass door and stalked in after his dogs. It slammed in front of Matt's face—luckily he was able to get it open before Vic might see. "I want that. That thing in the window. Two of 'em. For my dogs," Vic barked at a salesman. "For my little girls," he cooed, looking down. Matt lingered back and fingered a button-down shirt, flipping the price tag over in a covert flash. Ye *gods*. Six hundred for a plain white *shirt*.

The salesman returned from a whispered congress by the register. "I'm *so* sorry, sir, I'm afraid we're out of that item . . ." he whined, clasping his hands in penitence. "It's so close to the holidaaaays. But what I can do for you is I can order them, I can gift-wrap them, and they're *guaranteed* to be here by the end of the week."

"What?" snarled Vic, jerking back as if the man had bitten him. "You're *out* of it? No, that's fine, that's fine, I'm not gonna *order* it." Vic brushed past as if Matt were a stranger, the dogs swooping along companionably. Matt glanced stunned and sympathetic at the salesman, but the man was already cheerily tidying up a pile of cashmere scarves.

Matt ran after Vic and fell into step. It wasn't clear if he was noticed, but after a minute Vic opened his mouth again. "So," he said, "see where I'm coming from? I mean, your crowd is great, your numbers are getting there, but what we reeeeally need from you right now is to draw," he paused, methodical as Churchill, "from the NYU scene, from that population. Okay? You got it? Now, course you can't do that by Friday, that's all right. And next week, next week is right before Christmas, why don't you take the night off—college kids are gonna be gone anyway. But the week after that—the week after that I want you to be on just for New Year's. It's a Sunday, I know, but New Year's, in this business New Year's is all hands on deck. That's the big push, so forget Friday. All right? You got that? Good. You're a good kid." He looked Matt dead in the eyes, so serious, intense, he seemed to be about to declare his paternity—

Vic spun around on his dress heel and disappeared west, guarded on both sides by the alert and noble white dogs galloping fluently along.

6.

[33]Let the day perish wherein I was born, and the night in which it was said, *There is a man child conceived.* For the thing which I greatly feared is come upon me. Oh sure, Vic Spector hadn't fired him. Of course—not yet, nothing that simple, no. But could he be in any doubt what was to come next?

Matt leaned his head on a parking meter, holding it tenderly in both arms like a tether in a spaceship without gravity; if he let go he would float, all the way down Fifth Avenue. Touched his lips and chin: still there. A nausea set up a brisk tattoo, a little drummer boy in the tum; the ice was breaking, breaking audibly, in a moment he should fall through.

He let go the meter, fell down the avenue like a pinball jounced from

----

[33] On this day, Monday 11 December, I experienced a grave, hurtful shock of my own: Lisanne and I had a first of our „blow-outs," in the D'Agostino's of 21st Street. There we met the pompous Malcolm Barrow in his absurd checked jacket and exaggerated smile by the refrigerated cheese and after he left, I noticed how Lisanne's hand stayed on the same wedge of Appenzeller Swiss for the entirety of a minute, as long as I required to find flatbreads and one packet of the organic style of pita from the deli counter which I liked. And when I asked, not at all harshly or with anything but a friendly tone, what was occurring the corners of her lips turned down like a snake's tail, so that I felt a small chill at the bottom of my spine, and when I tried to take the cheese to put it in my basket, she dug her new maroon-painted nails into the back of my hand.

lamppost to lamppost. And to think he had actually believed his life was changing! Well, and haven't we learned this lesson before? Face facts, old sport! You are the perennial also-ran, the eternal *joke*.

Matt dipped into a diner on Sixth Avenue, ordered peppermint tea and toast. Come, now. Sir! What kind of brattish fit is this? The miasma of hysteria has distorted your vision. Let us recall, the man said you were doing a good job. It's merely that he wants college children from you. Simply draw up a plan. They *would* probably be coming back long before the official end of vacation on the twelfth of January; even Sophie was planning just two weeks in Chicago, and all the tristaters would probably zip down to New York for New Year's Eve; he might have thought of that before, no doubt would have if he'd ever been invited out to celebrate the night himself. Thank God Vic had told him now, with still enough time: last classes were this Wednesday, the thirteenth, and exams all next week; he would need to get his war machine on pronto. Today even. Tonight. He would simply have to find out what was going on around campus. Get the school newspapers, check all listings. There were plays about to go up, he'd vaguely seen posters, rock shows, whatnot. Figure out where the likelies would be. Draw upon reinforcements, perhaps; Sophie and Jason, if they were willing soldiers.

It could be done. It was even a bit exciting. Vic was forcing his hand, making him bring the club game to school—a thing about which he had been far too diffident, under the name of prudence, far too.

The waitress deposited a plate of toast, browned and buttered beautifully. And what could be better on this earth than bread and butter? How wonderfully the world rushed to his aid, filling his vacant places with material goodness. He nibbled the two toasts in grateful bites. Then he brushed off the crumbs and walked back to a payphone by the bathrooms, where he dialed Sophie and Jason. Agreed: rendezvous, his treat, seven-thirty at Belges Frites.

On this one he was not going down without a fight. After picking up paraphernalia at the stationer's next door, he marched purposefully down Sixth through the ash-smudged evening toward campus: when a familiar figure crossed his path.

That newspaper-boy cap—"Adrian?" Matt blurted.

Adrian stopped. Under a streetlight, the olive-colored cap showed covered with tiny *LV*s. "Hey, baby," Adrian drawled. Dark half-moons under eyes that flickered absently over Matt. "*Running* to hit CC before it closes." Snuffling, he ticked his head back toward a glass-plated office where fluorescent-lit men stood moored in line: CHECK CASHING blared in red neon above the door.

"Oh," murmured Matt, "me too."

Inside of ten minutes Matt was out on the street again, his check metamorphosed to three hundred in crisp twenties, pressing in a breast pocket against the heart where a new idea was beating. Adrian's cap: that was what had produced instant recognition. Some distinctive dash of outré sartorial *je ne sais quoi* brands one, bestows an image. Wasn't that what Adorno and Horkheimer had said in their old essay? *Today, a Hollywood actress . . . a simple cowlick . . . illusion of uniqueness . . .* something thereabouts. So with a trademark visual gesture, a signature This Is Me, when he strolled into class, or thudded down the steps in the crowd outside Meyer Hall, he might educe an automatic response in all lookers-on: *oh, that kid, I've seen him before; yes, he always wears that . . .* That what? What could be his cowlick, cap?

For almost an hour an uninspired Matt worked Mercer to Wooster: until it appeared, dangling mildly at the edge of a clothing rack, like a demure lady waiting to be asked to dance. And it was the first thing they seized on when he stood smiling above their booth at Belges Frites, Sophie snatching an end of the white scarf—blinding, cashmere, and obscenely lengthy: if Matt draped it about the neck, it brushed below-knees, turning him into Charles Lindbergh, a dashing aviator type with vaguely aristocratic bearing—to rub it at her cheek, while Jason, grabbing a ketchup bottle, began huffing as if to prepare for a giant squeeze.

"Don't you dare!" Matt screamed.

"Oh, get down here," Sophie squealed, dragging both ends to yoke him down to her lips, light as the touch of snow against his . . . "Now." She opened her eyes, let out her impish smile. "What's this secret meeting all about?"

"Ah . . ." He began tossing highlighters, index cards, NYU papers from his courier bag onto the table. "So, um, how's your week looking? Hmm? Pretty, pretty clear?"

Check: the suede-pants scene at the photo exhibit of Visual Studies seniors. Check: black-turtlenecked drama buffs after *Waiting for Godot* at the Experimental Theater. Check: cat's-eye chicks and horn-rimmed dudes hanging at the animation screening.

Now, here was the truly ridiculous thing. Here was the wonder of wonders. When he bounded, scarf wheeling, through the doors into a reception where the marks stood gathered like barnacles on the cheese-and-wine table, all he had to do was recall: calm, sir, take aim and shoot. When he'd sussed out the leaders-and-minions situation (leaders were taller, though not always; better-looking, though not always; more talkative, though not always: no, it was that lionlike freedom in their eyes as they crossed a room), he merely sallied up to one, uttered, *Hey.* No follow-up, no *What's up*—for he did not wish to be friends, this was not a conversation but an end-directed event, like administering a syringe; he had all the medicine ready at his tongue-tip—just *Hey,* delivered with a knowing stare of *I'm Like You:* then stop. Wait, like cars playing chicken . . . and they'd cave. They'd reply: arching an insecure eyebrow, as if, *Should I know you?* Those sitting ducks! Then out with the invite, tapping it against your palm as if at any moment it might be whisked back, and ask, *What're you doing for New Year's?* a query so onus-on-them that *I don't know* or *Hanging out with friends* was straight up out of the question.

But Sophie and Jason were appallingly bad at it. On Tuesday she had come along to an Asian Pacific American lecture-reception, but she went up so nicely, and to such *nice* people, no divas, she seemed to be recruiting for a school-spirit rally rather than granting a key to the coolest club in New York for New Year's Eve—who could blame when they outright refused or merely accepted the invite with a polite, condescending scan? At the Queer Union dance Thursday night, it turned out Jason got so riled up with Stan and Jorge over someone named Frank's hoochie new piece of ass that he forgot altogether for a whole hour, and when Matt arrived, dashing from the fashion show in Anderson Hall, his naive little buddy was, by the exit, simply passing out cards to partygoers bundling into the frigid night.

"What're you doing?" Matt hissed, dragging him into the hall.

"You wanted me to hand them all out, and I had thirty left, so I thought..."

"That's all right." Matt gave Jason's back a kindly pat. "All right. Here. I'll take the stack." Useless. Wonderful but useless when it came to that.

Saturday and Sunday, with exam week now begun, the main library was chockablock with kids, every carrel filled with piles of books and tapping laptops, and he, too, holed up, in a tiny annex room on the seventh floor no one ever seemed to enter. Luckily, his only two finals were World Cultures and Moral Reasoning—like taking candy from a baby: could there really be much head-scratching in distinguishing your Lady Murasaki from your Meiji?!—and then just the Expressive Culture paper, another in Freshman Seminar on *War and Peace*, ten-pagers he could knock out in five hours each, type 'em up later at Sophie's or Jason's.

So whenever the restlessness came into his knees, he allowed himself to shake his head clear, lift a quotient of invites, and plummet in the elevator to prowl about the water fountain and phones on the basement level, where exhausted break-takers were pacing, looking about eagerly for some momentary injection from the outside world. Then how like a doctor, how kindly, entering a battlefield infirmary with shots of morphine in his kit bag, Matt walked the hallway, choosing this one and that one from the melee of aimless strollers; he sidled up with an ironic smile to quiz, intrigue, and finally deliver unto their hands exactly what was needed. *Exams? Grades? Why, don't be so terribly blah-bourgeois, my friend,* his shrewd smile said. *Much more importantly*—"What are you doing New Year's Eve?"

And there was a little extra frisson in bringing the promoting circus to school, inserting, perversely, Magic Matt into the place where before was only lowly Matthew Acciaccatura. Besides, at school the danger level was do-or-die; you had to win over every last one to whom you opened your mouth, otherwise, the rumor could spread you were a loser—then, baby, say good night. Of course, it wasn't time yet to try his might in certain quarters, such as with the denizens of Third North, who, if they happened to place him as that anonymous nullity from Fourth Floor, would understandably fall prey to a fatal doubt. And certainly not Dwight et al.—no, Matt didn't want the prepsters even to know something was up; he was biding his time like Napoleon at Austerlitz in Tolstoy, waiting for the sun to emerge from its wrappings of fog, for the whole field to be lit brilliant before him until he may make his decisive move. Though once actually he caught himself automatically ducking beneath the rampart of the stair when he heard Taylor's pinched murmur and Carly Hale's pip-squeak draw perilously near: facing a puce wall in the paint-peeling underhang, Matt feigned a wearisome pocket search until the voices disappeared down the corridor.

Could they really get to him now, still now? Shaking, picking off bits of puce clinging stubbornly to his wool jersey, Matt marched into an elevator, jabbed morosely at button seven. Why should he care about that handful of loons? He imagined: Angel's gravelly laugh decimating the preps at the velvet ropes; she could be cruel, that kitten. "Not the look we're going for tonight," she had spat out the other evening to a pair of chunky B&T girls in slut gear, snidely unclipping the side rope so they had to withdraw into the street, tail between their boots. How lovely to unleash Angel on the preps! Welcome to *my* world, you blazered buffoons. Well, soon enough he would devise some way to put them in their place. Only not to rush: not to ruin.

Yet there was one old face from Third North he would have liked to see, was itching for, in fact—where was Scott Belfast, of the vintage rock Ts and perfect jeans? Neither he nor his lady Liza Andrewes was anywhere to be seen. Once Matt did spot the SB-hanger-on Myra Washington having a smoke outside the library but deferred, saving up his approach for the regal presence. Tuesday, when Sophie was at her kitchen table poring over images for the Ren Art test, Matt finally asked, "Will you—you'll see that kid tomorrow, Scott Belfast?" Maybe he could meet her at the exit, somehow strike it up . . .

"Oh. I guess I didn't tell you." She scooped up her knee, leaning forward eagerly in her chair. "He got asked to *leave*. Not kicked out, just for the year. He *plagiarized*. From his roommate. They, like, both turned in pretty much the same paper for ConWest. Can you believe it?" She rolled her eyes.

"Plagiarized," Matt echoed dully. "Asked to leave?" They were not to be friends? Not even now, when he had such prime goods to deliver up?

"How stupid. I told you he was stupid," she muttered, turning back to her book.

Asked to leave. Matt drew their cups to the stove for another round of green tea. So. Could *he* be king? Was he next in line? A veritable power vacuum. He could step in and lend direction. Who else did they have—James Marks, with his little rock band? Please.

Matt downed the tea and bent to kiss Sophie's cool neck. "I'll leave you alone, my fair studiette." He rubbed her shoulders, shoved invites in his coat pocket, and bounded out—to her protests calling back: *A punk show in the student center that I just remembered*—then down the stairs into a black night where giant pieces of snow were wheeling solemnly down from the mammoth sky.

Bring 'em on, baby. In this corner, ready for all comers! Skaters with long chains at the punk show, anorexics on the catwalk in Anderson Hall! Hotties at the La Raza dance, hotties at the film club's masked ball! What had he quailed in the face of, what could he not now accomplish? Like wily Odysseus outwitting the Cyclops—Nobody, my name is Nobody, and I shall ruin you with my gold tongue, by my *nous* that worketh wonders! NYU, do you hear me? Matt balled up his hands into fists and hit excitedly at his thighs, each stroke *yes, yes, yes*. NYU, you may call me by my given name, my name of Magic Matt! Flakes brushed his face, clung to the coat and vanished into the midnight-blue wool. Glittering buildings drew back from his nearing pace, their lit windows scanning him suspiciously like the eyes of silent fish through unfolding levels of dark water.

7.

Abruptly, the nine days of school promotion ended. By Wednesday, the dorm's population had definitely lessened; on Thursday, the day Sophie flew off to Chicago and Jason took the Metro-North up to Scarsdale, the place was practically a ghost town: in the bathroom, a stray flip-flop and towel lay on the lavender tile like objects villagers might have dropped while fleeing some catastrophe. Friday, when finals ended, when they were even going to shut off heat in the dorms, Matt awoke to find snow had come for real, a stock of splendid white stuff shaking itself softly over New York.[34]

---

[34] How well I recollect this magical snowfall! From the point of view of the night before: Lisanne and I had enjoyed an intimate evening, unusually, for hours in our studio and then, though late, perhaps three of the morning, we wished somehow to have fresh bread. We replaced our clothing and wandered east, where we came upon one bakery beginning to place bagels on trays. That scent of fresh baking! And how the snowflakes settled on her wavy hair. Tiny pieces of confetti, melting like the dark spot in my throat had earlier when, wishing to reproach her for a negligence, she came home from her final obligation for the term carrying a paper container with champagne and a gay mood and, glowing, kissed my shoulder mole while I stood at the stove over my garbanzo stew. I thought: see, Hans! *Ein kleines Wölkchen verbirgt oft die strahlendste Sonne*— a little cloud often hides the most brilliant sun: after some minor disturbances, are we not happy? are we not the identical H+L as before, adventurers in this strange country together, beloveds, man and wife, now that certain inconsiderable clouds have escaped?

I am grateful for the opportunity to reconsider these incidents, which appear in a new light to me. For perhaps the trajectory into which I then gathered all of these small

It was good. Everything was going right. He had sown the deluxe-size four-hundred-invite stack: he had doled out business cards past count: he had only to wait ten days to find out the fruits of his labor. All in all he was in a banner mood. Not even the delays in buses to Jersey bothered him. He practically whistled to the Muzak "Rudolph" blasting at the Port Authority. Snow was even brighter in the suburbs, covering the branches of leafless trees like heaps of crystalline sugar as he trudged along Lehman Lane; the air felt clearer, crisper here. At his front door, the melody of the tumblers turning in the lock sounded lovely-familiar as a favorite song. He made instant coffee and plopped himself under a quilt with his glossy picture book of Norse myths spread huge over his lap. Home. It did have its pleasures, this place, with its silence, its every-thing-relating-to-him. And stress-free, a total privacy.

Until his mother got here.

This vacation he was determined to be congenial, the soul of good-will. He would simply laugh aside any aspersions she might cast upon his fitness to live life victoriously and well. Thus he reflected, sinking on the couch around four into a royal nap.

Yet theory and dispatch—what worlds between! So did he see when she came home, bringing a bag of groceries from the A&P, her large, florid face, and—as she drew near to kiss and ruffle him, to gasp, "My goodness, what a big boy you look! My little college man!"—her scent of talcum powder, salami, and Lipton tea. Dear God: would he have to, impossible by now, get taller than she to grow out from her notion of miniature? "What is that shirt?" She fingered his newish D&G silk button-down, frowning. "It's kind of shiny, isn't it?" Her eyes rested on his chest, displeased.

"It's just silk," he explained, making his voice jaunty, cheerful. "That's why."

---

occasions was one made out of wish rather than right judgement—they now can be linked in a quite other line. As I have said elsewhere in regard to young Matthew, what was *Erlebnis* becomes *Erkenntnis*, what was lived through is now apprehended, recognized.

She lifted her fingers quickly, as if silk wasn't even nice to the touch, and turned to heft the groceries in her arms. "We used to have a name for guys who wore shirts like that," rang out from the kitchen. Pealing laughter: how joyless was his mother's laughter, squashed like a sat-on hat. Now her head popped back into the hall, naughtily gleeful. "We called them sleazos!"

"Really?" He adjusted a pillow under his neck, allowing his frown to refer to that recalcitrant thing. A woman of the world. "Well," he cleared his throat, "it's real silk."

She disappeared. *Ratchet, ratchet:* the usual sound of a can opening. "I hope it wasn't ex*pens*ive."

Oh, right, the groceries. He plodded to the kitchen. Milk into the fridge. Margarine. Biting his lip. Let it die. But—"Ma," he was ferrying the eggs into the rack with little repudiating clicks, "I paid for it with my own money. You know?"

"While you're home—" She broke off to grapple with the jar of Hellmann's, shaking an amused head at him when he reached to help. "While you're home, you should go to Burlington Coat Factory on Route 17. Did I show you my new coat? No?"

She reappeared in the kitchen doorway holding out a denim coat, thigh-length, inside lined with wisps of cotton fur that along the neck had sallowed yellow-brown. And her face beaming above the coat, as she shook it to better show him its shapeless shape—God, this was precisely the same face, tenterhooked, full of hope, she had when taking him to Chuck E. Cheese's, watching him unwrap a fake Cabbage Patch Kid that Christmas when all he'd wanted, when what he'd asked for, was a Dickens book (*I know the other kids all have this:* her plaintive explanation)—it made Matt have to blink to keep back weeping. Couldn't he be someone who thought that was nice? Was that really so much to ask of him?

"Wow." Dropping the cardboard carton, he stepped closer, fingering the denim under her cautious territorial gaze. "Let's see it on." Crossing his arms, a connoisseur: she blushed, tossed her hair bashfully. "Come on, Mom. I want to see you in it."

"Sixty-nine dollars," she crowed. She removed her light-brown tresses from beneath the collar so they fell toward her drooping mass of breast turned anyway by the coat into a sort of lateral footballer's padding, and gave him a dazzling grin. And there, disturbingly, like a fractal he distinguished: some white chip of his own freest, happiest, thousand-watt brilliance.

By the end of dinner (Ham Luau—*Your favorite!* she supposed), he was maybe five hundred calories over the daily max, and dangerously overdrawn on his patience too. He had donned the fox slippers when she'd shrieked at his sock feet. He had allowed his plate to be heaped with *plenty of good meat* and to her *cut it little, chew it good* had delivered his *Ma, I know how to eat!* tempered with a smile fashioned from pure Yule spirit. He had endured a barrage of questions: though not *How were your exams? How is Sophie*, or, at least, *how is—your friend?* No, instead: *Is Dwight going all the way to Minnesota for break? Did you ever go hear one of his singing concerts? What would you lose by trying out too? Maybe he could help you get on the team.* If she wasn't aiming to offend, if she had somehow not heard by a clatter of plate or fork, *Mom, I've told you, Dwight's not really my friend,* and finally, *He's actually kind of a phony, I really don't like him,* still, why, why did she ask about, instead of Sophie, Dwight's lady? Allison-from-Darien: because of blasted Emmalouise and her rich ex, this detail was lodged forever on the flypaper of his mother's brain. But he wouldn't condescend to sell Sophie with *Mom, Lake Forest is a rich town too.* Was it some subliminal or even conscious *fuck-you?* This was the labyrinth of questions his mother always led him to, a wilderness of half-truths that maddened and shut him in.

Thus, when she glanced at her watch and remarked, *Oh, wow. It's already past nine,* giving him a sympathetic look that all but said *Baby's up past his bedtime,* he found the path of less resistance in vowing that, hmm, actually he was pretty tired. Exams, you know. All that.

What did other people do in these situations? Sophie he'd heard on the phone; the bits not in Japanese seemed interesting, names of movies she'd seen, places her mother was presenting research papers. Jason was, well, a special case. They had a grand relationship, Jason and his mother, every week taking high tea at the St. Regis Hotel. "But what do you talk about?" Matt had asked in the fall. "You should come next time." Jason

shrugged. "I'm sure it'll be fine with my mom." And indeed, descending
at Grand Central in a dark brown fur, she had immediately drowned him
in rich perfume, gripping his arm and grumbling a warm, heavily
Russian *Hullo, pleast to meet you.* In the gilt-edged tearoom at the St.
Regis, as a mammoth harp caterwauled up and down the octaves, she
pretended to strike up a fight with the headwaiter over the number of
salmon sandwiches all the while keeping up a colorful conversation
about a sex scandal then overwhelming Scarsdale Country Day.

Salmon? Roe? Sex? Witty banter? Matt hauled himself onto the
comforter, lay cadaver-stiff staring at the eave over the bed, and fell
asleep, forgetting even to call and trade good-nights with Sophie.

In the morning, after a dreamless deep ten hours—annihilated time,
time X-ed out from the annals of the world—he waited in the sheets until the Camry roared, mufflerless, away. Then he crept downstairs, where
unearthly white reflected off the snow through the den's sliding glass
doors. Soon he was wheeling his bike out from the tiny back plot into
that whiteness, riding the cleared sidewalks beside powdery piles, off on
his annual Christmas errand. Ever since the time she'd brought home
plastic and twelve-year-old Matt cried, her "big boy" did the tree thing
himself; restriction: no higher than her waist. Dismounting at the stall
outside Wessex Drugs, Matt paced the rows of trees, finally edging up
beside a miniature pine whose splayed branches gave it a startled air. Ten
bucks, delivery please.

The next six hours he drowned in labor, pedaling to the gourmet
Italian place for risotto and sundries and homeward where the munch-
kin tree already stood startled on the doorstep, then arranging this on the
low den table, hanging balls, a string of lights detangled from its attic box,
chopping garlic, mushrooms—wouldn't she be pleased? coming home
from the A&P with the tree set, dinner made?—all the while racking the
mind for talking points. He was up to three (Emmalouise? Movies of
late? Sarah-Lu: new baby pics?) when the car boomed from the end of
the block, and he ran out of the kitchen, trembling as he hurried to light
the candles on the table: before she walked in.

"Hello!" He bounded into the hall. "How was work?" Aha: a fourth point!

She frowned. "Matthew? Your slippers?" She hung the denim coat on a hanger in the hall closet. Wrinkling her nose. "It smells in here."

"That's the mushrooms and garlic! I made dinner! It's all ready!" His arms were stretched out in a big ta-da.

She cupped his chin in her big hand. "Why did you do that?" Her eyes were sagging, tired or sad slivers of blue between leathery pouches. "Oh, that's the tree." She moved around him to face it, hands on her waist.

"Nice, huh? It's all the old balls and lights."

"And tinsel?" She spun her gaze at him quick, as if having found a weak spot.

"And tinsel," he repeated. "I didn't have to pay for anything new."

"Just the tree," she corrected. She tipped her head to one side. "Isn't it—"

"No higher than your waist." He beat her to it.

She sighed. "Well." Then: "All right," she relented, with a wan smile.

At dinner she pushed around the mushroom ragù on her plate, poking as if to find lumps of meat somewhere, and actually asked, "Should I brown up some hamburger meat?" but when he gritted his teeth, said, *No thanks,* she nicely dropped it. And the talking points worked well. Emmalouise snatched up a good twenty minutes, and movies always got his mom sparkly, especially vis-à-vis George Clooney. They were just turning to Sarah-Lu when clearing the table, and since it was only just eight—why not?—he proposed a game of Sorry! She clapped and said, "Really?!" with such girlish joy and appended so mournfully, "I haven't played that in so *long,*" that Matt's heart gave a little flop. His poor mom, alone in the dull house.... He set up the game on the coffee table beside the warm, winking tree and didn't even budge the radio from Lite FM.

It was not one of her best efforts; she looked on suspiciously when he booted her men from the board, which you practically had to tie your hands together to prevent. Besides, with only two players, the game is not much in the way of entertainment. So they talked between rolls, and Matt even pressed from poor teenage-mother Sarah-Lu a segue into school. "They gave us sex ed seminars in Orientation, and there's condoms with your hall residential leader. Supposedly," he added swiftly, insucking breath. But she simply rolled the die: *three,* tucking hair back behind an ear. Probably couldn't imagine he might be so fortunate as to have sex.

"Oh, I love this song!" She threw her head, beaming, up from the board. "*Do you know the way to San Jose . . . la, la . . .* oh, Matt. You should join that singing group. It would be so much fun. Get you out of your room. It's not good to study so much."

· Ah, that old saw. "I'm not really . . . so interested in that anyway. I do other things."

"I know you do, baby, I know you do. There's all kindsa things you like to do in the city," she tacked on absently, leaning from the couch to accept a queenly sip of Crystal Light.

As if it all were so twee, beneath her. Probably thought it was more nerdy art stuff. That unlucky day in twelfth grade, he never should have shown her the booklet of a Miró show; for months whenever he was off to the city it was "Going to see more exhibits of *Bird–Woman–Moon*? You figure out yet how to tell 'em apart?"

"Like for my job." He wrenched the die. "Six." He clicked along. "Like for my job," he repeated, looking her dead in the eyes. "You know? That kind of thing."

"With the—with the toilets?" Her brow furrowed, as if genuinely confused.

Matt let go an urbane chuckle. "Oh, Mom. You *know* my work-study job doesn't involve toilets. In fact, it's an office job. Or don't you recall?"

"Matt!" A snaggle-toothed volley of laughter. "Don't get so worked up! Honey! I'm just thinking of you! If you went to a school like Rutgers, which by the way is perfectly fine for boys in your school like Alex Hamilton, you wouldn't have to do this crap work. Oh, honey." Her face changed; again her eyes, searching his face, turned sad, tired. She put a hand on his cheek. "Don't be mad. I'm just thinking of you. Okay?"

And here he made his real tactical error.

"Mom," he whispered. He cleared his throat, blinked back what felt like tears. "Mom, I have a new job now. A better one. I'm really...I got very lucky."

"What is it, baby? Tell me!" Her hands skipped eagerly to her knees.

Now in one fluent gush he told her, how Vic Spector had picked him out as having something special, how there were business cards and wherever he went people whose job it was to guard the doors let him in, even treated him to admittance (he skipped the free-drinks bit), how in a single week he had earned upward of three hundred just for going around and having fun, how there were actresses and stars like Johnny Depp and Kate Moss at the club, it was a special place, not just a usual bar or anything, in case she was thinking that, in fact it was kind of like—ever heard of Studio 54? well, anyway, never mind—and there was a nickname, because otherwise people would never leave you alone, so everyone called him Magic Matt. Wasn't it fabulous? He reached for his first sip of the glass of Crystal Light she'd poured him.

"I've never heard anything so ridiculous in my life." Her elbow was propped on a cushion, her chin rested on her palm: for a long moment no fragment of her massive bulk budged on the couch. Then: "Where's the phone?" she said under her breath, standing up as if having totally forgotten him. She disappeared into the hall.

"Mom? Where are you going?" Trembling on watery legs...

"You got to be joking," she muttered. "This is disgusting."

He slid in on his slippers after her: too late. The cordless was in her hands. "What are you doing?" he shrieked.

"You can just forget about it. A nightclub? You are *not* working in a nightclub. With alcohol, and drugs—there is just no way."[35] She shook her head menacingly. "It's not your fault, baby." She punched her thumb at the cordless: a mournful dial tone entered the room. Then her face softened. "Does this Vic person know you're only eighteen?"

---

[35] Like the sheep who scolds her lamb back toward the shepherd's flock from which it strays, Robin Acciaccatura, perhaps with instinctual maternal close-mindedness, did not strike far from a right point. For it may not be denied that her son was more likely to encounter certain dangers in a night-club than in his custodial employment. *Ein blindes Huhn findet auch ein Korn*, even a blind chicken will find a corn.

"Mom, you can bartend at eighteen. It's thoroughly legal. There's nothing wr—"

"Oh yes, there is something wrong." Sighing, she dialed a string of digits. "Something very wrong. I mean, really. What could that man be thinking? What was the name of that club again, babe? The Movie Theater?"

"Don't you dare, Mom. Do not even for an instant imagine—"

"Are you threatening me?" Her gaze narrowed. "Yes, hello?" She squeezed the phone to her flushed cheek.

Flew up the stairs to his room—ripped the wretched bag open and threw in everything, fucking toothpaste, underwear, jeans—beat down the steps—

"Well, it's a business," she was intoning into the phone. "I don't have—" She cupped its mouth and called, "Matt, be reasonable! Be a big boy!"

"Farewell!" he yelled. "Merry Christmas!"

All the way down the road, while the white crust cracked angrily beneath his feet and he slipped and slid in his hurry and sleek-soled shoes, he felt the importance of what he'd done low in his throat, expanding to block his vocal cords. The slam of that door—how pure, he had never heard that noise before. He wished he'd gone and slammed the door a couple more times to really get the impulse out. With her harebrain she'd never manage to reach Vic. "The Movie Theater," that's wonderful, Mom; keep trying. Whatever you do to ruin my life, you will fail, and when you have failed enough times, you will have cut me off from you entirely as an island, and nothing you do then can touch me anymore.

Thus was the Christmas Eve and Christmas of '95 passed in his dorm. Later, he did, under the duress of Sophie's urgings and a slew of old-timey seasonal flicks watched upstairs in some unlocked jock's room, phone his mother and leave a message wishing her a real Merry Christmas. But when he missed her call the following day, he didn't bother to reply to her message for all the rest of what he styled *his dorm retreat*.

Which was frigid, as the heat was shut off; anxious, as he had to hide

from security: illegal to stay on over break. Luckily, his M&O key for
Hayden Hall opened the ramped back door by the garbage Dumpsters
of Third North, and once inside they couldn't catch him if he lay low
while they did once-an-evening perfunctory floor sweeps—then he was
free to roam his solitary arctic kingdom. Of course it was *insane*, as
Sophie phrased it, not to just go over to her place, but you must lie in the
bed you've yourself messed, and, anyway, this experience was: well, if not
fun, the way he claimed to her, at least so much more singular, ascetically
intense, with the whole of this fluorescent-lit palace all to himself. He
wore hat and gloves indoors; he was Shackleton, in the silence of the rim
of the world. Drifting down halls in his socks, reading Markerboards.
Exploring unlocked rooms; once he lay quietly still in a stranger's bed
pretending to be someone else, the someone who belonged to all these
smiling faces in the photocollage of friends, friends at prom, friends at
graduation, friends for no discernible occasion at all, lifting each other
up by a tree or lounging against a fence. Ah, friends; ah, high school; ah,
normal people, how quaint. Every night he ate Cracklin' Oat Bran with
skim milk in a plastic cup and made green tea on the hot ring. Afterward, he stretched out their floppy futon onto the floor, opened the
window, and, in the raw breeze, smoked deeply, staring up at the ceiling
where bewitching Christmas lights blinked down a sort of red and gold
empathy.

One night, when the suspense had fanned through his body like
fiberglass till he could hardly breathe from it, he rolled off the futon,
shifted the cigarette to his left hand, picked up the phone, and called his
voicemail at Cinema.

"You have six-ty-se-ven new mes-sages in your mail-box."

Saved. O gloria in excelsis this ghost in the machine.

8.

If New Year's has an epicenter, it is New York; if New York has a moment, it is New Year's. Space-time converges to this one point, finite and glittering as the disco ball above millions of bodies at Times Square gathered there to watch that sacramental fall. At no other time is New York so much itself, so freely rangy in its demesne; the event functions as a sort of estrus, seasonally brought on by a cyclical conjunction of stars.

Weather does its part. Beginning with the onset of darkness, the temperature drops absurdly. At this inducement, nasty skirmishes spring up between rival crews of coke-snuffed toughs with their shrieking, freezing women over that rara avis—bright yellow cabs darting through streets like red capes before toros. Although the streets are swirling with extra policemen, these reserve officers—perhaps cloned on some planet where they were trained to despise their puny human charges—do not intervene in the mayhem. Mounted atop steam-snorting horses, they merely instill a free-floating sense of violence, of occult and dangerous conclusions lurking in the butts of shiny nightsticks and gleaming riot gear. In this lawless zone, this primal power vacuum, packs rove block after faceless block searching for the next party, bar, scene. One girl in every group throws up—hardly a mishap; *au contraire*, it's a necessary ingredient, a ritual element. Auld lang syne, ev'rybody—who's got a noisemaker? Who's got my phone, the address, the keys? Patting their wallets, guys in beefy overcoats eye whatever ladies are still lacking action, while in the bowers of abandoned doorways, successful slyboots are already carpe-dieming up the panty-hosed thighs of maudlin women. All night, under the giveaway clocks emblazoned *Camel* or *Marlboro,* where hour hands climb, climb, climb impossibly high and then sink again slowly, inexorably, cruelly, the mournful owners of delis slide coins over a counter to tough guys who shove cigarettes in pockets and jog across the street to find their girls sobbing quietly, throwing down jeweled purses, taking off strappy shoes because those hurt, and, oh, alluva sudden—they don't feel so good!

And for Matt, the whole spectacular panoply appeared under that enchanting sign of its being his first time: inching through the streets in a taxi with Jason and Sophie, he ducked to peer through both side windows, devouring the city scene in big bites. *So this is the New Year festivity!* He squeezed Sophie's hand, bit her cheek—"Hooray!"

"Hooray, what?" said Jason.

"Just hooray!" He laughed. "We're going to have so much fun tonight!"

Jason grinned. "Sure beats what I usually do: rent *Auntie Mame* and wish really hard I'll find out I'm adopted. How fabulous would Mame be for a mom!"

Matt snorted. "Like *you* have anything to be adopted about. I'd switch mothers in a second. Anyway: forget them, every last mother creature! It's New Year's Eve!"

"*You're* in a great mood." Sophie ruffled Matt's hair.

"I am," he said, awed.

Not even the mess near Cinema disturbed his bliss, though they had to get out and push through the last two blocks—to where, befrazzled, Lacey was barely able to deal out ten drink-tickets, a New Year's bonus, before the crowd pressed angrily forward. Eyes widened, she hissed, would you believe it, they were starting cover at a hundred, making up prices on Vic's orders? A hundred smackers just to get in the front door!—yet still in the first few rooms the club was mobbed, completely, and with what Vic would call *uglies.* But in the Red Room, where the strains of Blondie's "Call Me" burst like rockets above, they threw off that crush and danced—even Matt!—raging in the electric frenzy.

Impossible to tell who were the other promoters on call tonight, summoned up for Vic's all-hands-on-deck. He, at least, seemed to be sitting pretty: seven, ten of his own kids were visible.

"Is that Heather Thorndike?" Jason dragged him down by an arm, jerking his head toward the front bar. "From your hall group?"

"Looks like it," screamed Matt over the music, still moving his hips. Must have been someone's plus-one. So: was it time for the crows to roost *chez nous*? Not so beneath her anymore? Though she laughed into her flaxen hair that first day, on hearing my *I like to take long walks* tale? Well, well. All the same, gracious, he nodded to each face he knew and even winked or stroked some on the shoulder.

The night unfolded like a time-lapse rose. They got champagne; they got a table. Nearby they spotted celebs; Sophie pointed out a Belgian model with sensitive eyes, the new face of Miu Miu. Then just before midnight, when Matt was rushing from the behind-bar staff bathroom to grab fresh holiday champers: an actual supermodel stood waiting for his stall, straight off that cover of *Harper's Bazaar* he'd seen all over random newsstands in subway and street. From a foot above she gave him a shy, kindly smile—beautiful even under fluorescent panels and built like a stallion; you could pat that long bony nose, offer it a lump of maple sugar. By the bar, waiting in the premidnight mob for three flutes, he was still probing, how you wanted her nude not even really for a lay but just to watch her moving, bones and muscles working through that fabulous ass and sleek tawny haunches, when:

"Matty!" Arms vised him from behind; Matt wriggled back an inch to see—Marshall's hideous face, made up with clown white: maybe meant to look geisha-ish but coming off more Kiss. "Isn't it so good to hug? You're so little! I've never hugged you before. Mmm." Marshall rubbed his face along Matt's shoulder, despoiling his black shirt.

"Aloha, Marshall." He squirmed free.

"Matty." Solemnly, with a closed Chinese fan, Marshall batted Matt's shoulder. "This is Jonathan." He struck the shoulder of a greasy-haired man standing beside him in a ratty flannel shirt and shitty jeans.

"Pleased to meet you." Jonathan raised a green bottle in toast. A wry half smile played on his lips, and his eyes looked sober, untouched by New Year's. Plus he was dressed not remotely festive, more, like, for a garage band. How on earth did he get in?

"He's been wanting to meet you. *And*," throwing Jonathan a giddy glance, Marshall bent to shout by Matt's ear, "can I just say: it's *to*tally *fab*ulous tonight. You don't get all teeth-grindy—pure, sweet M D M A. He'll give you some. Won't you?" Marshall stood up and smacked Jonathan's scrawny flanneled biceps with the fan.

"Eh? What's that?" Jonathan held his beer to the side to edge in closer.

"You'll give Matty some candy?" Marshall was rubbing Matt's back.

Teeth-grindy? Candy? But Matt kept his face airy, knowing. Of course.

"Sure, of course I will," Jonathan replied, calm, unsurprised. "How many hits do you need, eh? Like five, seven? How many are you?"

Check: I get it. Hits: drugs! "Three," Matt squeaked. Now what? Were they going to stab him from the back with a spurtling needle?

"Oh, give him seven. He'll be your best friend," Marshall sang out, both hands grabbing Matt's back and pushing him forward with maternal élan. "Won't you, Matty?"

Jonathan was fingering around in his pocket, his lips pursed in a bemused, ingratiating expression. Expecting something. "Put out your hand, low," Jonathan cautioned him, while Marshall pressed him from behind—

"Guys, I'm not sure I want to, I'm kind of . . . taking the night off!" Matt's hand was practically trembling by Jonathan's hip. "Okay? Maybe another time? Thanks?"

"Oh my God!" Marshall laughed so hard he had to clutch the bar. "Did you hear that?! Isn't he so cute?" he gasped to Jonathan. "Such a baby!" Wrinkling up his eyes, where the white makeup was beginning to pucker on the lashes, he grasped Matt's cheeks, pinching them chipmunk. "I could just eat you alive!" he howled, horrifyingly accurate. "Baby," he bent now to purl into Matt's ear, "you are going to adore Ecstasy."

Oh, *Ecstasy*. Hmm. Interesting. That British drug, the rave drug—

what they were always referring to in limey mags. So it's come overseas. Well, that wasn't much of anything; people did that all the time, apparently, office boys, ordinary sorts, not junkies either. Like, just a step above pot. Scaredy! When Matt walked back to the table, he carried three gleaming flutes in his hands and seven white pills in his right pants pocket.

"There you are!" yelped Sophie. "It's almost midnight! What happened?"

"Do you see that guy by the bar with Marshall? Look again. Wearing flannel—"

"Kind of white bread?" she asked.

"White trash is the expression," drawled Jason.

"The oddest thing just happened." Matt leaned in, smiling sheepishly, and began.

No way was Jason's response, clapping his plump hands, and *omigod, this is going to be the best New Year's everrrrr: I wouldn't mind,* chimed Sophie, a mischievous smile puckering her lips as she reached to lift a smoke from her pack. "But what's it going to do to us?" Matt wanted to know. "Is there any potential long-term damage?"

"Damage, schmamage," argued Jason. "Listen, you've got plenty of brain. What's one of anything going to do? It's not addictive, I've definitely heard that."

Sophie shrugged, picking tobacco from her tongue. "I think we're supposed to be fine if we just drink a lot of water. But I don't want to pressure you."

"Well, I do," Jason sniffed. "Come on, Matt! It won't be any fun without you."

"We're not going to do it without him," Sophie chided Jason.

"Think about how it fell into our laps. Weren't you just saying about tonight, best time? Think about how special this'll make it. It's like it was meant to be," he tailed off in a faux-sentimental breathy murmur to Sophie.

The boy sure knew how to play him. But, indeed: this had fallen into their laps, like a little golden key, a mark on the special door of New Year's Eve.

So right after the midnight cheers (drinking only sips: didn't want to dampen the X effect) and a big moist New Year's kiss with Sophie, they each placed a half-inch white pill of faintly alkaline tang on their tongues. And swallowed a storm of water. And waited for the "afterwards" to show up.

"Stop," said Jason the millionth time Matt asked Sophie how long it had been. "We just have to relax, I think. Stop stressing about it, you know? Either that or take another."

"I don't want to take another one," said Sophie. "Too strong." The sound slowly escaped from her mouth like helium from a balloon-blowing machine. *Onnggg*.

Matt and Jason glanced over at Sophie. At each other. *Hmm*. Back at Sophie.

"I, I," Sophie broke out. Her lips flushed and curved, her eyes dilated. "I think I may be feeling something," she purred, "a little something."

"Yeah? What does it feel like?" Jason demanded.

"I don't know. I . . . I don't know. Know."

Know? Or did she say *no*? Something trembled in his legs, and the arms were mildly, um: airborne. Curiously.

"Just . . . light." Sophie nodded.

"Yes!" Matt burst out. Dear, without meaning to; action without will.

"You're feeling it too?" Jason swiveled to face him. "Great. I don't feel shit yet," sighed Jason, playing with a match.

"Oh, you will," said Sophie mysteriously. She took Matt's hand and squeezed.

"Yeah . . ." Who said that?! Whee!

"Oh my God," said Jason, rising up like a cobra, "whooooo-oh!"

They laughed. "Are you feeling it now?"

Yes. The answer to any question should always be *Yes*. What a good word, positive, an approbation, an acceptance. Go with the flow, as they say, sit back and savor the ride. God. What a strange bird he was, always erecting barricades, trying to wall himself off from everyone else. As if one person, alone, could ever be an island unto itself! Really, it was all just like Marx—Hegel?—said years ago: the nature of being, it doesn't show itself up as severally; you have to think broadly, in parabolic waves.

Thesis, Antithesis, Synthesis. There's no such thing as *individual human fate*. No one is separate; all of us are working like mitochondria in a big world body. Boy—how long he had had it wrong.

"The difference between anyone," he blew out lovely smoke, "it's just semantic, you know?"

"Totally," said Jason, swooping his arms through the air.

Look at these *people*! God, everybody's so *good*. Open together, they're just opened and opening—how they're looking one another right in the eye, and hugging, passing something between them: a human wave, electromagnetic, a sort of force...ah, they're all on this, they are. Absolutely. How long has this been going *on*? It's *fabulous*. It's like an underground brotherhood, like some kind of communion. Yesss. It's the New Communion. Into redemption, the *vita nuova*, New Life with other people. Ha, not a wafer anymore—this tiny dry pill on your tongue.

This tiny dry pill.

They walked home as the wraiths of morning mist had begun to loosen from the piers. Fresh-squeezed orange juice shone in the ice-packed displays outside delis; they bought three and stood on the curb smiling, smoking, blinking in the bright sun. But already something was making itself felt: it was manifest to him as a whiff, a brooding.

All morning he lay buried alive. In a semblance of sleep at Sophie's: hands curled over his chest stiffly as the statue of a medieval king carved on some coffinlid of marble. The slightest sound—the heaters, even the air at his ears—formed into raw electronic music, alien songs. The days hung out before him, lifeless sheets on an old clothesline.

He curled into a ball. Suddenly a sense of free fall—vertiginous, helpless against this—*gravity* that whooshed him down, black stories—

It was night when he opened his eyes. Jason had to pull it together for some aunt's dinner, and Matt and Sophie sniffed out a meal of cheap Chinese up Second Avenue: where he shoveled piles of lardy beef until a stomachache set in. They walked downtown through the New Year's aftermath, bottles, confetti, vomit. Great pachydermic street-cleaning machines hummed across like moon buggies. He held her hand, he and

she silent, the last man and woman left in the calm after some cataclysm
has rinsed the earth of life.

The next day slid out between their fingers like silty water. The three
of them had brunch in the East Village, drifted to a thrift joint
where Sophie attempted ill-fitting sweaters, and flipped through record
bin after bin. Dizzy, Matt lurched from the store, sat on the curb. Down
the street a police car slid around the corner, lights whirring but no
sound; nothing to slice this gray gelatin fog that filled the world both
outside and in him. Even the smoke from his cigarette seemed to hover,
immobile.

"I feel awful," he had to confess when Jason and Sophie blocked out
the sky beside him.

"Oh, baby." Sophie bent to put an anxious hand by his neck. "Sick?"

"Not sick, just . . ." He stared at the bubbles of asphalt beyond his
sneaker.

"Down," decided Jason, standing stock-still behind Sophie.

"Tre*mend*ously," Matt agreed.

"I thought you guys knew." Jason readjusted the vintage wastebasket
in his arms, staring westward down 10th, where the sun was a purplish
wound punched in the haze. A fat kid holding a pink trashcan like the
only thing he wants to save from our botched planet. "You're supposed to
be, like, eating bananas and oranges to restore your serotonin after."

Matt held his temples with both hands. *How would we have known?!*
he felt like shouting. Though, true: it did ring vaguely familiar, from the
articles he'd scanned. "I thought you said there was no damage," he said
finally.

"No long-term damage," Jason corrected. "Post-Ecstasy blues. This'll
go away in a couple of days." But the sigh he let out sounded uncertain.

What a way to begin a new year. The only real event that Tuesday was
Vic telephoning that Matt had *done good*, that he had been watching the

crowd carefully and was satisfied Matt had done exactly what he'd wanted. Somehow this news only exacerbated the feeling of emptiness. Whatever the Ecstasy did *(never again)* blended into a general malaise, as day after day devoid of class, of activity, passed, and January showed itself gray, mild, pissy-mild. So much for vacation. His single project in those days that eroded away was to make up properly with his mom. He drafted a letter, but everything came out sarcastic and cruel—*I'm fine, hope your Christmas was good;* how could he say that and mean it too? At last, the Friday before school started up, he called, waiting to catch her right after the *Golden Girls* rerun at nine, happy-mood time.

"Hi." Her voice was simple: flat and small. "Do you want your present?"

"Do you want *your* present!" he repeated, trying to sound bright.

"Oh." Her heavy breathing. "Wanna—wanna come home this weekend?"

"You know, Mom, classes are getting under way; I was thinking—why not come to the city for lunch? That might be fun!" On his turf for once; why shouldn't she?

Silence. Finally, "Oh, Matt. I don't really feel like, it's just all the traffic, and nowhere to park..."

"Got it," he said tersely. "All right then. But we'll just...maybe have lunch." At least some form of compromise. "I can't stay the night."

So on Sunday he bused out. All through lunch at Spanakopita on that last day of break, neither said a word about his hasty leave-taking, his job, or anything but weather and tabloid gossip, old hat enough for them. It could have been any Sunday from high school, with the old people in the booth behind poring over the *Times*, the same familiar mustachioed waiter, the same spelling errors on the menu and vista of the desolate street beyond brown-tinted glass. Except: afterward she left him at the bus stop, with a kiss, a button-up and husky *Be good*, then drove on without him into that other life.

That night, though he was still stuffed on grape leaves and greasy mush, he met Jason in the dining hall for dinner, as they settled back to life in ye olde dormitory. "I'm kind of relieved," Matt sighed. "It's been such a long break."

"Your best friend is back," noted Jason, scooping up scalloped potatoes. "How relieved do you feel about that? I saw him with Taylor on the stairs. He asked what I did for New Year's."

"Really?" Matt raised an eyebrow. Unusually thoughtful for Dwight. "What did you say?"

"I told him we were X-ing our balls off. Just kidding. Take a chill pill! Like it would matter anyway. I told him we were at Cinema."

"What did he say?" Matt scrutinized Jason's face.

"He said, 'Oh, is that like a bar or something?' "

Matt snorted. "He knows. He has to know about Cinema. He was just fucking pretending, so he can keep his condescension."

Jason shrugged. "Whatever. Dwight's not even from around New York. It's totally possible he's never heard of Cinema before.[36] Now *Tayl*or, on the other hand," Jason spooned up a quivering cube of green Jell-O, "Taylor *is* from Greenwich."

"I just cannot wait for the day when I explode it in their faces. I simply can't *wait*." He gripped the table edge as he leaned in over his tray.

"What *are* you waiting for, anyway? God, it's been, what, more than a month! Like six weeks. Why won't you just tell them straight out? And fucking quit your work-study already."

"I *am* going to quit my work-study, thank you, but I am *not* going to 'just tell them,' as you so quaintly put it. Instead, I'm going to rub their fucking faces in it. I just need a tad more time. I want this to be a moment I can treasure forever."

"Hey." Liza Andrewes was standing by their table. Ludicrously beautiful: dressed in a simple white T-shirt and jeans, but, jeez—what legs! Like a giraffe! Head like a Madonna *del quattrocento* and oh, oh, oh. "You're Magic Matt." She shuffled her big tall-girl's feet. "I'm Liza."

Shouldn't he say—we've met? You know my girlfriend: Sophie, Scott, art class? "Hey," he sniffed, affecting ho-hum.

---

[36] Quite possible. I lived in New York for nearly one academic year before I had heard of this night-club.

"I came to your party the other night." She talked weirdly slow; Matt had to grope his way over each low molasses-dripping syllable. For a long moment (during which he may have said *really?* or *royal,* or simply *rule,* though in a firm authoritative voice) she held her head cocked, looking wayward at the ceiling—then straightened, nervy, awkward as some young swan in a land of geese. "I just wanted to tell you." She winked. Shyly, she touched the back of his hand on the table and bounded away. At the exit, she turned back for a wave; too late, he erased the slight, accidental smile from his lips. "Bye," she crooned, her glance loitering a moment on his face before she disappeared from the hall.

Jason twirled his finger. "*She's* a leettle cra-zy."

Staring down at the film of milk in his beige bowl, almost blushing, the skin of his hand a scalding-hot site of forest fire.

9.

The world began to fill again, like an aquarium after its regularly scheduled wash, as kids settled back from break. A new semester: it's a fresh start, a New World, a chance to erect a tiny utopia on virgin soil. Matt shaved his schedule expertly as a barber. No classes before noon, four core guts *sans* response papers, just final exams for a blitzkrieg cram-time at the end of the term. Japanese, it was true, would have to take a backseat until next year; our time, sadly, is short, and there exist such things as duties. In consolation he bought luxe notebooks with metal covers and hundreds of snowy blank pages.[37]

He quit his work-study position. Some kind of instinctual poor-boy in him had been scared of surrendering it on the chance that Cinema turned out illusory or fleeting. He well remembered filling out those endless financial-aid forms, and the excitement on learning he was going to have the chance, by brawn as by brain, to attend NYU, with a little elbow grease, a little standing on his own two feet. But with the

---

[37] What did our hero, in fact, study, at his famous university? I have reconstructed Matthew's schedule for Spring 1996: Conversations of the West (so-called „ConWest"); Natural Science II: Evolution of Human Nature (succinctly: „Sex"); Expository Writing („Expos"); and one elective beside those required MAP courses, The Greek Heroic Age (I like this one: „Heroes for Zeroes").

big New Year's check together with the week after racking up nearly a cool grand, there was no need anymore to push around rolls of TP. And what if someone saw?

For there was a brand name to keep up now, that much was sure. After break, there was a discernible difference in the nature of his relations to peers. First off, the surfeit of glances. Nothing obvious, no, but definite all the same. He had for months stalked the halls and walkways of campus like a specter; could he fail to notice now how their gazes lingered on his face just a moment too long? One day Jason shot breathless from the stairs to announce that Christine from his own ConWest section had asked, wasn't he friends with that guy Magic Matt? Because they had been spotted together. *Spotted.* As if he were a celestial body that materialized only in special moments. And Tuesday, didn't he halt a conversation in mid-flight? At the crook of the stairs, in Meyer? There instantly three girls had begun to preen, discreetly checking hair and nails: all too plain a giveaway for one who has specialized in covert surveillance.

He stopped going to meals in Third North. Too risky: he couldn't be seen dining alone, like your run of the mill loser, nor sharing in such a prole diet. So the days Sophie and Jason were taken up by class and couldn't make it out somewhere for lunch, he dawdled in stores, fondling leather shoes or squinting at the cut of pants, then at the last possible instant snarfed down a tray of sushi standing up in one of the Japanese grocers near the park. Funny how like the old days of fourth, fifth grades, squeezed between bookcases to eat lunch while thumbing through those lovely paperbacks of three English children solving mysteries. And wasn't that odd? As if celebrity were somehow inversely related to sociability, so the more he had of fame, the more solitary his days grew...

Well. Let's not get mawkish, now. And, anyway, not exaggerate: really speaking, it's hardly *everyone* you're so famous for. Just the artsos, trendies, ravers, speed freaks: fringe groups, in a way. While the whole indistinguishable mass of the common herd remains unmoved—besides: do you suppose the prepsters have heard of you?

Droll as ever was the suite in Third North, with its pure status quo of inattention. Josh, who still ignored Matt thoroughly to cast his pearls before Dwight, appeared to be growing in his mushroomlike fashion toward a group; he even seemed now to have a pale and bespectacled lady friend of his own, though this appeared more sisterly than sexual. Meanwhile, Dwight was thick in some dark business of fraternities. Strange cues in phone calls: rushing? And envelopes with Greek letters pushed under-door. (Well, fine, see if I care. Because I don't.) The few times Dwight crossed his path, the idiot doled the same condescending smile as ever. "The Sharps have a concert tonight, maybe—oh, you're going out? Great!" Beaming as if Matt had just taken baby steps or said a remarkably precocious sentence. The only real signal of newness in their relations were the increasingly frequent comments on Matt's sartorial choices. Once when Matt came in for a quick change, it was: "Wow, that's a long scarf! I bet it's really warm. Can I try it on?"

—And, with Josh gazing all gaga at Dwight, what else could Matt say but *okay*?

Instantly the badge of office was whipped from Matt's neck and slung on Dwight's body: buffoonish on the broad form, with its long-sleeved polo, Gappish bland jeans, and boat shoes. "What do you say, Josh? Is it me?" Turning his big chest this way and that, aping a girl before a mirror, while Josh, chuckling, lamented, "I don't know. It's kind of long."

"That's how it's supposed to be," Matt snapped, and "you can wear it a variety of ways," absently quoting the salesman's demo before he managed to catch himself.

Yet too late, it turned out. "I guess I'm just not such…a sharp dresser," remarked Dwight, handing it back with a good-natured smile.

From then on that became the code word, the cursed nickname! Even from the end of the hall, the blasted loon would call out, *There goes the sharp dresser,* in tune to "Here Comes the Hotstepper," that dancehall song so popular last year: so that Taylor or Adam Faire would cough to hide their laughs as they descended the stairs.

Clever, this Dwight. A worthy combatant.

* * *

"What's the big deal?" asked Jason the Wednesday after classes started, installed in a booth at Bretagne over a vat of hot mulled wine. "Do you really want to, like, go chill with those frat boys and pound some beer? Please."

"You fail to discern the point, friend. It's the *principle*." Matt blew on his cup.

"Ri-i-ight." Jason fished out the ladle from the crock. "What fucking principle?"

"If you have to ask..." Matt shook his head and lit a match. But he leaned in before touching it to cigarette. "First off, should my scarf be grounds for a joke?"

"Maybe he's trying to be nice. Friendly." Jason wiped his mouth with a napkin.

"Oh, so *that's* it," Matt scoffed. "Anyway: second," he took his sweet time to wave out a second match, drag hard, and exhale, "I don't see why we shouldn't have been invited to join."

"You mean *you*. I don't think frats are too keen on fairies."

How did Jason not see? *Now* how was he supposed to make Dwight cringe with repentance—when the creature had his own busy social universe, a universe that took no notice of the claims of Magic Matt? How could he claim a superior title, so passed over?

"Maybe you should invite him to Cinema. Maybe he's mad you never did." Jason folded his arms over his round chest. "Just for strategy, I mean."

Sophie was back from the bathroom and slid in next to him on the wooden bench. "This place rocks."[38] Her eyes shone. "There are reindeer heads in the women's room!"

---

[38] As a Bretonne, also Lisanne was unaccountably charmed by this, it must be admitted, inauthentic „rustic" bistro. But then, this liking came during that phase in which she refused to eat my cooking. Of course, one may comprehend that after lecture and office hours and seminar and committees she had no strength to join with me in the cooking, and what other labour did I have to do besides? Yet let us be clear on one subject, my food is both tasteful and satisfying, even though vegetarian. Let her try again my aubergine wraps, or better: my Moroccan *tagine* with plums. Yes, let her try it again! Lisanne, it is a dare! Do you hear me?

"Mm," said Matt.

She sighed. "Don't tell me you two are still on Dwight."

"What do you think?" Jason smirked.

"Well, he's always seemed nice enough to me." She gamely lifted the ladle.

Waigh waigh wauuugh—I ruv you, Rat. He kissed her little cold hand. *Never shall you know of what I must avenge.*

"Besides, I'm telling you, Matt, those frats are totally *not* anything. You would never want to go hang out there with those people." She wrinkled up her nose.

"So!" He pounced on her flimsy clue. "See? Even you've been to frat parties, haven't you? Just as I say: they're inexorable. And you both still claim they're not important?"

"Ugh. I was a freshman—I didn't *know* any better," Sophie squealed. "If I had thought I could get into Cinema with the famous Magic Matt . . ." She threw a napkin ball at him.

"Ugh, God." He clapped his hands to his head. "My mom. I'll so never hear the end of it. I barely managed to convince her I don't want to do a cappella. *Did you hear, Dwight got into his favorite frat? Isn't that nice? Oh—you didn't want to. Oh sure.*"

"He's hopeless." Sophie rolled her eyes at Jason across the table.

"Remind me again why we hang out with him?"

She studied Matt and pursed her lips. "Hmm . . ."

"Oh yes—free drinks." Jason slurped his goblet. "Of—candied wine." He cracked up.

"*Mulled* wine," said Matt. "It's something like mead. Surely you've heard of mead before. Top off, anyone?" Reaching for the ladle. "If you will humor me, lady and gentleman, I'd like to present for you a little dream of mine called *nemesis*. You know, the Greeks had this goddess, a kind of avatar of retributive justice?" he began, as Jason, toying wearily with his fork, sent a probing look across the wooden table to Sophie.

*   *   *

Oh. Dear.

Matt pushed up, jeaned and smoky, in the swaying sheets at Sophie's as the black clock by the bed flared the alarming time of close on noon. How? A note from her lay on the kitchen table—*Don't forget: the Chan at 4:00*—rather brusque, in sum: hopefully he hadn't annoyed too much last night? All that Dwight business; please, no one's interested in your resentments, sir. Well, now—a little present? Flowers? He could hang around after class and find her some treasure; try that junk store on West 3rd?

In the one o'clock ConWest lecture he managed to limp to, Simonson droned on about the Black Death, and the buboes, and the rats scuttling across the galleys of seagoing ships, until Matt felt it rise in his throat, a little ocean of his own from mulled wine, general bile. . . . Leaning a hand against the seatbacks, he teetered last out of the classroom.

And there across the corridor: Liza Andrewes, huddled with two unfamiliar guys.

He was still reaching for his game face and a scrap of clear head when she pushed off from the wall with one easeful kick and strode up on her stilt legs to him. "Heyyy." A flash of smile above her red quilted jacket, ruffed with white at the neck and cuffs. Her face was cream and rose, flushed with cold, wisps of blond curling over the smooth wide brow. Her topaz eyes were obscenely open, clear of the veils of common social modesty.

"Hey, Liza." He caught himself, added a bored glance. "It *is* Liza, right?"

"It *is*!" She grinned at him as if he'd referenced the memory of an intimate something just between them. Such an American grin: perfect white teeth, so simple with entitlement. "Which way are you going?"

"Um." Vague gesture to the exit doors. Now what? "Sullivan," he snapped.

"I'll walk with you." She fell in step with an impetuous skip. "So." They ambled down the stairs outside into a cruelly brilliant January blue sky. "Are you gonna have another party this week?"

"It's every week. Every Friday."

"Can I come?" She turned on him eagerly. *Can I have a pony? Huh, Dad, can I?*

He gave her an appraising look: she stared back boldly. Gorgeous, and knows it. "All right." He twisted back to face the pavement clouded with kids hoisting book bags, unlocking bikes. Were his legs really working? Oh, NYU—do you see? I'm walking with Liza Andrewes!

"Yay." Holding them flat, she clapped her fine long hands, a tiny replication of his bloody heart's hard pounding.

"I don't have any more invites." At least, not with him. "But, even better." He slipped out a business card, held it crisply toward her between two almost-trembling fingers. "Just leave a message, you plus whomever."

They were already at the corner of Sullivan and 3rd, among Italian cafés and garish T-shirt displays. "This is you." She softly kicked a bottle top with her big Adidas.

And if he hadn't done it so often with the randoms at Cinema, how could he have ever held himself steady while kissing both live cheeks of that radiant thing?

"Ciao, bella. See you tomorrow," he called, breaking into a lope away south.

What an unexpected turn for this hung-over afternoon. At least he hadn't said anything awry. Back at Sophie's he undressed, eased into her bed for a recuperative nap, but lay a long time awake—reviewing Liza's silty lashes practically brushing the tent poles of her cheekbones, feeling his way again over the strange jerks of her mood, now instantly manic-thrilled, now soft-voiced, now bold-eyed, unpredictable—and it seemed had barely drifted off to sleep . . . when the door opened.

The lady of the pad marched in to drop her tote bag with a crash on the kitchen table. "Forget something? It's four-thirty." Sophie stomped over to the bed, wearing an ugly pink pomponed hat, hands pinioned grimly to her waist. "I waited outside the Chan for half an hour! What do you have to say for yourself?"

Panicked, unthinking—"Oh no. I must have: slept through it. Slept till now."

She harrumphed, then sat down on the bed and gave him a grudging kiss, by the instant getting less affronted in inverse proportion to his own growing terror.

Why? Did he lie? To *her*? "I'm so sorry," he gushed, rubbing her back, trying to press her at his chest, oh, to pillow, block it all out. So much for buying her a present! Here comes Liza Andrewes, and instantly— hypnotized, brainwashed.

"It's okay." She was laughing, squeezing out of his grasp. "You *were* pretty drunk last night." She gazed at him gravely. "You were…you were really psycho, you know? Really obsessive. We could not fucking shut you up!" She laughed once again, but thin.

"Oh God." And now this perjury, inexplicable, hideous…"I'm so sorry." Reaching for her.

"Don't be sorry." She edged away, staring. "Only—maybe you should try not to drink that much. Okay?" She pushed up from the bed, gave him a glance over her shoulder as she passed, sighing, into the bathroom.

He ran to the bathroom door. "No, please: let me make it up."

"Just forget it." She giggled uncomfortably.

"What about this. Can you—Saturday night. Dinner? You've never really tasted my cuisine?"

"Don't you have to 'promote'?"

Was there a new coldness in her voice on that word? "Promote, schmomote!"

"If you really want to. But it's fine."

"It's not fine," he muttered, pacing in the bedroom, hands to his forehead. In no way fine. Stinking, cankered liar—all to hide how bewitched you were by that ditzerama, how you let that painted Jezebel turn your head? Even the blue and white circles on the wall accused him, the fake birds on the branches above the bed eyed him with a new, predatory stare. Look at me, world, I'm walking with Liza Andrewes: was that what you said to yourself? He released a dry laugh, covered by the toilet's whirlpooling flush.

* * *

That Saturday night, it was A Romantic Evening at home, *à deux:* "I can't believe you know how to cook this." Sophie's fork trailed in the delicate risotto *al* squid ink. "Where did you learn?" she asked, taking a timorous bite. "Your mom?"

Matt snorted. "My mom taught me how to use a can opener. Her notion of this is mac and cheese from the box."

"You're so mean." She bit her lip. "I bet your mom is actually super nice. Why haven't I met her?"

"Excellent question." He shot out a *voilà* hand. "What I can say is that it's through no fault of mine."

"Really?" Sophie's eyes widened. "So what does she say when you ask her?"

Ask? He was supposed to ask her? He coughed. "Hmmm?"

"You never *asked* her? You never thought of that?"

"Sssh." He raised a finger to smiling lips. "What you have to do is pretend I'm an alien. Pretend I don't know anything, and you just tell me what I'm supposed to do." He leapt up and skidded over, plopping on the chair beside her tiny ass. "Okay?" Wrapping arms about her middle, looking seriously in her face. And what if she *could:* tell, teach him? Tame him—yes, you wanted to give yourself up to that, like some mute beast walking timidly from the forest, who knows nothing of the ways of humankind. Only to approach; to feel her soft yoke thrown about the neck. Even sharing details about his mother just now with Sophie: it was a step, his hooves clomping awkwardly on the path toward her, toward the one human girl with sympathy for such an ugly thing.

"Okay," her plum-mouth whispered. "Know what we do now?"

"Do I carry you to the bed?" His voice cracking, hoarse. Nipped at her smooth earlobe.

"No," she corrected, with a laugh and a knee pat. Which pained him: why, was that silly, that idea of his? "Put on your jacket. We're going out." She stood up from their chair. "Not out like that." She frowned. "Don't worry about clothes."

By the door, he turned back to see her bundled in the new vintage white-fur coat that turned her into a Siberian princess. "Hey." Touched the hood. Along the cheeks and brow, Asian Blushing Syndrome blotches were breaking out, rosy stripes around the flashing black eyes.

"What is it?" She gave the hood a couple of bashful touches. "Crooked?"

"Nothing." He squeezed her hand. There was something, though, in his throat. "You're beautiful," he said quickly, leaning in for a closed-mouth kiss.

But that wasn't it, not quite. What was this strange feeling that absorbed his body? Outside, neon lights lasered through the crystalline-crisp air as she dragged him down Greene Street. At corners she pivoted eastward and south, pointing, a little army general—he simply clambered over snow-piles beside, on guard against speeding cabs, the red trails of taillights resonant behind like streaks left by some rocket. Ah, trust Sophie: right she was to take them out. Now he could silently give over control of his body, fit feet and mind into a cryptic minuet established by her while the world opened to either side of them, skimming fairy-tale pictures against their skin in gaudy ruby, in emerald, gold . . .

"Are we in Chinatown?" he whispered, agape beneath a veritable totem pole of signs in Chinese.

She stamped, clapped. "Duh!"

Chinatown: how different it was by night! Pigs swinging red-lit like stars on sticks in a charring rotisserie, the bare wooden rails of a closed-up fruit stand, a snack bar from whose door a gentleman now emerged; he picked his teeth and passed without even a glance at them. Yes, swallowed up and lost, they were blissfully forgotten for a moment in the furrows of nighttime Chinatown, its alley-wormholes that slipped one between worlds. Holding her hand: they were skipping down the Yellow Brick Road or dashing hide-and-seek in a movie set while the cameras went rolling on everyone but them.

"Here we go." She had halted at a door, above which was a pretty blue-lettered sign touting something called *Bubble Tea*.

Giddy, he followed her into a large clean room with wooden booths, slid in at the table of her choosing, and unbundled—too giddy even to read the menu, where there were glossy color pictures of drinks in sundae glasses festooned in pastel shades like prom queens on parade. He thumbed through dumbly, shut it with a happy bang. "You pick." While she scrutinized the photos, "You're so far away…" he mused, stretching out a hand over the big table, rubbing her freezing hands between his fingers. He wanted to give her something, to rip something out of his breast pocket and show her, as in *Here is my handkerchief on a platter, my ladylove,* but there was nothing there to give or say. "Oh my," he murmured when the waitress came and plonked down two tall glasses, sweating slightly, with beige creamy liquid and an enormous pink straw in each. His glass felt cool and lovely to the touch. "I love it already." He took a thirsty sip. "Oh! There appears to be some sediment at the bottom of mine."

"Tapioca balls!" she explained. "Yum!"

"Tapioca, no joke." He fumbled his straw over viscous globules: springy, alien. He could not eat this. Black as tar and squishy as, ugh, a kidney, a bladder. "Wow, don't they—give that to babies? So you, you eat them?"

"Just suck on your straw," she counseled. "That's why it's so wide."

"Up—oh, goes right through, hmm?" Disgusting squishy nastiness… Napkin, napkin; there we go, nicely done, sir. "Mmm. Thank you! This is fabulous!"

"I thought you'd like it!" She dragged on her straw with pleasure.

And now, while she told him about real frostbite in the Windy City, about the strange Polish girl in her 20th Century Art, he cleverly secreted twenty-odd balls into his napkin. But every time he looked back up at her tiny shining mouth chattering on: how worth it, how right and worth it, just to keep her like this. So evidently they couldn't come anytime soon to an agreement about appropriate food texture. Yet even that fact, that the machinery of her brain, the apple-sized muscle of her heart, prompted her to incomprehensible urges—it made you want to keep unwrapping toward her enigmatic nexus. The only other customers in the place were five kids, high school, obviously, maybe fifteen, the two boys haw-hawing on some salacious joke. And without her—wasn't it all so? How crude and dull was everything compared to her flashing eyes and wry expressions. She who could turn a walk of twenty blocks into fairy-tale adventure.

"Well, shall we go?" he said at last, when her straw hissed air. He motioned to the waitress. "Thank you again! This was wonderful."

"So you liked it?" Sophie nodded eagerly.

"Definitely!" he agreed, dealing money onto the table. "Really...a *treat*."

She slipped her arm in his as they walked out the door. "And the tapioca balls?"

"Oh—ah, very nice. I'll bet it's beneficial for you too. I mean, if babies eat it. Why else."

"Oh, Matt." She fell against a building wall postered up in red and black and white, laughing. Then she looked up at him, dabbing her eyes. "Wow. You didn't honestly think you were hiding it? You're a *hysterical* liar. And you were making the wildest faces." She squinched up her mouth and twisted it to the side, bugged her eyes.

"Ah-*ha*." He edged up and planted his arm to one side of her, like a jock by lockers in the movies. Her laughter scattered sparks in the alley. "So," he murmured, hoarse. "You like to torture me?"

"Of course!" She grinned, impish, clearing the hair from her face. "That was the best part."

She was beautiful. There under the streetlight. Everything was quiet but the bird in the breast which beat. He closed his eyes and leaned in over the precipice.

And kissed. You could take everything else away. It was enough. This. Point. Lips. Enough to have lived this. Kiss.

He pulled away and opened his eyes. She was grinning wider now, lopsided. "I love you. Oh!" That was it: what he'd had on his tongue, all night—but, God, why? Why force the issue? *Ruined.* He buried his head into wet mildewy posters covering the wall.

"Matt?" She tried to nuzzle her face into the space between his and the wall. "What's wrong? What did you say?"

Saved. By some stray city noise, a miraculous horn? She hadn't heard!

—Yet was that the way? And what will you do now, lie? Again? Make up some bullshit, what-you-said? When tonight, how you were feeling, wanting to come up to her like a wild animal out of the forest, eager for her light yoke: you'll go backward instead of forward, here at this critical juncture? And maybe it was obvious anyway; true, he hadn't exactly been shielding that *ahh,* that delight when she walked into a room, lavishing her very finger joints with kisses, not letting her sleep till he'd extracted his due of embraces. "I said," he began, turning from the wall to take two freezing hands in his. He gazed into her grave face, his heart clenched too-tight in his chest: but only to finish it. "I said, I love you."

"Oh, Matt." Her face looked shaken and flushed even by streetlight. Her eyes half-closed, weary. "I thought . . . I don't know. That we've been loving each other for a long time."

Did he hear right? *We?* "Can you just clarify what you mean by that, ahm, pronoun?"

"Oh my God." Shaking her head sternly, she clasped both his cheeks in her hands, drawing him down. "I mean, I Love You Too. I guess I should have said it to you before. Maybe. But I didn't want to push, Matt, I know how hard it is for you to trust and, you know, believe that other people are like you too. Sometimes I think you get scared, or suspicious, like you can't believe what's between me and you, or you and anyone for that matter. It's like it's all new for you. I mean, it *is,* isn't it? Like," she scanned his face, reflective, "sometimes I've wondered: when was the last time someone said *I love you* to you?"

Last time. I mean, there must have been some time. "Oh sure," he recalled. "My grandmother used to say it on the phone, birthdays, that sort of thing."

"That was the *last* time?"

"And then she died," he continued eagerly.

Now they had to laugh. The sound of that, in the alleyway, so forthright and cheery. "It's fatal!" he murmured (thinking: how did she know so much? how could she both know *and* love him?) into the crisp wind beyond her head. *Murder,* she seemed to purr (or maybe just *Mmrr?*) into his neck. "But you're not going to die from it, now, are you?" he exclaimed, hugging her harder, hugging a whole furred universe in his arms.

"Not if you stop squeezing me," she squeaked out. "I can't breathe."

And when he let her go, their mouths came together so they shared one breath. For a whole white instant. Then: "I love you," he said, and grinned his hot mouth. "Again." Well, now. While she wiped the lashes fringing her sleek lids, he looped an arm about her, dragged her gawky and half tripping along the slim pavement into fathoms of clear night air. Much easier said than one would have guessed, this *I love you,* in the end.[39]

_____

[39] And why should it have been so extraordinary for Matthew to participate in the love oath? Has he not, we may wonder, been engaged in a love relationship for months, even without the saying of this explicit phrase? Perhaps it is only, as Sophie suggests here, his lack of experience with words that come as second nature to many others; what may be a meaningless expression to them is for him a solemn and mysterious sacrament. I have had experience of the love oath only in a single relationship. When now I imagine that out beyond the walls of this detainment facility there are those who say *love* to two or three (or perhaps four? can such double-dealers exist?) individuals over the course of a few short years, I have the same sickly taste on my tongue as when by a boyhood dare I swallowed a teaspoon of Vegemite. Perhaps the truly wise man would, instead of joining his life to a woman, obtain a dog, or a cat, or a pair of large-eyed, sympathetic fish who never fail to respond to your overtures, whose constancy can never be in question.

10.

Love: one could dredge it out by the magnum, yet still fresh quantities bubbled to the mouth.

As January wound down toward the petulance of February, a glowering snowless gray season, Matt absorbed himself in the lover's rosary—for why was it one never came to the end of what was meant? why was it, even if patently obvious, saying this string of three words nonetheless *did* something, indeed each, every time mysteriously reordering the universe powerfully as a magic spell?[40]—and let the whole Cinema apparatus chauffeur itself along for a couple of weeks of his really quite sweeping salutary neglect. That Friday the twenty-sixth, post-Chinatown, through the haze of happiness he half-heard Lacey say ninety-six reduced and six comp had tallied on his sheet. Evidently, what with repeats, like an ab-

----

[40] „Magic"! Perhaps a charlatan's magic! An ignis fatuus? What else should this *love* be called if all that may be required for its illusion to depart is that someday a bald-pate, with tenure, from Seattle, encounter your wife at a reception after a lecture of obscene stupidity—if instantly it seems to her *he* is pleasing, *he* is desirable, and you are not? What then may you do with all the many precious vows of *love* you have stored up, ever trustfully? *Es ist nicht alles Gold, was glänzt,* it is not all gold, what shines! Some is iron with gold-coloured coating, which melts easily away!

sentee grandee, here one may reap without having sown more than a handful of off-the-cuff invites and assorted air kisses. And as that weekend continued, it was almost like old times, those six or so autumn weeks when it had been just Jason-n-Sophie, the Three Musketeers. They went to galleries in SoHo, brunched at Le Gamin on crêpes, holed up with the Sunday *New York Times* crossword. Toward Sunday evening, out of sheer what-else, Matt even managed to crack his Greek Heroic Age textbook to do tomorrow's reading—inspiring happy gasps from the couch, where Sophie was hand-sewing a pistachio-colored cap-sleeve sheath. "Studying? Are you feeling all right?" she teased.

"I love you," he replied. Then dodged the cushion that she threw. And lunged to pin her down until she relented to echo *I love you too.*

But he was, actually. Feeling uncommonly all right. Until, after a teatime section that Friday on the *Oresteia* (during which, like some sort of eager beaver, he nearly committed the faux pas of speaking), he drifted back to Third North for a rare visit. Josh was present, tapping at his desktop in the common room; he answered Matt's friendly *Hello!* with an abstracted grunt. There Matt puttered—making green tea, staring out the windows onto the courtyard below—before he passed into the bedroom, where he lay paging sleepily through next week's reading.

"Sfryu." Josh woke him, holding out at half arm's length the cordless phone.

"Hello?"

A receiver snatched up on the other end. "Magic, baby, where the hell have you been, I've been trying you for hours!"

"Oh—sorry Vic, I didn't get your message."

"No, genius, I didn't leave one, I didn't get that far. Your phone's been busy! Look—I don't know if you realize this, but we're a business concern, we can't tolerate this kind of behavior. I know, you're a college kid, mebbe you just can't handle this kind of responsibilities, so my mistake, we'll call it off, I just—frankly?—I just don't have time to babysit."

Call it off? My God! But how—call-waiting ought to make a *ring-ring* sound? "No, Vic, of course, of course I totally understand, I'm so sorry, I'm really really sorry—"

"Sorry?" Vic snarled. "That's great. What can I do with sorry, huh? Am I, am I gonna pay my DJs with sorry? You just don't get it, do you? I don't know *why* I'm wasting my time with you. Here, how's this, Magic: Sorry. You're fired."

"Vic!" he shrieked. A joke, a jest? But no—Vic's voice was as deadpan as that time yelling at the blond assistant-girl to fire whomever-from-Paris. "Listen, Vic, there was a malfunction with the phone! Of course I realize how serious Cinema is, and I take great pains to make everything run smoothly." Vic was still on the line. Breathe. "I will go out and purchase a cell phone this weekend so that this never happens again."

"Don't ever let it happen again."

"Of course. I will never let it happen again." The *Internet*. *Josh* must have been on the scabrous Internet!

"You see, I had a very important mission for you, very important, and I was just about to give it to somebody else. Wasn't I about to give it to someone else, Miranda?" Her voice chirped in the background. "Who was I about to give it to?" Two pert syllables. "You see, Magic? See how close you came? Don't ever let this happen again."

"Vic, I will never let this happen again."

"All right, here's the deal. Tonight we're gonna have some very special guests in from London, and I want you to take care of them. Astral's doing a show at Madison Square Garden; they're gonna come by the club after."

"Astral?!" Spin cover Astral? MTV award Astral?

"Oh yeah, they're old friends of mine. I've known, whatsit, Keith Aldren, I've known Keith Aldren since he was a baby. Fact, I, I gave him his start. Oh yeah. Years ago. So you just, you know, get them seated, the Red Room, I think that's really more their vibe, get them a bottle of champagne, whatever it takes. Whatever it takes, just, you know, keep them happy. That's your job. All right? All right? All right."

Vic vanished into optic neverness.

Astral.

Josh.

Matt placed the phone down on the bed. He was shaking. "Like a leaf," as they say; how true. He swallowed deeply. Try to keep the stopper on the test tube, sir. Why? That creature has nearly altered the course of our life. Oh, accident, schmaccident. Now that Dwighty has his own line, it doesn't matter, does it? That we *agreed* not to use the Internet during daytime?

He threw open the door.

"Um, Josh"—Matt draped an elastic torso along the colossal top of Josh's computer monitor, while Josh's gaze remained riveted to its screen—"ah, that was my boss."

"Mm," noted Josh.

"And . . . and he said he had some trouble, ah, getting . . . getting in touch with me today." Matt traced loose circles on the plastic, trying to calm. "Do you know why?"

Josh blinked.

"Jesus! You were on the *Internet,* weren't you! Didn't we agree *not* to use the Internet during the day?"

Josh sighed tiredly and stared at the screen.

"You know due to your wholly inconsiderate flouting of our rules I nearly missed a very, very critical assignment? Do you understand that, hmm? Do you get it? Hello, are you listening? Houston to spaceship, do you read us! Do you realize—do you realize that you nearly got me fired?"

Josh turned to Matt. That gray, moon-shaped maggoty face smirked back and mouthed, "I'm sure you can find another job scrubbing toilets."

Ohhh, now that was a low blow. So he knew? Did Dwight? Did they talk about him? And so scornful! Matt had walked away, made one slow circle on the floor, hands clasped behind his back. Now he stopped: from the opposite side of the room he stared at Josh's back. "Care to repeat that?"

Josh swiveled round, resting a dispassionate arm on the chair's back. "I said, you can always find another job scrubbing toilets. I don't think they're too hard to come by."

Matt opened the mini-refrigerator and took out one of those

quart-size plastic containers filled with viscous gruel Josh was always bringing back from Brooklyn. He slowly headed for the window and raised it. "Would you say that again, please?"

"Scrubbing toilets."

Matt dropped the container into the courtyard, checking first for pedestrians. Then he spun on his heel and strode back to the fridge. "Once more please—ah, dreadfully noisy day."

"Scrubbing toilets."

First of all, that wasn't what his job had been, but then of course Josh probably knew that! He took two more containers to the window. "I *almost* heard you that time."

"Scrubbing toilets."

He gathered up an armful and threw them as a unit down. A revolting stain, like a patch of whale vomit, was growing there on the concrete. It was too bad some poor comrade of his would have to mop it up. "You know, it's the damnedest thing—please, accommodate me. Once more."

"Scrubbing toilets."

And then Matt stopped listening; he moved into a frame of pure action. He took out a pair of scissors from Dwight's pen jar and slit deliciously along the y-axis of Josh's precious four-foot-long hanging calendar, whose two sides fell apart like broken wings. He took a small porcelain bell and a mug commemorating some social occasion from the top of Josh's bookshelf and dashed them to the middle of the floor, then jumped on the smithereening pieces. Just when he thought he might perhaps have gone too far, he saw Josh's sunglasses—or rather that clip-on thing that, ah, *le pauvre,* this sensitive-eyed mommy's boy liked to fit over his regular glasses. Matt bent them till each dark circle met its brother; he took the scissors to the plastic lenses and tried to scratch, then finally he tossed it smack into the vomit spot down in the courtyard too. *Finis.*

He fell back against the wall, drunkenly laughed. Then he coughed coyly. "I may as well tell you," he began, waving his hand over the room as if he were a magician. "I am Magic Matt, a key promoter at only the very hottest nightclub in New York City, Cinema. So the next time I have the mischance of speaking with you, you had better fucking look me in the eye like a human. Because this? *This I shall no longer tolerate.*"

Josh's pale face was trained down at the mess of ceramic. Now the faintest of chair creaks, with the slightest of sighs, was his only response.

Matt had passed through a waterfall. The world shone brilliant and hard. Down the stairs and outside Third North, taxis, baby strollers, shoppers went jerking quickly through blinding winter sun. He pulled out a Dunhill and fired it up; why, his hands were shaking, just a bit. With these hands he had snatched, viciously, and dashed Josh's precious things. Now they looked quiet, small. Unaccusable. The little hypocrites. Don't be ridic. Matt strolled across Second Avenue with hardly a thought to the traffic light blooming from yellow into red, to the cars that peevishly bleated by. Since day one there had been from Josh and Dwight a crime against humanity, namely upon that piece of humanity that was him. All he had done here was in the way of some just redress.

With a joyful foot, Matt stamped out the half-smoked cig, clambering into a cab. But by the time he slammed the door closed outside Sophie's—blinking excessively, with a burr in his throat that simply would not cough off: the familiar diagnostics of guilt. God, if only there were a way to be certain. . . . Surely he was not base as a berserker Viking, but an avenging angel, sword burning with righteous fire? Listen, sir. Later we will go into all this quite satisfactorily, okay? Now is a matter of great professional urgency. In less than five hours, Astral. And you.

"Keith Aldren is in *People's Most Beautiful* this year, you know?" pointed out Jason, casually drumming his fingers on the taxi armrest. At 10:15—insanely early—they were headed to Cinema in various states of unusual finery: Jason, a kelly-green silk button-down that actually was rather slimming; Sophie, a tiny Robin Hood hat with woodsman feather and short white lace dress that barely covered her privates; and Matt, his best Costume National black top and sleek wool pants (a tailored British look, he and Sophie had reasoned, futuristic with that edgy Vivienne Westwood sense of punk supplied by a spiked man-bracelet). A shortened version of the Josh affair at the traditional preclub dinner had elicited a few minutes of censure (*That's psychotic,* said Sophie; Jason, *You're so dead*), but then they'd successfully been diverted by the Astral news and began getting in the spirit of this new adventure.

Sophie bit her lip demurely, as if having learned her own boyfriend was in *People.* "He *is*? I wouldn't have thought such a mainstream..."

"What are you talking about? They, like, won a Grammy," countered Jason.

"Two," added Matt. "Trust me. I've just spent about thirty bucks and three hours on magazines." No fool, he had brushed up on his Brit stuff.

An arctic breeze was shearing off the river—Sophie screamed as she got out of the cab and ran headlong inside, leaving Matt to chortle with Lacey, pick up his drink tickets, and scan the somewhat thinned line (weather? season?) penned by the ropes. The next two hours—pointlessly in advance, but why not just check?—he spent mostly running along the path connecting the Red Room with the dais outside, where he would stand briefly with the bouncers to grumble at the frigid weather, occasionally spotting Vic.

"So this is where you hang!" joshed Matt in a conciliatory tone the first time Vic barreled out to draw Lacey aside for some instructional adjustment. "You're certainly never in the Red Room."

"Aww," sang the bouncers, shifting uncomfortably. *Now you gone and done it.*

"I'm everywhere," spat Vic, shooting Matt a manic Jack Nicholson glare. Pointing to his broad creased temple, then spinning the finger toward the crowd, Vic hissed, "You look but you don't see, kid," before vanishing inside.

"He don't like you to say that," declared Alex, the friendliest bouncer.

"It's true, though," said Roger, whose big, commanding face always had a mournful cast. "I've heard a lot of stories. That man gets around this club. Don't know how he does it."

And, as if to prove it, when, finally, sometime after midnight, Astral stepped black-sheathed and sleek from a limousine—in an instant Vic was there, crooning into the ear of one member of the party, who was listening with an absent air.

Keith Aldren, it had to be. Hatefully gorgeous, with cupid curls over his brow, a weary yet open, down-to-earth expression. And tall, an Adonis above stunted Vic. The man laughed gently at something Vic said, bending his head with a gesture of modest princeliness. So these other three must be Arthur Vigelow, James Nutley, Tom Cutter, leaving an extra man with voluminous hair and the anorexic blonde, clearly Keith Aldren's "bird."

—Suddenly the whole party moved up toward the steps.... Matt took an involuntary step back, brushed a bouncer, then pitched forward on quivery legs when Vic gestured to "my man Magic."

Keith Aldren fixed his thoughtful blue eyes on Matt.

And then there came a pause. In this instant—as long as it took before Matt recalled he had a hand to extend for the customary slap, a mouth with which to pronounce *What's up*—he fixated on one feature of the situation: namely, that a mistake had been made here, a real and deleterious error. It was precisely the same sort of gaffe as when, say, a well-meaning substitute gym teacher tried to get Matt in the game by asking that the volleyball be passed his way. What could Vic have been *thinking* to choose him for this errand—why couldn't Vic have left him, in accordance with his humble powers, idle, by the sidelines, content to watch the traffic of fitter forms before him? Was it possible to run with dignity down the dais, hail a cab, and lickety-split be at Sophie's? But finally: "What's up?" he managed, holding out his hand until it was slapped.

"Well. Shall we go in?" said Keith Aldren, with a head jerk to his "blokes."

All down the corridor, Matt kept darting around to make sure they were with him, which they were, untensed, absentminded. Loose. Done this a million times. They were hardly noticing. Maybe if he just kept his cool, did nothing too strange or intrusive?

In the main hall the situation was not such as to impress. A smattering of guido-y guys massed on the dance floor, muscle Ts, gold. "It's a little early," Matt chattered. "It *really* picks up after one or so." Idiot. Like they'd never been to a nightclub before!

"Mm," said Keith Aldren, nodding vaguely.

Matt led them through the back stairs. "I *wish* I could have caught your show," he gushed. "I just *love* your music. But you know how it is, *work*…" He bunched his shoulders and sighed.

A shadow crossed Keith Aldren's face. Shite! Gauche to refer to this as work. At last they reached Coco. "Here we are," he chirped, a touch too peppily.

The bird murmured something in Keith Aldren's ear; Keith pursed his lips. Was there a mote of suspicion in his eye? "This is… the VIP room, right?"

"Oh yes, of course. I mean, of course it's *one* of them—there's the Champagne Lounge and the Booty Den[41] too—but this is the one Vic told me to take you to. I mean, this is more your vibe. Most your vibe. Of the ones we have. Here."

Keith Aldren nodded. Coco opened the ropes, regally. And: what now? Why, what else but—the tables were all taken! He ran at the hostess.

"Well, are they here yet?" Sandi twirled her hair around an ear lazily.

"They're right behind me! Now hop to it or Vic will have your head!" He sidled back to Astral. The bird was squished against a wall, mashed by a vulgar woman doffing her jacket. "*Sooo* sorry. They're just clearing one now. Our staff…" He rolled his eyes.

"No problem," muttered Keith Aldren. Downright quizzical this time. No doubt about it. Tremors of suspicion about our suitability.

---

[41] The Champagne Lounge and the Booty Den are the two other rooms which on Friday evenings also contained parties organized by promoters in roles parallel to Matthew's. Though to distinctly different effects: the Champagne Lounge was in command of „Baby" Brett, whom we have once overheard Vic Spector phoning, and the Briton, Carl-B, who imposed a style of music and dress which has for its shorthand the simplistic, besides inaccurate, label „Euro"; the Booty Den is the place where flock those interested in dancing to varieties of African-American music, managed again by two men who appeared very friendly at first but whom I must have in some way offended, for I was swiftly shown how little I was welcome there.

Sandi appeared and led them to their table. They slid themselves down moodily, surveying the scene with dark glances. "What would you like?" she asked.

"Uh . . ." Keith Aldren raised his eyebrows. ". . . a bottle . . ."

"Champagne!" shot Matt.

"Ye-es, I think we'll have champagne."

He followed lockstep behind Sandi. "Why did you do that?" he hissed. "Don't you know who they are? We're always supposed to give celebs champagne!" But he was all glad hands again by the time, back at the table, she began easing the foam into six flutes.

"If you need anything else," she smiled, "just ask me. My name's Sandi."

"Oh yes," babbled Matt, hurriedly springing at the table (hello, my role here, I should think!), "if you need anything else, just ask *me*. Matt. Magic. Again." He half-felt the urge to bow. "So I'll be over there. Okay. Bye."

He teetered over toward where he'd left Sophie and Jason half an hour ago by the bar, en route lighting a cigarette, sweaty and desperate as a man escaped from prison.

"Hi!" Through the crowd, Sophie squeezed his arm. "How did it go?"

"Hey," said Jason, "are they here? Which are they?"

"Back left, see them? In the corner. Five guys, malnourished girl. See?"

"Wow, it really is them. Cool. C'you introduce me?"

"What was that? I'm sorry, I didn't hear that, I thought you said you were completely insane. Words to that effect."

"Ouch!" Jason grinned. "Hold on to this one, Sophie, he's a keeper."

He flitted, too nervous to sit. Intermittently he visited to ensure Astral's champers was flowing freely, which it always was, without his needing to intervene. In fact, a mild element of humor started to enter the surprised face Keith Aldren made each time Matt checked in, as he answered, "We're fine," or "Fine, thank you," or "Still fine!" But around two-thirty Matt felt a tap on the shoulder: that unidentified fifth guy, with the hair. "Hey," the man breathed in Matt's face, "d'you know where we can get some X?"

"The drug?" Matt jerked a look over his shoulders.

The man laughed through his nostrils. "Yes—The Drug."

He swallowed. So was it really so casual? Was that the way it was done? Like asking to bum a smoke. There, sickly and nasty as ever, stood Marshall's dealer, Jonathan, with a Heineken against the back rim of the bar, where it was dark. All this would require was to say a few words. The illegality of that could hardly be very great . . . or what would they say to Vic? *Your kid's a fucking prude.* And, after all, Vic had ordered him: *Whatever it takes, just keep them happy. That's your job.*

"Sorry, just zoned for a sec. Hold on." He dropped his drink and walked over.

Jonathan perked up instantly. "Where is he?" he demanded, darting his head around. Matt walked Jonathan over to the guy; then hands off, no evidence, he beelined away to the staff bathroom. Inside, Matt clinked shut the toilet cover and sat down. It was over. That simple. The hands, empty and light. He was grinning wide. *He got Astral drugs.* An intimate link, a fine yet indestructible thread. Astral. How far had he come from seeing them on the cover of *Spin* at CVS while killing time in the aimless autumn afternoons? These very fingers had touched those glossy faces posing in the studio with headphones, just four months ago.

Out of the bathroom, he found Sophie and Jason's table. "Well, *that* was too odd." He fell into a chair.

"Interesting," concluded Jason when Matt finished the story. "Hey, you guys," he bent toward them animatedly, "when are *we* going to X again?"

"Really?" Sophie murmured. A skittish laugh.

"Yes, really. It's been like a month—more, since New Year's."

"I don't know," mumbled Matt. "Last time it took me nearly a whole week to get over that blues thing." He shuddered. Just thinking about those gray days brought the ash taste back.

"It's just the *time*. You have to stay up the whole night, and then the next day is wasted…I think you can only really do it when you have vacation," reasoned Sophie.

"Well, I'd like to." Jason crossly folded up his arms. "One of these days."

"I'd be happy to ask Jonathan for you, if you…" Matt suggested.

"I'm not going to do it by my*self*," Jason huffed.

"Maybe you should ask Stan and Jorge, or something," said Sophie helpfully.

"Maybe I will." Jason sulked. Then his face softened; he scratched his chin thoughtfully, drew out a Newport. "Shouldn't you go, like, give them water?"

Though when Matt plowed with six freezing bottles straight to their table, there was only that guy and Tom Cutter, looking at their hands and laughing. "Hey." Matt set down the bottles. "Where're the others?" Let them be unhurt! Not on *his* beat!

"Oh." The guy beamed at Tom Cutter. "They weren't, uh, *up* to it. They jetted." He sniffed, shrugging. "Back to the hotel."

"Thank you," said—or almost sang—Tom Cutter, in a lilting Scottish brogue. "You've been brilliant."

Hmm. Still, it was something; twenty-five percent of Astral. "My pleasure. Well, here's a load of water. Should last you all night. Try to drink it all, okay? And have fun!" he added, washing his hands of the night's task at last.

"Heavens," Matt sighed when he was back by Sophie's side. "I need a beverage. A real one."

"Now? Isn't it time to *go*?" she exclaimed, exasperated.

"Oh please," he kissed her hand, "just one," he kissed it again, "fair lady," again, "I've been so crazed all night."

She clucked her tongue but smiled. "*Fine*. But just one."

He ran to the bar and ordered a, well, double; *one*. In that sense.

"Hey…" Liza Andrewes, leaning there against the counter. Splendor in the garden. She was half angel, half leopard. The topaz eyes drooped prettily under the weight of all that loveliness. Liza flashed up on her Ionian neck. "We're about to cut." Behind her stood a good-looking kid, jet-black hair, an ironic slouch, perfectly reedy like Keith Aldren in dark denim; how are some people just born with it? And a stumpy guy who was bent over lighting a cigarette, surreptitiously, like a flasher. "Jeremy, Marco, this is Magic! So, Magic," slow, serious, "do you wanna come hang? My place. Mercer and Fourth."

Want to come. Hang. An invitation, a palpable invitation—Liza with crew! To *hang*. Utterly different from just using him for entrée! "Huh; right by where I live," he mused. Or Sophie lived. Not to appear eager: one one thousand, two two thousand . . . "Maybe. Let me check with my people."

"Yay, good, ready?" Sophie reached for her purse when she saw him.

"Do you wanna go hang with these kids?" he fired off in a quiet undertone.

"Who?" she moaned.

"Liza . . . you know." He looked at Jason, jerking his shoulder back toward them.

Jason raised his eyebrows. "Sure . . . whatever." He shrugged to Sophie.

She paused, purse aloft in her hands. "Whatever." Shot Jason a glance. "Okay."

Down the corridor they barreled, ducking between bodies curled in shadows. By now, the main dance floor was mostly empty. A queen in a white pantsuit was roiling a balloon slowly through the air—air that stank, felt sticky, as if something viscous had exploded hours ago and was dripping down the walls.

Outdoors the night was full of February, ice.

"Let's go three and three," Liza declared. "Marco, you know the way, you should go with them." She pointed at Sophie and Jason.

Jeremy opened a cab door, and Liza trailed. Then him. The taxi bucked forward from the curb and he realized—forgot to peck Sophie bye as they always did, or even wave, *See you there.* How'd that happen? He was, perhaps, sinking into a warm golden bath of the scotch which flushed from a tight spot in the middle of his chest. And that was the tincture one needed: not these kiddie cosmos Sophie and Jason persisted in favoring. Yes, the edge was off his nerves. The edge was off his tongue, his mind; scotch had rubbed them smooth. Unzipped two fingers' width of his window as they sped past the Hudson—by this point of winter there must be ice floes out there, in the river that glowed inhuman blue under the moon. Inside the car was the same as outside, dark space, silent. You gave yourself up to this, the speed and space of it. Every second left behind, behind, behind, and he, whee, a kid letting go the handlebars of a bike, was merely transmitted like a signal between two ends of a wire.

The car purred to a stop at the corner of Mercer. He fumbled with his wallet but Jeremy paid, without even looking at him, while Liza strode on ahead; he followed into the lobby. "Hi, Rico," she growled to the liveried doorman, who seemed tiny under the resplendent chandelier. "I'm expecting some guests." Catapulting lazily ahead on her twin minaret legs. Behind Matt's back the past universe tingled; the unreturnable world.

She unlocked her door[42] and they floated into the space, a loft-style duplex with a half second floor. Jeremy wandered over to the stereo. "Portishead?" he called.

"Okay..." floated from the kitchen. They weren't boy-and-girl, were they? She was acting too queenly, too independent of him, some Boudicca, an Amazonian chieftess. "Lester...where are you, kitty? There you are, there you are, you must be starving..."

The music oared in, liquid strokes. Not a word had they said since the club, and still there was nothing to say: what exactly *was* "chilling"? If only he could for once, say, plant a tape recorder, find out. He stiffly settled on the couch and lit a smoke. Truly, this place was *immense*. How

---

[42] Liza Andrewes no longer resides here but, it is said, on the isle of Ibiza, where she is involved in the creation of a handbag/jewelry line. (To call this loss from my research disappointing is to state the case in humorously low terms, but one must bear with the limitations of a meagre budget.) The rather famous television comic who answered her former door allowed me to inspect this extravagant loft complex, still rubbing sleep from his eyes as my knockings had woken him from an afternoon catnap, and in fact shared with me a glass of very mellow Irish whisky as he tried to recall (unsuccessfully) whether he had met her.

rich is rich? Twenty feet at least stretched cathedrally above him. Languid scarlet drapes hung over what must be an incredible view. To think a freshman girl lives here alone. A pad like this must cost at least ten times his house.

Liza stalked from the kitchen, followed by a lean gray cat that walked like her, somehow—a wrenching torque of the hips that wrung out flashes of violence and elegance at once. She folded into a high leather chair, her legs tucked below the lithe ass and inscrutably smooth torso outlined by her clinging beige jersey. Head propped on the tall chair back's corner, she gazed down at him, half shy, half ravishing.

The door buzzed. Her long legs scissored open and walked her over to it; Marco padded in, followed by Jason and a shell-shocked Sophie. Okay, he felt bad. But did she have to look so horribly deer-in-headlights? Though she knows Liza: or, at least, they've met. When Sophie's eyes adjusted and lit on him, she beat it over to the couch and slid in, next Jason.

"Hey," Matt said, exhaling, noncommittal, tapping her knee.

Jeremy was packing a bowl with slim fingers. He tamped it, drew, passed it on. Matt dragged, hard; when he lifted his eyes, Jason was staring at him with an odd look of concentrated search: as if there were a shell propped to his ear, and he was trying to hear the sea.

"Where's your mirror, Liza?" whined Marco. Fetching it from the bathroom, he sat cross-legged on the floor to unpeel a square of tinfoil, dumping white powder. He massaged it with a credit card, coiled a bill into a tube, and snorted, threw back his head.

How *sexy*. Even on this midget, it was so *Miami Vice*. Nights of staying home those Fridays of fifth grade watching the show and combing his hair to look like Crockett flashed through his mind. For an instant the reflection of that ten-year-old lard in his mother's Dippity-Do whom he had been glinted out of Marco's mirror back at him. "God, you know Astral?" His head was spinning. He felt floaty and invincible as he stubbed out the smoke. "I had to, like, get them drugs tonight."

"*Astral* was there?" Jeremy looked up from the bowl, animate for once. "Rad."

"What kind of drugs?" Marco wanted to know, licking his finger and dabbing it into the tinfoil, licking and dabbing, like a lizard.

"Just Ecs—" Ahem, the cool word is *X*.

"Really?" chimed Liza, stroking Lester in her lap. Girlishly delighted yet not listening, her face just radiant with the gazing of him, golden. What in God's green heaven could a girl like her want from him. "That's *cra-zy*," she drawled, molasses-slow. Lester stared directly into Matt's eyes, that fine gray tail erect.

PHARMACEUTICAL GLOSS BY DR. HANS MANNHEIM

Now I intervene to douse what may be for some a question that flames. Do you scratch your head and say: what? How can persons purchase and sell ecstasy like one commercial item, and how can they „take" it? Once I considered such issues at a certain memorable cocktail party in the flat of one of Lisanne's colleagues. „You tell him, Joan," was the response of my wife, sighing as she reached for another date. And so the unfeelingly rude Joan[43] explained that Lisanne and she did not discuss some emotional or spiritual state of ecstasy but rather a recreational narcotic of the same name. However, Joan left so many gaps that I was forced to supplement her words with researches conducted on my own.

Ecstasy, rather 3,4 methylenedioxy-N-methylamphetamine, is a Schedule 1 Controlled Substance, which is to say that, on your Federal Drug Enforcement Agency's sliding scale, Ecstasy stands with heroin and cocaine as one of the most illegal drugs citizens can employ. In fact it was patented in Germany, in 1914, by the pharmaceutical firm Merck, as a dietetic medication, since Ecstasy (or let us call it MDMA) interferes with appetite; yet the drug was never manufactured by

----

[43] I hope you never received that associate professorship, Joan. In objectivity I may now tell you: you are boring and cruel and, in light of your pear-shaped rear, should in future avoid white trousers.

Merck. At this moment MDMA voyages from Germany to America, affixing itself in a new soil, as have I.

Important dates:

- 1953: U.S. Army makes trials of MDMA, as truth serum, reportedly.
- Mid-1970s to Mid-1980s: Psychiatrists give MDMA to patients, claiming users can communicate with others more intimately and unlock repressed memories.
- 1985: Drug Enforcement Agency forbids use; raises MDMA to a Schedule 1 status (ruling over the judge's recommended Schedule 3).

Those psychiatrists in favour of the drug's employment now complained that, unlike other Schedule 1 substances, Ecstasy was neither fatal nor addictive; the DEA countered by pointing to several young persons who perished on consuming it; the psychiatrists argued that such persons perished through secondary means (e.g., becoming „overheated" in a high-temperature dancing palace and failing to re-hydrate with plentiful water); but in the end the DEA, having no need of the psychiatrists' authorization, did as it wished.

There is a reason that I did not join the faculty of natural sciences; if you are like me you may be saying, Hans, enough with the chemical history! Yet one moment more, please: take a deep breath, and let us journey together inside the human brain.

I now excerpt from a text received by return mail from a kindly secretary in the toxicological program at the University of New Keene: *MDMA operates chiefly by manipulating levels of serotonin—the brain's regulator of mood, appetite, and sleep—as well as other neurotransmitters such as dopamine, by stimulating their release and inhibiting their reuptake.* So: in these respects, Ecstasy resembles Prozac and other Selective Serotonin Reuptake Inhibitors, which attack the syndrome of depression. When the brain is flooded by the serotonin, the user experiences elation, loss of inhibition, great sensitivity to tactile sensations, increased enjoyment of musical stimuli, a universal mood of openness with others. However, I continue: *Typically the on-drug experi-ence is followed by periods of depression and negative emotions, with as many as 90% of users citing what they call* midweek blues. . . . *Experiments have linked serotonergic nerve damage in laboratory animals to single doses of MDMA, with additional doses resulting in widespread loss of distal axon terminals . . . and an increasing body of evidence supports corresponding neuro-psychobiological damage in humans. Regular Ecstasy users frequently dem-onstrate: memory loss, deficits in higher cognitive functioning, impaired attention, a range of psychiatric disorders, reduced immuno-competence, sleep disturbances, appetite loss, and sexual dysfunction.*

But why then, if the studies are correct, do so many swallow Ecstasy? Who will wish to bring upon himself depression or rid him-self of natural delights in food and sex? There is a youth in my Tuesday reading group (James, Aggravated Assault) who informs me that in the year before his arrest, he swallowed some two hundred pills of Ecstasy. He enjoyed Ecstasy every weekend, by habit twice each week-end, often swallowing more than one pill in a night (as serotonin lev-els decrease, more stimulant is needed). He describes for me feelings of sensory bliss, of emotional euphoria, of extreme togetherness, telling me of parties where psychedelic films are played in vast ware-houses while total strangers approach and stroke and use electric massagers and mentholated ointments upon each other. I am re-minded of those riotous gatherings among primitive peoples Emile Durkheim outlined in his *Elementary Forms of the Religious Life*: beating drums, brilliant body paint and fantastic costumes, wild dancings, that sensation of no longer being one, alone, solitary, but bound into a larger Soul with others of your nature, a sensation for which we hu-mans are said to possess a fundamental hunger. Today, without shamans and human sacrifice, one pill promises such an experience to its taker. Promises, I say: I refrain from any claim about how well the drug fulfils this pledge.

11.

The rest of the weekend withered away from his grasp. Matt never left Sophie's except for some errands and a brief walk on Sunday evening, which turned out to be a slushy mistake. She was in a foul mood; she kept stalking around the apartment in socks and flip-flops, sighing and picking up pieces of paper. She even broke a mug, most unlike her, most—then, kneeling to pick up the shards by the counter where it had slipped, she blew up the hair fallen in her eyes and glared at him; venomously, as if it were somehow his fault. Had she picked up on his minor infatuation with Liza? Fine, not minor, but, say, mild? Or a touch over mild... Liza. She simply electrified, with her topazy eyes, she just—"*Ah.*"

"Mm? What's up?" From the pillow on his lap, Sophie's eyes drilled into his.

His heart tripped. "Oh, just some think-thought. You know. The whole Josh debacle, what I'll do Monday."

Her gaze went aimless and casual again as she lifted fingers to his hair. "You're mental. I told you, you should have already apologized. Go there. Or call him."

The notion was distasteful. The release that had come in that room had been so pure, so out-of-body ecstatic. He felt changed now, woken up a wolf after years as a sniveling sheep. Yet how could he possibly go on living there if he didn't at least simulate some regret?

In point of fact, the situation turned out to be entirely out of his hands. Monday at eleven, on a surreptitious mission to retrieve his note-books, he discerned a brazen red flashing on his answering machine box: the message hailed from Saturday afternoon. Dirk Proctor would see him today at one. On *a disciplinary matter.*

"As you probably know, this can't wait. I've checked your schedule online and you should be free then; if you have any other commitments (sigh), I seri-ously advise you to skip them." Click.

Matt managed to stay calm long enough to drag himself up two flights to Jason's. Two hours to go. They scrapped the idea of class and headed to the diner on 7th for a plot out session. And here, over French toast and fries, Jason persisted in the delusion that he had a cunning plan. Viz., that Matt should play this in terms of responsibility. That he should explain to Dirk how necessary his job was—after all, "I mean, my God," Jason waxed outraged, oratorically righteous, "you're putting yourself through school, and here's this fucking little shit, doesn't have to work a *day* in his life, and he's about to cost you your fucking job, so *wham*! You lose your temper. You're *so, so* sorry, it's not like you meant to do it, it's just a—a crime of passion! Haven't you said Dirk, like, grew up in butt-fuck, dirt schoolroom, blah blah blah, outside of Atlanta somewhere? You just rock that angle." Jason snarfed down a last handful of fries, tossed some cash on the table. "C'mon, it's quarter-to, I'll walk you over."

But what would they do to him? Useless to fantasize that Dirk might grant him any benefit of the doubt; Matt knew how this one went. Historically, all interactions with discipliners had lacked something in the way of justice—from as far back as the first grade, when Kyle Gordon had taken off Matt's pants and thrown these on a bookshelf he could not reach. For though it seemed obvious to him no six-year-old would wish to store his pants in a high place, Miss Penny did not see the matter in the same light.

"I wish I could take you with me," Matt moaned at Jason in the lobby at the bottom of the Third North main steps.

"Don't be so melodramatic." Jason gave his shoulder a brisk pat. "It'll be fine."

Matt plodded one by one up the heartless stairs.

Dirk was waiting for him; Matt had barely touched knuckles to the door when it swung open, revealing the familiar face wearing a familiar disappointed expression touched by—well: was that rage? "Come in," demanded Dirk gruffly. As he shut the door, his expensive-looking robin's-egg-blue shirt rippled, releasing a dizzying waft of cologne. Inside, beneath a window of winter brilliance, another man was sitting in the leftmost of two leather armchairs facing a small wooden one. Now, *this* threw everything out of whack—what on earth? "This is Dr. Saarsgaard," explained Dirk, gesturing toward the pale man dressed in a light-gray suit, woolen V-neck sweater, and limp checked button-down. "Our Resident Coordinator in Third North."

Of course it is.

Dr. Saarsgaard was holding a clipboard above crossed legs. Late thirties, though worn-looking, and very thin; his blond hair bled into his pallid face, his thin lips blended into a raggedy sketchy beard and mustache. Beside him on the maroon carpet lay a rather used-looking brown leather briefcase, abraded white here and there. "Hello," he said in a tense, high voice that seemed to strive for a pleasant note. "Have a seat."

Matt gingerly assumed the little wooden chair. "Hello."

Dirk threw himself into the right armchair, crossed his arms against his chest, straining the opulent shirt over his biceps, and lunged in so hard the chair inched forward along the carpet. Next to fey, frail Dr. Saarsgaard, he seemed a mammoth Mount Rushmore of a person, and sparkling new, a just-minted penny. Throwing restless glances at Dr. Saarsgaard, Dirk squirmed in his chair, the fists pushing down powerfully on the seat as if trying to find an outlet besides punching Matt out. Suddenly he clasped his hands and declared, "Dr. Saarsgaard is the first circuit for disciplinary matters."

"Well, you *could* put it that way," Dr. Saarsgaard informed Matt, a frozen half smile on his lips. "Apart from the many *student* RAs, who revolve every year, each dorm has a Resident Coordinator, a certified counselor. With specialized training[44] and," he lifted a hand, let it drop on the clipboard with a weary, submissive gesture, "all that."

---

[44] I fear that I cannot place much confidence in New York University's „home help," the Resident Coordinators. My opinion has not been improved by the course of Dr.

"Right," Dirk assented humbly. He scratched his jaw, emitting a manly rasp. Then he blurted, "Well, you know why you're here."

"Why don't you tell us," asked Dr. Saarsgaard, keeping his eyes fixed pointedly on Matt, "why you destroyed your roommate's things?" Like a child's psychologist, that's how he sounded, desperately trying to keep his voice guilt-free and bright.

Matt looked down timidly at his own linked hands. *They made fun of me:* ha, that useless old saw. But now how to play the responsibility card Jason had plotted, with this strange doctor-person? Still, he was likely better off than alone with disdaining Dirk.

"Michael," continued Dr. Saarsgaard, "I'm not on anyone's side. You can talk to me." The words sounded as threadbare as his ugly sweater: sheer overuse.

"Sir?" Should he even correct? "It's Matthew?"

"What?" Dr. Saarsgaard blanched, impossibly, further, glancing at his clipboard.

"It *is* Matthew," inserted Dirk hurriedly, looking over the man's shoulder to point.

Dr. Saarsgaard gave Dirk a bitter look. Then, "Matthew. I'm sorry. Please, go on."

"Well. You see, I have this job. I depend upon it. I take it very seriously. I work very hard. It's a lot of . . . responsibility. I am putting myself through school; I'm here on scholarship. And what happened was, I thought an action of Josh's cost me my job."

"An action of Dwight's," corrected Dr. Saarsgaard evenly.

"No, no, that's not . . ." Dirk hovered over Dr. Saarsgaard's clipboard.

"I have it right here," Dr. Saarsgaard snapped at Dirk, a little hairy

Saarsgaard, who by the time of my research had moved to the state of Florida, where as I understand from the office I phoned he now performs management seminars for business executives and where he lost no time in peevishly replacing the receiver on each of my attempts to question him. How many youthful tragedies needlessly occur each year through lack of properly skilled hands in these vital official positions, it may not be numbered.

fox terrier snapping at a mastiff. "Dwight Smeethman. It says it right here on the incident report."

"But I didn't..." Matt looked beseechingly at Dirk. "I didn't touch..."

"You see, Doctor, his roommate Dwight Smeethman—now, Matthew, you have the right to know this," Dirk nodded at him, cold-eyed, "Dwight Smeethman filed the report, but the victim"—he reached to thumb through the papers—"it's the other boy in the room."

Ah. *I'll take care of it, Josh.*

Dr. Saarsgaard moved the clipboard to the left, out of Dirk's grasp. He turned to fix Matt with a steely glance, as if focusing all his energies on blocking out Dirk from his side altogether. Then he glanced down at the clipboard abstractedly. He seemed to be unable to take in this new piece of information. He looked again at Matt, an ingratiating smile on his lips. "Why did the other roommate file the incident report?" The question was obviously for Dirk, though Dr. Saarsgaard kept his eyes trained forward. A desiccated laugh escaped him, sounding more like a couple of joyless gasps.

"I don't know, sir," Matt piped in meekest mouse tones. Sheer evil?

"—technicality," Dirk was saying in his booming confident voice. "I'm sure by the time it goes to Judicial Affairs, we'll have an incident report from the victim."

"Technicality." Dr. Saarsgaard's pen tapped spitefully at the clipboard. "But it won't *go* to Judicial Affairs," he nearly shrieked, "if we don't have an incident report from the victim. Because it should not have come to *me* without an incident report from the victim." Dr. Saarsgaard let the words roll off his tongue in a kind of childish singsong, evidently deriving a great deal of enjoyment from repeating this formula.

"But, Doctor." Good-natured, eyes atwinkle, Dirk manuevered his ripply body before Dr. Saarsgaard's. "Surely we can get one. I'll just call Joshua in here."

Whatever Dirk was doing really was not working. Dr. Saarsgaard was staring at him, his narrowed eyes shooting daggers of derision, his lips pinched. "You'll just call Joshua in here?" Dr. Saarsgaard asked, raising his eyebrows ironically. "You'll just badger a student into entering a formal complaint? Is that what you suggest?"

There was an opening here. A vista of escape. Well, it's all we have: you may as well try. "Sir?" Matt began, taking the cue to studiously avoid Dirk.

"Yes, Matthew, what is it?" All benevolence again, Dr. Saarsgaard turned to Matt.

"What does this mean?" Matt asked, plaintive. "What is an incident report?"

"Well—" Dirk sprang forward in his chair.

Dr. Saarsgaard glared him down. "You see, an incident report is what I have right here." With one agitated finger he poked at the clipboard pages. "Whenever a dispute between residents arises, whenever there is an accusation of any wrongdoing, the victim can come to his or her RA and file a formal complaint. The written record of that complaint is called an incident report." Dr. Saarsgaard was growing voluble, eager, as if what he'd most wanted all along was to explain the arcana of his job. "Then it's my job to determine the truth of the matter, which can often be very complex, you know, which is why I *hes*itate to call myself a *first circuit*," here a ghastly gummy smile, faintly sinister, "because anyway these matters are not remotely like court cases in the criminal system, and it's not as if I am simply passed over in later stages of the process in favor of higher *circuits*. You'll find that in almost every instance, even when incidents go all the way to Judicial Affairs, *still*, it's the recommendations of my*self* and of my *col*leagues that form the basis of their decisions."

"Because you're the experts. That makes sense," answered awestruck Matt. Nodding as if the whole world had generously deigned to become much clearer.

"Yes, it does," said Dr. Saarsgaard, his voice strained dangerously high. Then he clasped his frail arms above the elbows, looking dreamily off as if savoring the truth of this statement.

Dirk cleared his throat. "Doctor. What do you advise—what do you determine..."

"Well, I don't advise badgering the victim into making a complaint, if that's what you mean. That is absolutely not the policy, that is no iota like the policy of New York University."

Now: intervene now, before some actually fair solution might be found. "Sir." Matt sighed. "I think maybe I know why. Why Josh didn't do it." Sounding powerless as the true victim here.

An exultant flash pulsed through the man's face. "Can you tell me?"

"Maybe I don't know why," said Matt, looking shyly down at his hands. He knew this one from debate: give them something, whip it away, make them reach for it like a cat batting at a piece of string.

"Michael—Matthew." Dr. Saarsgaard's vexed flicker of chagrin transformed into an even greater show of warmth when he hit on the right name. "You can trust me."

Matt stared pleadingly at Dr. Saarsgaard, tossing a couple of timid peeks toward Dirk. *I can trust you, sir, but not . . .*

Dr. Saarsgaard caught the hint. "Would you like to speak privately?"

"Oh." Matt pinned his gaze to his knees and sucked in his breath. "I don't want to trouble . . ." He shrank his body ever so slightly Dr. Saarsgaard-ward, as if terrified of some physical reprisal that might explode upon him from Dirk.

"It's perfectly acceptable to request a private conference. Don't be afraid."

Matt lifted eyes full of moist gratitude. "O-okay?"

"Dirk," Dr. Saarsgaard announced, "would you mind giving us fifteen minutes?" Then, "Will that be enough time?" he asked Matt, warming to the role of a white knight of children everywhere. As soon as Dirk walked out the hall door—thrown out from his own suite, how about that!—Dr. Saarsgaard's mood lightened considerably. "Is that better?" He seemed downright cheerful.

"Much." Matt smiled a fragile, abused-boy smile. "Thank you. This is exactly what I needed without my having to—being able to say," he marveled.

"Well, yes. Part of a counselor's training is in psychology, you know. And of course, your typical counselor has been in conference with students you just can't imagine how many times over the years. We try very hard to be perceptive about our students' needs." But suddenly the man shut his eyes disgustedly. He scooped his thumbs along the crinkled lids and cleared his throat. "So, Matthew," his fingers linked around one skinny knee, "why don't you tell me what you couldn't say in front of Dirk?"

"It's like, every time I talk to Dirk, all year, he always"—Matt swallowed back what someone might take for a sob. "The first time I—I had a problem here, in my room," not exactly true but who cares, "he, he basically made me feel, like it was me who, like I was..."

"He thought it was your fault?" Dr. Saarsgaard raised an eyebrow. *I knew it.*

"He said I should go seek help. That I was just *homesick.* But I wasn't, Dr. Saarsgaard, I swear."

"I'm listening." Dr. Saarsgaard frowned.

"So...when I started having more problems, my roommates harassing me—"

"They harass you?"

"—saying really derogatory things, I mean, terrible things, about how I'm poor," well, *scrubbing toilets,* sort of, "and all this stuff, I mean, what could—like, I couldn't go back to Dirk? So, I didn't have anyone to go to. You know," Matt leaned in rapturously, "I had no idea about you until just now?"

Dr. Saarsgaard grimaced at the ceiling. "That's the trouble. What you say does not surprise me, Matthew. Not at all. Students who need me the most, like yourself, there's just no good way for them to know I'm here."

"You mean I could have come to you?"

"And all this time you've been talking to some corporate-lawyer-in-training instead." Dr. Saarsgaard threw up his hands. "It doesn't make any sense to me either. I mean, what on earth does a *cor*porate *law*yer know about fostering..." Dr. Saarsgaard dismissed the remainder of this statement with a wave. "Well, Matthew," he gloated. "What was it again, why your roommate didn't come forward, did you say?"

And because Dr. Saarsgaard was so obviously entering this incident in the great record book of his victories of tedious years at NYU, was even perhaps inventing a few extra things he might have said to this *cor*porate *law*yer Dirk—Matt contented himself with small facts and dark hints, steering clear of outright bald lies that might have woken the man from his pleasant reverie, from his noddings and *oh*s and sympathetic, automatic *That's terrible*s. When Matt was bemoaning the lack of *class sensitivity* in his roommates, Dr. Saarsgaard did tune in long enough to fill him with blab about how Matt would have no idea just how entitled, and spoiled, and privileged some of these kids were at NYU—and although that was in effect what Matt had just been talking about, he neatly switched gears, showing himself properly astonished. *Wow. Really, Dr. Saarsgaard?*

"Nine years at this school," Dr. Saarsgaard was saying. "And let me tell you something that might surprise you. In all that time, if there's one thing I've discovered, it is that when victims do not come forward, there's a very *good* reason. I'm not talking about sexual assault: those cases are the exception. In that event we work with counselors to help the victims come forward. Because we *never badger students* into a complaint. But as a *rule*," he said, craning his neck out unnaturally on *rule*, "in all other disciplinary *mat*ters, whenever the victim does *not* come forward, the advising center, the counseling center, and my*self* and my *col*leagues, operating in *tan*dem with Judicial Affairs and the Dean of Housing, have developed a policy." Dr. Saarsgaard's lips curled up in a triumphant smirk. "And do you know what that is?"

Matt shook his head. Capital punishment?

"We do this." Dr. Saarsgaard undid two pages from his clipboard, neatly banged them together, and mimed a swift rip. The whole event had had an absolutely salutary effect on the man's complexion; now he looked almost flesh-colored. "I tell you what, Matthew," Dr. Saarsgaard said, apropos of nothing. "Why don't we transfer you?"

What on earth? "But—sir. I really like NYU. Mostly. You know, it's just *those* kids. Privileged kids. Like you were saying."

"No, no, no! We'll just transfer your *room*. I mean, it doesn't sound as if you can go on living there, after what you've, you know." Another wave dispatched the troublesome uncertainty of what might have been said. "Would you like that?"

"Oh, absolutely, sir, absolutely. That would be so wonderful!" *Thank you, Dad! This is the best Christmas ever!*

"I'll go back to my office." Dr. Saarsgaard was shoving his clipboard into his crappy briefcase. "I'll make a few calls. *That's* what," he added to the briefcase, "we have *real* resident counselors for." He fished in a side pocket for a card. "It probably won't happen till tomorrow, you might want to stay somewhere else tonight. Do you have somewhere to stay?" he hastened to ask, as if having just remembered his caring act.

There was a knock at the door. "Come in," Dr. Saarsgaard called in a sterner, stronger voice; a chastened Dirk entered. "I'm moving him from your hall group. Thanks for all of your assistance." He was having some trouble hoisting his briefcase and looking official at the same time. "Come along, Matthew." Struggling to get the door open. "You'll get my report," he noted to Dirk—then, just before the door closed, still within Dirk's hearing, he added to Matt, "So you've got my number? You'll call me tomorrow?" And the man in the gray suit trotted off along the hideous mint-green floor.

My hero. My wimpy, petty hero! A miraculous travesty of justice had just gone down, a benevolent wind fanning the flames of flagrant insecurity, vindictiveness. And we have done our part! Found a weakness, trod heavily on that shaky ice—until the whole thing surrendered with a fulminating detonation. Promoting really set you up for life. Valuable skills. A manipulator's training. Matt melted down the hallway, floating along on fumes of pure exaltation, but by the time he touched his hand to the doorknob of 403, crept into the deserted suite—ah, farewell, old shithole, how we loved you not!—this was slipping from him, replaced by up-currents of what was certainly bitter hate.

Dwight. Dwight, smiling Young-Man-Responsible Dwight, Mr. Politician, Mr. Student Body President. Well—your little conspiracy's gone awry, hmm? So much the worse for *you*. Oh, how you shall *suffer*.

Matt tore about the suite. He ripped out a handful of garbage bags from the box on the fridge. Spend another night here?—not under *this* roof, no, sir. Grab whatever possible, return Wednesday or Thursday, midday, when they were never here: not to see them again until he'd exacted his vengeance. The bloodguilt, drop by drop—there, that phrase satisfied. *Drop by drop*—he echoed it in his mind as he threw open his wardrobe. Should have realized Josh could never be capable of this on his own. Yes, *scrubbing toilets*, idle words, but this was outright warfare—to knife him behind his back, not even allow him a chance to make up: and what had been destroyed? Containers of gruel. Fine, a mug, a pair of shades. But straightaway on Saturday, or maybe even Friday... to try to assassinate, snitching to Dirk? That took some dastardly, bald-faced shyster—should have instinctively smelled the foul hand of Dwight Smeethman from the start. But...

Whosoever the malefactor: this treachery was a poor failure. Poor? An embarrassing failure, a failure of the highest order—*bro!* Matt twist-danced on the wooden floor, then sashayed over, grabbed his three bags, flicked the light switches, and shut the door on that whole eviscerated dorm world.

When in the heavy gold suffusion of the following afternoon Matt taxied to the curb before Eleventh Street Residence, the bitter bird of irony and revenge sang sweetly from the topmost branch of his inner pear tree.[45] From the front, a perfect slice of cake, salmon-pink *pied-à-terre:* through a deep-green door with gold knocker and knob, the small entrance hall drowsed in carefree afternoon light. A slick serpentine rail snuck sinuously up the stair; three flights, my darling, and it's a dark-wood corridor where, all the way at the end, tucked on the right, a heavy oak door opens into—

A room. *His.* Flung himself backfirst on the crisp white bed—*bounce!*—the mattress clean and soft to the fingers and—ho! His very own bathroom!

Matt whipped his things from the bags: then it was out to make his purchases. Two hours later he was on the sidewalk of 11th Street, arms full with a case for the cell phone bought Saturday, champagne, berries *du bois,* and a bell-mouthed vase spotted on his way to the liquor store

---

[45] I note in passing that with this displacement Matthew has shifted significantly nearer to my own residence of that period, 108 E. 18th; a mere seven streets separated our two flats.

where they didn't card. He would float rose petals in it. Fill it with champagne sorbet. Tomorrow he might squeeze in a trip for a nice blue silk Japanese dressing gown. Or should it be a red plush smoking jacket?

"Hey!" Liza shoved his shoulder, grinning. "You've got a lot of stuff!"

A beauty of rare eloquence and grace. "Ciao," he air-kissed. "I just moved in to Eleventh Street." His stomach had reduced to a gelatinous ooze: stay calm, sir. "My old roommates..." He shifted the packages and rolled his eyes. "From another planet," he explained, neatly ripping off Vic's line.

She cocked her head. "Didn't you live with Dwight Smeethman? Who goes out with Allison Carleton?"

Matt blinked, long, and studied the curb with a snide gaze: to cover the terror that was exploding tiniest ball bearings through his veins. Small world, to say the least. He ought to have remembered that from her facebook précis—one of those precious New York prep schools, a ritzy address, a sailor's profile down to the veriest detail: why wouldn't she know Dwight's patrician wench? *"Voilà,"* he snickered finally, when his mouth could be trusted. "So you know *exactly* what I mean." Please say yes. Please let this not get ugly.

"God, *Allison*..." Liza moaned, kicking at the curb.

Attagirl! Matt snorted empathetically. "How do you know her?"

"I went to school with her for a couple years, so..." She shrugged. "They were all like that." She looked at him wistfully, *did he understand*... "You know, finally you're like—arghhh!" She thrust her hands round his neck and choked him back and forth.

"Ha-ha," he said, recovering his balance. That was very, very close to capsize.

"What *is* all this stuff?" Her eyes widened. "Are you having people over?"

"Ah, just, ah, couple. Want to? Come?"

She lit up, clearly mistaking it for some top-list occasion. "That'd be *awesome*."

A stolid guy in a houndstooth sport coat approached and laid a hand lightly on Liza's red satined arm. "Liza, hello! Now, this is a rare pleasure. We missed you the other night, uptown." Turned entirely toward her, ignoring Matt, even craning his head down nearer to her on *uptown* as if he didn't want Matt to hear.

Fine. "I'm jetting," Matt sighed. "It's number forty-seven, if you still want to join us."

"Okay!" She waved eagerly, twisting back toward him while the eyes of the guy beside her rested, interested, on Matt for a second.

Jason and Sophie were sitting cross-legged in the hall. "*There* you are," said Sophie, jumping up. "I thought you said eight o'clock!"

They oohed over the whole place. "You have your *own bathroom*?" Sophie gaped disbelievingly. "Oh my God."

"Hello?!" said Jason. "A fucking double bed?" He tackled Matt onto it and pummeled. "You are the luckiest motherfucker I know! Mother-fucker!" Jason propped himself on an elbow, his hair all sticking up in patches. "How did you talk your way into this?"

"Holy shit." Sophie had sat, dazed, on the edge of the bed. "You know you don't deserve this."

They threw the goodies onto the desk—Sophie tossed Swedish Fish, wasabi peas, and her signature melon candies into the vase, while Jason set up his Discman and portable speakers. Then, with the Magnetic Fields cranked and the champagne popped and poured—indeed, hardly spilled at all—there came a knock at one of the side *(closet?!)* doors.

This frightened him so much he squeezed his plastic glass so that it fissured.

"Is that another entrance?" Jason squinted at the door.

"Are you expecting anyone?" asked Sophie, hurriedly smoothing her hair and white eyelet-lace skirt. "Aren't you going to get it?"

Matt dabbed toilet paper at the stain on his gray wool pants and turned the knob.

"Heyyyy!" Liza leaned in the doorframe. "There you are. Guess who it turns out is your new suitemate!" She jerked a slender thumb dismis-sively over her shoulder.

There beyond her shoulder was a large room, outfitted in leather armchairs and sturdy side tables, with an enormous marble fireplace, like some Edwardian hunting lodge. Now the guy in the houndstooth jacket moved from behind Liza; he put out his hand cordially. "Welcome to

Eleventh Street Residence. Glad to have you here." His words fell flat, like slabs of fudge, as his solid hand pumped Matt's.

"Ryan, *Matt;* Matt, Ryan." Liza tossed her tawny hair and barged in, leaving Ryan in her wake.

"Hello." Sophie had come up shyly beside Matt; she gave Liza a nod. "I'm Sophie," she added to Ryan, extending her small hand. "Matt's girl-friend." Jason stood from the bed, diffidently waved his cigarette hand. "Jason. 'Sup."

"Pleasure to meet you," Ryan replied. Perhaps he might have said more, but Liza, already bounded to the desk, now lifted a glass and called, "So let's get this party started! Ryan, champagne?" over the chords of defenseless music. "Oh my God, Swedish Fish!" She jammed her hand into the bowl and dug out a red netful. "I haven't had these since I was, like, *ten.* Who brought these?" she demanded, whirling to face them urgently.

"That would be me." Sophie tilted back her head to fix Liza with a strained smile.

"They're the best," sighed Liza, biting off an aspic-smooth head.

12.

In the morning, the room was still there. Lit up brilliant now and with Sophie breathing, hair spread over the pillow beside him, which meant it had to be real.

The sheer absurdity of it abashed him, that he might be living in this jewel of a Manhattan town house. He collapsed back against the headboard's solid wood. It was quite possible that his mother had never even been inside such a beautiful domicile her whole life. Matt tucked arms behind his head, like a millionaire on a raft in a swimming pool, umbrella drink to hand. A fresh breeze blew in the window opened last night to clear out the smoke; distantly he heard the stirring of cars, but in a soft blurred way, romantic, pleasant. No other noises: no human commerce, the sounds of people going out, those half-caught conversations that invaded and despoiled your mood.

Scratching his bare ass, he felt his way into the shower, groggy with lack of sleep and the weight of last night's events, or dreams, or just the liquors' residuals. He dressed, combed impassively in the mirror. Sophie was still sleeping in the sleek black river of her hair, which he wanted to climb into, close himself inside. Strange to see her there. Well, yes, that was it: they'd never slept together anywhere but her place. This would be a different era for the two of them. He might actually want to sleep in his "own room" at times; it would change things.

Last night he had, admittedly, ignored Jason's and Sophie's dismay at the arrival of Liza and Ryan, and then Liza's Jeremy and Marco from the other evening, and Ryan's friend Isaac to boot, so that even when Sophie followed Matt from the common room into his bathroom, where he was refilling a water glass, and hissed, *How long are they going to stay?* he'd merely asserted, *Probably not too long,* but done nothing to effect it. But surely that wasn't disloyal? Ryan *was* his new suitemate; rude to ignore him. At least Jason seemed to have a nice time with Marco, certainly more than on their first meet at Liza's, though God knows why, that sullen golem. But brightly Jason had asked, *Did your gaydar pick up on . . .* with a subtle toss of the eyes toward the hall, before skipping out the door to rejoin Marco for the walk back to the dorm. Yet his ladylove: who else had there been last night for her to play with? No wonder if she fell asleep before everyone went, splayed on his comforter, the black stocking legs all tangled up in her funny skirt.

Matt ripped three squares from a piece of paper and wrote *I. Love. You.* Attached them to the footboard under her toes so she would see them when she first woke. Then he kissed her and, armed with his new cell, headed out the door.

There was one errand he was itching for: to stop by, see Vic, mention the move. After all, between this cell phone and living alone—how much more ready, standing at attention could he be, for whatever professional mission Vic wished to lob his way? And besides . . . maybe just to find out, ahm, a hint how he'd done with Astral the other night?

He found Vic kneeling on the office floor holding strips of rare beef above his dogs, playful, shaking out their ears coquettishly as they reached up. "Heh heh," said Vic, more to the slavering dogs than to Matt, "do *you* feed your dog Kobe?[46] I didn't think so, I didn't think so," Vic brayed. "Here, c'mon, give it a try, give it a try." Vic was shoving cold

---

[46] Also called *Wagyu*. At one of the unendurable cocktail parties to which Lisanne began increasingly to draw me this second semester, I sampled a morsel of this overpriced cow's flesh. You may recall I am a vegetarian; I am ashamed to admit I tried the meat in reaction to one guest—Malcolm Barrow, who appeared to laugh disrespectfully, then said, in the hearing of several present, *Oh, I forgot, you can't eat this.* I smiled and accepted a piece. Mm, I replied, though it was revolting, and even lukewarm, as if from the living cow.

raw animal into Matt's hand. "Sashaaaa. . . . So just hold it out—don't be scared—just take it right by her . . ."

Teeth closed over the fleshy ball of Matt's palm—"Aaaah!" Devil spawn! Did the monster draw blood? No, but Jesus Christ: look at those puncture marks.

Mouth open in what might be a smile, yellow-eyed Sasha fixed her manic glare on him while gamely bobbing her head.

"Now, you were scared." Vic was scowling at Matt. "Sasha can sense that, she's a very intelligent dog. They're Australian sheep dogs, they breed 'em for that. People will tell you border collies are the smartest, but lemme tell you, my dogs—aren't you, girls? Aren't you just the smartest?" As Matt washed the wound in the little kitchen sink, he could still hear Vic crooning, "That's Magic. Magic. He's gonna run a room. What do you think, girls? Should we let him?"

The dogs swayed back and forth on the couch uncomfortably, faintly whimpering.

"Magic," Vic was raising himself up heavily to his feet when Matt returned, "I'm glad you could make it; c'mon—step into my office." Could make it? Though they had no appointment? Vic tucked himself excitedly behind the desk. "I have some very very good news for you. Are you ready for this? You're gonna have your own party." Puckering his lips, Vic deposited his chin on a palm. Then he opened his hands wide, as if acknowledging the obvious. "The Red Room—it's all yours."

"Are you serious?" His own room? To have and to hold, to shape and to form, whichever way he pleased?

"Marshall's just not, you know, I'll be honest with you, he's just not cutting it anymore, you know?" Vic eyed Matt warily. Then a roguish smile broke out over his face. "Should I tell you? Last week—that whole Astral thing? It was a *test*. I wanted to see—c'mon," he vociferated in patriotic tones, "I needed to know, for the sake of the club, if you could handle that kind of responsibility." He cocked his head. "I had my eye on you the *whole time*. Did you guess?"

Spied on? "Ne-never." Ah, exactly how whole is your *whole*, sir? And the bit with Jonathan, that little biz?

Vic tittered coyly. "I told you, kid, I'm everywhere, I see everything.

You don't see me, but I see you. Oh my God, it was hil-a-rious." He passed his hand in front of his face in disbelief, peeked out cheekily. "Oh my *God*. But you did great. Getting them seated, champagne, getting them comfortable, whatever they need, see, that's what stars expect from us. Making sure no one gets in their face, they can do whatever they want to, let down their hair a little. Right? Well, you did great. I didn't even have to tell you what to do. Did I tell you? You're a natural."

Why don't you just come out and say Ecstasy, if you mean Ecstasy? Just say it: You got Astral Ecstasy; good.

"Anyway. So congratulations. You know, this is a *huge* step for you. Unheard of for a kid your age. I must be crazy. Am I crazy?" He cackled to the ceiling. "I must be. I mean, even Sasha can tell you're scared. You can't do that," he pleaded, suddenly solicitous and intimate. "A promoter can never show fear. Fear is what you wanna make other people feel. You got that?" Matt nodded slightly. "Well, don't worry, kid, luckily *people* are a lot more stupid than my dogs. All right. Now, the invites for this week, they're obviously print-ed, and the next week, unfor-tunately," he shuddered in disgust, "we'll have to get rid of 'em. I want you on for next Friday, which is what?"

"The sixteenth," he croaked.

"Sixteenth of February, that's what I thought. So," Vic thrust a business card forward like a tiny stop sign, "this is Andy Wilton, our designer, okay, just tell him Vic said to call, you're Magic Matt—he'll know who you are. Do it im*me*diately, soon as you leave here. You're gonna have total control. Find a name for the party, an image, you'll probably want to do the first two, three invites, get more of a jump on things than Marshall, but any extra, I wouldn't advise it. You want to stay con*tempo*rary. The vibe of downtown, it's always changing. It's like what they say about the butterfly. You know that thing, the, the Butterfly Effect?" Vic catapulted himself back in the chair at Matt's shake of the head. Then he crossed his arms, canny. "What do they teach you in college, anyway? This is why I didn't need college. You learn more about the real world from me." Vic jabbed the desk: real. "So, all right, okay..." But he trailed off, gazing beyond Matt dreamily. Suddenly his shoulders violently shrugged and a burst of mechanical laughter exploded from his chest: a frightful jack-in-the-box. "I just can't be*lieve* you never heard it before—that's all. I'm, like, dis*ori*ented." But evidently the empathetic smile on Matt's face was not enough. "Miran-*da!*" he rapped out in a reprimanding tone.

"Yah, Vic?" Her voice arrived an instant before she did, trim in an olive and burgundy knee-length dress.

"Tell Magic that thing about the butterfly. The Butterfly Effect," Vic demanded.

"How a butterfly flapping its wings in Japan can start a tidal wave in New York?" she deadpanned, smart-alecky. When Vic threw up his hands she flounced away.

"You still don't believe me!" Vic was incredulous. "Watch this. Adrian—*Adrian!* Is he there?"

"What, Vic, I'm in the middle of . . ." droned a voice from farther off.

"Whatever you're doing, Adrian, is not im*por*tant." Vic rolled his eyes at Matt. "Get over here."

Sound of trudging. Then Adrian appeared, in shades and a tailored shirt and pants, evidently post-party ravaged yet still gorgeous. "What?" he snuffled.

"Tell Magic how the Butterfly Effect works."

Adrian scratched his temple. "You mean how like a butterfly, if it's flying somewhere, like really far, can start like winds or like a hurricane . . ."

"That's enough, Adrian, thank you." Vic waved him away. "Ha! If Adrian, who doesn't know *any*thing—believe me, you must be the last person on earth," he crowed.

"Wow," remarked Matt, trying to fit an appropriate amount of startlement into the word. How tiring it must be to work in the office here.

"Anyway, the *point* is how all the little things together can be powerful. The vibe downtown is like that. It registers everything. The wind's always changing. That's what makes this profession so exciting." Vic raised his arm out proudly, as if, having climbed a mountain, he was indicating the extent of his domain. "I wouldn't trade it for anything. And I would know, I've done everything—*you* know, I've told you, right?"

"Oh, yes. You were a stockbroker," Matt elaborated appreciatively.

"A broker?" Vic's extended hand now flipped over in the air dismissively. "Kid, that's not even—let's see. You wanna hear? You ready? How 'bout I used to do protests with the SDS and the Black Panthers in Oakland? Then I was on a compound in Moroc-co for a couple of years, the seventies." Vic ticked these off on his fingers, smirking at each. "Oh my God, I ran a punk store in London right near Vivienne Westwood and Malcolm McLaren's, I started my own art gallery in the eighties here, I'm talking early, when it was still legit—" And just as he might have called the humble pinkie into service along with an implausible fifth adventure, Vic stopped. He slapped the desk and a giant smile absorbed his face till he seemed possessed, addled. "And this is it. This is the center of the world, I promise you," Vic said huskily, as if he'd been waiting all his life to disclose this secret to Matt. "All righty, Magic." He stood up and held open the door. "I'll see you when I see you. Call Wilton."

"Oh—Vic, I, I wanted to tell you; I got my cell phone and I, uh, moved. I have my own place. Now. I. Got it. So."

"Would you believe this?" Vic punched the door, swerved his head out into the corridor as though looking for witnesses. "I love this kid! Always thinking ahead."

If that's what you prefer to call it! The dogs flew whining at the door just as Matt walked from the office. Fuck you, you twisted dogs, and fuck your whole fucked inbred species! *I* have my own party. Oh, it was too much. Was he giving off some strange new pheromone? The Dirk thing was blessed enough, and now this. *Two* new rooms!

He rang up Sophie and Jason on his new cell, but no one was home. So he bought a sixteen-ounce Diet Mountain Dew and, electrocuted by the caffeine, strode all down Eighth Avenue like an emperor at the head of his triumphal march. Regally he surveyed the cars fleeting past in bright colored waves. The sky was astonishing at this hour, blue-gray clouds in one mammoth blanket up to a dramatic line—after which was pure pale gold, so pale it was almost white but everywhere, without distinction, shining with odd irradiation. Right now were there people leaning out of office buildings above and around him, were there other people staring from hospital beds at that flag of grace, that pale gold im-material fabric? And why should explorers sailing on the ocean not have seen such a thing and known it for paradise, not felt how if only they could scud the waves over to just past the cloud line they would enter that palpable grace? And why should unbelievers everywhere not have seen such a sky and known, without reasoning, with only a revolution in the coronary valves, that God exists, that anything else is deception?

Now the first seed spore of the idea began blooming inwardly, walk-ing down Eighth, which turned into Hudson, which passed by a tiny baseball diamond where kids shrieked, whose sounds dissolved like bits of snow rising up from the earth into that sky. Paradise. The theme for the party. He would turn the hell world of Marshall's Down Below into Paradise. A new decor, with a painted ceiling, spots of gold light. Then the name of Vic's designer, Andy Wilton, turning over in his brain like a whirlpooling twig suddenly made him think: the Wilton what-was-that? Diptych? That English painting he loved so much in tenth-grade European History that he had paid three dollars for a color copy? With cobalt-cloaked angels bending their wings in a meek, elegant line around a slender maiden who was supposed to be Mary. As wonderful as any an image for the first invite. There in the room he would give everyone a feeling of earthly paradise, a haven where all fantasies became material, fabulously real. And wouldn't it really be such a paradise for him? The ending point of struggle?

Matt didn't leave the streets until darkness had shaken all its soot over the world and the enchantment of the luminous sky was blotted out to black.

13.

The sun revolved on its wire. The moon too. There came a dread chill that sheeted your hands in glacial cold should you step outside a bar to take the air for a smoke: then, just as rapidly as it had arrived, the frigid tinge to the weather melted off, leaving in its stead a balmy atmosphere, an unseasonable season, so that when Matt—sodden by drink, he was napping until five on the evening of February 16—flashed open his eyes sudden as if some finger had pressed his button, what he smelled was a faraway and chimerical spring.

Let the wild rumpus begin.

For tonight scores of those kids across the city to whom he had dealt invites—at midnight in a crowded cocktail lounge, at eleven in a corridor of Judson Hall—all this last week were diving into bags or lifting magnets from refrigerators or feverishly looking around their pads for a postcard Lucas Cranach Adam and velvety Eve, a Master of Umbria luminous soap-bubblelike Eden, a Bosch *Garden of Earthly Delights*, upon the glorious gloss of whose verso one could read PARADISE and MAGIC MATT PRESENTS.

Now, at his directives, the Red Room was metamorphosed to heaven by tacked-on lapis panels radiant with halos above ardent angels, and underneath the star-pricked vaulted azure ceiling it hummed and buzzed with black-dressed drinkers and smokers and dancers and laughter! Betwixt the walls' chiaroscuro arches framing open Mediterranean sky above ideal green fields, alongside the faux-marble bar where V-mouth glasses clinked, among the gilt-edged ivory couches heaped with sleek bodies, between the very notes of dancey, ambient music loosed by his brand-new DJ in place of Declan's '80s hit parade, Matt flew, air-kissing here and there, across the space—while the surprise of salary Miranda had just handed him thumped in an envelope nestled in his hot breast pocket. Who would have guessed the raise? Weekly base pay of seven hundred fifty smackers on the little white line of a check made out to you-know-who-yes-him: him, the center of the swirling Heliogabalan universe, so let us raise the names of praise, let us wrap our flesh in flame—

"Your kid just *fucked* up bigtime!" Jonathan twisted his shoulder violently backward, flinging Matt round. Barely a foot off, the stringy hair hung disheveled about Jonathan's sweaty face, and his upper lip was curled. "Your fucking Jason just came screaming at me, 'I wan' some Ecstasy! I wan' some Ecstasy!' I mean, in front of *people*! You just can't do that, eh, I mean, the club is cool, but c'*mon*!"

Dear: Jason must be trashed off his ass. And Xing again: didn't he just? "I—I'm deeply sorry, Jonathan," Matt stammered. "I'll talk; it won't happen again, I assure you."

"That's not good enough!" The lines of Jonathan's mouth quivered in rage. Wow. Louche, laid-back Jonathan was utterly vanished: in his place, this spitting hydra. "You know, it's really *your* fault!" He stabbed a long pasty finger at Matt's chest.

Matt jumped ever so slightly: but no one behind him seemed to have noticed. "*My* fault?" he hissed. I mean, really. Enough is enough. "How's that?"

"You gotta step up to the plate!" Jonathan practically yelled. "Look: look, eh, we probably should have had this conversation a long time ago. Before Marshall fucking—shit. Such a *stupid* thing for him to do, it just—it endangers *e*verybody. Really, really stupid." He checked over both his shoulders. "Whatever. Eh, I guess we shouldn't talk about it, at least not until somebody finds him. All right?"

What on earth? Somebody needed to *find* Marshall? And what could possibly be endangering? Did Vic know about this hush-hush stuff? Vic must—though, *Not cutting it,* that's all the info he'd been provided.[47] But Matt nodded as if in the know too.

Now Jonathan closed his eyes. When he opened them again they were less horror-movie. Still, there was something out of place about him now, vulnerable and off-kilter in the changed room, as if he were a bit of trash barely clinging on while the tide of Marshall's skeevier era ebbed away. How long had he been here? How long had he known Coco enough to slip by her at the ropes, with an innocuous hand wave? Yes, that was the odd thing: as if in looking so innocuous, Jonathan actually stood out, the one shadow-spot in the room, the one auditioner that was not projecting but slinking across the stage. "Listen. Having your own party," he started in a strained voice, "it comes with a lot of responsibility. I'm sure Vic told you."

Matt nodded. Responsibility, yes.

"Well, what do think that means?" Lighting a smoke, Jonathan picked over the crowd with a worldly glance. "I mean, think." He paused, looking Matt carefully in the eye. "What do you think, eh," Jonathan said, "would happen to this room if there were no drugs? Or shitty drugs? Say someone comes here to party, and instead he gets some speedy crap? Eh? You think that person's gonna come back?" He flitted his gaze over the crowd again and smiled cruelly. "I like what you've done with the space, Magic. And your new DJ—he's pretty good." He sighed, turning toward the bar. "It's so tricky running a party. Especially at the beginning. You wouldn't believe how fickle some people can be." He shook his head consolingly—then stopped, dragged deeply on his cigarette, staring off into space stone-faced; chapter closed on all that.

In the vacuum after Jonathan stopped talking, Matt heard the noises of the crowd come from very far away, washing over him and blithely

---

[47] And if Matthew had learnt of Marshall's disappearance and the serious criminal actions which as it is commonly supposed caused him to flee—what should then have occurred? The course of Matthew's (and therefore our) life may have run in a different stream-bed, so to say, if he had perceived the risks of certain schemes.

receding, like happy voices on an island he was trying to swim to: so lovable, so human, endearing; their link suddenly endangered. "No," he said simply. Surely not.

Jonathan gave Matt a stagey smirk. "Think. Use your head. What do you think Vic hired you for?"[48]

There was perhaps still that unanswered question about Astral and exactly what kind of "test" he had passed with such evident flying colors. There was now also this strangely incriminating incident with Marshall—why *had* Marshall been fired? Why hadn't Vic wanted to explain it all plainly?

Jonathan waved at the bartender; Lucie popped a Heineken, coolly deposited it on the counter. Now he huddled over it, taking a couple of moderate sips, casual as any workingman enjoying a brewski after shift. "But it's no big deal," Jonathan noted to his bottle, whose label he was regarding like an interesting, intimate message. "I mean, luckily, *luckily* I've been working with Marshall for so long I already know most of your crowd, so they come to me directly. It's just other people. And by the way, I should have told you, I don't mind sharing the wealth. I play fair, that's how I've always done it with Marshall, five bucks a head, if everything's going well. So they'll approach you, because it's your room. They'll ask who's holding. And all you do is just screen: you make sure they're cool. Then you just put us in contact, but *discreetly*. You know, like you did with, with that guy the other day. Eh? That was just fine. That was great." He turned back to size Matt up, but tenderly, like the mother of some kid with skinned knees; can he go back to play? "Know what? I'm

---

[48] Expertly done, this drugs-dealer Jonathan's exploitation of Matthew. 1) There is no evidence suggesting Vic Spector knows of the Ecstasy sales; still less is there evidence suggesting Spector wishes his employees to become involved in that trade. 2) Yet Jonathan has only to gain from Matthew's misapprehending the scope of his tasks. 3) Therefore, the criminal makes use of what may have been Matthew's obvious weak spots: a) a desire to succeed in his position, combined with b) a willingness, as evidenced elsewhere in the exchanges between Matthew and Jonathan, to play along even when in a position of ignorance. From start to finish, therefore, Jonathan's representation here may be one virtuoso piece of deception.

gonna give you *five* hits, for free. Eh? You just make sure that little shit gets one. 'Sides, if we're going to do this right, you may as well have someone to sample. If you want, you know, to test. When I get new supply." He grinned as he pressed Matt's hand.

Finally. *Someone* to put it into plain English. For who has time for these ludicrous guessing games? Obviously Marshall had been doing this forever; perhaps Marshall was even supposed to have explained it to him but had been too zozzled all the time to do so. It really did make sense now. *Whatever they want, you take care of them*—precisely what Vic had said about Astral. *Whatever:* a mighty broad hint, you dodo. And maybe Marshall's *not cutting it* for Vic had to do with this X stuff too: failing these responsibilities, letting events happen like what Jason just did; Marshall certainly had been way too cracked out to make a system like this run smoothly. Well, it was about time he'd had this little talking-to. How easy: probably Jason, if asked, would be a happy sampler, given the way he and Marco seemed to be snarfing X down these days like candy corn. The rest of it was merely bringing two ends together, supply-demand, just screen and point—then a little extra greenback in your wallet; at this rate, he was priming to be a young rajah. So later, when Timothy from Marc Jacobs and Yeoh-lee from Indochine came to ask, *Where could we,* he, gladly, knew exactly what to do with himself, at last.

THREE

1.

Every evening it began—in gilt lamplit lounges, among a maze of velvet couches—clear jewels of young teeth glittering in laughter; a glass of champagne being raised; the DJ touching his headphones tenderly and lowering a tiny needle.

"*Hi,* gorgeous..." "Omigod, Magic! It's *so* good to see you." "This is *fabulous*—who is it, Margiela?" "I think you should do an invite with *you* in a fig leaf—wouldn't that be *hot*?" "Magic, you remember Kimoko, Eri..." "They were amazing, amazing, I just, wow. Save me one for Friday night." "Is that my phone?" "Of course I'll hook you up. I always have enough X for my people at my party." "Darling! I had *such* a great time at Paradise last week."

Magic staring out the back of a train, subway tracks dissolving away. Magic losing a glove somewhere in Midtown. Magic in an elevator, trying to recall the apartment number, trying to recall the last name, holding a bottle of wine. Magic taking pressed pants out of starched gauze paper. Driving down Fifth Avenue in a taxi through the winter evening rain. Magic lifting up the collar on a camel-hair coat. At Battery Park, a green haze hovers. Magic copying down names from his voicemail, drawing up a seating chart. Magic buying a billfold at Costume National. Magic telling Jason to just sample the Doves for Friday night. "I only want the best quality." Feeling a manhole cover under his feet. The reassuring rush of the sewer system, its veins purring, electric.

And the subway whine, far off, underground, crying away...Magic organizing his shoes into rows. The lights change, the taxis go. Magic at Viva, strutting past the line. "It's Magic. And *you* are . . . ?" Magic shooting through campus dragging on a smoke. "Is that my phone?" "Whose apartment is this anyway?" Magic brushing lint off his coat, hard. "I need a comp bottle of Cristal for the back table." Magic with mother-of-pearl-tipped Cartier cigarettes. "Just tell the doorman the penthouse." "Oh my God. Those Doves you tried were heroin? Are you sure? Ugh, Jason, I'm so sorry. I'll absolutely talk to Jonathan about this." "It's *gorgeous*! And it's crocodile?" "Of course, we met at the Ghost after-thing." Magic raising an arm to hail a cab on West Broadway in the rain. "Hello? Sophie, I can't hear you—the signal's really bad in here—sorry, can I call you later?" Heels on sidewalk, heels on rubber halls, heels on the red carpet, no noise at all.

There were certain incontrovertible facts. 1) He was Matthew Acciaccatura, formerly of Teaneck, New Jersey, honors student, National Cum Laude Society, Mu Alpha Theta Society of Mathematics, Bergen Valley Junior Forensics Tournament medal-winner (j.v. and varsity), Edward J. Bloustein New Jersey Distinguished Scholar, Rutgers College High School Scholar, etc. 2) He was a college freshman. A freshman at New York University. He was an NYU student with one girlfriend, Sophie Yamamoto, and one best friend, Jason Kirsch. 3) He made .75 K base pay per week as one of five key promoters for Fridays at *the* nightclub of New York. 4) "Ecstasy is the spirit of a new generation of club kids"—*Village Voice.* 5) He possessed a Dolce & Gabbana suit with minimal lapels just like Johnny Depp's. 6) He was profiled in *Time Out.* They printed a two-inch photo of him sitting at a Red Room banquette beneath the sweeping bosom of a painted angel, a cocktail in his hand. Caption: "The King of Club Kids." 7) He constituted one of three most talked about members of the freshman class. (A Real English Lord and an '80s sitcom child star—who was only half-time!—also got nods.) 8) Did he mention he was profiled in *Time Out*? 9) Did he mention they were going to print on the back page of the next *Paper* a photo of him by the dance floor, "Cinema's new phenomenon"?

Eh, *phenomenon*—exactly right. A thing that appears, that seems to the senses to be opening out in disclosure . . . and *seems:* thank the good

Lord for *seems*! For wasn't it so much luck? or the lucky word of others? Yes, the image-work was his—conjuring the room into a garden of earthly pleasures, or slapping pics on the invites, jewel-toned medieval illuminations that smacked instantly different from your run of the mill slick article. But, besides: what? Merely he had fit into the system Jonathan had in situ—at his leisure after Paradise Jason sampled whatever Peace Sign– or Red Dot–marked cargo were handy, by Wednesday came approval of this fresh batch of X, then Friday Matt simply screened, brought the have-nots over to daddy—and if Ecstasy was the spirit of a new generation, so much the happier for all and sundry *chez nous*! Merely he had liked the sly, morose face of DJ Future and picked him to supplant Declan after a quick demo-tape listen, without having any notion that Future's "mixture of jazzy breakbeat from San Francisco with a slowed-down London drum & bass" was a style of music "no one else was bringing over to the mainstream" as the gushing attendees and media people soon gave Matt to believe.

A handful of fortuitous accidents! And it was astonishing, even, for one who had passed hours copying listings from the magazines into his address book to impress other incoming freshmen, something in the way of disturbing, to discover just what a bogus rumor circus the whole thing was now that all sorts of enterprising reporters, having seen the Page Six mention of Bjork's visit, came scrambling to cover Paradise.[49] Though Matt played the opportunity: if *New York* or *Project X* inquired into how the boy wonder had known this hybrid house music was what the club scene needed? He stifled a yawn, then regurgitated some of Vic's lingo. "The vibe of New York . . . it's always changing. A promoter simply has to take the pulse, feel which way the wind's blowing. A single butterfly flapping its wings . . . meteorology . . . a tsunami . . ." And bingo: they slipped Filofaxes filled with sound bites into bags and asked for an invite, this Friday, please.

Setting aside questions of *why, Lord; thank you but why me?*: well, it

---

[49] Just so—and they would turn on him with equal suddenness, equally willing to leap for conclusions.

could not be denied that he put his humble shoulder to the wheel. Daily he pored over fashion magazines and hip boîte listings even in foreign cities, just for ideas; nightly he preened and booted up and took himself out to the VIPs of bars or clubs where, like a diver chipping bits from some fantastic coral reef, he went up and down mining beautiful people. And he did not stint even in paying calls of politesse (which had the convenient benefit of extending his reach) by attending those parties he was being invited to reciprocally: a soirée for a new couture store in SoHo; an after-party for a screening in Tribeca; the birthday dinner for the model girlfriend of a Cinema promoter and all her model chums at a little French bistro in the East Village, where everyone drank kir royales until they got so affectionate and familiar that when a quivering butter-colored Lab puppy was passed round the table, there seemed no better, more sensible thing than to lavish this infant king with hugs and adoration, letting it lick your face, nestle its soft pawlets in your lap.

In the face of all this welter, a strange thing happened. Now, if Sophie would have consented to stay out a weeknight past ten, instead of claiming she got too tired, didn't feel like dressing, and anyway couldn't have more than a couple of drinks before her face went red and she began to feel sick: if Jason weren't always stuck hanging out with Marco (*platonic*, Jason insisted; *narcotic* was more like it), like a penned animal, rooting among coke-filmed tinfoils in the perennially lightless, soiled limbo of his-or-his quarters, where he could not be parted from nappy sweatpants and melancholy records, or hanging out with Marco's wastoid crew, Amber, Julian, who could bother to keep track—sure thing, they would have been his first-chosen companions.

But as it was, under these circumstances, whom else could Matt really bring?

To give her due props: Liza proved the perfect wing-girl. Yes, in uncountable ways. With her bod, she managed to look dressed up in so much as a wifebeater and jeans, and struck right in the bullseye each time with what you were supposed to wear, whereas Sophie could veer between genius (her futuristic Courrèges getup) and daft (let's not even talk about the Victorian nightgown thing). Liza drank like an adventurer, like someone seeking the elusive white whale of happiness through the churning seas of liquor, and to see her drain a pint glass and plonk it on the bar—smoothing back her tawny waves about the rose-flushed face, where her topaz eyes were starting to go wonky, reel with sheer plucky derring-do—made you want to clap for this brave, dashing gallant, all fitted out and bound off on a voyage for parts unexplored. Therefore she did occasionally get into scrapes, but mostly of an eminently recountable variety, such as snogging madly with that fey, pillow-lipped excuse for a British Calvin Klein model shrouded by all the privacy of a security camera, so that at Cinema first the bouncers, and then the tech staff, and then even Miranda and the accounting folks had viewed Liza's very own soft-core. With that male bimbo, such an airhead: how unseemly; come on, Liza, really!

Yet when confronted by this trenchant tale? She made a face, she raised a gazelle-graceful brow. Then she said: "Oh well." So ironic and deadpan. So vulnerable and poignant?

For that was her best trick, her real genius, her only (besides her looks, of course) (well, besides her money too) true gift. She could wring enough meaning into a single syllable that it meant alpha and omega. You'd be shaking your head, musing on her excellent riposte to a discussion topic and realize—maybe—that the only word she'd uttered had been *Ha*. But what a *Ha*! Throaty, and touched by every note, like a harpist warming up on mellifluous strings of gold, so that you gave up trying to make sense of the profusion, just surrendered to the pleasure of such unearthly scales. And it was because of this talent that Liza was most valuable. For he could stroll in at a fete with Liza by his side and air-kiss someone, and when that person launched into a story of having been all the way uptown at Barneys when it started to *absolutely pour*, while Matt's mind was racing toward possibilities of what on earth could be the point of all this blab?, Liza would dole out such inimitable *oh*s, *oh*s full of pity and at the same time awake to the absurdities of the world that he would actually soften into something like calm watching the satisfied interlocutor's face soften too. Let's face it: preferred girl or nay, Sophie would have fucked it up from the first faux kiss.

For these signal services rendered, Matt repaid Liza in kind. Besides whatever good she claimed about how wonderful-strange it was to have a guy friend who *for once,* ugh, wasn't trying to get in her pants (with an Atlas effort of empathy, Matt could almost grasp the tragic nature of that fate: though...come on, really? was it so very ghastly, her irresistibility affliction?), there was the little matter of entrée he offered. You would have no idea how boring were the people that she'd known from childhood, she wanted him to understand. Narrow-minded, WASPy, Upper East Side; there were actual debutantes in this world who needed couture dresses for their coming-outs. Or didn't he believe her? Well, didn't he? Well, did he want to see?

"I'll show you," she declared one Tuesday evening. "Tonight there's a party at Peter Kent's I wasn't going to go to, but if you want..."

At nine they were speeding in a taxi along monumental Madison Avenue. She was dressed down, in a shearling coat, white go-go boots worn over jeans tight as shrinkwrap, with a black tie-neck sweater, which surprised him till he realized: posturing, to show her old folk how far she'd traveled from prig world. Now he was wishing he had thrown in a mark of rebellion of his own, his leather punk-kid bracelet, perhaps, among the camel-hair coat, trademark scarf, and black silk button-down shirt. "So they have this stupid private 'club,'" she gloated. "It's every Tuesday. You should *see* Peter's place." She shook a disdainful head: "It's un*real* he lives there by himself." Though a wire of excitement thrummed through her voice, and—suffering perhaps a case of nerves?—she cajoled the Rasta cabbie into letting her smoke.

Was it gauche to ask how Peter's parents had their money? Oil? An invention? A sugar plantation in some impoverished Latin American republic? The taxi turned left at 83rd, then inched down Fifth Avenue until she recognized the number. Okay, now, come on. It wasn't the awning or the liveried doormen. It wasn't the marble floor. It was the *urn*s, the ridiculous ginormous urns made of who-knows-what, malachite, alabaster, Mars. From behind, Liza appeared to be a tall prostitute, as she scissored forward among the astonished doormen and he—a glimpse in the gold-framed mirror before they hit the elevator—a small, meticulously dressed troll, vaguely green-complected.

"Should we have brought something?" he inquired in the chryselephantine elevator, trying to sound worldly, for he had recently learned this thing, apparently a rule of "common" etiquette. "Champagne?" Checking his nails.

She snorted. "No." Gave him a glassy condescending glare, which seemed to say he should know better than to think that Peter Kent needed hooch from the likes of him.

PH: Penthouse. And out into the Oriental-carpeted hallway, whither the noises of cocktail talk swirled tepidly round. Now she put her hand on the gold doorknob and, bending slightly, pushed her way in.[50]

So to stay aloof, not to gape about, he kept his eyes riveted to her back as he followed, which made it a little difficult to take in the scene, though he was aware of something like twenty people standing or sitting in groups of various sizes around a room that, given the opulence of downstairs, seemed maybe a touch small. It was done up, like the elevator, in white and gold, with gold sconces on the walls and lamps over white couches, and a few heavy tables with massive animal-faced legs and dark marble tops, outrageously ugly and burdensome like coffins. Right smack dab in the center, isolated on a white armchair like a polar bear marooned on a chunk of ice, sat a guy in a dark-green sweater, his black-panted legs crossed to showcase one sullen brown shoe. When he recognized Liza from afar, his expression underwent a change. A sly smile crept into his lost face while he tipped forward, pressing a hand down on the armrest as though about to get up, then fell back again inside his luxurious throne. Not drunk exactly, but clearly wrecked from hard use: his skin was grayish, and his close-set eyes were almost shutting, and did shut, to open again without much vibrancy. "Liza," he said when she finally reached him, drawing her down into an avuncular hug.

---

[50] I did not succeed in obtaining access to the Kent family flat (prevented by some efficient porters on each attempt); in this, as at certain other regrettable points, we have had to rely upon others' accounts. And was it too much to hope that Peter Kent himself would meet with me, he whom Matthew regarded so kindly? Or at the least make his refusal personally?

Looking past her now at Matt, he curved a hand around to pat her hip as she giggled and readjusted the shearling coat in her arms. "You know I've known this girl my whole life?"

And with that: not half bad, this Peter Kent. Ludicrous, yes, such a judgment, given that the whole point of this evening was to flesh out Liza's scorn with *tableaux vivants*. But there was something so marvelously unsnobby about the way Peter Kent looked him in the eyes and talked as if he were already a friend, without fussing, just being genuine, that Matt whipped off his sniggering face, ashamed. "What's your name?" Peter asked, without affectation, without even a *dude* or *bro,* and inclined his head, thoughtful as a real College Man. Even Liza looked delighted with him; standing behind his chair, she petted at one dark-green shoulder (only a delicate half closure of Peter's eyelids registered he felt this) while fluently depicting some cofamily vacation. "I still have that catamaran," Peter mused. "I haven't used it in years. I just don't get to Cape Cod." He let the words drop slowly, like pieces of something, money, a letter, dropped onto a river just to see them wheel blithely away among the water's burnished greaves. Now he shook his head as if at the gloomy paradox of what he'd just said and waved toward the far side of the room, beyond the entrance. "Go get yourselves something to drink." But first he reached to shake Matt's hand.

"I *like* him," Matt announced, challenging her, as they stood by the bar table pouring Macallan's into crystal tumblers.

She halted her breaking off bits of ice. "Who, Peter?" A frolicsome toss of her ponytail. "Peter's a sweetheart." She turned to angle her glass at the room. "It's the other people you have to worry about." She rolled her eyes, then deposited the glass on the bar and released a tubercular cough into her slender black-nailed hand: so *La Bohème,* so ruined heroine! *Brava,* encore.

Artificial though she might be: correct nonetheless. For nigh on half an hour he glided along the carpet among a species as strange, as startling, as a race of dwarves. They were kids: they went to NYU, or some of them did, at least: but they were enclosed in the costume and manners of forty-year-olds. Girls who could not be over twenty had their forearms weighed down by gold-locked frame bags more suitable to *grandes dames* as they traded wisdom about how to tie Hermès scarves into bandeau tops, *the way they always wear them at Cannes.* Guys murmuring about *Merrill Lynch, Goldman Sachs, private equity* demurely maneuvered crystal tumblers into the same three or four established positions, as if those were the gentleman Ken doll's few possible poses; they kept their free hand rigid in slacks pockets at a perfect forty-five-degree angle, in a way that made their navy blazer's back vent peel open yet let the flap lie neatly firm against the body. They resembled the Caleb- and Taylor-preps; there was certainly overlap in the conventional clothing and general honky atmosphere; but these were so much more *advanced:* little replicas of jet-set socialites and Wall Street types, preternaturally joyless and formal beyond their years. Why? It didn't even look *fun,* to wear pearl necklaces and flat Ferragamo shoes, to talk in low, stilted tones about the recruitment trends of investment banks on campus. While two girls, both in twinsets and plaid pants, gamely tried to sway along in a corner, softly in the background Dr. Dre and Snoop Dogg extolled the virtues of rolling down a street sipping on gin and juice with their minds on their money and vice versa.

And, *voilà,* indeed: one short girl with dire blue eyes who had attached herself like an earwig to Liza looked interesting, dressed in sleek black and intriguingly nineteenth-century china-doll pretty with her white skin and jet hair, but when Matt caught up to the conversation on the parquet by the bar, he realized that she was, in all seriousness, recounting a nightmare in which her father had disclosed there were only ten million dollars coming to her at his death. "What did you do?" Matt interrupted rudely. Please: someone needed to stick a fork in this! Not like they'd ever see him again. "I mean, that must have been a shock." He crossed his arms, cocked his head with a scrutinizing air, while Liza badly covered a smile with her scotch glass: and that's what she'd wanted from him, wasn't it, tonight. For a moment Dahlia, the short girl, rested her striking cobalt eyes impersonally on Matt, as if deciding whether to see him or merely gaze in his direction. Then her shoulders executed a slight and implacable shrug, queerly threatening, like a WASP version of *Wanna start something?* "Well," she tossed her glossy raven hair, addressing Liza, "it's kind of strange. I just looked him straight in the eyes," now her terrifying eyes annihilated a foot of wall, "and said, 'Well, then it's a good thing you're not dead yet!' " She barked a laugh, shot Liza an invitation to go smoke, then barreled toward the place where presumably the smokers were billeted.

Not just the smokers. In a child's bedroom—a little girl's, from the look of the elaborate dollhouse set up on its own wide pedestal—were another seven or so people, strewn about the bucolic grass-and-daffodil-printed window seat and the white brocaded bed. One guy on the window seat was focused outside and kept gesturing excitedly, *It's hailing, it's hailing, you have to see this, in the park, it's hailing,* but everyone in the room was busy concentrating on snorting white powder up their nostrils, so that, still staring out the window like a dejected dog, he finally broke off. Snorting? Not just that but combing it, assorting it, re-sorting it into lines with something like the affection that the mistress of this room must have had when at work braiding her dolls' hair.

In one fluid workmanlike motion, Dahlia dropped to her knees and swayed forward over the bed, where whatever she did was discreetly curtained by masses of black hair. Then Liza balanced herself sideways on the bed's edge and leaned wide like a trick rider: a moment later she was fondly touching the coronas of her nostrils.

Well. Not as if he hadn't seen coke happening before. But so far, really, only Marco and Jason over these last weeks, mostly in places so familiar as their dank dorm rooms. This scene was utterly different: the pederastic thrill of sprawling on a little girl's bed to engage in blatant evildoing, for starters. And so many people at it—the difference between having sex and an orgy. What a bizarre combo! Sordidness, like greasy faces in a neon-lit *Miami Vice* drug den, mixed with its total opposite, the security of money, the freshness of youth, the endless future possibilities of all these scions—gathered in one place, soon to disperse maybe to every corner of the globe. The best doctors had slapped their asses into the bright world; the best tutors had leaned over them, coaxing; and with astounding negligence, in fact with a marvelous industry, they were blowing mind and body to Timbuktu. So how bad could it be for you, then? I mean, I'm sure these kids aren't playing Russian roulette with ODing. Just watch how they do it and opt for a little line.

Liza turned a glazed face toward him and offered her cold hand, drawing him over. Kneeling, in the instant before he dipped his nose, outfitted with a dollar-bill straw, to a porcelain platter, he spotted on the far side of the bed, high on the wall, a Venetian mask with gouged-out eyes and lunar skin: like one of Sophie's masks, but this one obviously real, an antique. Creepy—like some roving witness, part of an underground network of spies on humanity, with a clearly disfavoring cast to its crimson lips, to that unforgiving, adamant blot that was its black beauty mark. . . . He thought of sitting up,[51] giving back the straw, collecting his coat, and walking out in the hailstorm down below . . . then he had shoveled starlight inside the mother-ship, was incalculably high.

For as long as it took to leave the sanctum and wait in line for the bathroom, and pee and wash his hands, he tried to put all thoughts of what it was like out of his mind and just *whee!* along with the exhilarating ride; Don't Talk and Just Feel, Sophie and Jason had badgered him on Ecstasy. But when he was outside again in the corridor, wiping moist hands on his pants barely fifteen minutes later, the feeling suddenly dropped off, into crash. He went back into the room for another pull— ah, already Liza was patting her nose again: so obviously second helpings must not be risky now—and this time it lasted longer, maybe a good twenty minutes of euphoria, sliding his ass onto the bed, the window seat, remembering to look for that hail but the sky was absent. Then: crash. A terrible mania, his heart beating wild, fingers stiff with anxiety . . .

Calm, now: another scotch? Calm, now: what's the matter with you? By the bar he was trembling trying to pinion out a couple of ice cubes with the tongs. Maybe just to be alone, for a few minutes, would help? Matt walked himself and his fresh glass into the hallway and tried a shut door: the kitchen. A man and a woman in gray-and-white uniforms were sitting at a table, eyes stuck on a television where two officers were crouching over the white outline of a vanished corpse. Without taking his eyes from the screen, the man stood, extricated a bottle of champagne

---

[51] Yes, Matthew, rise! But we who look over these pages of his life are mere witnesses, powerless as that mask.

from a giant silver refrigerator. "N-no," Matt mumbled. Blasé, still look-ing at the screen where a lab-coated woman now examined a curl of hair beneath a microscope, the man dug in the fridge and replaced the cham-pagne with a bottle of Chimay ale; this Matt accepted, so as not to dis-turb further. Then he passed back into the corridor, headed to deliver it at the bar.

Beside the counter, two blond girls were grilling a handsome, talka-tive guy in a beige suit with a jaunty black collarless shirt about some name. "I don't know him," said one of the girls, patting back a satisfied yawn. "Do you, Emma?" Emma sounded almost sad to admit she didn't either. "They're almost all freshmen this time," the first girl went on, in tones of exquisite somnolence. "I don't know freshmen."

"Well, you'll know them now, Megan," the guy rapped out cheerily. "Right?"

"Maybe." Megan let slip a sleepy ripple of laughter. "So—tell me again? Tell me all of them."

Well, let him see. There was Taylor Harrison. There was Walker Jones. There were a whole host of unknowns—

And there was Dwight Smeethman.

"No," came Megan's groan. "See, it's hopeless. I don't know him either."

Jesus! *What* about Dwight? Matt pretended to examine a bottle of Pimm's.

"Hello, suitemate," Ryan declared warmly, but so loud and sudden that Matt jumped. He did the downward-scoop move with his tumbler that Matt recognized from earlier, some sort of ritualized greeting ges-ture. "I didn't realize," Ryan coughed apologetically into his hand, "you were a member?" Looking pained, regretful he'd asked.

"N-no, just came with Liza," Matt explained. His words were com-ing far too fast. "How're you?" He chewed a cube of ice to steady his mouth.

A girl approached, woolen coats and scarves piled on one arm. There was something so monstrous about her, Matt needed instantly to take a sip to cover his fright; he tried to turn his step-back into a kind of friendly opening-up. Her face—like a Hapsburg portrait—so inbred, addled: the chin all jutting, the round mushy nose; it was a crime against humanity to go on breeding people this way.... "Hello," she said pleasantly.

"Eleanor, this is my suitemate Matthew!" said Ryan, as if she were an old golfing partner he was proudly introducing to his college son.

"Weeell." Eleanor took it in the same spirit. Her gray eyes twinkled as she studied him, a smile on her face that said, *Every garden is beautiful*, untroubled, trusting in the upward growth of life. She reached out a hand and pumped his merrily. "Nice to meet you!" she proclaimed in a sprightly, precise walking stick of a voice. "Finally! We certainly should have met before now!"

Yes, yes, they should have. Though he was always so busy with his work, and Ryan was busy too, and it was the first time he had come to Peter Kent's, and really they rarely saw each other around the dorm because it's very different when you don't have a dining hall in your dorm, you know, I don't know if you have a dining hall in your dorm but it's certainly very different from where he used to live, Third North, though he was infinitely grateful to have shifted over and "wasn't the building just an absolute gem?"

Oh. Now you've gone and done it. I knew it. This cocaine is not good for you at all, at all. Ryan and Eleanor were staring at him with gentle, faintly worried expressions. "Whew. I'm sorry. I'm feeling sort of strange. Would you excuse me?" And the noddings and pats and waves, and Eleanor beginning to bend over the pile of coatstuffs on her arm, her forehead creased with puzzlement: Matt whizzed past to the other side of the bar. Thank God at least he'd managed to quell a shout-out: *Katharine Hepburn—that's who your voice reminds me of!*

He swallowed back the last fiery draught, filled his glass again, still hyperactive-manic, then examined along the wall a series of framed illustrations where red-jacketed gentlemen on beautiful horses sped forward among a horde of silken-haired dogs. At the end, when little plumes of smoke were rising into air from ancient guns, when he wound up beside the couch where a guy clearly recognizable from newspaper pics as student-body president Arthur Brody was explicating point by point in a stalwart, officious drone the storyline of *Barbarians at the Gate* to a guy who nodded, nodded his neck broken like a hung man's, Matt wheeled on his heel over to where Peter Kent had just said goodbye to a pair of girls and was now propping his head with one hand, weary king.

"Matt," Peter remarked, once again tipping forward as though to get up, but not managing to. "Sit down, have a seat."

"Where's your sister?" Matt asked, sounding nonsensically urgent as he pounced onto an armchair. "I saw her bedroom."

While Matt assiduously drank tumblerfuls of scotch, Peter Kent generously explained his life, and just to keep the steady stream of it in motion, just to listen to something, a history in which everything was already inevitable and you didn't have to think, act, worry, Matt leveled a series of questions about the smallest cog and flywheel in it: how competent Annabel's French was for her grammar school in Paris, when exactly the opportunities for Russian oil had arisen for people like Peter's father, what the order of the courses was like when Peter went to visit his parents (evidently first-class), how the slippers felt and the tilt of the seats, to which Peter seemed to cleave with particular fondness, leading him to declare finally in a reverential tone, *Sleep*, then examine Matt with a rueful, sympathetic look. Sleep: yes. Exactly. Like speaking of innocence or childhood, a country whose gate had closed on you forever, which other people, simple people, people outside the gold and the ivory of this living room, who had never been poisoned by this eternal drone of Arthur Brody's syllables entering your ear one by one like a line of black ants, were still enjoying—wasn't that incredible!

Whether Matt would ever be allowed back into that land was still in doubt at ten and then eleven that morning, shivering in the white eiderdown, hands clasped around his knees, having thought *I'm never going to try coke again* almost continuously since taking the cab home at three. But finally Sleep, like an injured queen, forgave him, so a white door opened—he was falling upward into oblivion.

2.

Then it was a gray, sodden four o'clock. Slept through Sex lecture. Matt had a bad moment until from a corner of the room he managed to dig up the pristine, rarely seen syllabus and discovered: Friday, the midterm wasn't till the eighth. Now he clambered back onto the bed, facedown, with one thought in mind—or it wasn't *thought,* just image:

Jason, the other night at a table at Paradise, looking anxiously to see where Marco had gone, nodding *Uh-huh* along distractedly with one of Matt's little evening vignettes.

This was cocaine. One could be fairly certain of that now. The itchiness, the flicky gestures, eyes roving like the kids' last night, lines of tension in the face like fissures in porcelain. Because of the quickness, and the ineluctable draw after; one felt it even on a first try. Jonathan was absolutely on-point not to deal C or H, *a bad vibe for the room,* the man had said, *all sorts of problems.* Should he call Jason? Check in with him? Matt stood and made for the shower, undressed, let it pelt him. When was the last time he had spoken to Jason? Well, last Wednesday, for sure, to get Jason's thumbs-up on the new crop of X; then of course Paradise, though barely talked then, what with that splendid, unexpected stroke of Liza's childhood friend Natasha showing up with a whole bevy of her comodels from Ford. Perhaps it was time to invite Jason out? Get him away for an evening from Marco and Marco's wastoid crew—Devin, whomever else it was he had met that night of the party in Marco's room.

Some party: a bunch of kids frenching bongs, sitting cross-legged on the floor in enormous baggy jeans.

See, that is your problem. So willing to criticize them for being tacky, lame. That was why Jason became so defensive at anything you happened to say knocking the "new friends." Like when you asked if he actually liked that girl Amber after she flounced away in a spasm of moronic laughter—and Jason had merely sneered, *Whatever,* as if to say *What, she isn't cool enough for you?*

Matt zipped his trousers, looking up at the fine ceiling with its scrolled moldings at the rim. What had Amber really said? Simply complimented his shirt, said she was having a great time at Paradise. Nothing out of keeping for, say, a Liza, grateful to get in to Cinema for the first time. But it was the way Amber did it that rankled: her stringy hair falling round her face, teeth manically gnashing at the speed in her E. The way she flopped her body self-consciously among the cocktail tables, trying to be all sex kitten when, let's face it, she wasn't even mildly pretty, with that broad-shouldered footballer's physique. Well, so she was failing, attempting to seem more gifted in looks or charm than what God had allotted—was that all? If so, Jason was right to throw the comment back in his teeth.

But they just seemed so *stupid.* There: that felt good to say! Matt gave the lace ends of his sneaker a satisfyingly sharp tug. Always *Rad* this, *Rad* that, or *Right on* when you least expected it, not even with any feeling but in a single monotone breath. And what was their talk? Gossip, gossip from the most rancidly banal butt ends of a party's leavings, and pot-growing tips, and wouldn't it be cool if + some totally inane scenario, like video games in bathroom stalls.

Okay now. Matt slipped the cell into his gray wool pants, lifted his key loop from the desk. Now you're just being petty. They're *his* friends. Just—give him a ring.

So Matt tried Jason: once on his walk over to and once from the drear puce-colored basement of the library (useless tonight for going out anyway, might as well shake a leg for Friday's test), he left humble messages on Jason's machine and even beeped him, but heard no word back. It was all of twenty-four hours later, Thursday afternoon after his interview with a man from *Index,* that he discovered a sullen message from Jason on the machine: *sorry he was so late, the stuff for tomorrow was great.*

And why the room phone? Was Jason avoiding him? Matt tried him once, twice (*Jason,* please *call my* cell), also beeped him, with emergency digits (911911911), and at last rang up Liza for Marco's number. But "I don't think he's going to be home," Liza mourned.

Oh no?

"They're all going to karaoke. It's Lauren's birthday. Isn't she so annoying?" Liza hissed. "I'm so staying in. Unless—did you want to go out somewhere?" Innocently.

"Who's Lauren?"

"Jeremy, Matt's asking me who Lauren is," she lowed off the phone. A muffled masculine expostulation, then Liza's *heu-heu* laugh. "God. She's this girl…" Liza trailed. "She's this girl…" she repeated, clearly having difficulty: her hard drive overheating…

"That's okay," inserted Matt smoothly. "Do you think—Jason will be there?"

"Probably!" Liza blurted. "Hey baby, do you want to come over? Jeremy and I are cooking dinner." And when Matt confessed he had a test, "Good luck!" she sang with dramatized revulsion, as if what he'd admitted was a case of herpes instead.

Not until Matt clicked shut his phone did Liza's *Probably* resolve itself into what it was: a burp of disdain, a sort of *Ugh.* About his own little bud? *But he's not like them,* one wanted to say. And yet all evidence would flatly contradict this. These days, to an impartial eye, Jason was glum-guy, sulky, or nattering about nonsense while "X-ing his balls off." Or again recovering, like, say, a slug fallen off some low perch—dazed, self-involved, feebly resuming its oily crawl. Or trying too hard, wearing billowy silken shirts like an overdressed burgher, breathlessly asking *What? What?* and grinning along inanely after jokes that weren't meant for him. Poor Jason. But why wasn't he calling?

Finally, at eleven on Friday, just as Matt was racing up the steps of Meyer Hall, mind swirling with tattered worded scraps like *asexual reproduction* and *gametes:* "Did you need something?" Jason inquired over the line, almost sarcastic.

Well, now. And no apology?

At this point, given the nature of human frailty—in other words, the dreadful inflammability of all this emotional brush with which Matt was stuffed—there was nothing else to do but studiously freeze the boy out! Mention as if in passing that he hoped Jason would make it to Cinema tonight, a marvel of iciness, and goodbye. No slouch, Jason responded by flouncing in at Paradise with Marco, Amber, Devin, Julian, a probable Lauren, and two guys it didn't even seem like Jason knew: having, as it turned out, prevailed upon Lacey in Magic Matt's name to give them all (eight!) comps. Acting as if he owned the place, in a gauche black blazer like some garmento. Now it was Matt's move. And he responded by— yes, the slightest bit pathetic, but still it was a crafty stratagem, in its way—having Sandi inform Jason that *these tables are bottle service only,* a rule normally forgone for Matt's number two. But Jason had a counter-coup: ordering a bottle of Stoli. And was he really going to use his parents' credit card at a nightclub? For a two-hundred-dollar charge? "I think that's just sick," Matt bitched to Sophie.

"I think you should talk to him."

"Ho! He should talk to me. Who's the one not returning calls?"

"You're making such a big deal out of it. Probably just some sort of misunderstanding," Sophie sighed, digging in her silver cocktail purse.

Matt rolled his eyes. Did Sophie *always* have to be so goody-goody? So do the right thing? There was a small leopard in the room of his heart's core, pawing, turning tight circles. And what were you going to say to that creature: let's put the matter aside, let's make up nice-nice with Jason?

Ostentatiously, Jason danced with his crew; ostentatiously, he lolled at his table, smoking, flip-lighting his Zippo, and grinning possessively around like a rap star with his entourage. Luckily the photographer from *Index,* who required Matt's acumen in framing a few crowd shots, succeeded in distracting him awhile from that revolting pageant.

"I think I'm going to leave," snapped Sophie, when it was barely one o'clock.

"What? Sophie. What a pretty dress you have on—did you make

this?" Naively fingering the tiny pistachio sleeves. "You did, I remember it!"

"Nice try." She smirked. "But I'm not getting in the middle of this. I'm out of here. Hey—how about don't wake me up tonight, okay? I think I really need some sleep. Maybe you could go sleep at your place?"

Fine. When Sophie ditched, Matt stood round the bar with Liza and Jeremy, who, unless he was mistaken, were suffering a rift of their own, in re: Marco. "Oh, look," Liza said once, cranking up that blanched cedilla of an eyebrow toward the dance floor, as she lowered her mouth to a martini glass. That was all she needed to say. Out there was Amber working hard at the slippery beats, arms doing odd Aztec moves, face set grim.

A gulp-laugh erupted from Matt. "What's *wrong* with them? I mean, actually. This isn't a rhetorical question."

They liked that. Jeremy coughed, smiling into his fist; Liza lifted her glass in a cheers with the air, and called, *Hear, hear!* But it wasn't humor he intended, or criticism really. What *was* wrong there? It couldn't just be animus on his part: Matt had caught Robert, the reporter from *Index,* from his prime table throwing quizzical glances at the Friends of Jason. There was something hard and desperate, forced, about them, shouting, throwing territorial looks around as they snatched off raver backpacks, playacting their enjoyment. And could Jason really prefer that crew? To hanging out with yours truly?

"Let's dance!" Liza cooed, when the music erupted into a swirl of sirens and whistles; a triumphant DJ Future rocked the record just finished high over his turntables.

Instead Matt absorbed himself in working the room, ferrying that girl Chen over to Jonathan, greeting some model from the other week and Stefan, her French filmmaker beau, a man with a giant schnoz and an insistent, self-promoting conversational style. Matt had just extracted himself from Stefan when someone tapped him on the shoulder.

Jason.

Close up, Jason looked still worse: the satiny white shirt beneath his blazer shining pornographically, like lingerie, his face a plump pudge above. Dark hollows under his eyes made the overall skin look ashen, even in this dim roseate light. With one hand in a pants pocket, Jason's padded shoulders slumped so the blazer sagged, warped—too big for him: some boy dressed up in his father's clothes. Yet the sulky cast of his familiar face was endearing, brought suddenly near, with the always warm brown eyes now grown almost unbearably open and unguarded. Matt was on the verge of reaching out a hand to straighten the blazer when Jason threw his head back, defiant. "I need my sample now," he whined.

"Well," said Matt, his would-be friendly hand instead seizing his scotch from the low marbleized table where he'd placed it. "That's early, isn't it? You know, perhaps, perhaps we don't need you this week, after all." Improvising, his fingers tapping lordly at the glass. "Sophie and I will try them ourselves. For her birthday tomorrow. Thanks, though," he added, a crowning indignity, before making as if to edge by.

"What?" Jason's eyes twitched, incredulous. "But—you don't even *like* X!" He looked hastily over his shoulder as though afraid of who might have overheard.

"Maybe you were right," soothed Matt, asinine, "maybe she and I just need to give it another try?" An evil grin. "Please excuse me."

Jason's hand caught Matt by the arm. "You're a fucking asshole, Matt!" he blubbered, spraying a monstrous vodka wind.

"Ssh," hissed Matt. "You're making a scene."

"You guys don't even *like* X," Jason repeated, quieter, as if that were the main point to get across.

"What's the big whoop?"

"I promised my friends." Jason blinked. "They're waiting." Now they both glanced about fifteen feet off to where the crew sat in state about a circular table. Though Julian was saying something in his ear, Marco had his gaze fixed ahead in their direction.

Bingo. So: they were waiting for Jason to bring them free drugs. The desperation in Jason's face—didn't want to disappoint, couldn't come back empty-handed. "Jonathan . . . still has some, for sale," Matt began feebly.

"Matt," Jason begged, "I can't. That'll be, like, two hundred dollars. I just spent," he looked up gingerly at Matt, "two hundred on that bottle."

"More with tax," Matt muttered automatically. They weren't paying for—anything? And eight—was Jason crazy? A sample of *eight?*

"And tip," said Jason, with a sheepish grin.

"Jason. Why are you the one who has to . . . ?" He peered intently, trying to discover the truth hidden somewhere beneath the panels of Jason's skin.

"Oh, it was my idea," Jason hurried to explain. "I told · them— we could. You know. I just, um, suggested we all come here and X." His voice cracked slightly. "I mean, I could buy a couple. I know eight's a lot."

It was coming to the surface, but not quite there yet. Who started this? Jason, seeking to impress? Or did all these loons ask for it, using him—and he couldn't say no? Look at the steely way Marco was staring. But how to broach the matter with Jason? How to do it so it wasn't too paternalistic, know-it-all? Especially after our track record.

"Where's Liza?" Jason asked politely, looking about, just trying to placate.

"Okay," said Matt. Exhaling heavily. It would be cruelty to go further with this now. We can pick it up another time, when he's not so on the line.

"Okay?" Jason's face began to light up, in sections—first the eyes, then the cheeks, the mouth opening in a tentative, delighted smile. "Really?"

"Come on." Matt patted Jason's shoulder. "Let's go over to Jonathan."

"Oh, Matt. This is so great: thank you!" Jason's relief was becoming glee. "I'm really sorry about tonight. I was just, you know, pissed, from the phone today, and then you were ignoring me; I guess I was being a *little* passive-aggressive. Just silly, I guess, I mean, I know I was being silly. Hey Matt," he gushed from behind, clawing at Matt's arm after they crossed through a clot of bodies by an ivory divan, "guess what?"

"What's that?" said Matt, inclining his head back.

"I came up with a club name! Finally. You know how I've been trying? Or maybe you don't know. But, anyway, what do you think—of J-Force?"

It was lucky that Matt was facing forward, so that in the instant before he turned he was able to wipe clear the slate of his skin. Jason was evidently not kidding: under the rose and blue spots his face shone eagerly, manic. As if he had come finally upon some magic key that would solve all, at last throw open a closed door on happiness. He was standing ramrod straight, like a statue beneath which the word J-FORCE should be graven.

—What else could Matt say? "Really nice! I like it!"

When Matt left Paradise close on four, Jason and posse were still drinking water in long tugs from bottles, dancing, patting one another where they sat, and generally having themselves a good old X party. Matt watched how Jason balanced Amber on his lap, how he grinned ecstatically into Marco's face while jabbering on and on about something evidently of marvelous import. Well, he looked all right. Happy. Didn't he? It didn't quite seem bad, when you saw them all together—Amber dragging Jason up with both hands to the dance floor, for example. And yet: it was somehow like the time Jason had described his friends from high school, the double life of his closeted days in Scarsdale, even faking it with a girlfriend, *Wish I'd never done it,* or words to that effect. Why had he, then? Simply to have friends? Well, you couldn't knock that as a legitimate objective. I'd probably have become friends with a chair leg if it had let me.

J-Force, though. Really? Did he have to go that far, to please them?

There wasn't time to properly mull the question. For in less than twenty-four hours, mostly spent in preparation, he was lying supine on the luxurious sheets of a suite in the Plaza Hotel, having made a dreadful botch of Sophie's twentieth birthday. She was lying to his right, had finally stopped crying, had finally stopped withholding the cause in silence and finished discussing, in a tear-made-husky voice, what he had done wrong. A suite at the Plaza *Hotel*? That wasn't her, not her at all; and if she had wanted not to have a party, wanted only to spend some sim-ple time with him, what gave him the notion that the Plaza Hotel was the place to do it in? She wasn't some mistress, some gold digger to be impressed by all this disgusting luxury, so impersonal—"It's like you don't know me at all! You might as well give me a mink coat," she had snarled moistly at him, " 'cause obviously that's what you think of me." Then she had gathered herself, pressed up from the bed on trembling fists, her face a wet red mess, and announced that she was taking a bath. During which time he had occasion to draw himself over to the bathroom door, collapse on the soft clean carpet, and talk, and agree, and interminably apologize.

Though he half-felt: what was the problem here? Yes, if he hadn't been so frazzled with the reporters and his midterm this week, he might have spent longer pondering what to do. But everything had been neces-sary, except I guess going with Liza to Peter Kent's. Besides, what did she want from him, an opera composed in her name? Listen: the *Plaza Hotel*. Who couldn't like the idea of a suite here? Who couldn't like champagne and chocolate and orchids? It's the fucking *Plaza Hotel*—wasn't it a trip even to walk into the lobby, stride right up to the massive concierge sta-tion, and, just as they might begin to examine you with suspicion, de-mand the key? to your *suite*? "You, you liked *Breakfast at Tiffany's*," he had allowed himself to suggest timidly, after she'd accepted his apologies and subsided into an exhausted rancor. (And didn't she like *Eloise*? But not to mention, in case he was wrong about that.) "Oh God, Matt, that's different!" An angry splash from inside.

Now they were lying one beside the other, wide awake, in silence. Matt strained his ears toward the not quite inaudible heat system: a kind of *tstssshh*, breath on the curtains. The champagne in its handled silver bucket by the bed's foot must be utterly warm now, floating in a bath of ice-flecked water. And maybe it would indeed be better to be far away from here: Matt saw himself being drawn, backward, like a filmstrip set in reverse, down the magnificent stairs, out the revolving doors, at that corner of Central Park so favored by pigeons and scented of the horses standing yoked there in immobile carriages. Then drawn farther, down-town to Sophie's, beyond, right to the tip of Manhattan—and off it, into the sleek waters reflecting in rills the city lights, then lifted up high, by his back, like a kitten being carried by the scruff of its neck, toward the moon. So all of New York City would disappear in the dark like a flashing coin being thrown into the sea.

"Sophie," his dry tongue pushed out into the motionless, oneiric space. For wouldn't this please her, at least faintly? "I talked to Jason last night. After you left."

"That's good," she approved. "You made up?"

"Sort of. Yes. Tell me—do you like his new friends?"

"Why not?" Tinged with a little malice.

"Do you not want to talk about it now?" He flipped over to face the curved back of her body, naked but for a tank top and panties.

"No, it's fine." She rubbed her nose. "What's wrong with them?"

So Matt began, starting with the most recent, the hullabaloo over the X, then working his way toward the remoter past, giving an account of the party at Marco's and his interpretations of that whole posse, and finally forward again to: "He came up with a club name. J-Force. Isn't that strange?"

"Ohh." This one struck home. "Poor Jason."

"W-why *poor*?" A nervous laugh. "He doesn't need all these, these idiots. He'd be perfectly fine—*better* off—without impressing them. Or trying to."

Now she sat up cross-legged on the bed. Her face looking calm and sage and definite: how he loved that expression, two lines suddenly graven between the eyebrows. "I can't believe I have to tell this to you," she declared airily. "Jason's trying to imitate you. He's jealous. He's like a little brother. Looking up to you."

"That is ridiculous," he swore. Sort of.

She blew hair out of her eyes. "J-Force? Who else has a club name? Come on."

"But I *need* a club name."

"You're not getting it, Matt." She shook her head. "That's the point. He feels excluded. You have a role: at the club. But what about him? You get to be Magic Matt. But who's he? And now that you're so busy..."

As much as he loved it when she looked wise and wide-knowing of sundry matters—prescribing bananas for his upset stomach, interpreting the pink couch in a dream as a symbol of his mother—there came a point when you had to take such sagacity with a megalithic crystal of salt. I mean, it just all fit together too neatly—like a complex straight out of a Psych 1 textbook. *Club Promoter Envy.* "Hmm," he said, unfortunately at the same time letting slip a bemused smile.

"Fine, if you don't believe me, why do you bother asking me to explain!" She hurled herself down on the bed and peremptorily flopped away from him. But it wasn't *anger* anger; you could see it even in the way her eyes went looking for him to come and surround her in a flurry of kisses, hugs.

"I do believe you, I do," he whispered into her left ear, wrapping his arms around her body and digging his lips into her neck. Well, even if her hypothesis wasn't correct, it might not hurt to include Jason a bit round the old farm. Give him a couple of chores to do.

The old farm. His small and perfect Eden!

3.

Yet when Jason received Matt Monday afternoon, in the gray-lit bedroom where the one window left open to clear out the smoke was letting in line after line of fat, placid raindrops, his manner could only be construed as tepid. Yes, tepid, as he opened the bag of oranges and bananas Matt presented him (quite thoughtfully: this was a boost for the little gremlin's poor, serotonin-squeezed axons), and flung it on the pilled couch beside a stack of battered, damp magazines, and lit a smoke, and scratched his chin, and made such a pathetic attempt at smiling that Matt had to wonder—well, maybe the boy just doesn't like us anymore? Simple as that?

But plug right on, soldier. Now, Jason, the other day, that club name, it got Matt thinking. I mean, why shouldn't Jason pick up a few responsibilities around Cinema? In short, well, would Jason like it, or, rather, wouldn't it, um, in fact be really awesome—for J-Force to join the staff? in some capacity? which they could figure out?

"Oh." Interested. Jason combed up the hairs off his nape with a furtive hand.

"I don't know why I didn't think of it before. There's tons of things you'd be great at doing around the club. That is, if you're interested..."

"But like what? I mean, I'm not," now the corners of Jason's mouth twisted up, ironic, "*Magic Matt*. No one picked me to be their protégé."

Aha: score one for Sophie. "Oh no. The club would be lucky, I'm sure they'll be really glad to have you." Or, rather, maybe wouldn't care too much, if the job proved small enough. "I mean, Vic's always said he could use people with brains. I'll just ask him."

That notion seemed to ruffle Jason further. He stubbed out his half-finished smoke. "But I don't even know—what could I possibly do?" His voice sounded a forlorn note in the fusty room.

"Well, I don't know yet! That's the thing. I don't know every last, last role around the club. I just wanted to check in with you first, see if you were interested. I mean, there's no point to asking him if you're not! Right? But, hey! I think you'd be totally fabulous! At whatever there is. Eh?"

"Sure. Whatever." Jason hungrily dug out another Newport. "Why not."

"Can I bum one?" asked Matt, not that he wanted menthol but just for the extra convivial feeling . . .

"Help yourself." Jason tossed the pack over to the bed.

All right, then. Not *exactly* the effect he'd intended—was a thank-you totally out of order here?—but good enough. By the time Matt got sick of the menthol, Jason had warmed sufficiently to give an account of the X party the other evening, how in the bathroom he'd stared at a candle flame for what felt like half an hour but turned out only to be five minutes, and have you ever really stared at a flame? I mean, really looked, and seen how it seemed to be dancing, to a kind of beat, only you couldn't hear, though you almost, that was the thing, you almost *could*—

"Whatever." Shrugging. "That's how it seemed."

Matt bobbed his head empathetically. "I think I know what you mean."

Jason smirked at Matt. "Really?" Shrewd.

"I think so." Matt blinked, smiling, dazed. "Sure. I can imagine it."

Jason drew an arm over his head and leaned back, taking his time, an overfed he-odalisque in grimy white T. "So why don't you X, Matt? *Never?* Like, the other night, when you said you and Sophie were going to . . ." He rolled his eyes at the implausibility of banal, decorous Matt daring such a bold venture. "Like you ever do that."

"Well. I've told you! I get depressed, after. Evidently you don't, don't need those treats." Matt gestured broadly at the black plastic deli bag. "But me—whew!"

"Right," muttered Jason quietly, bending to ash his smoke. Then: "I'd like to X with you sometime, Matt." He quickly lifted his head to fix Matt with a serious stare. "Just you and me. I think we could, could..." His warm brown eyes open, searching.

Aww. "I'd like that," Matt agreed, curling up his arms across his chest eagerly. "Absolutely. We'll find a good night."

And that was that. A good deed done there, sir. What a devil is insecurity! All you needed was a little tête-à-tête, an I-Still-Like-You-Buddy, Of-Course-You-Are-Someone, to set things in order. "So I'll talk to Vic, figure out some possibilities. I'll call you later in the week."

"Right, right," Jason murmured from the couch, rueful, waving.

With a light mind, then, over the phone that evening Matt reported back to Sophie on the success of the stratagem. "He really seemed to loosen up by the end. He told me some stuff, about X-ing, actually wants me to do it with him one of these days—"

"Really?!" Sophie squealed. "What did you say?" Like it was the most scandalous part of the story.

"I said yes. Sure. What?"

"Mmm, and you're going to?" Sophie chomped on something excitedly in the background.

"Who knows? The point is, I mean, I couldn't say no."

"I guess so." A bowl clinked at counter. "But it's a promise you can't keep."

"Well, I *can*. It's not like I'm allergic. I mean, if it's such a big deal."

"Right. Well, good, if that's how you feel. Hey, Matt. So tonight, I got the best film out of the library, this black-and-white gangster movie, French—"

He groaned.

"What?"

"I really have to work tonight. Can I, um, interest you in hitting a few bars?"

"Ahhhhhh: no. Not likely."

"Sophie. Come on! I have to. It's already Monday..."

"All ri-ight. Say hi to Liza for me."

"Hey, now. It's your own fault if you don't want to come with me."

"My fault! Oh-ho. It's your fault for having this fucking, flunky-ass job that—"

"Not fault, fault. I just mean: I'd a hundred times rather be with you, my sweet."

"Oh yeah?"

To convince, on a whim, on a blessed inspiration transmitted from celestial radio waves straight into his voice box, he picked up the chorus of Hall and Oates's seminal *"Because your kiss, your kiss, is what I miss—"*

"Goodbye!"

"When I turn out the li-ght..."

And the last thing he heard before hang-up was a beautiful glass blossom of breaking laughter.

But just as Matt had opened up the matter of where to stick Jason came another snafu vis-à-vis staffing at Paradise. For when he stopped by Cinema close on five to pick up the week's invites, who should be coming out the silver doors but two attractive African-American gentlemen in sports shirts and jeans—one of whom squealed and pinched his shoulder. "There you are!" he (she?) crowed, batting his eyelashes, considerably less effective a gesture now...Matt was still groping, trying to reassemble the familiar face out of his/her soft powdered cocoa-colored nose and mouth, when Coco—Carter—launched into the tale of how she was leaving, joining the staff of a club in Paris, "called *Les Bains*. Which means *The Baths*. So naturally, I said—"

"Girl, you said, count me in!" the other man shrilled.

"That's right!" Carter dissolved in effervescent hysteria, a hand flapping over his chest as he jumped up and down. "Magic, actually I'm soooo glad I ran into you, because I wanted to tell you myself—"

"Huh, you wanted to tell him *Good Bye*," said the other man. "*See* ya."

"Oeur voir!" Coco yelled gaily, pumping her arms as she hotfooted it from the dais to the street. "Good luck, baby!" She blew air-kisses from her long brown fingers.

If only ropes were right for Jason! But his tubby buddy in gauche clothes, trying to seem imperious…Who could take such a VIP seriously?

The call came the following day, when Matt was still in ConWest lecture (which was on, not altogether inappositely, Machiavelli's *Prince*): Miranda, letting him know Vic was sick but wanted to take a meeting at his place to deal with this replacing-Coco situation—at three, if Matt was free? Well! So Vic wanted his input on this issue. Why, yes, yes he was clear for three indeed.

The address surprised: it was that nothing-zone of lower Fifties on the East Side, and from the front the building looked like an ordinary, haute-bourgeois brownstone, but inside—not remotely Biedermeier, a zigzagging set of minimalist stairways leading to open floors off from a large, high-ceilinged room artfully done up with futuristic plastic furniture. Very '60s, like Sophie's spaceship ashtray: a maroon couch set of modular curved separates dominated the room; behind it, pink plastic lamps sprouted candescent pearls atop a long black plastic sideboard; ten paces off, by the kitchen, hovered a globed aquarium in which, when Matt arrived, Vic, dressed in a black cashmere robe left open at the top and showing a fecund field of chest hair, along with a tiny, very tasteful silver crucifix, was dribbling bits of fish food.

"Magic, there you are," Vic announced proudly. But he sounded sinus-stuffed, and the half-moons under his eyes looked dangerously bluish. From one robed arm he continued to shake, magisterial, translucent particles into the aquarium: rainbow-colored creatures wheeled through the water, their sinuous bodies disappearing and revealing themselves, practically half folded to open again like banners among the varieties of subaqueous rainforest. "Thanks for stopping by. I never get sick; for me this is, like, *whoa*. The world's coming to an end." Vic slammed the fish-food cylinder onto the kitchen bar, then walked to a framed kelly-green psychedelic Pop Art print on the far wall. As if in response to some question Matt had posed, Vic addressed this bit of art and then another, marching round the room; *I bought this in 1979, oh yeah, I knew them all, Warhol, Keith Haring, Basquiat, I knew Basquiat when he was still a baby spraying graf-fiti on, like, sub-way trains,* though the pictures themselves didn't seem to be Warhol, Haring, or Basquiat, just lovely pieces of late-twentieth-century anonymity. Maybe upstairs? Then the room ended at a glass wall: beyond, Matt spied an extensive terraced garden, but Vic refused to even let him really look, let alone go out there. "My garden is a work of *art,*" he declared. "Now's not the time; you'll come back in a couple weeks."

Oh? That sounded promising. Amiable. A good mood all round.

Vic blended himself a drink with pineapples someone had sent from Hawaii, then that reminded him of a whole load of lox that someone else had sent from Sweden, which he couldn't try now, too sick, it would be a waste: and before the word *Coco* had even been floated, Matt, perched uncomfortably on one section of the extravagant couch, had completed a plate of Scandinavian lox with flatbread and heirloom tomatoes and cream cheese. These were from specialty markets he hadn't heard of, yet Vic never tired of making astounded faces at each profession of ignorance as Matt was forced to *mm* and *ah* upon every luscious, singular gift of nature and cultivation that had been fussed over only to find a final resting place right here in his very own belly.

At last, Vic swooped down on a chair beside the couch. "So, Magic. How do you feel about your party?"

"Fine," he squeaked. Play it safe. He coughed. "I feel fine."

"*There* you are." Vic's arms folded awkwardly over the large chest. "See, someone like Carl or Brett, they would just be telling me how fantastic their party was, nothing like it in New York, filling me with bullshit, you know, because it's not as if I don't have eyes, it's not as if I don't know what's going on in my own *city!*" Looking at him darkly as if that were indeed just what Matt had been claiming. Now Vic tilted his head sideways, amused. "You know, the other day, when Donatella Versace came to Paradise, you know what they said to me?"

Matt shook his head.

"Well, Brett, Brett just went ballistic. Blaming everyone from Lacey to Coco. *Someone should have told her to go to the Champagne Lounge!* Carl, you know how he is. By the time he got it in his thick skull, that guy is so stupid, you have no idea, it's unbelievable, finally, he goes—" Vic sat higher in his chair and in Carl's mincing British pronounced: *"The commoners shouldn't be talking to the upper clawses."* Now Vic collapsed, dislodging, as if from a noisemaker somewhere in his chair, a series of raucous, ferociously unsick guffaws.

Matt's fingertips burned, his palms, his arms. "Ha-ha," he gritted out finally. He mimed dabbing tears of mirth from his dry eyes. "So they're funny. I didn't know that!"

"Oh well. You have to understand. They get desperate. They're like dogs. I mean, not like my Sasha or Mila; they're like bulldogs. Doberman pinschers. You're on their turf—they growl, they snap.[52] There's no *think*ing going on there. I mean, it works pretty well. They've been around, I don't know, ten years. That takes work. You're young." A gently corrective smile on his face, Vic gazed at him, almost greedily, as if through his hazel eyes Vic could suck out whatever in Matt was young. Now he popped a hand over his face. He peeked over the top cheekily. "I almost *forgot.* Here's what Brett said: *When you go fabulous that fast, you're finished.*"

"Finished." Oh, I. See. "Talk about finished. How about Carl's Whitesnake hair." Matt sniffed cruelly. Certainly knew that look from Jersey.

Vic chortled. "Oh, you're terrible." He scratched the stippled underside

---

[52] Only by grossly inflating my German accent and hinting—well, let us be candid each with the other, it is after all not a crime—rather dissembling that I served on the staff of a well-known women's magazine based in Berlin was I able to persuade Brett Nevers into an interview lasting no more than fifteen minutes and composed exclusively on his dog-hearted part of ruthless „pot-shots" aimed at our hero. Those sympathetic among you may be pleased to learn that, due to an all too foreseeable attack of clumsiness by the office exit, I succeeded in knocking over a spoiled orchid in its sumptuous glass container. (Is this a crime? Impersonation? I note in passing, it is amazing what a European accent permits in your country.)

of his jaw. "The thing is, they do have a good crowd. Even if they bring me twenty people on a Friday night, if I get one Amber Valletta out of it, it's worth ten of your college punks." Vic raised his eyebrows significantly at Matt. *"However,"* he went on, looking off as if to ignore the rage that was taking over Matt's face (please—hadn't Vic specifically asked for college kids!!), "the fact of the matter is, you're doing really, exceptionally well now. You're really firing on all cylinders. And our PR people are, like, ecstatic about you, all the press you've been doing. As a result, taking all of this into consideration," a sage Vic linked his fingers together around one robed knee, "I have decided to give you a raise. To a thousand a week. Which is, as I'm sure you know, exactly the same as Carl and Brett get," he explained primly, flicking a bit of lint off the couch. "Besides, you're at a new level now, you're coming in on hiring. I mean, we have to think about your new ropes girl. *I* was thinking—what about your girlfriend?"

Sophie?

"I mean, she's hot—what is she, a model?" Ah: Liza. "She seems to know everybody." And how would Vic deduce this: was it all done with one-way mirrors, security cameras? That mysterious look-but-don't-see thing; he had certainly never caught Vic anywhere in Paradise. "She's young, she's beautiful, she dresses," Vic nodded defensively along with each criterion. "I think she'd be perfect. Fresh face. We could give her— three hundred a week." Vic crossed his arms. *Not a penny more.*

"Oh. Well, the money wouldn't matter to her..."

"An uptown girl, huh?" Vic disbursed a salacious wink.

"And she's not—she isn't my girlfriend. My girlfriend's, um, Japanese."

"Aha! I shoulda known! Nothing but the best!" The robe fell apart to reveal an expanse of leathery forestland as Vic reached over and batted Matt powerfully on the shoulder. "My girlfriend's Korean. You know what they say—*once you try sushi!*"[53]

---

[53] Disgusting joke. We may be grateful for the blinds of innocence protecting Matthew from perceiving this vulgar jest.

Whatever that means. Matt nodded weakly.

"All right, Magic." Vic got to his feet, drawing the robe around him and tightening the belt with a peevish tug. "Call your *friend;* she says yes, you call Miranda, get her on payroll, we can use her this week. Let me know by this evening, otherwise we'll get one of our alternates, I've got people to call. All right? All right?" Vic had walked him over to the door; now he stooped suddenly at a thick paper bag. "Here you go. A little present. Dom. Some idiot gave it to me. Shows how well he knows me. I. mean, what am I gonna do with this stuff? Just a waste."

"You don't . . . drink champagne?" Feeling moronic even as the words came out of his mouth.

"Magic." Vic pursed his lips sarcastically. "Have you ever seen me drink? I mean, I'll have a *sip,* if it's really something special, but in this business, believe me, you just don't, when you've been around awhile. And now that I'm sick, it's just, *ugh.*" A phone began mewling from somewhere back in the apartment: Vic waved, more to shoo Matt out the door. "Right, Magic," he mimed a phone, "call Miranda." Then Vic hurried off, the robe floating around above his heels like a cape.

And would now be a good time to mention Jason? But—Vic's busy, sick, probably not the best moment. Besides, shouldn't we think this out first? Come up with a plan, present an appropriate position to Vic. *She's hot; she dresses:* not exactly Jason's skill set, that. Ugh, but what *was?* Matt clicked the door shut behind him and tripped down the four steps outside, swinging the bag of champagne under a leaden March sky.

The idea of Liza at the ropes was taken as different strokes by different folks. Liza herself, when he phoned just after six, let out a low caterwaul of pure delight. Vic Spector wanted her, really, he knew of her existence, had seen her? (Flattered, obviously, and indeed, as he himself well remembered, it was like having someone pick you from some celestial lookbook in which you never knew yourself enrolled.) Really, but Vic Spector thought she could do the job? Well, absolutely! Matt encouraged her, thinking: hardly brain surgery. Merely check to make sure whoever came by had hands stamped by Lacey or Angel; if not, use her best judgment (on whether hot or not, dressed versus dull). "Maybe I'll wear my satin sleeveless shirt, you know, with the ruffles on the side? And, wow, you haven't seen these, I just got the most awesome blue suede boots, I'll show you tonight at Ciel Rouge...or maybe red, this backless Alexander McQueen thing?" Matt left her flicking hangers relentlessly through the closet of her mind. "Thank you," she murmured after they set up a plan to meet at nine. "You're welcome," he said, a bit awkward. Because in truth: he was queerly disengaged from the whole matter, certainly hadn't been seeking out a way to signal her with favor.

That was the angle he tried to spotlight on the phone with Sophie immediately after. He shied away from any hot-button terms that might reveal he understood that what it really meant when she stuttered a jumpy laugh, said *Liza!* and *Wow, I never would have thought she would be a...good person for that,* was: my Sophie, afflicted by a little jealousy, aren't you. "I'm not at all sure about it either," he agreed, assuming a worried voice, "but Vic just basically ordered me—he has such weird ideas sometimes."

"Totally. I practically have déjà vu. Weren't we last saying all this about his hiring you?"

"Well, I've turned out pretty, pretty well." He stiffened before he realized: she's pushing your buttons out of insecure pique; just hold on till the tantrum blows off. "Anyway, we can just try Liza, see how it works out...and, I mean, I knew *you* would never want—"

"Oh, *never*," she broke in. "You got that right. Ugh. Actually, I was thinking. Um, how would you feel if I didn't go to Paradise this week?"

"Really?" Now that was taking it too far.

Her voice softened. "It's just, then I could leave for break a whole day earlier and get to Chicago Friday—because, the thing is, my aunt's driving up on Saturday and I could be there before...I mean, I'll come if you want me to. Totally. I just, I know my family will be really stressed out, picking me up."

And then, to bundle the whole conversation up into a little unhappy ball that could be hurled away, he relented.[54] "I'm going to miss you," he averred. "It's going to seem so empty, so unParadisiacal!" Though: easier, probably. Yes, true. On a night with Liza debuting at the ropes, with that reporter from *Interview*, having to minister, to run back all the time to Sophie's table and pep her up when she was feeling bored, tired, would maybe have been a little much. "But you should definitely do what you have to."

"Thanks," she said quietly. "Hey—did you ask Vic about Jason?"

"Well, he was sick. So. It didn't seem like a good time. And I mean, shouldn't I figure something out first? Like, what Jason's suited to do?"

"I guess so." She sighed. "He's going to be pretty bummed out about Liza."

"W-why? I mean, not like he'd be a good ropes person! He can't expect *that*."

"No, I know. But I'm just saying—his feelings are still going to be hurt."

"Well, I'll devise something for him soon. By Friday, let's say."

Afterward, Matt folded up the phone and fell back on the suggestible bed pillows. And *why* had he raised the possibility of working at Cinema with Jason without thinking it through first? God. Should he tell Jason in advance, somehow prepare him?

Oh, let's just let it slide away in silence. Matt tossed the cell to a corner of the bed. Better not to foment an issue; just see Jason Friday, introduce the matter offhand. And after all by Friday we'll have thought up something for him to do too? Done. Matt catapulted himself toward

---

[54] But this is not the way to nourish a fond love-relationship! So: I see this now, though not then, when also I gave way to silences, similar makeshift measures to maintain a peace I was desperate for. Readers, perhaps you will think I make some joke, but often I feel that being placed in a detainment facility for seven months (seven months and eight days; only twenty-four such days remain to me!) while I await a trial to determine all my future is an advantageous event in my life. After all, how simplified my day is made! „What shall I buy at the market for dinner?" „What film shall I view tonight?" Such lesser questions vanish, so I am left to turn over the leaves of my own past under a clear new light, an instructional experience.

the shower—only an hour until Liza in red, or in cream, would be waiting for him at Ciel Rouge tapping a blue suede boot in the air with her customary show-impatience. Ropes girl. My God, she was practically in his employ. I mean, she *was*. Who would have thunk it, to see her gliding past him on the waxed hallway of Third North, first day of the world, a millennium ago! A blot of warm pulsed through his pelvis, stirring it faintly as a lake fern.

CHRONOLOGICAL GLOSS BY DR. HANS MANNHEIM
————————————————————————————

So perhaps you sit in Oklahoma, or Idaho, or Guardalavaca, and you are saying to yourself or to your loved ones, great God! This small child, this unskilled labourer Matthew Acciaccatura, earns $1,000 each week in base compensation for luring students to a venue where they may dance and drink and make use of recreational drugs, besides, now let me tell, he can count an additional $500 in revenue from sales of the drug named Ecstasy (for he profits $5 from each of the 90–100 pills sold at $25); also he receives bonus of $5 per body he draws; at this rate, he may make some $150,000 in the year 1996. Am I in a sane frame of mind? This is what you say. Yes, I appreciate your dismay. May I remind you that during this identical period, I, one academic doctor, lived with my wife (also academic doctor) in a „studio" of roughly 3.5 metres by 5 metres, not to count kitchen and bathroom, and, though a trained professional, could discover no employment?

So you dig for your railway schedules or telephone the long-distance bus lines such as Greyhound and Red & Tan. You are saying, I wish to partake of these riches as well. Well, you cannot. Why, you say? So the child Matthew is talkative and possesses expensive clothing; why cannot I do the same? Because this world we discuss is gone.

Allow me, please, to rewind your timepieces once more. In 1996 we danced along to the merry „Macarena" and „No Diggity" and wept with The English Patient and Shine, „feel-good tearjerkers." In 1996 elections were held in Bosnia, and the Taliban captured

Afghanistan. TWA Flight 800 exploded. And, what concerns us very closely, in this era Mayor Rudolph Giuliani launched a „crusade" against New York night-clubs.

Please comprehend: in 1996 a night-club like Matthew's could service 10,000 patrons in two weekend nights; over a year, New York would host approximately 25 million such patrons and gross an approximate $2.9 billion in admission and alcohol sales. In 1996 there existed a civilization at its height, led by youths such as Matthew and fueled by Ecstasy, which kept myriads dancing all the night, many of their veins racing with the additive methamphetamine. Let some anthropologist with access to a greater library than mine study how very widely this subculture was covered in the magazines and newspapers, how high songs with the electronic background and rapid beats of so-called techno rose on the musical charts. Or yourselves perform a search—it is so easy, in this present computerized era—upon the names *Richie Rich*, *Suzanne Bartsch*, *Michael Alig*, and you will locate the vibrant atmosphere in which Matthew operated. Dressed in tinfoils and large fairy costumes, or wearing minks costing tens of thousands of dollars, the inhabitants of this country went to large-scale night-clubs and stayed to dawn, then they attended after-parties and stayed through the afternoon, next they went home, they swapped the news of their entertainments, they went shopping for their subsequent ensembles, and were anxious in every way until that time once more approached to enter the dancing palaces.

It was a world. But then something changed: the „Quality of Life" brigades of Mayor Giuliani laid their chilling hand upon this bloom. Thus what I speak of, what you hear of in these pages, is as an Atlantis now.

4.

In those three days before spring break, crocuses unfolded from the meager dust. Magnolias bloomed. One marvelous prematurely vernal evening—Wednesday, this was—sent everyone hanging out windows, reclining on stoops, reverberating the downtown streets with the noises of clicking shoes and late-night chatter floating free as dandelion seeds. And the one dark spot in all of this:

What To Do With Jason.

Oh, Matt tried. Bartender? No, he might as well help Jason into a busboy's uniform as suggest a thing so beneath him. Office staff? Er, the little matter of daylight, responsibility, attention to detail. Then what? Security guard? Tech crew? Skills—why did so many jobs require actual skills! Did they need another person stationed outside the club...ah, please. Like Jason could represent the club's image? And just imagine: Lacey and Angel—they'd rip him to ribbons. Sir, I think you're just spinning your wheels.

—Well, it wasn't exactly our fault! The boy has: a structural *flaw*. Lose some weight, you know? Hercules helps those who help trim their own waistlines first.

"But you're not going to say that to Jason" was Sophie's dry comment when they were spending a last fifteen minutes at her place before she took a shuttle for the airport.

"Of course not." Nodding along fluently.

"Because that sounds pretty superficial and awful." Her serious eyes scanned his.

He sighed. Picked a white fluff from her lashes. "It's just the truth, though. Realism. Dry-eyed materialism. Nature, red in tooth and claw," he babbled on, while she remained silent and grim. "You're really to blame, you know."

"Me?!" She blew up her bangs out of her face angrily. "Why?"

He was grinning, mischievous. "If I hadn't mentioned it to him . . ."

"I was just—wakening you to your fucking senses! And you *asked* me!"

"Sh, sh, Sophie." He lavished her neck, cheek with pecks. "I was just kidding!"

But the joke never took. And her goodbye kiss by the door smacked the faintest bit cold.

Now what? Stranded in the empty pad, Matt passed a dull forty minutes poking through some uninspired magazines and downing sesame snacks. Before Liza phoned and in conspiratorial tones revealed an urgent scheme: "Do you want to get facials?"

What?

"My treat." Her voice breaking up, husky, on the *ee* of *treat*.

"Isn't that sort of . . . ladies only?"

"Oh, Matt." As if: how could he be such a shy egg, such a naïf? "My dad does it all the time." A lambent pause. Then: "I won't tell anyone if you don't," her breathy whisper loosed through the earpiece like smoke into Sophie's studio.

There was this facial; there was the bottle of prosecco Matt drained afterward, curled on the couch with electric Lester, watching Liza walk out in at least twelve versions of outfit before she settled on a brown crinoline dress with spaghetti straps (real spring Prada, she let him know over a shoulder). And so, rubbed thus with rich unguents outside and in, as Matt lolled on the leather, lifting Lester scruffwise to stare into his sublime and omniscient green eyes—while outside the day went plunging from languorous spring evening into irrevocable black and dark—there seemed indeed no righter place to be than precisely here. All cares sculled far off, driftwood, in the darkness . . . so that even when Jason's name came up on the cell-phone screen, Matt saw no reason why he shouldn't press the green button to *Accept*. "Jason! Hello!"

"Hey, Matt." Heavy breathing.

Oh, crap. "I wanted um, to call you—Vic's been sick this week." Jerking up hastily, Matt jammed the phone to his ear. "So I haven't had a chance, didn't seem like the right time. To ask. But as soon as he gets better—ow! Jesus Christ! Stop!" Lester had seized this moment to dig claws into his shoulder.

"Wh-where are you?" A discomfited chuckle.

"I'm at Liza's. Helping her dress. Well, not like *that*, just the old what-to-wear."

"Right. Yeah, I heard she's the new Coco."

Of course: Liza: Marco: Jason. Though wasn't she on the outs with him these days? So: all cards were on the table. "Vic's idea. I mean, Coco just quit suddenly, so it was a, a staffing emergency. I had to go over to his place—that's how sick he is. And maybe something will open up for you, like this! Or we'll just find something; let's talk tonight—"

"Well, actually, that was why I'm calling you. I'm feeling not so good, I think I'm not going to come to Paradise."

"No! Maybe it'll—make you feel better? They say alcohol—"

No, he would stay in. No, he didn't want any OJ or soup, thanks anyway, would sleep, try to take an early train to Scarsdale. Yes, he would say hi for Matt to his mom. Sounding calm and self-possessed, if a bit stuffed up, when he pledged, "You have a good break too."

And: *click*. Well, that was easy! So much for Sophie, fantasizing all sorts of dire conclusions. . . .

"Who was that?" Liza wondered, strolling on bare stilt legs back into the room. "Oh my God, Matt!" Slapping at the ripply hip of her dress. "You drank the whole thing?"

From its dark-wood coffee table, the bottle radiated a vacant green light into the dim sitting zone. "Er . . . whoops?"

"Dude, you mooch..." Sighing, she patiently headed back to a cabinet.

"Mooch..." Coming up behind her to lean against the threshold to the kitchen. A beautiful word. Moon and smooch. S-moo—

"Here, you do it." Whirling on him, she pressed the fresh bottle to his hands. Her flushed underlip bit, her cold fingers brushing his, her atmosphere of smoke and a musky French-ish perfume suddenly veiling him in... before she mussed his hair and winked. "Be a gentleman." And sashayed past him to fidget with a CD in the five-disc changer.

The music transformed into samba. The cork gave way, complaisant, in his palm. And when he eased into the spot she patted beside her on the couch, when he spilled the foam into vintage etched glasses, when Liza smiled at him, it was a smile tipped out of the corner of her mouth and eyes, then reached over to light his cigarette—flash of black polish and fluted marble—Matt thought: oh, it was impossible not to: this is the life. This is what it's all about.

"So listen," she yawned, one arm triangled atop the couch back, her white flesh dipping a hollow in its gleaming black pelt, "my birthday's coming up. Three weeks from today, April fifth. Which is a Friday. And I was thinking—can I have a party?"

How easy to make her happy! She clapped her hands, holding them upright, stiff and straight, and let out the softest, hoarsest, most delicately restrained *Yay*. She wanted a birthday cake big enough for all comers, to pay for everyone's hits of X that night all by herself. She wanted to wear a flapper's beaded wig and a dress with tassels. And why not? Why couldn't Jonathan sell a fat load in advance (at a discount, even? surely no kickback for me)? What had she asked of him, these last weeks, trucked hither and yon, aiding and abetting him from the goodness of her meretricious heart?

"It's going to be the best party of all time! Yee-ow!" Liza vaulted her arms like an Olympic gymnast, bucking her torso in the direction of the far wall. But then—"Thank you," she murmured, turning demurely toward him. And with her head tilted back, her eyes lowered beneath curled lashes, her gaze on him felt as if the shyest, most elusive unicorn crept up to you and at last laid its modest head right in your lap.

* * *

Spring break turned out to be boring. Spring break turned out to be mind-fissioningly, unutterably stultifyingly dull. A whole half semester's worth of catch-up lay sterile on the shelves of his sturdy bookcase: but the will, alas, was lacking. And how could he ever have thought this would be a swell plan? *I'll just stay in the city. By myself. Go to a few museums; annihilate the overdue reading.* Please! If the contest was between *The Sexual Habits of Primates* and staring vacantly at the ceiling, those swollen randy bonobos would come up short every time.

Plus, sans Sophie, where was the point in treating oneself to a savory crêpe at Le Gamin? Sans Liza, uncooperatively absconded till Friday into the wilds of Nantucket, did he really want to show up at the opening for the flagship store of a chichi leather-goods firm, stand aimless in the fern-shaded emporium among throngs of faintly familiar faces? No, truly: Matt stepped out from his cab, peered a moment through the plate glass, then turned on a heel to walk southward down Madison.

Though: "I'm getting so much done, Mom," he swore over the phone after a dispiriting matinée of *Contempt* at Film Forum. Oh no, he really couldn't afford to come out to New Jersey—I mean, he *could*, but, um, what sort of position would that put him in for the end of the semester?

"You mean you can't bring your books here?"

"Well, but the thing is—it's research, you know? So. I need to use the library. NYU has a *really* amazing library; I mean, all these documents, and microfilm—"

Microfilm did it. The magic pomp of technology swept her every time. "Oh yeah, I bet they don't have that even at the Englewood Library—"

"—or at least not the same selection!"

"Gee. They work you too hard there," she decided. Then: "I guess you're almost done anyway. What do you have, a coupla months left?"

Right, right, something like that. And he vamoosed off the line before landing himself in a fresh pot of boiling water.[55] Christ! Surely he wasn't going home this summer? He must stick that on his list of things to think toward.

As it happened, Sophie was full of all things summer when she and her new pageboy haircut returned on Sunday afternoon, having spent the stay in Chicago diligently dispatching applications for internships at emerging indie designers around the nation. Around the nation? "What do you mean?! You didn't say that part on the phone. Where are these places?" he wanted to know.

"Chicago." She shrugged. "San Francisco." Musing over where in the kitchen to place the emerald-green artisanal blown-glass vase he had just presented her.

"You're going to Chicago for the summer without telling me?"

"Matt! I'm telling you now. It's a possibility, for a few weeks," she commented, matter-of-fact, as she stepped back, hand on hip, to admire her vase on the window ledge. "And you know, it wouldn't hurt for you to try applying for an internship either." He rolled his eyes. "At least start thinking of your career path." His fingers drummed at the side of the table. "I mean, it's not like you're going to be a promoter your whole life!" She glanced over at him, a clear, blameless expression on her face. "Right?"

Now, how many people did she know of who had been interviewed by *Index* at age eighteen? Was that anything to sneer at, say? Couldn't she once be glad for him instead of twisting his accomplishments to seem like so much inconsequential crap? "Who knows? Have you ever met Brett and Carl?" he asked airily, though of course she hadn't. "They're, like, thirty-*five*. They seem to be leading a very nice life."

"Thirty-*five*!" She rested the vase on a shelf above the sink. "You're not going to do it at thirty-five." Now she turned, serious. "Are you?"

---

[55] I was not so fortunate. My father's seventieth birthday occurred on 18 March; thus I was summoned, at incredible expense, in an absence I would later learn was exploited for abominable ends, back to München for a difficult celebration.

"Maybe."

"That would be very, very sad," she muttered. Then she marched over and plonked the vase right back on the original window ledge. "I think it looks nice there," she declared tersely.

That was the beginning of their tiff: which ended, like spring break—they finished off just as the minutes drained to midnight—with an urgent bout of X-rated make-up, rather spicier for that basis than their sessions of late. The one real event of his wearisome vacation.

And perhaps he had run to seed a bit over these humdrum, solitary days. For he didn't quite have his thinking cap on when, a mere thirty-six hours after school began again, he discovered that word of his birthday favor to his new, evidently motormouth of a ropes girl was not without consequence. It began with a telephone call, on his cell, after ConWest lecture, Tuesday, at two.[56] "Heyyy," a snazzy male voice said. "Is that Matt? Do I have Magic Matt?" An affable laugh at Matt's morose *yah*.

---

[56] I cannot help but note it was on this day, 26 March, that also I received signals of a portentous nature. Or rather, I made the acquaintance of someone who would later be the source of much trouble. This occurred at a reception given for him by the psychology department after one of the most absurd lectures I have heard, I do not recollect the title but can inform you it dealt with a Freudian reading of a popular, vegetable-themed children's toy. He and I were standing some metre apart by a table on which those standard American cocktail items were lit up by the same ceiling fixtures that caused the bald ellipse on the centre of his head to shine with sweat. All at once he looked diagonally behind me with an expression of dull interest: I turned and saw Lisanne entering the room in her navy sheath dress, carrying her blazer over one energetic, jogger's arm, her beautiful thick wavy hair straining at the metal clip where she had forced it into a chignon. She was drawing to my side—or so I only thought, because she walked two paces past me and put out her hand to shake the clumsy paw (even from my distance I could see it was clammy and without force) of that „celebrity" visiting us for the evening from Seattle, chair of an entire department of toadies and frauds with whose numbers my wife, ex-wife, now counts herself among. Amazing now to consider that for weeks I kept an alert eagle-eye for any exchanges she might have with Malcolm Barrow: though, in all fairness, as I should have seen, my quick-witted pet could do no more than dally briefly with one so simple-minded, such a common Jack-a-dandy. Yet arrogant youth errs in dismissing as romantic rivals its elders, with their floppy bodies, besides lack of hair. Thus Malcolm Barrow stayed the focus of my suspicion/surveillance—while the real threat grew like one mandrake-root beneath our marriage-bed.

"I hope you don't mind," the voice continued, in a free and easy tone suggesting he was certain that Matt couldn't, "Liza gave me your number. David Breck. We met, for just a moment, the other week at Peter Kent's?"

David Breck. Matt squeezed against the wall, letting a rush of kids stream past in the corridor as he flipped through the mind's Rolodex. Was it maybe that guy in the beige suit? Who'd come over and said good night to Peter at one point, Peter's best friend from St. Paul's? Hadn't Liza described him as the son of a big Hollywood producer?

"I'm sorry we didn't get a chance to talk more then," the voice went on, smooth, genial. "But I was wondering if you had some time over the next couple of days . . . there's an idea I was hoping you could help with." No, definitely better not to discuss it over the phone. Oh, whenever Matt was free. Was that all right? It wouldn't take up too much time. He would be really grateful, David Breck explained, though so self-assured that he sounded rather to be doing Matt a favor.

So mysterious and hush-hush. And evidently to my advantage, this idea, most definitely the intended vibe. Hmm. Well, I mean, obviously the guy was friends enough with Liza; and Peter, churlish to refuse *him* . . . "All right. Do you know Café Gitane, Mott Street?"

Matt waited to reach home before calling Liza, catching her in the middle of a nap. "Oh, did he call you?" she mused. But she had no idea why: David Breck had given her the same business about not discussing over the phone. "I'm sure it isn't anything *bad*," she claimed. "Peter likes you. And they're, like, one person. Remember I told you that party was part of this thing, this, like, social club? Anyway, the thing is, it's really David's baby. I bet you anything it has to do with that. David's *super* into it. He's like obsess—" A delicate sneeze away from the phone. "Obsessed. I'm so sick, Matt," she moaned. "I don't know if I can come out tonight," though, in the end, she decided that she *would* really like to see the inside of that new bar Caramel, grippe or no.

David Breck was already seated on the banquette when Matt threw open the door at Gitane and got his tall, elastic form up cheerfully, extending a hand for the shake. He let his other hand rest on the back of

Matt's a longish moment, smiling broadly, two winsome blots of blood glowing in the apples of his cheeks. "Thanks so much for meeting me." He gestured to the chair. "Please sit down."

So patrician. *Please sit down.* Hello, it's a public place—which *I* picked! And as Matt bent over the menu, David's manner continued to chafe: the "charming" way he bantered with the waitress, coaxing out a smile from her sullen face; how he generously twirled his fingers at Matt reading, indicating he would let Matt take his time, sensitively watching over the ordering process as if it were all happening under his auspices.

"Now, Matt," David Breck began, serious, after the waitress scooted off. But then a brilliant smile split open his face. "Isn't this place great? I've never been here before, thanks for the suggestion." He lifted an eyebrow to commend Matt's discerning taste. Jeez, how much *gayer* West Coast guys could seem. "Well, Matt. I wanted to talk to you on serious club business." He leaned back against the wall, in his ivory turtleneck sweater all Handsome Young Man.

Serious club business. Like you know from serious club business, you fop.

The waitress brought their lattes; David lavished her with another screen-test smile, then crooked his bendy-straw of a body back toward Matt. So, how much did Matt know about their little club? I mean, it was nothing much, it was only that when he and Peter came to NYU, they were disappointed. By the social offerings. At Harvard, did Matt know, there were final clubs? Right, and at Princeton, eating clubs. At Yale, they had secret societies. At other schools frats, good frats, not these . . . David Breck searched the ceiling with a profound expression of disgust. Well, Matt knew what he meant, no doubt. And that was back when Peter's parents first moved to Paris, so they had this perfect space, just uptown. Why not start their own club? David beamed at Matt in pure *Eureka!* A place where, every week, you could hang out, meet new people like yourself, as guests that members brought, for example. Like how he had met Matt! David's hands shot up to signal how very fortuitous that meeting was. There were all those other advantages, like forming a network for later, but David shrugged these away. Though, it was true, how else could you get so connected to people who would be helpful after college. . . . David took a sip of latte, looking off into space as if drawn up entirely into the vast network he was building there. Then his gaze lit on Matt: it was just really *too bad* that they hadn't run across each other earlier! Because this round was over, they were just doing initiations now; an apologetic smile. But next semester, as early as September, get in touch, and of course Matt should come along anytime with Liza as a guest . . .

Matt began to protest, to show how little he was interested in such a connection, *please*, when—what? "Liza's in the club?"

David looked slyly embarrassed, as if out of modesty he hadn't meant to show that ace in his hand. "She didn't tell you? Last fall she joined us." He failed to hide the beginnings of a designing smile by blowing on his mug. "She doesn't come much anymore, though." For a moment, David appeared off, blinking inappropriately, before he lathered on the white-wash of a fresh smile. "From what I understood, the other night, it seems as if maybe what she used to get with us she gets at your club these days." David tilted his water glass deferentially at Matt. *Touché.*

Now this was all turning out awful, terribly sordid. Plainly David had some sort of poisonous crush on her. Jesus, I'm not stopping you! "Maybe it's the nightclub setting," Matt noted diplomatically. The slightest bit different—wouldn't you say?

David began a rapid, overeager nodding. "Oh, absolutely. The other evening she was telling me everything about when she goes to Paradise. And *that's* actually why I asked you to meet with me today. Because I had this idea." It was *Eureka* all over again, David waving both hands by his head—*Crazy, I know, but with the right studio, this project could really fly!* "Matt." David stared right at him with benevolent intensity. "I want to buy some Ecstasy for our initiation party."

Lickety-split Matt swiveled 360, making sure no one was near. "I'm not a dealer," he hissed across the table.

"Oh." Calm. Undimmed. Folding his arms again. As if to say, *Why not? Why aren't you what I want you to be?* So typical rich-kid. "But Liza said," David paused, lips curled vaguely sinister, *I'm smarter than you think*, "that you always get the best—"

"Ssh," Matt spat. The waitress was speeding by from the bathroom, but she didn't glance over. "Yes, yes, but I am not—that." Jesus!

"Sorry." Stubborn, in an affronted voice, David went on: "Maybe I should explain. It's very in-house, very discreet. April fourth. Just our initiates, and about ten core members of the club. I could even give you a list of names."

"You're not listening," Matt singsang. I could just leave, stand up and flee—wait. Names. Remember, that night at Peter's? Those two blondes? He cleared his throat. "Who are they? The...initiates?"

Yes, yes. In a tally of ten or so girls and guys, among whom Matt again distinguished Taylor Harrison and Walker Jones, was that other he'd overheard at Peter's.

Of course. How could he have failed to connect the dots? But afterward the events of that evening, when he was so drunk and coked-up, had just seemed nothing touching reality. Well. So appropriate! So Dwight! Sneaking up the social ladder, insinuating himself like a rock climber...While we've been wrapped up in Paradise, he's steadily ascending in this land of the limitless rich! God, how did he manage it? No pedigree, not the scion of a noble house: a hick, sweet Jesus, a hick from Buttfuck, Minnesota! And now: initiated!

—Or was he? Let's see. How very badly did David Breck want this Ecstasy? Maybe we could stipulate, *Let's make a deal: you nix Dwight and you've got yourself a party.* But no, no: what kind of revenge was that? So whiny, so weenie-like. Surely you can invent better. With or without X, Dwight's joining, unless you...Nine days to come up with a stratagem. You're a bright boy. "You know," Matt breathed out, "the fourth, did you say? Well—I can't promise. It's not what I do, but as a favor..." Really, how hard could it be? Jonathan sells, you resell. "I'll look into it. I think I might just manage it."

"Excellent!" David laughed happily. "I know Peter will be thrilled. He was really excited by the idea. Everyone will be. Thank you!"

Of all things. Ecstasy. Coke, sure, but impossible to imagine X in that place, the chalky pills on the marble tabletops, raucous beats of house music quaking the frail golden sconces. And when they stumbled out, before those liveried doormen! I wonder if David knows what he's sign-ing this in-group up for. Now David was paying the check, handshaking, blabbing how thirty or so tabs (tabs! as if it were LSD) would be great, money no object: a dumb, officious aedile to the very last.

In the taxi, speeding westward along Houston, Matt emitted a little cackle, startling the driver into glancing round. Back in the room, he threw his coat at the chair, dove headfirst onto the bed. By all standards he was dancing o'er the green graves of the prepster mafia. Downtown was practically pelting him with invitations and presents: and, lifting a flute of champagne at a fashion-show after-party in a SoHo loft, climb-ing the spiral stair at a triplex penthouse in the Chelsea Hotel over a rau-cous magazine launch in progress, giving his name to the list girl of a cocktail thing at Cipriani's Downtown to celebrate some record release, hadn't he had occasion to reflect, *Ah, me*, apropos his success relative to the preps? Yes, by now he was nearly a household name at school, kids made up stories (that he was really the black-sheep son of an Italian count, was fornicating with Liv Tyler, was fabulously rich with villas at Ibiza, Majorca); indeed, he even intimidated—all around NYU kids got nervous, blushed, looked back to see if he'd noticed them, evidently won-dering if he knew their names. He was unstoppable, he was a juggernaut, he was riding three horses at the forefront of the Golden Horde—

Yet there was still one kid to KO.

For almost two hours, like a miser about a pile of gold, Matt capered about the hearth rug, plotting revenge. There was planting the pills on Dwight, somehow calling the police: but certain to rebound on him and, anyway, far too grisly. Not expulsion, not criminal charges, just an em-barrassment, some suffering, mayhap not getting into the club. But how? What action would they consider too much? Perhaps he could arrange for a massive breakage of some expensive thing, have the blame fall Dwightward? The dollhouse? But no, what a recreant he was to even consider ruining poor unknown Annabel's toy. Ditto with insulting the servants in some shape; don't drag other people's misery into this. Or get Dwight to disobey some rule . . . Did they have any rules? But how fool-ish, how easily explained: and to have Dwight slip publicly through such a clumsy noose? Not a breach of protocol: something no one could talk his way out from, something incontrovertible as science.

Use that gray matter, can't you? Or just think of the alternative, if you miss your chance here! Dwight beyond reach, fancy-free forever! Will you really pass him the wafer, will he really close his eyes as he joins in communion with them, by your hand?

—That's it.

He couldn't resist pouncing on the phone. "Jason," Matt hissed when, miraculously, the boy answered! "Um, hello, how are you. I was wondering—that bad X. The Doves you sampled the other week. Do you still have a few?"

"Marco and I didn't take any more, if that's what you mean. After throwing up all night, ugh." There came a wan laugh. "God, if that's heroin, I am so never trying again."

"That's not my question," Matt snapped. "Did you throw them out? Do you still have them?"

Ah, and he did, he did, he did.

5.

In the daytime the Dwight plan was definite. It was the plane on which Matt walked, darkly glittering as asphalt over water. In the nights it was more cloudlike, a fever's haze. Sometimes he grew sick from the idea, nauseated off the toxic fumes of this venom roiling in his belly, or suddenly afraid of detection. Then he might almost have been convinced to relinquish it, knocked down by the feather of some minor argument. Who knows? If Jason had bothered to palpate his flimsy excuse (trying to do that Stefan guy a favor, since Jonathan didn't sell H at Paradise: hardly the soundest of stories) or mentioned it to Sophie, and Sophie so much as *looked* at him hard with her sane dark eyes—who knows.

But classes began and ended at their appointed hours, nights took their habitual roller-coaster course, and as for the Paradise of March 29: well, it was as if some god of good-time had blown the room full of happy-dust, gold and swirling, infectious; even Matt could hear how Future didn't mix one wrong beat, seemed to be conjuring an unbroken soundtrack to total joy out of the elements of beats and notes, and diva moans. Jonathan didn't blink when Matt turned over the brick of David Breck's cash in the staff bathroom, and though the tin of Smiley-Face-stamped Ecstasy rattled disconcertingly in Matt's jacket, Sophie had long ago left the club for the night and all those who swept him into an intoxicated embrace that evening seemed not to notice how he flinched, angled away. What anyway could they have guessed about what for all the world looked like a case of breath mints? So for nine whole days, nothing blocked his way. The signposts led squarely to this precipice.

April 4!

Matt arrived at Peter's early, after leaving Sophie holed up on a long-distance telephone date with her best childhood friend from Kyoto. In the main room, two girls in tucked-in silk button-down blouses chattered urgently, sneaking glances in the direction of a couch where three guys wearing neat dress shirts, navy blazers, and khakis sat trading comments in low voices beneath the prints of hunting scenes; otherwise, only from down the hall toward the bedrooms could the buzz of talk be heard. Matt visited the coatroom, then obtained a scotch and drew over to a window in the wall opposite the front door. Through the pane: a patio, a walkway bordered by side lanterns leading to a kind of Belle Époque iron-and-glass cabana lit by what appeared to be flickering candles.

"There you are, baby," murmured Liza, striding right up. "I need a drink, God." She grabbed his scotch off the sill and nuzzled it. "I can't believe you're doing this," she teased, a vaguely malicious fire in her eyes.

For an instant—jeez, and would it be like that all night? all life?—a bubble of fear rose from his stomach to burst in his gullet: how did she...? But then: of course not, just doing this favor, she means. "Keep that. I'll, ah, get us fresh ones. And then—a smoke?"

"Why not," she growled into the glass, nipping at the side with her fine teeth.

As she drilled her bitten, black-polished nails on the bar counter and tapped one wayward boot against the parquet, Matt tried to keep his gaze sutured to tongs and ice, the crystal decanter he was manipulating. One trusted her, though. Even if she could afterward put it together: what allegiance did she feel toward Dwight Smeethman? Or anyway: who cared? Who needed her, or anyone else here who might suspect? Just so long as no one told the police. But they wouldn't do that—would have to admit they'd bought drugs, these princelings. No, the plan was cut on all sides like a crown jewel. Yet his breath still caught, raspy, in his chest. Ten o'clock it must be now: two more hours.

"I'd rather be," she began, leaning her elbow down on the counter, *très intime,* "with you at Ichor." She snatched up a purple grape from a bowl, lobbed it into her mouth. "You know it's some kind of Rite of Spring party there tonight?"

"It'll still be going on when we leave," he sniffed, passing one of the tumblers.

"You think so?" Fluttering her lashes at him like a true ingenue. "So we'll go?"

"Of course we'll go, we'll go." Blathering on about a future in which nothing would matter anymore. "Now, how about that smoke?"

Out on the patio, they sat on a stair above the slate walkway and smoked, gazing at the glass cabana animated only by tapering candle flames and the bright white haze in the sky that was all the lights in New York. Well, he had thought it through. For, sure, there had been stirrings of remorse, when, incredulous at having even thought such an evil up, he had nearly laughed it off: a joke, merely a hypothetical fantasizing, didn't anyone get I was only messing? Because, let's face it, he talked a big game, justice and fate and nemesis. But never once—hardly creditable, but true!—never *once* had he premeditatively *set out* to hurt a soul. Which was what had always amazed him in high school and before—how sometimes they'd planned for days, maybe even weeks in advance, the exact instant and manner by which to rush him all at once in the locker room with duct tape, or for hours the precise corner where they would meet to beat him so he walked on bawling and stinging and half broken (but not broken!) home. And how did you carry that much evil around, while drifting toward the land of Nod, while accepting your brown-bag lunch and a forehead kiss from your faithful mother? How could you live with yourself all that while—with a rope in your bag or a camera to take the humiliating picture, with a spring in your step as you passed that spot where two streets cross, the scene of an as-yet-uncommitted crime, or visited the locker room, unblinkingly, as if it were not the stage of imminent horror? And yet wasn't that exactly what he was doing with this heroin and Dwight?

Really? But just for once? And in justice? Not picking on an innocent but one whose insolent ribbing, and let us not forget the knife-behind-our-back to Dirk, surely merited this. Who said we must always be the martyr? *The meek shall suffer,* that's all that's sure in their future. Why else should fate have arranged things so perfectly as this, as though delaying a revenge till this juncture? Perhaps naive, precollege-he would have lacked heart or stomach or enough experience of the world for this deed—I mean, can you picture someone like Mary Fawzi from Third North all Lady Macbeth–like rising to the role? Ah, that poor weeper would crumble at the mere thought of such a scheme. It's up to you to deal a blow here for all loserkind.

"Earth to Matt." Liza was waving her hand. "Aren't you done yet? Here." And she held out her empty glass for Matt's butt.

"So," Matt tossed back the last watery contents of his scotch, "let's do the grand tour, shall we?"

Back in the main room, the crowd had grown measurably: guys in neat shirts and loafers, girls in matronly leather belts, the pearls pressed into the fat purses of their earlobes hideous as teeth. A whole host of WASPs ruddy with money and privilege, rows of aristocratic noses, sporty and perfect shoulders, here a conservative silk tie or scarf brandished like an affront, like tribal colors worn both to assert credentials and punish the excluded at once. He sucked in his breath as he shoehorned his way around: was it the mere closeness of the room? Or could so many NYU kids still not know who he was? They noticed Liza, yet no one glanced at him with anything like interest. Imperturbable, they let him pass by, calmly stationed in a serenity of order as neutral as the laws of heraldry. Dahlia Warner, the short girl with lasery blue eyes, stood by the bar, ranting toward David Breck's chest—he was in a black suit with a rainbow-colored button-down, looking rather with-it, actually. On the near side, sunk into an armchair, wearing the same unfestive dark-green sweater as last time, sat Peter Kent, but now so surrounded he could only raise a glass, shoot Matt a sympathetic eyebrow lift.

"Oh, look, he's not white!" Matt sniggered, faux-excited as he nudged Liza toward an Indian guy some paces behind.

"Noooo . . ." Liza groaned. "That's just Ashok Something. I can't remember his last name. Like the richest family in India. He has more money than God."

They really found them, didn't they. As if they put out some signal, a huge dollar sign in the sky, like the Bat symbol. You could only see it if you were loaded.

"I'd like to go powder my nose. You?"

"I'll come," he assented, "but—might make me kind of jittery. I'll just smoke."

Clinging to Liza's heels, he rambled restlessly and, yes, sick of himself, with this dire act unhatched in his breast . . . and when at last they pushed into Annabel's room: empty, inhabited only by white gauze curtains streaming irregularly from the open windows. "Fabulous," Liza sneered, dropping to the window seat, showily lighting a cig.

I'm going to stay in this room forever, Matt thought, falling on the white brocaded bed. Or, no, better: I'm going to tie these sheets into ropes and, Rapunzel-like, shimmy down from the penthouse. Then I'll run across the street into Central Park where no one can find me, not with their lanterns, not with their hunting horses and beautiful dogs, their rifles shooting plumes of smoke. Come on, now: after all the world has done to bring this about? You'll flinch back from the brink, *I'm sorry, I wasn't ready, I can't,* wah-wah, sobbie-sob, an incurable milquetoast? Now will you choose forever to be Doormat Boy?

And maybe that was part of why it'd happened in the first place: they had scented *wimp* on him—kindergarten, first grade, like a pacifist in a prison yard among hardened criminals, who'd get the shit kicked from him to Samoa. *No, guys, stop, I mean it, come on, give me back my book . . . my bag . . . my life . . .*

No. Not me: no more. This is the end, my friend. This is the last of that road.

"What time is it?" he mumbled, sitting up.

Liza turned her wrist to peer at her ridiculous gilt watch, which with the diamond ring were the sole accessories that showed: still Daddy's Little Girl. "It's midnight. Time, right?"

But David Breck found them first. Out at the end of the corridor he was stamping and rubbing his hands together. "Hello, hello!" He threw his arms low about Liza, kissed her cheek. "Having a nice time?" he asked Matt, still holding her back while she giggled awkwardly, squirming, straightening her tresses.

"Absolutely." Matt waved his glass between them, not trusting himself to say more.

"Excellent!" David looked giddy as a little kid. "So, are you ready, man?"

Somebody was paddling wildly inside him as he followed David's stretchy form through the patio door and out into the night. The door of the cabana was ajar; now he peered into the candle glow—they had arranged cushions about an Oriental rug, were sitting on the floor. Dimwit David must have thought it "groovy," appropriate for a "mind-altering experience." The music, too, was trippy in a pseudopsychedelic style; over the cheese of ersatz Gregorian chants and saccharine synth scratched the excited chatter of girls and guys dying to lose themselves for a few hours. Matt circled the space distributing nods, pep-up remarks, and pills from a cache in his right pants pocket.

Dwight was ready for him, cushioned on the marble, one leg extended as if in the midst of an athletic stretch, an expression of compassionate understanding on his face. And everything else in the room went low, snuffed out. Their voices, the music, even the sense of space blurred into one black brushstroke, irrelevant at the periphery. Matt shook his head, feigning perplexity. "Oh—hello! Dwight!"

"Hey," Dwight said, husky, mano a mano, Sensitive New Age Macho, reaching up for a hand clasp, "how—how *are* you?"

"Fabulous." Funny how one freezes up in such a situation; he ached to get away.

"How's—how are . . . things?"

Please! What could be better? I've won! Admit it, you phony! Why won't you ever admit it? " 'Things' are pretty fabulous too," he replied. "And you?" Bending down low.

Dwight sighed deeply, as if the world's sufferings hurt him personally but he bore on nevertheless. Insultingly healthy, the leader of some Mt. Everest trek who tries to console one fallen by the wayside: you understand, the team's got to go on. "Listen, Matt," Dwight's voice cracked— nice touch, "I wanted to tell you . . . I'm sorry about the way things happened. Just wanted you to know . . . I feel for you, man." Dwight clapped his arm athletically to Matt's inclined shoulder.

"Don't sweat it, 'man,' don't give it another, any second thought. You did what you had to do—that's as it should be." Matt grinned broad and touched Dwight's upper body with something that might pass for earnestness.

"Great." Dwight squeezed and released his shoulder. "That's really awesome. Wow, I'm so glad we got to talk. I guess—that's what this drug is good for, right? Brings people together." Dwight laughed. "You would know."

"Ekstasis," Matt explained the Greek, " 'out of oneself.' "

"Community," paraphrased Dwight. "That's so awesome."

Matt nodded blandly. The sap. *Got to talk:* what a grand tête-à-tête, all of five seconds. And as if one widget of Ecstasy were working in him right now. "Well, don't get ahead of yourself! You're going to be feeling . . . ahm, even more that way in about a half hour." And he slipped out the Dove from his left pocket.

"Of course." Dwight opened his hands wide as if to grant Matt free movement in the little glassed-in world he owned. Now his palm closed over the pill. "Thanks for this, man," he vowed, and gave a last wink.

So it was official. History melted down to this instant; it pinholed to a point, blotted out to dark. Matt slunk back up the walkway, through the rooms, sated. And he was proud! He wanted to pass out cigars and share! Sprinting forward, he pushed his way to the bathroom and locked the door. Flushed rouge in the mirror! Hello, genius! You devil! You did it! Beaming, grinning, the lips nearly puckering as if on the point of kiss. Shall I tell you a secret? He leaned over the sink and kissed the figure in the mirror, closing his lips on that metallic cold—before abruptly exiting, letting the door slam behind.

Because there was no Liza towering about the main room, because, Jesus Christ, a drink, was ever a man so in need of a nip of whiskey, he hightailed it over to the bar, mixed him a little mischief. Standing just three paces off was Dahlia, the one whom he had interrogated on his last visit about her dream of a chintzy ten-mil bequest. "Oh, come off it," she was saying in her gravelly voice. "Just come off it. I'm calling him a dud because that's what he is, he's a total tool. And it's one thing if you want to be nice to Allison by inviting him, like as a *guest,* okay, but to, like, bring him in as a member? I mean, I ask you, what's the point of being in this club if guys like that can get in? I mean: who is he? That's all I have to say."

"He's a nice guy," some kid in a white sweater and cufflinks protested.

A bold snort was her first retort. "Who Is He?" She stamped on the parquet with each monosyllable. "I mean, you know! He's from, like, Missouri."

"Dahlia," reproved the guy. "You're such a snob."

"I am not a snob! Okay, so maybe I am." Guttural rupture of carte blanche laughter. "But let me ask you: what did you think when you found out that *tool* was getting in?"

The kid said something closer to Dahlia's ear that caused them both to peal.

"See what I mean? And you're trying to make me out like I'm some kind of, kind of monster. Hey, you." A snapping of fingers in Matt's direction. "You. Liza's friend."

Matt merely let the scotch purl about his gums to acquit him of eavesdropping.

Dahlia's ghost-white face pushed before his, Muppet-like, head back; the cave of her mouth brutish, red. "You're Matt, right? Magic Matt?"

"Hm-mm?" Matt coughed, blinked laboriously slow.

"You used to live with him, right?"

"Who?" Matt chewed ice, causing him unfortunately to drool.

"Dwight Smeethman!" She stamped again and tossed her black hair.

"Mm-hm?"

"Explain to him, explain to my *friend,*" and here her hand clutched at a white-sweatered arm; she drew the guy, reluctantly laughing, over to the bar, "what's wrong with Dwight Smeethman."

Matt rolled his eyes. Please go away, little girl. You're hurting me. Please just back away, slowly.

"Let me ask you this," she continued, lapdog-style, not letting go of a bone on which it scents flesh. "Would *you* let him into this club?"

There were all sorts of possible ripostes to this. Matt was reaching for that line, wouldn't want to be a part of any club that—that what? Something about me for a member. But as nothing came to mind, he simply took a meek sip. "No."

Yet evidently comedy is all in the timing. For Dahlia and even the politic guy discovered something singularly hilarious in this damning with faint blame.

"See! Thank you." Dahlia leaned back against the wall where the two had first been. "I'm coming to your party tomorrow night, by the way. For Liza's."

Speak of the devil: she pulled up alongside. "What's that, lady?" Liza droned.

"I said I'm coming to your party tomorrow night." But the way Dahlia barked it and raised an eyebrow, the statement was less tribute than warning. *It better be fun.*

"Let's go," Matt commanded, banging his glass down on the tiled counter. "Babe. We're going to be late."

6.

At Ichor there were orchids, organdy, champagne—Liza pulled him into the main room, where a whole disassembled grove of birch trees appeared, leaning over the tables their silvery skin, skeins of green flags fluttering faintly. From across the way Matt recognized Carl and Brett sitting with a troupe of model sorts—*six-footers*, to use Carl's term—all combed hair and vapid smiles; he tipped a flute toward their table: courteously returned. "Ah, thank God," murmured Liza, removing her white sweater to reveal a backless, sleeveless black thing, more sash than shirt, incredibly bare in fact, kind of cancan dancer/dominatrix with suggestive straps. Had she been tanning? Or was it makeup? The molded shoulders and lithe ridges at the collarbone looked touched with gold radiance, brushed by strays from the upswept mane: she was someone's mistress at St. Tropez, discerning, young, pampered; bought. "I don't want to be hung-over for tomorrow, but, ah!" Lifting a brazen arm to sip cheerily at her champagne, the square diamond on its middle finger winking liquid lights. "Isn't this going to be so much fun?"

Yes, one would think so. Matt finished his glass, filled it from the bottle in the bucket beside. It will be. Only—why should that evil bitch have spoiled it? She merely agreed with you anyway, *Dwight's a tool, Who Is He*—well, but who are you, missy? Just because you have gobs of money? Your parents' money, stacked in some bank depository, in the dream storehouse, where malicious, acquisitive, you count up your coins? "Who's that girl Dahlia?" Matt blurted out, slurry.

"Dahlia?! She's—I knew her at Spence." Liza fixed her attention on her beaded purse, drawing out her new slim silver cigarette case. "Here," she urged, practically pushing one in his lips.

"But who is she?"

"Why, do you like her?" Unsmiling as she lit his and hers.

"No! Hardly. Rather, I dislike her." He reached for the bottle.

"She's pretty..." mused Liza, shrugging one globe of a shoulder.

Matt snorted. "The girl looks like a Muppet." Did he say that? Ouch. But "Heu heu heu," Liza chortled. "Good." She reached out a cold hand to his forearm. "You scared me there a second."

"Really? Why?"

"Ohhh, no reason." She lolled farther, dropping an arm behind the chair's back. Her smoking fingers neared and departed from her lips; smirking guiltily, she raised one hay-colored eyebrow. "No reason at all." Setting her chin on a palm, she flicked her cig shyly at the ashtray. The table was shaking: she was kicking a restless boot. "Or—maybe I'll tell you later, if you really can't guess. *Any*way, let's for*get* about Dahlia, and Peter, and—oh my God! David Breck." A spectral blue beam had shot up from the table. "He's calling me. Right now."

"Don't you want to get that?!"

"Why?"

"I don't know, might be important. Jeez, Liza, get it already, he'll hang up."

She looked over at him queerly, then fussed over the keypad and delivered her customary morose, "Hello?"

Matt examined Carl and Brett at their table across the way: but stop, stop staring. He investigated the birch branch hanging beside and over his head, lifted an itchy finger to peel at its papery scales. *No,* she was saying, *no way. That's really weird. I'll ask him.* "Matt?" she said, holding her hand over the phone. "Dwight's feeling really weird, they don't know what's wrong with him, he—"

So. Here we go. "Tell him to throw up," Matt advised, mouth numb with cold champagne tucked under his tongue. "Can happen to anyone, bad reaction to dopamine, it has to do with your enzymes and your serotonin, how the transmitters..." blah blah blah, the stuff Jonathan had tried on Jason. No point in being sorry now. He's going to throw up a lung, be fine in the morning. "Happens all the time. Too bad. I'm sorry."

"O-*kay*," she murmured, defensive. Brows knit. Hesitating an instant, as if to say more before uncovering the mouthpiece, bending in to give out this diagnosis.

What's the big deal, really. So he'll toss his dinner.

—But: Dwight in his stupid boat shoes, his mediocre Gap jeans! Why didn't we see he's not in their league? Plain, in plain sight, yet never spotted it till now: so caught up in our own brainish fantasies, making him out to be a captain of the planet! To think of poor Dwight—earnest, a naïf from nowhere, when you really thought of it—oh, all of his dogged confidence exposed to their scorn, to that Dahlia-girl's pointing finger, hideous laughing. And they roped you in, complicit in making fun of him too. There by the bar effectively you mocked right along, with a more extreme cadre of snobs: when Dwight might even have believed we were on good terms now. And you on your high horse, dealing a blow for all loserkind? Look in the mirror, pal. Ugh, that horrible mirror-kiss! You make me sick.

"That's weird," concluded Liza, pressing the hangup button. "Isn't it?"

"Not really. Trust Dwight." Matt shrugged, impassive, keeping his gaze locked to the back of a brunette at Carl and Brett's table. She had just turned eagerly to a man bowed over her. The guy, topped by a fringe of blond poodle curls, was staring down on her, bemused, one muscled arm extended to grip the back of her chair as if to impress her with his health, youth—ugh, just check yourself in to some foul motel. Just fuck and get it over with. Fuck porno-style, leave lipstick stains all over the pillow, and forget each other's names in the morning: that's all you want, right? "Some guys shouldn't do drugs," he sighed, not checking to see if he'd ashed in the tray.

"But why just Dwight. I mean, all these times of doing Ecstasy, I've never even heard of someone at Cinema . . ."

He turned to fix her with a vicious glare. "Happens all the time. Happened to Jason a few weeks ago, actually. *And* Marco."

"Really?" Now her cat's eyes narrowed. "Mm. I didn't hear that. But they don't, don't have a problem taking *Ecstasy*."

And could she have heard about the Doves from Marco? Through Jeremy? Please tell me there hasn't been some thaw in their Cold War. "Maybe it was a bad hit," he backpedaled. "That happens too, you know. Jonathan's getting sloppy. Did I tell you he's thinking of leaving? Did I tell you he's Can*ad*ian? Have you ever noticed how much he says *eh*? It's really crazy."

She laughed. "All right, Matt. Have it your way."

"What do you mean?"

"I mean," she purred, drawing close and taking his face in both cold hands, lavishing it with a gaze that was tenderly solicitous to his lips, his brow, the side of his cheek, "don't you think I know you by now? Enough to tell when something's up?" Suddenly she looked him right in the eyes and burst out into a sunset-at-the-end-of-a-highway smile. "All right?"

She was lovely. Her eyes liquid, searching. Radiant—it was the look from that first night at her place, the look that ravished him, offering herself, open, in a chalice ... "Don't know what you're talking about," he got out, in the crushed, salivary voice of drunk-boy, his jaws mallow-soft.

"Have it your way!" she jeered, twining bare arms across her breasts. "Here," she shot out, refilling their glasses with a careless hand, plonking the bottle scornfully back in the silver bucket. Now she rested her flute against the flushed lips. "Not like I even know how, exactly. Whatever. But I wish you would trust"—she cocked her head, peering down at him out of doe-lashed eyes—"I'm on your side." Her whole face again turned instantly, impossibly dazzling as she bounced slightly on the chair and brought her smooth brow toward his. "Okay?" Now her hand mapped over his right knee, squeezed ... wheeeee. Her hand on his knee was a jellyfish.

"Okay."

She fired up a new smoke, slinking down ever so slightly and curving it into her chest. Lit, she blew, while looking around the room: then whirled upon him with a shrewd smile. "Does Sophie know about this?"

He coughed. "N-no, and you can't, can't, absolutely, tell—"

She razed the ceiling with a triumphant glare. "I'm not going to *tell* her, Matt. Besides, uhhh ... I don't think she likes me very much. Oh!"

She laid bronze fingers over the insubordinate lips already curled in a smile, stagey, as if the matter she'd slipped were an irresistible in-joke of theirs. "Um. That's not what I meant. Oh, Matt." Suddenly, urgently, she enclosed him in a delirious hug: one perfect round breast pressed between them like Eve's gold apple. She lifted her mouth to whisper, "It'll be our secret."

It went through him like a wire, convulsing him tight. *Secret,* in her husky breath, *secret,* by his neck…could she just perhaps say it again? He wanted to catch the gas of her words in a bottle, lift it to his nose and sniff at whim. *Our secret.*

"But what Sophie maybe doesn't understand," one hand was rubbing in a scoop of his back, "which I do, is that sometimes—it's natural. There are things we have to do, and they're Not Al-ways Good." Tapping a finger on his shoulder. "You and I—listen. I know you. And I know me. Mm. Can I tell you a secret? Since you've told me yours?"

"Tell away," he managed to say, lips accidentally brushing the skin at her nape. Oh my God. "S-sorry." But so smooth, and the sound of his voice—low and intimate, so man-and-woman, here in the little space between her flesh hugging his.

"It's okay," she gasped, nestling deeper in his neck. "So—oh, I can't," she insisted, burying her brow into his chest. "No, I have to. I've been wanting to say—and now I've got you all excited. Okay. What I was going to tell you before. My reason. About: being scared. When you were asking me about Dahlia. Can I tell you?"

Might have nodded, might have shuddered—

"Because it seemed like maybe you liked her. But the thing is: I want you for myself. Right now, I want to take you back to my place and do very, very bad things to you." The lobe of his left ear: cinched in the tines of her teeth, quick. "And by bad, ah, Matt, I mean *good.* You have no idea."

No idea. No sense—no thought to catch at: a door ruptured open on a black hole, an impossible world where, perverse, everything turned opposite-day, inside-out. And something in him had burst: tears surged up to his eyes, there was a flooding in his windpipe. "You don't mean that, Liza." It came out like a sob from the broken trapdoor of his mouth.

"Why not?" she mused, one hand creeping up his pants leg toward the plane of his penis, which had lifted, stiff... "I've always wanted you. Aha." Her slender hand had closed over him. "I can see you want me too."

He shut his eyes—the room was an ocean of voices and tinkling, and above must be the birch leaves, yes, still quivering, in benediction of, what? spring? the Rite of Spring! The clash and cymbals of it, this room, this city wherever anyone, anyone was not sleeping, in a bar, a bedroom, all arrows pointed here, to this paragon of hot, premier, top-shelf; everything wanted him to take her back to Mercer, throw her down on the bed in her loft. What else was it all for? What man, Carl, Brett, the guy with poodle curls, would not do that? But how had he tricked her, how could she possibly think—[57]

"Sssh. It's okay. You don't have to say anything. We don't have to say a word, all night."

All night. Well. All right. Okay. All night. Thinking ahead. Nice touch. That's good. Holy mother of—

"Come on," she whispered by his ear—then brusquely, standing, grabbing his hand on the table, turned all business as she nipped up her purse and sweater, commanded, "Let's get out of here." Hoarse. Not even looking at him, as she placed her silver case into her small purse and zipped it.

He was on his feet, shaky, his heart whirring wild, a mechanical bird spurred out of control. The doorman nodded; Matt forced on a mask of grim sobriety, nodded back. *Ciao,* he graze-kissed the girl at the ropes. All the time trying to keep up with Liza, on her high boots speeding forward, she knew exactly where she was going—

"Let's get a cab," she said, breathless. Dear Lord, of all the luck, the girl can stop a cab in the Arctic. He slid in after her. She called out her address, added "sir," the sort of surly "sir" that doesn't mean "sir" at all.

The car shot into the avenue and tore off, throbbing beneath him.

---

[57] Oh, Lisanne! Is that how it began? Is that how it felt for you?

She was staring at him, biting her lip, her rosy, cherubic lip. Jesus, was anyone ever so *alive,* burst open as a ripe fruit, brimming—aaah! Her hand was tucked over his. Think quickly. Think quickly. Is this what you want? Is this really what you want? But she liked him! She chose *him*! To leap into that saddle—intended for others, for kids like *Scott Belfast*?

God, no: she had his fingers to her lips and blew on them, and blew a tiny hurricane; he like a house was rising up, all its terrified windows alight.... Now she kissed, each press planting mines, each press infecting him. He squeezed shut his eyes. Over, it's done, you've made up your mind. Haven't you wanted this all this time? Or won't you always wonder: a woman like her? You're going to be grizzled in your invalid bed and remember such incomparable flesh; toothless, you'll be laughing, clapping your wrinkled hands. Bed. I bet she's very very good there; wild-woman—*You have no idea.*

"Matt," she moaned. He flashed open his eyes: in the taxi, shuttling headlong beneath streetlights, the space was silver-edged black, a celluloid filmstrip coming undone into black-and-white frames hurtling across a screen at breakneck pace. Her white face, her hair full of light above the high-necked black coat, kept lunging closer at him whenever, strobish, the car flared bright. "Matt"; now she had swallowed the space between them and was at him, arms clasped around his back, fingers stiff as basket weave up along his nape. And now she dipped, dipped; evidently her rose lips found something here, in his open neck, at the upraised ridge of his collarbone, enough to their liking that they wanted a sip—

He threw his head into the vinyl seat, while the car, like a wire, pulled him deeper away. High through the rear window, a round full moon hovered over those grainy streets of Alphabet City. So pure, casting wavy oceans of milk into the relentless black sky! It was a wise face, a face infinitely patient, trained down right on him, seeing.

And now as they hurtled east they were heading toward someone else too: Sophie, sleeping, no doubt, mouth open in that adorable fishy way of hers as she breathed her clear breath all over the pillow.... He hurled his head forward and gasped. "I can't do this. I'm sorry. I know. It's just—Sophie—"[58]

"Oh, Matt," she began. "Listen—just listen to me—"

But there was nothing to listen to. Nothing forthcoming from her mouth but fulgurant peacock flashes, emerald-and-sapphire-dusted brushes along his neck, in the hollow below his ear—nothing but the nixieish lure of watery sinkings; now his lobe had descended, ah, now even half the span of his index finger went, sucked in without warning. And in the place of words, as at the beginning of the world, before the humans detached themselves from the beasts and rutted in a fusty cave, another kind of logic was supplied as, dumb-show, silent like mimes, she drew his hand toward her and laid it beneath silk straps on a mound of succulent and melting snow. Would anything he'd touch in his life resemble this precious treasure-door breast again? God, smooth and so cool, a drink of water beneath his burning palm.

The lights were bright outside her building at Mercer. Brilliant in the lobby where from behind his marble-topped desk the doorman nodded at them, incurious—and what would there have been to suspect here unless perhaps the man had caught the tinkle of her laugh, the flash of her white hand as she grabbed Matt's to skip up the last couple of steps, whisk him round the corner? Onto the luxurious Persian carpet running the length of a corridor studded on both sides with mysterious doors. "Oh, Matt," she repeated once more, as if those were the only words left to say in this world. Snatches of her tawny hair—when had she taken it down?—splayed over his neck, reaching into the open collar of his shirt as she pressed hot mouth to the side of his head, with both hands wrenched his ass so he fell against the enchanted delta of her pelvis...a fabulous delta, lush greenery, jewel-eyed tigers peering at him out of awesome, palm-shaded depths.

"Are you okay?" she wanted to know when she had sat him on the leather couch, laid her long, jeaned legs crosswise over his trembling lap.

---

[58] Did you think upon me? Did you once mention my name? Did you attempt some stop on yourself, or him? Lisanne, do you listen?

"Does this feel...okay?" Perhaps it did? Or was it more like red-hot lashes against the side of his neck? "Don't be nervous," she felt the need to command him, as her fingers worked at the silver square that appeared to be his belt buckle, "it's going to be just fine. Mm, I take that back," she decided, lowering her head shyly by his ear.

"You do?" At last reaching his hands up to meet around her sinuous— God, yes, it was backless, this shirt; warm skin pressed against his palms.

"It's going to be much. Much. Better than that."

7.

Matt woke facedown on a leather couch, shirtless, but with his pants still on and a pressure against the back of his head: which on investigation turned out to be a cat. Lester, who leapt to the wooden floor and, tail erect, turned round to reprove Matt with a look of offended majesty before gliding off toward the kitchen.

He pushed himself up on a fist—difficult on the beaten, tanned pelt of the couch which gave way beneath his weight. There were gray smudges of ash on the dark-wood coffee table. Two tumblers part full of watery scotch. His button-down shirt open on the floor, its black arms twisted, reaching out toward nothing.

Mother of God.

There were something like a hundred shut doors in his brain, slammed and permanent against some better version of him. Someone utterly left behind yesterday, someone capable of saying on the phone he would be late, but not too, not terribly, who had planned when he was done with the work of the night to sleep beside Sophie. Matt's hands were trembling as he buttoned his shirt over a chest that was beginning to burn, to radiate out an insane heat from the splotches Liza had touched, bitten. Evidently she had slept upstairs, in the loft: the black sash-shirt hung out over the railing. Right, that's right. *You're impossible*, she had said when at last he'd managed to push her off him, picking out the fingers she was digging in his waistband. *You're impossible:* tossing the words over her shoulder with a look of disgust—before she flounced up the steps, lifting off her top to reveal a fantastic curved and swaying Amazonian back along the way.

Mother of *God*. He was moving quickly now, hopping as he tried to squeeze his feet back into the boots collapsed like war dead on one side of the couch. This happened, you kissed her, repeatedly, probably for as long as ten minutes if not considerably more? And where else were his lips: but around her ear, in her scented neck, taking the long voyage to beneath the plunge line of that shirt, which opened so subserviently, which let him lift her out of the extravagant bra—ah, it was all slit like a razor blade into the tissue of his brain: her golden peninsula of skin, the luminous white globes offered to him—her hot and liquid mouth, the coiled asp of her tongue, striking deep—

Automatic, mechanical, the door made a definite and irrevocable click when Matt shut it behind. Down in the dim nether regions of the corridor, a woman gave him a dubious glance before coaxing a large, cottony dog into an invisible apartment. And perhaps it was obvious here what style of scene he was departing from: eight A.M. yet dressed for the evening, not to mention roped in with smoke stench, besides wreathed with unseen but nonetheless palpable stains. The sun was a red gouge in the sky surrounded by a few sullen pewter-colored clouds as Matt skirted Washington Square Park. In their trench coats, clutching briefcases or paper bags with coffee, they passed him, the good people of this city, so definite and going incredibly fast.

Everything was strangely the same in the room when Matt limped through his door—the wooden desk and the stiffly made white sheets of the bed took him back again cheerfully, as if nothing had altered, as if he were precisely the same figure who had checked his image in the mirror and clicked shut the light before leaving last night. Well, but what a night. First Dwight. There was intentional, premeditated evil in that, and yet when it had still been a stratagem, when it had still been mere plan—he could have stopped then, satisfied it was in his power to do, but in the clear, crime-free. Lord knows what hours Dwight must have spent over the toilet, with his guts being pulled out his mouth. Then Liza. The reverse of Dwight, in a way: unplanned, unchosen, really, unless one were to count the dozens of nights spent together these last months which must have been encouragement, yes, aiding and abetting of a sort. Because she had to have known. It must have been in how he looked at her. It was certainly in the lurch of his viscera whenever her name came up on his cell-phone screen—which so many times, blinking long and slow, he tried to hide from Sophie, who must also have known.

Damp and naked from the shower, Matt crumpled onto the bed. Ah, God. What more do you want? You craven apostate? He rolled over onto his stomach, pressed his face into the pillow: a sour smoke smell simpered out. Yes, everything poisoned, everything graffitied over by your blasphemies. Over again Matt flipped onto his back to face the incurious screen of the ceiling: black, it felt, the heart in his chest, like some kind of tumor, some meteor matter that had fallen and lodged there in place of what should be red and pulsing with truth. Simply, last night, as Sophie lay ten blocks away, blameless in sleep, he'd taken the stick of her-in-him and snapped it.[59] What now?

"God," he said aloud, but it sounded hollow. A reflex action, nothing behind it. No one taking the call on the other end.

Counsel was needed: someone to take confession. That fact revealed itself incontrovertible as the hours ticked by in the unfeelingly brilliant room invested by a spring breeze, almost showily naive, from the open window, where Matt paced, sat creaking on the chair, lay facedown on the bed, and cried hot tears on finding his old notes from the first night here, fallen between footboard and mattress: *I—Love—You.* In a circle around his *Love,* Sophie had written with small capitals FOREVER, and from this drawn the flames of a sun. How could he, all these weeks— Christ, man, are you *alive?*—never once have found this here? I'll tell

---

[59] But I would have forgiven you. You know this, do you not? You know your Hans, who does not begrudge, who is gentle—I would have disregarded everything, if you had asked only.

you why: Paradise. When he came home nights after hitting the scene, he hardly even bothered to turn on the light.

Not anymore. This note he tucked into his breast pocket—a totem, a flag of his devotion, a shield over that quadrant of his chest where a desperate, battered muscle was squeezing and letting slip its fistfuls of blood—when, close to noon, he dressed, headed out toward Third North: let Jason be up now, Lord, please. I realize I am in no position for requests. But who else might one talk to? The sulky walls, the blue sky?

Just then his cell phone began to tremble, to peal...

"Magic, baby," Vic barked. "What's this I hear, you're throwing your ropes girl a birthday thing? Glad to see you're thinking, trying new things with your par-ty, don't get me wrong, but your ropes girl, I wouldn't advise...and covering for her at the ropes, kid, take it from me, it doesn't look right for you to do that. You shoulda told me, now it's too late to call one of my alternates. Even yesterday, if you'd—listen, it's busy now, but stop by, come by early tonight and find me. All right? We'll talk when you get in."

Cinema? Tonight? Liza? Like he could possibly stand at the ropes, click-clack with the velvet barrier, screen out *uglies*, make chitchat—and for *her* party, of all creatures? "You know, Vic, I'm actually—not feeling so well. I wonder if there's—are you sure it's too late for a replacement?"

"What did I tell you, kid? This is a business. You hafta be professional. I don't care what kinda partying you do in your spare time, but when it comes to *my* club—"

"I know Vic, I know, it isn't that, just there's something personal, very imp—"

"Miranda!" Vic yelled, muted, away from the mouthpiece. "What did I tell—"

"Vic, please. Look, I can't, I'm not in the right frame of mind to absorb a *lesson* just now...."

Silence. Then: "Where should I send the flowers?" Vic snapped, asinine.

"What?"

"Because somebody better be dead or in the hospital. Magic, what the hell is with you? This is not—"

"Vic, can we maybe talk about this another time? I'm really, I'm not able to . . ."

"You know what I think? I think Carl and Brett are right. Take it from me. *When you go fabulous that fast—*"

"—Vic, I really, gotta go—"

"You're FINISHED!"

Matt pressed the little button marked *End*.

Was that an adult, the well-respected leader of a major nightclub? *Somebody better be dead.* Why were people so evil? God, but only to reach Jason. Ah, jeez. If Jason wasn't up . . . could he, would he mind so much being waked? Since we are in An Extreme State?

But wide awake and strangely unsurprised: "There you are," murmured Jason, when Matt appeared at his stinky cave. Cleaner than usual, in a white button-down, though some general puffiness showed he'd had a long night. Holding the door barely ajar, Jason studied Matt curiously, as though trying to piece together someone he'd only heard of or seen in photos: then sighed and walked heavily inside, leaving Matt by the door. "Come in, I guess." He fell solidly onto the couch, rubbing hands against his pants legs. "Since you're here."

What? "Okay?" Matt gingerly assumed a seat opposite, on the foot of the bed.

"I wondered if you might come by." Jason fumbled with a cigarette. "Wondered what you might have to say." He looked over at Matt soberly above the Zippo's large flame. "Because I'm sure you know," the lighter snapped shut, "you've gone too far on this one, Matt. You just *have*."

Could Liza—have told Marco? Already? Was word of our botched fling spreading that fast?

"You don't fuck around with heroin. I could have told you that." Sadly, Jason tapped off his ash. "But you didn't ask me. Naturally. You just fed me that bullshit about Stefan: such *obvious* bullshit. And why didn't I ask you? That part is my fault. Like I was afraid of you or something. I mean, not that I thought you were suddenly interested in trying heroin. But, motherfucker, Matt!" Jason's fists clenched up. "I'm a good person!"

Oh. "This is—about Dwight?"

An odd, indefinable expression entered Jason's eyes as he peered at Matt, as though trying to see a different facet of Matt's face from a new angle. "Yes," he said finally, very calm and slow, "this is about Dwight. Don't tell me—you didn't come here to pretend you had nothing to do with that, did you?"

"N-no, of course not, I just, I'm surprised to hear that you know..."

"Or tell me to keep my mouth shut? Is that why you came here?"

"No! I just told you, I didn't even know you knew. How—"

"Walker came over last night. Said they saw my light. He had Dwight down the hall in his room—they couldn't get him to stop throwing up. Supposedly they just brought him home from a party where you sold X: very interesting, I thought. So, did I know what to do? Since they knew we were 'friends'—did I have any advice? Because otherwise they might have to take him to the hospital, but they didn't want to, didn't want to get anyone in trouble... and I had to stand there, over Dwight, while he's shaking and crying, and spitting up, saying all kinds of crazy shit—*I don't want to die, Oh God, I wanna call my mom.* I had to stand there and say, 'Oh yeah. You just gotta wait it out. Same thing happened to me. That's just—just Ecstasy. Some times. Some people.'"

"'I don't want to die'?" repeated Matt dully. *Dwight?*

"That's right." Jason stubbed out the cigarette morosely. "Actually, he told us he had ulcers. I almost did have them take him to the hospital—he kept clutching his stomach, saying it *hurt*. And what if he had—ruptured his lining or something?"

Dwight, pale-faced, moaning on a stretcher. The ambulance outside Third North, silent white-dressed assistants loading him in... Dwight shunted along on a gurney, gripping his stomach, as surgeons in green masks bent toward him, holding up scalpels—

"But you probably didn't even consider that possibility. It doesn't seem like you waste much time thinking about anything, or I mean any-*one,* anymore. You certainly weren't thinking about me when you made me, like, a fucking accessory to your plan. Here." Jason reached over to the bookshelf by the couch, lifting a tattered white envelope. "Here are the rest of your hits; pretty sure that's everything. You can find yourself another slave to sample your shit." He tossed the envelope to the bed. "I'm out. Done. I'm done with you."

"What are you saying, Jason? You can't just—we're best friends."

"Best friends?" Jason's head whipped back in disbelief. "Sure, every now and then you throw me a bone—'Jason, J-Force, whoever you are, how would you like to help out around the club?' As if you had any intention of that. And one more thing—"

But Jason never got a chance to say what this was. For now there came a flurry of bangings at the door and someone—Marco?—crying, *I was right, I was right,* in pinched, elated tones. "Come in," Jason declared, exhausted. Evidently Marco couldn't hear above the chorus of Billy Idol's "Flesh for Fantasy" he was now singing. *Flesh*—bang—*flesh for fantasy-hee* . . . "It's open," Jason called, a bit louder but still weary and reluctant.

From the far end of the room came the noise of the door wheeling to slam at the wall. "Hate to say I told you so . . . but: somebody is soooo *busted*!" Three finger snaps crackled out as an invisible Marco apparently took his sweet time walking down the tiny corridor. "Guess who Amber saw coming out of Liza's building this morning at eight A.M.—" And now Marco was standing before him, astonished, with a hand clamped over his mouth. "Oops," he said, beginning to titter. "Now, this *is* embarrassing." Though he didn't look embarrassed in the least as his whole body discharged little shocks of ill-spirited hilarity.

Jason was searching Matt's face. "Really?" His gaze darkening.

"I think I need to go now," Matt breathed. "Bye."

8.

From the dorm to Sophie's apartment was thirteen city blocks down-town and several large avenues west, which Matt was having difficulty tallying as he estimated the time that remained between now and the end of all life. Twenty minutes. More; closer to thirty, especially if he kept up at this trudging rate. No hurry, really. Only there was nowhere else to go: but there, and finish it. Or maybe he didn't even need that. He could just turn left. Walk across the Brooklyn Bridge and head for the green fields of Long Island, right to the tip of Montauk Beach, which Sophie had al-ways wanted to visit, make a raft of some kind out of reeds and nettles and float away like a kid in a fairy tale, like King Arthur taking ship for the isle of Avalon, which is to say the island beyond life . . .

Oh shove a sock in it, sir, and pick up the pace.

Sophie was sitting rigid at the kitchen table when Matt crept into her studio, below the line of windows, all ajar, where a breeze stirred a few ambrosial-smelling jonquils in a vase on the sill: the sole moving feature of the oddly stationary room. Immediately she hustled up—attentive, affectionate, giggling queerly high-pitched as she pecked him with little kisses. "Hi," she murmured, taking his face in her hands. "I missed you last night." Grinning. "God, you look awful. Was it—are you hung-over? Do you want some juice or water?" Wheeling at the sink before he even responded.

"A bad thing happened last night, Sophie. A few bad things." Where to begin? "Oh, God, Sophie. You have no idea." *You have no idea:* Liza's whisper! The virus of it was still in his ears. He put his hands over his eyes.

"Ssh," she decided, sinking into a chair beside him. "Come on." With her small, definite hand she pried one of his, to hold it on his lap. "Matt?"

So he started in with the less incendiary of the two matters.

Weirdly, she seemed more melancholy than mad when she heard about Dwight. "Wow," she reflected, shaking her head. "You guys—you guys really need to stop with that stuff, you know? It's no joke to feed somebody heroin. You give out these drugs without thinking—even X can be really dangerous. Did you hear about that guy who died at a Supersize rave in San Francisco? Or that girl who overheated a couple of weeks ago in St. Louis? It was in the *Times*. Matt, she was only *fifteen*. Aren't you worried?"

Matt stared at the mica tabletop, its scattering of dark flecks. Hardly the highest of worries here. Besides, the people at our parties have the good sense to drink water when they're feeling thirsty, that is to say dehydrated, folks, have you heard of the word? But, delicately, so as not to inflame: "Sophie. Wouldn't you say, probably more people die every year from alcohol poisoning? But it's not, no one takes it as the responsibility of the liquor-store guy who sells that last quart. Right?"

"Right. It's not their *responsibility*. I didn't say it was. But: don't you care? How would you feel if someone you gave X to—what if they *died*?"

How would we feel? When at the end of a night Jonathan forked out his bills in the staff bathroom, under the fluorescent beams: your kickback, blood money. Well, that's a little extreme! *Ecstasy*, not crack here. No?

"Well," she sighed. "Maybe you've learned your lesson. I guess it sounds like Dwight's going to be all right. I'm glad you told me, finally." Brightening, she squeezed his hand once on the table before lifting his glass for a refill.

While she let the water plunge into his glass, Matt's mind stayed fastened in the birdlime of one desire: that she remain there, just so, with her back to him, engaged in this act that, if you thought of it, was testament to her affection, and therefore a thing such as might never happen again, because this instant was the last moment in which she would not know, this second, passing now, the last in which she did not see she had been betrayed, by him.

Just like that: it was over.

"Matt?" she said, taking a step toward him, the clear glass held out in her hand like the picture of her own cleanness. "Are you crying? Matt? Is it—because of Dwight? Or what I said? I'm sorry. I didn't mean . . ." This just made him blubber harder. "Did you have wine last night? I told you wine messes with your mood, you're always so sad the next day." And that was her in spades, prescriptions at the ready, plus so caring she noticed each least thing about his person. "Come on, Matt." Even she was beginning to look unsettled. "It can't be that bad." Well. It *could* be.

And was.

First she was calm. She laid both hands on the table and inquired frankly into every detail: which he gave, blathering on, and for a moment it seemed as if Sophie had a store of hitherto unknown and impossible maturity, such that this story could be taken in and annihilated simply by being accurately conveyed. That moment had definitely passed when she started shouting, with curses, turning circles in the little kitchen, and was just a dim foolish memory by the time she was sobbing in a heap on the floor at the foot of her bed—kicking toward his ankles each time he approached with arms outstretched. Time passed. Matt begged. He offered penance. For example, he could sleep on the floor for a month. Longer, if she wanted. Or anything else she saw fit. Only not to, not to—

"No, it's good," she concluded finally. Wiping her tears, beginning actually to smile. To *smile*? Yes, indeed; remote and vaguely chilling. "You've made your choice." Looking at him almost proudly, pulling back her head as if to study him from an even greater distance. "And I've made mine too. Come here," she said, getting up to standing and walking into the kitchen. "I have something to show you." From atop the windowsill she produced a ripped envelope.

What nice stationery. A beautiful crest. The University of California at Berkeley.

"This came Tuesday. I haven't known what to do. But now: it all makes sense. You want something else, which isn't me, and you'll always want that. And I want to get out of New York. I don't even want to be *near* anyone who's heard of a place called *Cinema*. It's good," she said, taking both of his hands in hers, raising her smooth brow till it touched his. "You made it easier," she whispered. "We'll just part ways." Though her breath caught there; she was beginning to cry again, silently.

"But I want *you*," he insisted, squeezing her hands.

"It doesn't seem that way," she gasped. "It hasn't seemed that way for a long time."

"But it's true," he urged her.

"I wish it were," she murmured, firm, in control of herself again. "Goodbye, Matt." She drew his head farther down and pressed his forehead with a sisterly kiss.

He reeled away from that gesture, banging against the sink counter by the fridge—

On the refrigerator was a new picture among the art postcards, evidently clipped from a newspaper. And in this picture was a girl. Suddenly that girl had entered the room with them, was watching from one side: though not her but a flat version, flimsy as a slide, as a scale off some snakeskin. Mary's round and soft and black eyes were trained on something outside the frame; her lips were pressed together, tense. It was her photo from the facebook, the long-ago-pored-over facebook, blown up to monstrous size and converted to coarse newsprint. Granular, blurred: which made her look like some sort of a fugitive, a *WANTED* criminal, or one of those kidnapped children reproduced above the words *Have You Seen Me?* But what could humble Mary Fawzi from next door in Third North have done that she should be scissored and pinned among Sophie's painted Marys, Marys kneeling for Annunciation, reading, bending their gentle flaxen-haired heads—like some sort of icon? "What is that?" he asked timidly, approaching, while a sense of doom went blossoming up from his gut.

"What does that have to do with anything?" Sophie pressed a fist to her hip, blank-faced.

"I'm sorry, I just need to know—where did you get it?"

"It was in the school paper," she sighed. "That's that girl who killed herself, remember? I told you I went to the memorial service last week. Or I thought I did."

Oh, that girl. That's all. "Can you... tell me a little more? Please? I don't—remember." There was a haziness in the corners of his eyes, as if the periphery had gotten dusted with a particulate soot, like these pixels, these blots from the newsprint.

"She killed herself," Sophie repeated. "Where do you want me to start?"

"I don't suppose you have the article still?" he asked meekly, batting his enormous eyes, his eyes suddenly as large and unwieldy as palm fans. He was prostrate against the sink when she laid it before his gaze, saying, *Here.*

It was a tragedy. It was a mystery. A nice girl, involved in her studies, valedictorian of her class at the international school back in Alexandria, Egypt. At 12:03 P.M. on March 24. Five-story building. Home for spring break. No one had heard anything, no one had heard a sound. The family would not comment. The family was her mother, Sonia, an architect and public planner; father was deceased. No friends had commented either, but that was because there were no friends, guessed her roommates, guessed R. Kurt Schoonmaker '99, who often saw her eating breakfast alone in the dining hall of Third North. Roommate Carly Hale '99 guessed she was homesick. Roommate Marcia Brandton '99 guessed she was lonely. Professor Macalester, who taught the astronomy class for which Mary passed so many hours at the observatory, judged that you couldn't find a kinder girl. Trace Edwards '97 often saw her at the library, where he was a checker, but you never would have been able to tell something was wrong; even if sitting quietly by herself, she was likely to be smiling. "She always came across as very rational, lucid; she is the last person I would have expected to be driven by her emotions like this." "Still, set against comparable universities, NYU has an excellent record of diagnosing and preventing at-risk students." Dirk Proctor was compiling a memorial book. The Wellness Center was organizing grief-management sessions and adding extra sessions to its regular rounds of anxiety counseling. A pair of sandals had been left lined up on the balcony.

Waterworks spurted automatously from his eyes. His brow touched cool linoleum. *No.*

"Matt?" Sophie was behind him. "Matt?" Kneeling on the floor beside.

The story surged up in chunks. How he heard the first time her crying, so strangely, such an odd, pure kind of absolute sadness in the middle of the night. Then afterward, almost keeping a sort of vigil, wanting to be with her in her loneliness, which he understood; as if it was one thing he could do for her, witness, keep company. But in the daytime: what do you say? I heard you crying? I know you're sad too? It's going to be okay? All those times watching her eat corn chips in the hallway, smiling as she lifted a stack of books, walking past him with the tail of her soft cotton shirt brushing the back of his wrist—that's when he could have done something! Started a real conversation? Invited her to lunch? Or at the very least told someone, he could have informed, gotten Health Services involved. But: nothing. Hadn't even talked to her since sometime in the autumn. And moving rooms—just left her there, alone. Vigil over! When listening had been the single action he'd ever done for her: that *gesture.* That *beau geste.* That worthless piece of . . .

"Oh wow," she sighed, wiping his eyes with her sleeve, craning his head into the bony splay of her collarbone. "I'm sorry. I'm really sorry for you." One arm pulled him into the nets of her hair.

He nestled deeper, listened to the quick hare beat of her heart. And she was alive, this Sophie. She was the opposite of *No:* that was everywhere evident here in the preciousness of her against his head, his chest. The inimitable spindle of her, this moving mechanism of blood and bone and right thoughts, and the fantastic imaginations of her singular mind. Good. She at least was still undamaged and safe; for her it was not too late. Let her go on to Berkeley and leave him behind, bagged up like so much trash. Let her find love with someone who could give back all that she needed, all that she merited.

Yet now there passed in the magic lantern of his brain limitless Sophies, a Sophie in her snowflake-printed shirt digging her arm through his and tilting up her face for a kiss as together they crossed a winter-damasked street; a Sophie brooding, pure sagacity and intellection, over a café table on which there lay some variety of art-history text; black-eyed Sophie beside him in bed, a shyly excited smile on her face as the spider of her hand went tracing the verge of his shoulder, over and again the round loop of his shoulder, as if in all of time there was nothing more they would ever have to do but this, forever, this gazing and touching—because in her eyes there were still forests and countries, whole bodies of water and nations he had never explored, not yet met—

Yes: yes to her, yes to that, yes. Wasn't there a sliver of chance left?[60]

"Sophie," he croaked.

Her body stiffened under his head. Her hand stopped stroking his back. A long pause, interrupted by the plash of a drop into what sounded like a glass of water in the sink. "Why are you smiling?" she said at last.

"I'm not smiling."

"I saw you," urged her voice, steady, strong.

You certainly did!

There was a way: beyond this white ceiling, beyond the atmosphere, there was darkness, clear infinite darkness in which the stars stirred. Matt squeezed his eyes shut. Beyond these walls to his sides—weren't they flimsy, couldn't you reach and punch them down? A series of caramel-colored home-movieish images began raving across his mind. Sophie with her set of retro airline-style luggage, sunglasses on, pushing

---

[60] Do you remember this moment, Lisanne, this same Friday's grey afternoon? Do you remember the fight we had, when I came home from waiting for you at your office and found you putting on black hose? And you said, „We are going out," only you said, On sort ce soir, and I said, Pourquoi? And you murmured under your breath, Fou, le con, or was it only Fout-le-camp? Then you brushed past me and pointed to the calendar, Malcolm's cocktail party.

Another cocktail party? At Malcolm's? Why why why couldn't we be alone for once and do something real, like love-making, instead of standing up with small glasses of Gewürztraminer by tables feeding endless pieces of cheese into our mouths whilst chattering about nothing?

And what a cocktail party it was. That ox-brained gossip Joan was whispering in your ear all night while Fritz Haven, like a one-note trumpet, wanted to tell me about the Goldberg Variations, on and on, which do you know I do not think are so very good after all? And I said, let us go, it is already midnight and I believe in America the cocktail party ends much earlier, and you snorted in that pig way you get when you are evil. „In America, in America,"

a cart through an airport, checking backward to make sure he was following. Her beside him in a beat-up old car, riding up a mountain in the crisp air of evergreens and redwoods. Her before an immaculate sunset, wearing shorts and hiking boots—smiling, cheering!

Matt's eyes flared open. Are you confused, sir? A little brain-touched? It's totally and completely impractical, I can tell you that right now. And your scholarship? I suppose you'd like to fling that out the window—goodbye, future! Now, sir, that's being somewhat overdramatic, wouldn't you say? I mean: let's face it. You *are* a National Merit Scholar, after all. People take years off all the time, and transfer, just fine. And what will you do in this alleged "year"? I don't know. Work in a bookstore? Read philosophy? Cook up California produce—in some invisible kitchen, with her?

This was his chance to start fresh, free; he must take that risk. Not to fail with Sophie as he had failed with Mary: and she was above still, on the fridge, her picture, like a beacon shining clarity into the room. Here there was still an inch of time, here it was not too late. Would he really let trivial stuff prevent him again? From Sophie? What else was he for— but her? This special, miracle girl: with a single laugh she made the air scatter with magic sparks! Imagine not to have to don the costume of his clothing, to walk with a supercilious mask sutured to his face about

---

you tapped your fingers against your wineglass, „you know *so much* about America." Your eyes glazed over. „Yes, I do. Or I am trying to." „Ah—you're *trying*," you said, „is that what you call it?" „Yes," I said. I was confused. Someone was calling you in the other room and you ran off like a skipping schoolgirl. I saw the open door and the lamplight on the bed and it was Joan, and next to her was just a man's leg and jacketed arm but he was cut off from my view. Joan was sitting on the bed holding something in her hand she wanted to show you, and you started laughing. You were laughing wildly, and I came up behind to see too. „Oh," I said, „do you have a headache?" For Joan was only holding six pills of aspirin. I was next going to tell her that she really should not take six pills of aspirin at once, particularly if she has had more than three alcoholic drinks since that is so damaging to the liver. But they were laughing, Joan and Malcolm, and also you. Malcolm coughed. „Rich," he said, offering Joan a handkerchief to dab at her eyes, „rich." „It's Ecstasy," you hissed, and glared at me. Did you want me to pretend I knew what Ecstasy was? You should have kicked me or found some other expedient; you did not do a very good job. Then when I asked about what they meant regarding ecstasy, they were laughing again, until finally

NYU, to make chitchat with brainless strangers; no, of a Friday to stay in, read side by side with Sophie, not to have to sweep himself under the carpet of these catchwords, desperate, inveterate loser. And that must have been the hunger Vic had seen, from the beginning: *I'll do anything, make me a slave if need be.* But when you understood it finally for what it was—why couldn't it be escaped? Even just thinking so: his body suddenly like a river shooting everything in it toward her! "Sophie," he panted. "Close your eyes, okay?" Obediently, she shut her tear-ringed eyes; she seemed to be wishing, holding her little fists abstractedly tight. "You know what it's like, Sophie? It's like punching; remember, from our first day? When they poked through the paint so all the gold underneath could show through. That's how I feel right now. Because I feel how much I love you, completely. And I want to come with you to California, if you will let me."

"Really?" She flashed open her eyes. Her face was lit within as a lantern. It was a face he had maybe never seen before: red, wet, newborn-fresh. Then suddenly her gaze clouded over. "So: what. After last—don't you think I'm still *mad*? You think you can just—just—" Just what? He was waiting patiently. He could wait, so long as he was facing her, inhaling her presence with his gaze, with his chest that tingled at her warm nearness, just drinking in inexhaustible bottles of her. . . . Yet now her lips melted into that lopsided smile. "Really." She grabbed his hand, nipped

---

you made Joan explain what it was. „You feel good, open, you feel like talking," she said at the last. „You feel like dancing," you said, your eyes flashing. „Oh, that's *you*," said Joan, „I don't get as dancey as you." Ssshhh, Malcolm and you said, and then Malcolm coughed. How much I hated those self-satisfied coughs. „We had a little party before," he said, and coughed!!!!!! again, „while you were away. In Germany. A couple of weekends ago."

„Oh, I see," I said, but of course I didn't see because you were staring across the room at an absurdly huge photography book of Robert Mapplethorpe sitting on the tiny table at the far wall and would not catch my eyes. „And you swallowed Ecstasy," I said to Malcolm. „We all did, chum," said Malcolm, „not a big deal, just a bit of fun." And he coughed. I wanted to press against his stomach so hard that whatever was making him cough, whatever fluid was trying to get up and out, would feel my pressure and come flying from his mouth so he could never cough again. „Wasn't it, though?" said Joan, and coughed!!!!!!!!!!!!!!! „just a bit of fun." „It was nothing." You looked me finally in the eyes. „So you swallowed too?" „Yes, I ,swallowed' too," you said, and made an exasperated

playfully at its back. "Okay." Squeezing him, she was nodding, her whole body was a sort of nodding, even the way her moist lashes curled at the edges was a kind of assent, serious, joyful. "Okay." She rose from the floor, her smooth fingers lifting him to standing; slowly, they drew him over to the bed, rocked him back on the white sheets. "You are crazy to do it, you know that?" she broke off to sigh. *Yes, yes.* "Though I think actually you're doing the right thing. For you too. Get out of New York, Cinema." *Ssh, ssh.* He dove into her neck with his mouth. Thickets of rippling tendons, plateaus of unmarked beach. And there shone her face: still so brilliant red, so lucent, open; his own just felt the same, like a thimble, outfitted with dozens of tiny windows. Holy shit. As if the body had a trick in it, a secret button—if someone pressed it, the scales on your body clicked open: and goldenness, and just pure *you* went streaming through. Love. This, this at last deserved that name.

And, compared to this: what? What other concern could there possibly be?

"Wow," he muttered, "you look so different."

"You do too," she gasp-giggled.

"How?"

Now she threw back her head into the whiteness of sheet to see him, her fingers grazing at his cheek. "You kind of look like you're on Ecstasy."

---

smirk as one hand shot up from your knee into the air while Joan gave a little giggle. „Anyway, are we going to do it, or are we going to talk all night?" you asked them.

That was when I realised that you meant to do it again. Ecstasy? I don't even like it when you would smoke marijuana with your friends from the H-E Conservatory. Now you wanted to consume a true illegal substance with these silly people who weren't even our genuine friends, this Joan and Malcolm and God knows whom else here too? „Would you excuse us?" I said to Joan and Malcolm, and you groaned and got up and followed, your smart new heels clicking down the hallway after me as we passed the living room, where Fritz Haven was pulling out a record from its paper jacket, no doubt another ridiculous *Goldberg Variation* recording, and pushing his glasses higher on his toucan nose. Then we were in the kitchen, and you came from behind and jumped up on the travertine counter and said, „You can do it or not, but I'm going to."

In your face I saw nothing sorry, apologetic, not one part of you sad that you were keeping things from me and mocking me openly in public in front of your new, so wonderful

9.

Before Matt passed out in a lather of limbs and sheets while the afternoon sun still pressed white fingers against the west-facing windows, he had fancied something naive about the imminent sleep. Something equivalent to pulling a plug on a tub of dirty bathwater—just like that, with this nap, Vic Spector, Liza Andrewes, not to mention the very edifice of Cinema, would go swirling down the drain away from him, forever.

But when he woke, Sophie was holding out a luminous cell phone, her brow creased with perplexity. He rubbed his eyes with both fists like a child and the room went radiant with stars. "Hello?" he groaned.

---

psychology-department associates. „Oh, you are," I said. I admit it, I was not very expressive. There seemed to be nothing to say. You had made up your mind. „Then I will too."

What else could I do? Leave you to those vipers Malcolm and Joan so you could laugh at me all night in that bedroom? „Hmm," you said, and hopped down, „you don't have to. You could go home." You looked up at me and you seemed very short and yet powerful, like certain dogs with chests like barrels: this was not so becoming, it must be admitted. „No," I said, „I think it is going to be fun." „Oh, you do?" you said, and I think if I am not mistaken that you were being as lack-of-words as myself. „Well, let's do it then." You walked from the room towards the bedroom and jerked your head backward at me as you said to them, „We're both in." „Isn't that nice, then," said Joan, I think authentically glad, as if my presence would enable her to have more Malcolm for herself; that woman, formed like a building crane with the lean top and the overwhelming bottom, was nothing beside you. And then Malcolm went into the other room while you were sitting with your knees bent on the floor and I got down cross-legged opposite Joan. I thought, I want to be with *you, you, you*, Lisanne, and at each *you* I was as a little boat that

"Magic, where the fuck are you?" Angel's gravelly voice crackled over the line. *"Are you calling him?"* squealed Peter Boï in the background, happy-scandalized.

"Um?" He cleared his throat. "Home?"

"Are you as*leep*? Are you fucking sleeping?" she hissed. "You are such a cocksucker, Magic! Get the fuck off me, retard," she screamed past the phone. *Bitch!* Peter Boï screeched dimly. "Listen, Vic's having a shit fit, I'm covering for you at the Red Room, Lacey's out there all by herself, Liza's bitching about something with her party, and, let me tell you, I just got my period tonight so I am Not In A Good Mood." *"Yuk, you didn't have to tell him* that," came Peter Boï's heavily nasalized contribution. "Get your Skinny Little Ass over here!"

As soon as he pressed *End,* Sophie was shaking her head. "You're *going* there?" Incredulous. Affronted.

"Sophie." He pulled her down to sitting on the bed's edge. Rubbed at her shoulders through the apricot T-shirt—when did she get dressed? how long had he been out here since their melting session on the bed? "I can't just phone it in. Isn't this the ideal time to quit?"

"You're going to Liza's birthday party. Is what you're telling me."

He balanced his brow on her shoulder. "I'm telling you that I'm coming with you all the way to Northern California. But first I just need to

----

is scraping against the dock with a wave that is pushing it toward shore; I want to be with you even if you will do something stupid like this. You were examining your new bangle, and I think you were seeing how many of your small black freckles it was obscuring on your wrist for that long moment when none of us was talking.

I heard people leaving in the outer room—Shireen Winters; her husband with the bizarre paunch that makes him seem as if with child—and then Fritz and his wife appeared in the doorway and waved goodbye and so did some other people I had never met, although one of them had produced a very bad impression on me earlier when she reductively dismissed Jung as a collaborationist fraud. And it was she who winked at you and Joan and said, „Have fun, you guyyyyyys...mm," with that broad American accent which, until coming here, I had always thought was only a comic thing actors did for cinema and television productions.

Then Malcolm was in the doorway, he said that we should enter into the living room. Everyone was gone and the lights were switched off except one low lamp above the dark-green leather armchair—an imitation or perhaps real version of Tiffany; it must have cost a great deal of money, along with his other ridiculous antique furniture—and several lit

pass by my workplace, take care of a few matters, and have a word with Vic, so neither you nor I ever have to hear the syllables *Cinema* again. Right? Let's say, what, like an hour?"

"More like two hours," she commented drily. "Though that's not the *point*."

"Sophie." He pulled back to gaze at her face—all deflated now, crumpled. Well, and who *was* to say that it couldn't be phoned in? As if Vic would ever refrain from cutting him loose by molting carrier pigeon, if that were most convenient. Why shouldn't he fall back asleep here with Sophie, simply redial Angel: sorry, I'm unwell? But we are not Vic; we are not some Marshall, careless, flaky. Besides, did he want to start the new life by fleeing headlong from that whole world: instead of marching up to firmly shut the door? Ah jeez. No right answer here. "I put it in your hands," he sighed. "It's your call."

"What does that mean?" Her eyes went wide.

"Or do you want me to flip a coin?" He reached down to the carpet and fumbled in a pants pocket. "If you can't decide? Heads I stay? I mean it, I'm leaving it to—"

But as the silver went up flashing toward the ceiling, she tackled him backward into the sheets. "Oh, just go," she groused. "Or you'll totally guilt-trip me."

---

candles wavering in the breeze from the open window. There were cushions on the floor about the small round table in the centre of the room and a tray with glasses and two pitchers of water. Except for the water and an opened packet of some obviously high-flight tobacconist's black cigarettes, it looked as though we were going to have a séance, because you two sat down on the cushions while Malcolm stood in a very important way with his hand up. „We have six hits," he said. „Now, I am going to take two, because I really do need two to feel anything, so which one of you would like the other extra hit?" He turned to Joan and raised his eyebrows. „Not me," she said, „I don't want to go crazy." She laughed, I think nervously, at you, my pet. Then she tucked back her short hair behind her clumsy ear and turned to me; Malcolm and she were looking but you stared dully ahead at the water. „Same," I said, „I will only have one." We all looked now to you.

„I'll do it," you said. How did I know you were going to say that? I remember the time we went mountain climbing in the Sauerland and Werner's shirt got hooked on a branch in a place that was dangerous and hard for his large body to squeeze into, and though there were seven of us, men and women who practised this often, and though it was your

"Why don't you come with me?"

She smirked as she eased off his chest "For Liza's *birthday* party?!" She rolled her eyes, smoothing her hair.

"You could sit in another room, and I could run over and kiss you after every thing I finish tying up?"

"Please!" Though there was a smile-glimmer burgeoning at the corner of her lips. "Just go. It's already after midnight anyway, I guess."

All that remained in Sophie's closet after so many nights spent at Eleventh Street lately (and what to do with this absurd wardrobe now? arrange a little sidewalk sale, a Send Matt to California fund-raiser?) was one sadly stained and smoke-infested canary-yellow button-down and a pair of gunmetal pleather pants, which would under the circumstances have to bear up. Over it all he fitted the leather jacket where, after showing it to her, he patted their joint notelet of love in the breast pocket: his *Love*, her FOREVER burnished with triumphant sun flames. "Maybe you'll still be awake when I get back?" he wondered, kissing at both sides of her neck. "Maybe I'll be in California by then," she grumbled. But he jammed his jacket hard against her torso until: "Ow! ow! Okay. I take it back!" Still spluttering as she kissed him goodbye.

Matt ran from the door downstairs into the fresh, misty air, and darted neatly across Sullivan to nab a cab stuck at the corner. Every-

---

first time, you said the same then. „I'll do it." I remember watching you scurry along the cliffside, finding your handholds, a natural, like a spider, biting your lip with concentration. Of course you would take both pills, my dear, your brash little voice claiming it like a diminutive fist. And it seemed that it must be the dim lighting or a breeze lowering the candle flames strangely, because for a moment I thought I saw Malcolm's eyes gleam and his face flash excitedly. Then he placed the pills in our palms, and I saw Joan watch you carefully, as if to make sure you'd taken yours, and you tossed your head back twice, triumphant, and banged your empty hand on the table. Then Malcolm grinned and took his.

I put the pill inside my mouth and, in the moment when I forgot about the water, tasted its chemical flavour. It seemed almost to be made of metal, and as little flakes of it were peeling off in my mouth, I thought of them as pieces of metal, little slivers like the metal splinter I once received from my skis' edge when I was fifteen, which had to be removed with a very painful pair of scissors. Then you said *ugh* and placed your head on your knees while Joan kindly (okay, Joan, for one time you were kindly) passed me a glass of water. So I swallowed and it was gone. And I realised with a small shock it was over, it was

where along the streets, his favorite sort of tree was in profusion and bloom, scattering infinitesimal white dots into the gutter, along the sidewalks. . . . Matt rolled down the window, trailed his left hand through the spring breeze beside them. How do you not know the name of this tree by now! That's the sort of existential info a human being should fill himself with. Perhaps in California he could buy a manual, spend his first days identifying *redwood, eucalyptus*. Yes, just as once you identified *swank* bars, *hip* clothes. And pored over those magazines as if they were field guides to your *vita nuova*. Was it time to burn those notes? In a bonfire—like post-graduation, with his high school, college-prep stuff? Goodbye to all that, a riotous blaze?

He was wondering where such a fire could legally be staged in this city when the club emerged silver out from the deliquescent night.

It looked very much like nothing. Seven or so security guards in puffy black jackets standing around on a rather simplistically constructed platform, hands in their pockets, trying to appear fierce, bored, before a pair of unremarkable silver doors. Down at ground level, Lacey, a frail figure in a trench coat, kept back the hordes behind velvet ropes by plying the tool of her authority, an ordinary stationery-store clipboard—humble as the chair with which the circus tamer keeps his credulous lions at bay.

And yet. These people had taken taxis, plotted evenings around this

---

too late. I could not now change my mind. This metal was inside me like a seed and was going to germinate in my stomach and spread its metal vines through my bloodstream.

But of course I didn't feel anything though I waited anxiously. We were all being jittery and nervous, except for Malcolm. You lay back on the Persian carpet with the cushion under your back arching it so your breasts stood up and open deliciously, and you put your hands just beneath the lower vault of your ribs as though you were indeed concentrating on letting whatever was in your stomach grow over you. Joan was busy drinking more water. „But I shouldn't drink too much, isn't that right?" she asked Malcolm, „because that'll wash it right out?" Yes, for five, ten, twenty, forty minutes it was it, this unsaid thing, this mystery to me, it. „Do you feel it yet?" you three kept asking one another. „I can't wait for it." It sounded like God, like some Messiah. Perhaps that was because you attributed it to strange actions, *I can't wait for it to come, for it to start, amazing when it takes over . . . remember last time when I thought it peaked but then it just kept going and going . . .*

Then you felt it first. Your face was flushed, unbearably *rouge* as after our very best, best incidents of sex, glowing and warm so that I almost wanted to come up to you and open

event; they had searched for invites to bring along or got nervous about their chances of getting in: as if they *wanted* to believe in this charade, that was the only way to parse it, deliberately shut their eyes to jump through whatever hoops were offered here. Why? Boredom? Pheromones? Of all the places to be, in this country, this planet—why should they care? What angel had painted this portal with an unseeable signal, drawing so many varieties of animal, lumbering or scampering or flying from all quarters of the wilderness of this city? And there were all of those other people, so many of them—busboys, janitors and bartenders, the sound-tech crew, Miranda and Adrian and God knows who else in the office, those women hunched for whole evenings in the two window booths collecting money and slipping out admission tickets—who earned their bread from precisely that, the lure, chimerical and transitory as a soap bubble, the smoke and mirrors of this place, the double-talk people like him gave to magazines; they lifted milk cartons from grocery bags into unknown kitchens bought in part with the money he made from his mouth, from this ridiculous getup, his prima donna outfit. But now one of their leads was quitting: definitively and final, he was detaching himself from their vast panoply, tonight.

Matt marched forward, apologized to Lacey, and gave the bouncers an unusually warm greeting as he pounded up the stairs.

---

the buttons of your tight ivory sweater, but it was curious to see you looking like that alone, not just without me but without anyone, as if you were having sex with yourself, or it was having sex with you. „Oh my God," you said, your lips curved, rocking back and forth on your cushion in an equal, regular motion, „I feel it." You looked at Malcolm and smiled, your face glowing toward him with—no, I know now, I know it was my mistake: not love but ecstasy. You reached out and gripped his hand above the table tightly, and then Joan said, „Ohhhh," and gasped, and you reached out your other hand and gripped hers too.

What could I do? „Ohhh," I said too, though I did not feel anything. And it worked. You and Joan ungripped and reached for my hands too, Joan cackling, saying, „Mm-hmm." „What does it feel like?" Malcolm asked me; perhaps he was having doubts. „It's—it's—" *did* I feel anything? *nothing* „it's—" „Ha-ha," said you and Joan, „he feels it, all right." And you were nodding like black women in a gospel meeting. „Mm-hmm." „All right." Then you broke my grip and Malcolm's and reached for a cigarette. „Lise!" I said, without meaning to, because I had not seen you smoke since you quit more than two years ago.

"Someone's in a good mood!" Alex, the friendly bouncer, nodded jovially.

"Ain't gonna be in a good mood too long once he see Vic," specified one of the new guys, a shorter man with a boxy, tough-jawed face and rapid eyes.

"Aww," the others laughed together, bobbing, shifting their enormous feet.

All righty, then. Matt hightailed it inside the silver doors. So it was like that. Evidently the entire staff knew he was slated to be Vic's whipping boy tonight. Well: what of it? In an hour or so such an issue could hardly be too vexing for him anymore.

Now as Matt plowed through the rooms for the last time, through the Opium Den, through the Technicolor savanna, through the Champagne Lounge, the waves of rock music, hip-hop, even the cheesy Eurotrash that broke over him waxed strangely nostalgic, endearingly lame. So Potemkin, so miniature: something only seen through the telescope of memory, in a galaxy far off. Matt blew past Angel out at the corridor (*Sorry, hang tight,* he commanded); in the Red Room he checked in with the team—Sandi, the bartenders, and a sour-faced DJ Future, livid about being nagged by Liza on his play-list: "I'm not some wedding, some fucking bar mitzvah DJ!" "Of course not, Future, of course not,

----

Luckily you did not take annoyance at my reproving outburst. „Smoking feels *great* when you are on Ecstasy," you said, „you should really try it," this despite the fact that I have not smoked since I was first at university, „the smoke goes right into your lungs, it feels like," you lit the black cigarette with Malcolm's ostentatious palm-sized lighter, „ahhh, as if it's going inside each room, each space in your bronchial passages, it makes you feel *fabulous*." Then you grinned at Malcolm. „Thanks for this," you said, making the cigarette vertical a moment, „thanks for *all* of this." You grinned wider, and while Joan murmured, „Yeaah, of course, *thank* you, Malcolm," you rubbed Malcolm's arm with your free left hand. „That feels great," he said, and eyed you so openly, I think if any man did that on the street you would be forced to call over a policeman. „Keep doing that."

And of course you did, but first you put down your cigarette. „Wait, wait, I can do better than that." You started rubbing his back and he was making sounds, *Mm, ohh,* and then Joan came up and started rubbing you on the back and you were making the same sounds, *Mm, ohh,* and then even Joan, the idiot, was making these sounds even though

play whatever you want," Matt soothed. At last, having summarily halted glum Paul White, the chief PR guy, in his complaining about how that *Interview* piece might turn out after all kind of small, valiantly fending off a number of brazen raids of the usual palaver—*Magic, what up. Baby! Thank you for the other week, those Yin-Yangs were so sweet*—he slipped past Liza swooned in a chair engrossed with some new dandy of a male model, and was just about to search out Vic: when Gabe the bartender waved him over.

"Um." Poor Gabe was visibly discomfited at being the messenger of such ill tidings. "That was Vic on the Red Room walkie-talkie." Rubbing desperately at the side of his nose. "Wants to see you up in the office? Um—kind of—"

"Pronto?" Matt began walking away backward, while Gabe nodded fervently, relieved. Fine. So much the better for me. Matt was actually whistling as he passed the staff bathroom and turned the knob to the back tunnel. At the end of this corridor: at the end of this dingy limbo zone: freedom. A weightlessness invested his legs as they took him farther, underneath the fluorescent panels, which buzzed their alien hum. Now he laid a hand to the right wall, letting his palm go over the bubbles in the paint, into the scoops between the bricks, flaking off white chips here and there to reveal more of the sea-green layer beneath. This

----

no one was rubbing her, so that there were so many sounds I wondered with the open window whether Malcolm's neighbours might not think we were having a sex party. Joan got distracted by looking at her hand and she suddenly jumped up, almost toppled over, and declared she wanted music. Then she was leafing through Malcolm's records and found something she liked, and as she turned around to take it from its jacket, I saw how you were surging toward him as you rubbed his back so that your hair was deliberately playing across the nape of his neck, and then he looked up at me and grinned.

I do not know whether the Ecstasy had its one effect right then on my temper, but I was certain of two things in that instant: that Malcolm was the Lucifer, and that I needed to leave the room and go far enough away where I could not hear him saying *mm* and *ohh*. I raised myself up and walked to the hallway and turned right toward the kitchen. Malcolm had put out all the lights but there were long white tapers, two in a cylinder, in three places around the kitchen. One cylinder was on the counter by the sink, and I went there and turned on the taps, and even though there was water in the other

Monica Ferrell

ancient paint! Like a school gymnasium, this tunnel, or the hallways of one of those random schools where he'd gone to take SATs, with his pencils, and his water bottle, and every shred of him fixed on one thing, the dream of escape. And once these walls, these very drab, buzzing panels had witnessed him, or rather an early-stage, an embryo him, following behind Adrian—nearly stumbling as he tried to sashay!

Matt grinned and punched at the wall, the stripe of pain a pleasant shock on his knuckles. Vic, who had plucked him from nothingness and reposed endless trust... Really speaking, it wasn't Vic's fault. He must make sure Vic understood just how grateful he was for the opportunity, for all the opportunities and mentoring given; quitting was only a personal move, not in any way meant to knock Vic's kingdom. Love, you know, it had called: and such a call you had to answer. That's how he should put it. Then they would shake hands, swear to keep in touch— and when Matt visited, of course, he would be thrilled to stop in. And if Vic ever went west, absolutely, please look him up! Matt's love-smile— *Love, you know how it is, Vic*—was already bursting open his face as he leapt the last pediment, threw wide the office door.

Vic was sitting in the main part of the office, across a table from an elegantly dressed black man.

"Hello, Vic! You called for—"

---

room, the beautiful streaming water glinting and twisting under the candlelight seemed so wonderful that I put my hands in it and started cupping it to my face, cool, long smooth draughts that were so sweet in my mouth and throat and on my hands that I put my face in too and let the stream wash over it, turning my face again and again to get the different angles of the water.

That was when I decided that I wanted to put my whole body into it, and I thought, why not? They are having sex play in the other room; I think it will be acceptable if I take a shower in this stranger's house. I went to the bathroom, outside there was a linen cabinet and I took a big, huge, firm bath towel, still folded up neatly, and stepped inside. I put the toilet seat down and placed the towel nicely on it. Then I took off my clothes and let them fall to the ground. I remember not caring about them, I remember trodding them under my feet on purpose, kneading with my toes my only good wool dress pants that I had „dry-cleaned" the day before with those little dry-cleaner bags in the launderette along with a batch of your clothes for next week's seminar. I turned on the water in the shower and watched it stream, through the clear transparent curtain, as I waited for it to

"Shut up, bitch," Vic snapped. "Can't you see we're playing a game of chess!" He threw back his head: the huge hazel eyes blared engorged, inflamed under the track lights.

Now, that was unexpected. Matt's mind cleared of his words like dust blown off from a book. The black man chortled. A light, even laughter as Matt fell back against the kitchen counter. Grumbling, Vic had suddenly grabbed a tall white queen in his fist—the ivory crown tipped, the whole tall idol shone like a bone in Vic's hideous mitt—and stabbed it forward.

"Ignore him," Vic grunted, "he's just one of my promoters." He waved manically at the other man, who, with a serene expression, as if to humor Vic, gracefully lifted a pawn and moved it one square.

But the sight of Vic with that bone in his hand had done something to Matt. It was sticking, like a still from a movie, even though the reels went wheeling forward, projecting images too pale to block it out. With that hand Vic fed raw meat to his dog, watered his plants, moved about these obscene speechless statues here in the think room, the club's brains. And apportioned out all his little acts of cruelty—remember Xavier's stricken face, the very first day? "I'm quitting," Matt said in a quiet, definite voice.

"Look over there," Vic replied, waving to a table behind him. He was

---

heat up. There was a knocking sound, not the door, something much lighter, lighter even than knuckles, tinier, like a skinny fish bone tapping against a plate. I looked up to the window. Another two long tapers were arranged in a cylinder stationed on the windowsill, casting a circle of light against the closed glass. My beloved, you will not believe me if I tell you it was a luna moth tapping against the pane within the circle of light thrown on that glass. You know that I have always wanted to see a luna moth, and you know they only live in North America, and you will say that I am inventing this. You will remember that luna moths only live in the summertime, where they are eggs, and then they cocoon, and then they gestate, and then they break out and when their wings are dry they open them, fly away, mate and die—all of this in the months of June and early July, all of this in deciduous forests where they can find hickory or walnut leaves. But I am real and the moth was real. Both wings were only just smaller than my hand, and it was greenish, a light pale green lighter than our celadon bowl from China. I opened the window and the luna moth hovered outside, inquisitive, it seemed, about the flame but not coming any nearer out of its fresh darkness, only flapping there its two huge wings,

still facing the other man, so Matt was surprised when the guy didn't turn. But now Vic smirked at Matt. "I said over there, you idiot, not at me."

On the table behind—Matt had to approach, to make sure—lay a gun. Between stacks of invites, some discarded hand-stamp machines: not a pistol, not a rifle, but one of those in-between varieties, that sort you see in movies, with a silencer. Was it real?

Vic had folded his arms. "Bradley picked it off some guy you negged from Paradise last week. Take a good look, now." Vic extended one hand in gun form at Matt, squinted shut an eye. "Pow."

The other man had turned to give Matt a genial look. "Pow," he said softly, seeming to find this funny.

"Bradley was in the navy," Vic explained to the man. "They're good security, those navy boys. I recommend, you know, if you ever . . ."

"I'll keep that in mind," the man replied thoughtfully. Though his eyes were dancing and his silver ascot was filled with merry little lights.

"Sometimes: you know, it's kind of refreshing to find this. As many years as I been in this business, even I can still make a mistake. Of course, the last time I made one was prob'ly 1988. Huh. But you see that little shit? That little shit in his bright, yellow shirt? When I found him, he was nobody. Worse than nothing, I mean you practically had to hose

----

ungainly and beautiful at once, alive. I watched the moth flap and dart in the square of black framed on all sides by the white of the window casement; I watched it I do not know how long, and as it shook its gawky large wings together and then suddenly raised, blew off, flew up away, for the first time in months I felt my heart surge outward out of my body toward it with what was real supernatural love.

I put my hands on the cool porcelain sink and lifted myself and placed my bare feet there; sweaty, they readily gripped the slippery porcelain; then I managed to get one foot on the narrow windowsill, and—amazing, so tiny a square, but in just a moment I flowed easily through. Then I was standing outside on the fire escape and I saw not the luna moth but the city spread out everywhere, or rather I saw darkness, perfect ermine black in the midst of which lights shone out like stars, and I took in big breaths through my nose of the wet breeze and shook with both hands the fire-escape railing, which made a whole line of droplets fall down into the below out of sight. It seemed strange that I caused them to fall, quite accidentally of course, and then I wondered about them lying stories below on the pavement or if they had touched someone's head and what would happen to them

down the Jersey off him, wearing mook boots, reeked of the fucking *mall*. He was, like, *contagious*, guido, that's how bad I'm talking. I bought him his first pair of shoes. I took him in. I gave him his own room. And everybody's going, 'What are you doing, Vic? The kid's a loser,' I mean, he doesn't even have a face. Look at him, he looks like a fucking frog. But I took a chance on him."

"You're a businessman."

"That's exactly what I am. I am a businessman. I saw potential and I took the risk. I mean, you had to see"—now Vic started to laugh, a raucous laugh that made the buttons on his white dress shirt glimmer like blind ivory eyes beneath the track lights—"you hadda see how he looked at me at first. So desperate, like a fucking puppy. Well." Vic's thumbs rubbed out tears of mirth. "Let's see: 1983, 1988 . . . I guess that's three."

"That's pretty good."

"Pretty good! Are you kidding? Who else has that track record? Oh, by the way, kid," for Matt had edged back toward the door, "just so you know, in case you're wondering, you're eighty-sixed, from my club. From any place," Vic raised his arms over his head, linking the fingers and stretching upward; then one hand came down blandly to cover a yawn, "worth going to in New York. You might look into *Queens*."

----

now, I fantasized that they would droplet-walk over to the Hudson River and be happy there, streaming with all the others like them.

That was when I turned back into the bathroom, where I dressed and closed the shower-taps. Do you remember what you were doing when I emerged into the other room? Joan was turning circles, her arms in the air—I suppose she had managed to feel dancey after all—while you and Malcolm were staring at each other, very near, and you told me, Ssssh. „You ruined it," you said after another minute of motionless staring. „You distracted me. We were trying to remove our masks and gaze at each other without any boundary between us." „That is funny," I said, „because do you know what the Greek etymology of *ecstasy* is?" „Mon Dieu," you said, and fell back on your cushion and started to laugh in small eruptions, irregular, as if land mines were exploding in your stomach, blowing it upward without mirth at odd intervals. Malcolm had picked up a cigarette and I could see he was cupping the lighter to his face to avoid letting me see his smile. „What does it mean?" asked Joan, still swooping her arms in arcs through the air, but bending closer a little to hear me. „Ek-stasis, the state of being put out of place, being put out of oneself or beside oneself. It has an interesting

"Goodbye." Matt turned on a heel and passed out of the office.

It was just so...unbecoming. Such a fool's act, lashing back like a lovesick girl. *Eighty-sixed from any place worth going to in New York*. Like that would really make us keen and quake—oh, take it back, Vic, please! But that's all the man's nerves were wired to see: nightclubs, and VIP hot spots, and mook boots, and *ugly fucking disgusting* or *beautiful people*, that tired dichotomy. Now it welled up in Matt, it pushed him forward like steam in his engine—getting faster and faster as he flew down the stairwell and along the tunnel, back into the party.

He was all the way to the center of the dance floor before the familiar universe ranged into place around him—ivory couches above which the red dots of cigarettes darted, bodies parting out of shadow when the mechanized lights splashed them full of bright, Future raising a record high, rocking in time, his glazed eyes only half-seeing the crowd, evidently lost in these tinny beats, shrieks unwinding in a splay that wrenched him fathoms down, through ocean whirlpools...Now, do it right now. What reason was there to delay like this? Oh, he wouldn't long-goodbye, explain he'd quit: much faster to just give out good nights. To Gabe the bartender, to an astonished Angel stuck manning the ropes. Olympia, the coat-check girl, most beautiful once-man woman he had ever seen, her delicate mouth and sorrowful eyes dark-shadowed and

---

history as a psychological or spiritual term. Paul—" But Joan had already said *oh* and moved on, absorbed in the flights of her arms.

„Well, my dear," I crouched next to you, „I think I am going to go home." „You are?" You opened one eye and looked at me from its glaze of blue. „Yes," I said, „I am tired." You started to speak, but I broke in. „You can stay." „Okay," you said, and began walking me to the door. Good night, Malcolm, Joan. Then I saw you standing, I was outside on the stained red industrial carpet and your body was inside, your hand resting on the doorknob, your hair unkempt—when did you take it out from your rubber band tonight?— gorgeous, lustrous and wavy, spilling above your smooth brow and down over your shoulders as you bobbed your head, tossing it, uncertain, your hand still on the brass knob and your one socked foot unconsciously toying with the long scarlet carpet runner at its edge where it met the hardwood floor, and those two sweet feet, in their white athletic socks you'd hidden so professionally all night with your ankle-height boots—had hidden, it seemed, from me all year—those white athletic socks reminded me of days of

Spanish, very *fado*, very *duende*, always about to cry; he squeezed her slender swan arm good night. Good night to Peter Boi with his clownish lips and perennial happy-time. So easy—just to walk out, free! He exited the double silver doors. It was good night to Lacey's round kickball of a face at the outside ropes. Well, good night, all, and thank you, thank you for this ridiculous ride! A scatter of the usual late-night chatter, *What a night, Can I have a light, There he is,* not even spoken but awe-whispered out behind him, *that's the kid who runs Paradise...*

Who said that? Matt whirled to face the dilatory crew lined behind the stanchions and ropes. Only a woman in a pair of shoddy thigh-highs and pink chinchilla, her face beaded with sweat as she leaned her head onto the much lower shoulder of a guy with bad roots. Two heavy men in business suits, one gazing forlornly at a beeper. Three underage girls in baggy pants and T-shirts, giggling, pulling on their ponytails.

And what are you going to find inside, friends? What are you hoping your twenty bucks will let you discover?

Well: whoever said it, goodbye to you too. What a gorgeous fresh night it still was, loveliest April. A purple cloud was massed right overhead, a dissolving amoeba with many licking tongues: now the red lights of a helicopter dimmed as it dipped inside that violet-colored miasma. Matt skipped down the six stairs, not touching the handrail, and barely

---

studying for our oral examinations together and how you used to draw pictures of Freud and Jung and Erich Fromm and pin them up on the wall with caricatures of what they'd written, just to keep our spirits up besides the coffee and the chocolate and the sex, the sex, sex, oh God, the sex; and remembering that girl you once were, I leaned in and kissed you, but as I did—I must have been imagining it, I had seen you drink glassful past glassful of water, besides smoking those nasty dark cigarettes—tasted that chemical, the metal flavour sunk into the flesh of your tongue.

„Goodbye," I said, even though I'd only meant to say good night. You nodded, looking down at the floor, and your long slim nose and fair hair and strange stiff pose reminded me of a Meister des Marienlebens *Visitation* you would have seen if you had ever wanted to come home with me to München, the left arm angled up, the right held down straight along the door-frame. Whatever has happened afterwards, that is how I will remember you, poised at something, uncertain, on the threshold of what we all know is inevitable. Then I turned and travelled down the hallway and the three flights of stairs outside to 16th Street,

restrained himself from skipping down the street. Ah! but after a few paces he just *had* to raise his arms in the misty springishness. La, lucky— he waved across the avenue to an idling taxi; oh, taxi, I wish you could bring me straight to Berkeley. A year off, then a transfer; no sweat. Not that his grades of late were the kind one might flaunt but, you know, he had hope and faith, and with a little elbow grease, with a little luck, he could be stepping without difficulty over the threshold of the new life with Sophie, toward a place where they could actually see the stars at night! Such trembling celluloid scenes had spooled sporadically before his inner eye all this evening, the two of them in Berkeley reading in the dank serious coffeehouses or splitting ice creams on the bright good sidewalks cleft open by tufted grass or driving again and again over the Golden Gate Bridge, taking pictures from its scarlet height toward the foggy headlands and beyond these the gray-lit gorgeous sea, immovable and moving, *soon,* it would be soon, was so close in the air the lashes of it were almost touching him now.

"Pardon me," said a voice behind him, "I believe you have lost something."

---

where the atmosphere was fresh and rare and breezy, and as I descended the marble steps of the pediment into the rain, I heard myself singing, *Luna moth, luna moth,* wondering where in this strange city, over what block, the Columbia University, the nearby St. John the Divine, or tacking eastward, perhaps, in the direction of Central Park and all of those mansions constructed like Gothic palaces which line the side streets about Fifth Avenue, or perhaps farther east yet, above the East River clotted slick with oil and the refuse outpourings of factories toward the Atlantic, yes, it might be, the slate-grey Atlantic, where in this weird universe right now it was flying off.

It is enough, is it not? May not the narrative be snipped here at this urgent point? Why cannot the sheet of silence be drawn over the horrific details, when by now all must be cognizant of the consequence of Terry Ford's visit to the Cinema night-club late in the night of 5, or we may say early in the morning of 6 April 1996? Can any among you require to hear extended relations of blood loss, of the various noises which those nearby have testified to hearing, of the time the ambulance was ordered, the time it arrived at hospital or when he was registered as breathless clay (perhaps this only: thirty-four minutes past five)? Such matters of fact have been recorded extensively in the New York and national newspapers and weekly newsmagazines throughout the whole of that month: there interested parties may derive a satisfactory summary of the night. Certainly, the media reports distort Matthew's person (I recall one insidious headline in particular: *Teenage Drug Kingpin Slain, Retribution for Deal Gone Wrong*), yet nonetheless they accord a wealth of information, especially with regard to the killer's determined course; indeed, they served well my early researches. For while the brief note Ford left slung about Matthew's neck provided some slender indication of his motive, truly it was the investigative reporters, with their impressive press-badges and newspaper titles, that convinced those from Ford's St. Louis orbit to part with richer details.

I provide some recapitulation of pure facts. That Katherine (Katie)

Ford at fifteen years of age „overheated" pursuant to a dose of
Ecstasy near eleven in the night of 19 March at St. Joseph's Hospital
was already a matter of public record over two weeks before Ford em-
barked on his fateful drive. Ensuing statements by fellow students
from the elite Mary Institute revealed the source of the tragic drugs to
be Katie, who had shared out to friends at an informal dancing-party
five „hits" brought back with her from a spring-break stay with the
sister of her late mother in New York. It seems the industrious Ford arrived upon this conclusion by means of independent analytical labour,
as may be understood by the vivid scene police officials discovered in
his suburban home, or, more precisely, in the room of his late daughter. Here he appears to have located and, with that accuracy of a
madman, organized a series of magazine cuttings on the subject not
merely of a certain downtown New York night-life culture but specifically of Matthew, „Magic Matt," the „King of Club Kids," several of
whose clipped pictures Ford left assembled into a pile on Katie's ex-
travagantly cushioned pink and white bed. I note in passing that even
in photographs this bedroom, with its ivory carpet, white leather armchair, antique ivory telephone, and bedside commodes upon which
sit matching pink tasselled lamps, poignantly testifies to what degree
Ford's only child was cherished as a little princess. (The conspicuous
newness of these objects suggests moreover they were acquired after
the death of Ford's wife, Carolyn, caused by breast cancer two years
earlier.) In striking contrast to the atmosphere of privileged schoolgirl's decorum yielded by these furnishments are the posters along
the walls—the smirking protagonist in bowler hat of *A Clockwork
Orange*; slouching, those black-dressed members of a band given the
caption „Charlatans U.K."; another of „Depeche Mode"—and the
few accounts that have surfaced concerning Katie's relations with
forbidden substances. In November she had collected a „citation" on
being found in an intoxicated state by the officers who raided a
school-fellow's party. Over Christmas recess, at a condominium in
Naples, Florida, let to Ford and his daughter jointly with another
classmate and her father, Katie returned one night in the company of
an elderly couple who had found her vomiting repeatedly on the

beach—an event which provoked Ford to demand her to stay indoors for the rest of the holiday and write repetitive oaths never to commit such an action again on the nearest available paper surface, a set of flower-printed paper plates. Most recently, school-friends describe hearing her boast that though she had been punished by „ground-ing" upon her father's discovery of cigarette refuse in the garage rub-bish bin, she was enabled to evade that penalty by climbing through the window in her room. In photographs, the outline of this escape route is clearly visible behind a set of gauze curtains embroidered with a mauve floral motif, to the left of her bed and above the white desk supporting a Webster's College Dictionary, a variety of sta-tionery tools, and a teddy bear wearing a miniature Mary Institute jersey. May I remind you that she was just fifteen at her death.

Plainly Ford had decided on Matthew as the fountainhead of his tragedy as early as six days before he proceeded to New York. On Saturday 30 March he made an unexpected call at the home of Anne-Marie Dobson, that school-friend who had first telephoned him from Katie's hospital room; catching her at the bottom of the footpath in her front garden, where she wished to check the family's mailbox, Ford directed her to enter his car, and there impelled her to confirm his surmise. On this point, I confess, my imagination has often fas-tened. Miss Dobson was not a witness to Katie's purchase of Ecstasy in New York, nor, by her subsequent admitting, had she been told from Katie who sold the illegal substance. Yet nonetheless she con-sented with Ford's hypothesis, which she has attributed to her fear in the face of Ford's strange behaviour and erratic driving gestures: he navigated the car at high velocity through the tranquil streets around her home, halting at stop signs so suddenly that she was required to hurl out her arms to break her forward impulse („I thought I was going to go through the windshield," she has stated somewhere; perhaps the New York magazine?). What might Ford's actions have been had Miss Dobson refused the logic that he urged her to accept? But perhaps Ford would have selected the identical course all the same; besides, any wit-ness of Ford as he was in those days, imposing in size, with a rigid jaw and a type of iron-willed resolution in his blue eyes, along with the uncanny suggestion—yes, truly this was it—that he had nothing more of value in this world to lose, scarcely could fault Anne-Marie for doing as he bid. In any case, testimony by those friends from summer-camp with whom Katie passed a New York Friday less than one week before her death has demonstrated that—however deranged by grief, however bereaved by the losing of this second and final member of his nuclear family over the space of two years—in fact Ford was correct in his guess that Katie attended the Paradise party of the Cinema night-club, where she may well have acquired her drugs-supply.

The execution phase of Ford's plan is easy to chart. The supervisor at the bottling corporation where Ford had by two decades of devoted employment risen to a mid-tier executive has noted that the killer requested leave on 5 April for a „personal day"; this date was the second anniversary of his wife's death, and Ford had done exactly the same the previous year. Police records demonstrate that the gun employed was one of four registered to Ford; acquaintances indicate that while Ford could not be called a shooting enthusiast, he had been raised in a hunters' family and was known through his adult years casually to practice marksmanship in an empty field outlying their town. (When blackbirds possessing an infectious bacterium responsible for several cases of infant blindness afflicted the oak trees outside a First Baptist church, Ford was one of three men called on to rid the community of the pest by skilful use of his firearms.) The lone signal of Ford's irregular state of mind in the days before the murder derives from a statement by Sam O'Hearn, of a barroom called „Sam's," who recollects seeing Ford at his establishment, an uncommon event as Ford was a teetotaler, and notable also for his peculiarly fine mood („It's good to see you smile a little," O'Hearn has spoken of declaring). It might have been difficult to establish the trajectory of Ford's journey to New York had he not, first, sped through a toll-collection booth at the entrance to the Pennsylvania Turnpike, where mounted video cameras recorded his number-plate, and, second, paid for petrol at the Sunoco of the Joyce Kilmer rest-stop in New Jersey with a credit card toward the middle of the evening. Three parking tickets provided to the car Ford abandoned on the street-side opposite the night-club resulted in its towing, then ultimate search, which disclosed an elaborately packed skier's bag including several changes of shirt, an extra sweater, a toothbrush, shaving implements, and a torn cardboard box holding enough shells to annihilate many times more Matthews than this world was ever fortunate enough to possess. Why, perhaps those ignorant among you may ask, do we not know from Ford's own mouth words of this event? Because he became deceased.

First of all you must know that I did not shoot of my intention but at Ford's own urging. We have in German the term *der Gnadentod* (grace- or mercy-death); here you call such a thing euthanasia or assisted suicide. There are diseases of the spirit as serious as those of the body, terminal, incurable sicknesses. I do not suggest that were I faced with the identical choice I would perform equivalently today. For, second, you must know also that I was not in a state of normality when shoved into the vortex of events. These two circumstances are among those the amiable and estimable Mr. Allen Eisenberg, J.D., wishes to make clear in his opening arguments four days from this one. That is accurate: in four brief days I shall find myself in a courtroom to determine my liberty or my guilt. So as not to alter the outcome of this critical event, I believe it shall be prudent to send this final note in an envelope whose seal is to be broken at the conclusion of my trial. If you now read these words at the close of the relation of Matthew's life, my faithful, also long-suffering friends, this should mean I am either a free person or I am created guilty beyond saving.

Yet let us pause one moment. Does this episode not belong to me as well? May I not then tell it „my way"? Readers, the staggering, ironic incident is that I was not arrested for my crime. No, it was my study of Matthew which endangered me. For I was halted in connection with a crime to which I had no relation; in May 1997, the New York University, shameful of a „security breach" and the several rapes which certain of you may have read about occurring in dormitories that month, caused myself and several other men to be taken into custody upon the grounds of various vain suspicions. Indeed I possessed a master key, indeed I owned a false identification card and a custodial uniform, indeed I was even seen in the hallways where the rapes occurred—for I was forever in the hallways for research, not only ones with rapes! Naturally in the police house no victims identified me from a „line-up," but once my fingerprint was cast, all damage was performed. I understand that advanced computerisation of files has made matches greatly more efficient, so much the luckier for me. Yet—perhaps there is no need for sarcasm on that point. I mean to say: perhaps the linking of myself with that fingerprint *was* a stroke of good fortune? If not for my arrest, would I not have spent my years imprisoned by this secret itself? Here I shall disclose all.

Picture with me, readers, once more Matthew's last night on earth, when I attended the Ecstasy party at the flat of Malcolm and witnessed the phenomenal luna moth and stood on the fire escape although I am fearful of tall heights and left my wife to fornicate with a strange and personally mocking man and was capable even of cheerfully singing to myself as I stepped the last few stairs down from the pediment outdoors. Yet I did not walk directly home when I exited Malcolm's; I turned left on the sidewalk outside not right, that is to say away from my flat. The night was so unbelievably fresh and dark, the light rain had dazzled the pavements into seeming new and beautiful, veins, special trails, I wished somehow to follow those droplets on the voyage I had imagined for them over to the Hudson River. It was not far, only a handful of avenues west; comprehend, Malcolm's flat was already nearly at the Ninth Avenue. I did not feel tired. Allen wishes to tell this as sign of a continuing Ecstasy influence, but I do not credit that ascription myself. The black girders of certain buildings pleased me, and the red brick, glowing warm and inviting in the streetlights, and the neat black or dark-green painted doors, shiny and some with large shapely knockers. I was enjoying them so much that when I neared the Eleventh Avenue I did not cross to the river but stuck toward the buildings, where even at this tardy hour of nearly three, enchanting couples were getting out of taxis and skipping across streets into such buildings' doors. It was either north or south and I chose north, but indeed I did not go more than a few blocks when I actually stopped a man with silver hair who was smoking and asked for a cigarette—I, the same Hans who had not smoked in seven years since that rebellious era of my first moving to Berlin, and for a few instants I enjoyed this, before it caused my stomach to boil with nausea; I crushed the cigarette on a lamppost, cradling it curiously in my palm as I walked five and one-half more haphazardly selected blocks.

Where a thing happened which absorbed me completely. Are you ready to hear? When I had reached several blocks north and west of Malcolm's, I noticed a brightly-lit platform where a number of black men were standing in dark jackets, below which a girl was sitting on a stool in a leopard-print dress like the clip Lisanne sometimes wore in her hair. Also a very few persons were on the sidewalk, perhaps five. I turned right to walk past and examine—why not; after all, it was a curious location for so many people to be at that late hour and right by the river, where, I think you might know, the streets normally are forlorn. I may have been whistling. I recall hearing the crack of broken glass under my formal dress shoes; Lisanne had ordered these. I was on the north side of the street alongside and beneath the platform with the tired girl and men. And then the silver doors peeled open like the covers of a silver book, and a boy came out on the stage lit up under the wash of spotlights.

You will never have noticed the resemblance, for even were you to witness photos of myself at a youthful age and so knew our same swollen lips, our wide blue eyes, our hair toward the browner side of blond, our narrow frame, there likely remain in your minds these trappings of my personality, all these life-turnings you know I have taken—becoming a devoted scholar, a husband, a divorcé—all of which make it difficult to imagine me as something other than I am. Yet I remember what I was before those path-branches, what I am in essence, and therefore the linking was easy, even instantaneous. This boy was dressed in such queer clothing—a leather jacket with many metal studs upon it, shining tight pants in which I do not think one could fit so much as a coin, clothing I could not see myself within, and he had just kissed a girl with spiky hair good evening and waved to the black men, and I wondered, how is it to do this, to be young and in this joyful universe, triumphant, without care, a little god, as if there

were some other twisting fork I could have taken so that I was not between the constricted walls of a pathetic existence where, after seven
months in this crushing city, I could not excite even so much as an interview for an academic position, so that I was not out on the pavement walking away from the place where my wife played happily with
those who scorn me? I was certain that this child would not ever be
forced to endure a single afternoon watching the grey-face women of
the launderette folding their terrible large undergarments piece by
piece, fold by fold, as the light sinks through some drain in the sky, or
undergo even so much as one of Malcolm's supercilious coughs. I
wished to know *how* all this could be so, I needed to see what those
small pale hands would do (understand, he was not three metres
away), or what path those lucky feet in their shiny black boots should
take.

Therefore I followed him. I tried to make my shoes very quiet as I
grew closer, but even with the gritty noises my step was still making
he did not once turn his head inquiringly. He seemed to be staring up
at the moon, and then he performed what seemed a bizarre act: he
opened out his hands to either side of his body, then suddenly one
darted up as if he meant to grab the moon from the sky. No, merely
gesturing to a taxi with glowing lights—those number-plate figures
swim before me now, I can almost make them out but of course I
cannot, not really—idling far down the street across the avenue; its
driver must have seen him, for it glided slowly toward us. I was going
to lose him in moments. „Pardon me," I blurted out in a hoarse
voice, spotting a feasible pretext, „I believe you have lost something."

The boy wheeled round and gasped when I pointed to a scrap of
paper on the ground. But by the time he had come perhaps three
paces closer, his fingers had worked far enough into a breast pocket
to ascertain whatever it held was still present; under the bluish streetlight also now it was plain to both of us that the scrap on the pavement was quite moist and must have come to rest before the
evening's rains. „Oh," he said, „thank you, but it isn't mine." His face
was in shadow and all I had a clear glimpse of was a flash of teeth by

which I presumed a smile. We resumed walking again. Heel-toe; heel-toe. The taxi was halted at a red light. It is so rare that I follow a whim—or rather it was rare then, I think I am improved now—but, I did. One advantage of a German accent is that it puts everyone at ease in this city, or perhaps it was my clean and neat appearance, for he did not seem frightened of me or hesitate when again I said, „I am sorry; excuse me," but turned politely around. „Do you have fire?" I held open my palm where the slightly smoked cigarette lay cradled.

Now, now that it is afterward and the night is long past, I am astonished that I did not recognize him—at least a little? Readers, I may, I must have seen him dozens of times. For did I not frequent the very same Japanese shops south of the Washington Park where he enjoyed his sushi? Did we not live, at least after his move, a small handful of blocks away? I do *perhaps* have now certain impressions of seeing in the Meyer Hall a slight fair boy hanging nervously about water fountains and notice boards where I sat nervously also with my back to Lisanne's seminar room, trying to pretend all was well when I knew the whole sand castle of our love and my life was coming apart, yes, a finger of water had entered so all was crumbling from inward. He stepped toward me, patting his pockets, his pants, his jacket, now his jacket from the interior. „No, I'm sorry, I don't." He took another pace and we were really centimetres away, we could clearly see one another. How curiously radiant and open he appeared. Not even the moon-like streetlights could overshadow this strange gold illumination pulsing out from the inside of his face. „But here," he slipped out a yellow packet of cigarettes from his chest pocket, „you can have these." He smiled a wide warm smile as I have in a certain photograph after I have played first oboe in the Mozartfest at Hochschule. „I'm quitting." A small piece of paper fluttered toward the ground like the luna moth, flapping and light, it was yellowy and whitish and almost see-through in the streetlight.

„Oh," I said, and bent, and with two fingers lifted it from the pavement, „now, this I have certainly witnessed you drop." The paper unfolded in my fingers as I held it out to him, and I saw the word *Love* in large letters and about it, I proceeded as far as FORE before I comprehended. *Forever?* The innocence of this, the youthfulness, the unawareness of how many millions of others have written such words and had those words turn into lies as false as counterfeit currency! Did my wife not once pen something so trite and mendacious on the beautiful taut expanse of her abdomen and lift the white sheet to show me one morning when I woke in her first flat in Berlin? Perhaps even now she was whispering something as noxious, as corrupt, into the ear of Malcolm, when she had succeeded in *taking off the mask* or whatever ludicrous thing they had been doing and it, the Ecstasy, the metallic substance which turns blood to mercury, had more completely diseased and shuttered her thoughts.

„Thank you," he uttered, blushing. „I don't want to lose that."

Now I opened my mouth, my brain racing with images of laughing, lying Lisannes with white torsos and mocking mouths, my tongue searching for English words of searing cynicism, something Nietzschean, jaded, severe. All I could discover were phrases in the vein of „Ha ha, little boy," or „Your naïveté..." but I did not progress further. There under the streetlight, as I viewed his resolved, radiant face so near its breath might brush mine, my throb of disbelief pained, melting. „I see," I said.

Two events occurred at nearly the identical instant: one, the taxi he had waved to, which had been stopped at the traffic light across the avenue, picked up a fare, blurry girls, I could not distinguish how many there were; then, as it turned left to speed away from us along the avenue downtown, two, a voice behind my back uttered, „Freeze."

There is much I do not recall very clearly after this moment. Scientists write that adrenaline disrupts the production of proteins which encode our memories; Allen will, I am sure, claim the interference of my pill of Ecstasy. A large, hairy man with an unseasonably dense woodsman's jacket stepped forward holding a gun in his left hand. He stepped directly for the boy. I should have left them then, I should have raced past those two to turn the corner. I would like to tell you that I meant to save the boy by staying, but that is not so, although at the time I did have a vague sensation that like some wonder-worker I could interpose myself between them and not become deceased though many bullet holes, which I imagined like pox sores, should open in my body. The man discharged a spray of angry words at the boy, none of which I comprehended properly. Only the word *Dead*, occurring with large regularity, drilled into my skull, also the phrase *You did this, you did this* and *her*, so that for the duration I had some mistaken hypothesis that the man was striving over the love of a girl. This notion may have been influenced by the current of my own evening, though also, of course, the man was shaking a photograph of a girl in the air; if you will believe my stupidity, when the photograph dropped upon the pavement I bent and retrieved it for him. Could I not have caught his legs? Could I not have effected a swift, saving gesture? Like a dunce I handed the man the photo, which he took to hang upon the boy's chest. When the noise occurred, for a moment I thought, oh, it is I being shot, and this was strangely pleasurable; my life, this night, all was ending, in this very moment I should become free, a ghost. Then the boy folded up like a picnic-chair. His lower half collapsed, a camel sitting suddenly down; his head followed, a balloon dragged on a string toward ground. Later, in the scores of months since, I have tried to recall the face—but perhaps mostly I avoided regarding it? for I only possess a clear recollection of the eyes, their mixture of reproach and horror frozen in that head which was falling. Do I imagine hearing the spatter? Perhaps. Because I saw this on the ground in some seconds. Not all blood is red. This blood was darker and the way it shimmered under the streetlight reminded me of a petroleum slick, flowing and stretching where the pavement was lake water. I tasted bile in my mouth. Still, it would have been simplest for me to race away then; I suppose I had some fear that the man should assassinate me from the rear but I do not think this concern was very grave, because he appeared to be so occupied with the fallen boy. Yet I did not move, my legs seemed as steamed asparagus. Then the man placed the gun in his mouth. A stream of nasal mucus shined on his chin and neck. He choked, spat upon the ground, coughing. He arranged the gun against his chest but his hand was shaking so powerfully it did not remain in the right vicinity.

„Come here," he uttered. My turn first, then; of course. I felt myself vibrating like a window under the blasts of forceful winds. He required both hands to press the gun into one of mine; I could not comprehend what he was doing until he stepped back again and lifted his vacant hands. „Do it," he pronounced.

I have never owned so much as a play pistol which emits loud noises and brimstone. The main sensation of the gun was outrageous heaviness.

„He killed my daughter," the man said simply.

„I do not know how to operate a..."

„Here." He stepped forward. He pressed his body at mine. He shifted my hands over a spot on his chest. You see, he insisted on it— Allen will make this clear, he must—„You can't miss," he said to me and smiled.

In retrospect I should have wiped the gun when I left it in his fingers. Even the most dim-witted observer of television police dramas can indicate that every killer must wipe his/her pistol. It amazes me that I thought to dispose of it at all, especially when I reflect that my primary concerns at the time were two divergent practical matters: whether my arm would recover from the nasty jerk it had had while travelling backward, and how rapidly I might leave that place of gore. Perhaps I preferred his suicide to be correct, apparent; perhaps I did not wish to rob even some dead man of his gun; perhaps I merely desired to rid myself instantly of that killing weight, which seemed to prevent my forward motion like some leg-chain. With both bodies, there was little amount of movement, altogether distinct from how death-throes are pictured in certain films I have witnessed. Touching the trigger down, friends, this is like entering a woman: you feel it give way, you feel the slight tension, you feel its longing to give way completely. I did not even pause to ascertain death by pulse or breath. Somehow I imagined that I should see them, this man and the boy, springing up like actors and meeting me on a street corner halfway home, though for now they lay on the pavement like bulky pillows behind me.

Those among you interested in concerns of public security should grow disturbed how easy it was for me to depart from that scene, walk more than a dozen blocks home (seven of these long avenue-blocks) without encountering so much as a siren. In the flat I put on water for chamomile tea but the fluid burned up underneath my nose and scarred the kettle so badly I had to place it in the rubbish bin. Then I washed my hands. I took a shower. I rubbed down my skin with a moist terry cloth. I placed Swiss eucalyptus drops in a stockpot of boiling water on the stove to wake me and soothe me at once. I considered opening and drinking the large bottle of Chimay Reserve that had waited near the rear of the refrigerator almost a month for a special occasion. In my pyjamas I performed yoga poses on the floor; I performed upward dog, I performed downward dog, I lay for much time in child's pose, pressing my forehead to the wicker rug until the burning on my brow felt like fire. I wondered whether I might telephone someone back in Germany. For some reason I kept considering Herr Prof. Blum, but the desire to call vanished when I pictured in my mind that way, if I had bungled some aspects of my field research or an academic presentation, he would sit behind his desk, take off his spectacles, and press them unfolded to his temple, as if to say, Hans, you were born an idiot, there is nothing to do with you. Envisioning Herr Blum, I moaned—my first utterance since the event. I felt that I had not shot but swallowed a bullet. I continued to experience that sickening sense of the man's body rearing away from me to fall down like some wall of meat. I lingered above the toilet bowl, hoping to vomit. I passed back into the kitchen, popped open and poured a glass of the Chimay, but I did not drink. I stared at the cork on the countertop. The cork made me displeased. I held it in my hand; how uncomfortably large it felt closed inside my fingers. This badly-shapen knot was a sort of heart, and when I put my ear to it I could vow I heard it beating.

I placed the cork under my pillow, lay down on the bed and closed the covers over my head, over the „day of the crime" itself. As if I could! And yet, the astonishing fact was: in the morning it seemed even this wild wish had succeeded. For when my wife slipped into bed beside me, so late that the starlings had long stopped peeping beyond the window, and I made my breath like a sleeping man though I was quite awake, had been awake seeing for hours on the underside of my eyelids all that had happened this night—or in the afternoon when she rose from the pillows and walked directly to the bathroom and showered without a good morning, without providing me even that usual pained peck on my cheek, and when she entered unutterably healthy, rosy, and lifted the lid on the pan where I was keeping warm her breakfast and she grunted, what a crucifying sound! as if I was not deserving of speech, I thought: not even *she* can tell that a murderer has been supplied in place of her humble Hans. I thought, if one's own wife cannot distinguish this, am I not safe? Am I not free?

No, hardly. Gentlemen, ladies, I do not know if you have ever had the opportunity to kill another person. I have enjoyed many conversations on this score with certain messmates of mine in West Facility. The killing itself is fearfully facile. One depresses a trigger; a noise, in some cases a flash of light, a back-kick. Once while visiting my uncle's farm in the Alsace I witnessed a horse with neck cancer being put to death. At the time I did not believe the animal could prefer the bullet, and I stayed in my room all the evening, refusing to partake of dinner. Yet when the victim is a person, after killing how much more the event grows upon one. One is populated first by a moving army of images, then of questions. Is killing the killer of a beautiful boy wrong? Is killing one who ardently wishes to be killed wrong? Or, the worst, did I cause the killing of the beautiful boy by causing him to linger? Might he perhaps have raced across the empty avenue, slipped into that taxi and flown safely away from that place, had I not, with my needless *Excuse mes*, invented the tethers that moored him there for his death?

And why did I require to bother him? Why should I, an adult, the possessor of an advanced degree and, at least in my homeland, a mounting professional career, have resorted to pursuing a boy of eighteen years, suited up in a costume that marked him out as a ridiculous popinjay, if not a streetwalker? What could I have possibly found to envy in this small boy? But do you not find it too? When I encountered in that night this vision, this boy mysteriously glowing, and then when under the streetlight with that slip of paper the source of his joy became revealed, what I witnessed in this gold-lit person was a—youthful, naïve; certainly, you skeptics, but nonetheless—a radiant exemplum of some love such as I fear I have never, not even with Lisanne, experienced.

How many of you, my faithful kind readers, have loved? This is a real question I ask. Oh, indeed certain songs, certain poems on that topic have made me cry, regularly, for more than two years, yet I know: this crying is not as it seems. Where did I create my first error? Was it that when I followed my wife to America, I possessed insufficient love? For it is true that what I contained in my heart was less desire to be with Lisanne than the wish not to be alone. Or was the mistake made earlier? Why does any thing happen? Queerly I see now the first meeting of myself and my wife, ex-wife, that silly ticket, my foolish gaffe, an error of place which brought us together, a momentary confusion, the street, the Trebbies zipping past and the mint syrup, my sweater, the grey day with big drops of water that fell fat upon our cheeks, then a tea-party, a wedding dress, a ribbon pulled from her hair, several large suitcases, an argument with pots ending with making love on the wood floor of our flat...

It is coming back to me. They are opening in me like raw lesions, the memories. We were happy, once. Of that I am nearly sure. What else could her gaze, grown almost violet-tinged, that I view again directed at me—tenderly, with a sacred kind of excitement, a sort of animal excitement such as one sees in foxes who step toward each other, curious, sniffing, before they fall to their painful, inexorable sex play—from beneath a flowering tree on the Kastanienallee at the height of spring: what else could such things have meant? But by the era of our arrival here, there was just the echo, the spoors and hairs of that heavenly time left behind: for me to collect, and whimper over, playacting the role of one wronged. What a loveless marshland we lived for months—a torture for her, torture for me though I smiled my coward's smile through it all, not stepping one centimetre nearer a conflict that would set her free for I did not want to set her free, you see; this may be my deepest crime.

Yet now I feel unusual, I feel cool. A starlight is shining in my skull.

Now there is something else. I regard in its full size a detail of the evening's events. Of we three who stood beneath that glowing street-light, have I not been spared? I am alive. For me to walk my days always mourning Lisanne or mourning what amounts to a deeper deficit, a lack of love in myself, would waste the strange mercy of my saving. And now I feel I must enter that unknown which opens inside me like a portal to another world: I must take on the venture of real love. I shall. Maybe there exists a woman who can take and treasure me with all my foul secrets, who can unfold them in me as so many fists and kiss the open hands. And Lisanne: may you forgive me for that hopeless clutching at you I have done, besides my bitter words (and certain unwise telephone calls: yes, you were right for suspecting me) (also loss of some personal objects: very sorry). I forgive you. My Hippolyta, my marvellous warrior-queen, I give you over to the happiness of your future.

This reminds me of one more story which it is perhaps right now to confess, to abolish in the telling. For though I adhered to the condition presented to me for Jason's cooperation—readers, be joyful: he is well, he is drugs-free, he is studying again after a year's leave and misses his friend Matthew, whom he has long forgiven!!!—that is to say I complied entirely with the letter and most of the spirit of the injunction against contacting Sophie, who wished to be left alone in her grief (justifiably), there was one occasion on which I performed a thing which may be considered a form of disobedience. My air ticket and hotel in Seattle were paid for by Lisanne, or by her eager fiancé for that is what he was to her by then, so she and I might glare over a table while our lawyers shook hands, trading golfing invitations as the sky outside thundered like a primitive drum. Therefore, once having unregistered from my hotel, there was the additional expense only of a day's extra rental of my auto, besides petrol for the long drive down and back the coastal road from Seattle where I traced that ocean which Matthew never in this life managed to see. A blazing March afternoon when I drew into Berkeley, where I drove through streets overflowing with children in T-shirts, red-cheeked children greeting one another with jovial shoulder pats—this was a Friday, you could read it in their relieved smiles—a population of careless children in the land of plenty, a land overwhelmed with oranges, and wine-grapes, and rich pastures for milk cows, and roses even at that tail-end of what is commonly considered winter. I drove past the red-tiled roofs of university buildings and the stucco facades of optimistic mission churches; I drove into the Berkeley Hills, where a real stag halted my progress in the midst of a mountain road as much with his serious, solemn eyes as his prodigious antlers; I drove along the spine of land that links on high Berkeley to Oakland, which gives a view onto a fantastic thing, the bay stretched out as a plate of silver converted to bronze here and there beneath the ribbons of its bridges, and finally turned down again out of the evergreens and cypresses into that portion of town where Sophie lived. You see, it was easy; a trusting Jason had failed to conceal among his memorabilia that envelope which contained her return address. So at that hour, I could not have better planned it, when the afternoon dilates fully to a throb of gold, the „magic hour" as I hear it is cynically called by wizards of cinema, I circled a lake spotted by the spindly bodies of white egrets and families of ducks defecating upon the lush greenery surrounding it and turned up a lane, and turned up a second lane, and coasted my labouring vehicle along a rise to stop opposite her flat on Capital Street.

What was I wanting to see? Nothing was concealed from my gaze; whatever architect devised her building had evidently no fear of peepers, for it was constructed primarily of glass, like a greenhouse; by changing his position on the street, an observer could peer clearly through three of its four walls. Would I have wished to see her interior decoration dominated by portraits of Matthew, lovingly framed and arranged about the living- or bed-room? For the walls were largely barren, excepting some brilliant pieces of cloth, dresses and I do not know what else, hung against the plaster. No, that would have been too much. Under the increasing spell of anticipation/fear should I be discovered, I sat in my plastic car watching her rock slightly over a desk where an enormous textbook lay outstretched, and where she at last helpfully switched on a lamp when the sun had vacated the flat. I watched her yawn, stretch, stand, and pass briefly out of view then back again, now in the bedroom, where she sought a sweatshirt from a dresser, put this on; vanished. The bathroom? Soon, it could have been a few minutes only, out of the decibels of silence, among lit windows, in the domestic atmosphere of that time when children are welcomed home, suits are removed to be hung in closets, whole families are sitting down to dinner, I distinguished some strains of music. I crept up a set of cement stairs to the rear of the building; a gloomy dog fenced behind wire in the neighbouring yard eyed me but said nothing, replacing a heavy head on folded paws. There: there in the kitchen, engaged in slicing up aubergines and onions and preparing some variety of stir-fry, merely two or three metres from where I crouched breathless by a tall window pushed wide like a door. *There may be trouble ahead*, sang a suave male voice from the radio on a low table, to which Sophie's little feet began to tap, her tuneless voice to croon. *So while there's moonlight and music*—here, or at least I will say it was here, her back started to sway before the stove, her tiny hips rolling—then suddenly, all at once—*let's face the music*—she swerved toward the center of the room, facing me, with my heart instantly in my mouth, petrified but she was aflame with light, you see, while I invisible in shadow—then, lifting a leg in the air, *and dance!* she rocked backward in a solitary swoon, with no one to swing her in this old-fashioned dance-move, that was the thing, no Matthew which not I nor anyone in this world with all our words could do one stroke toward replacing. Yet: *Let's face the music and dance*. She turned back to the stove, and I to my car, and to the highway, and to the airport, and to the plane, and to New York, and to this jail, and to this moment in time and to all those unseen moments, unnamed and unknown in the future which has not been written for us.

After a protracted eight months in custody, briefly at the Manhattan Detention Complex and then at Rikers Island, Dr. Hans Mannheim finally chose to plead guilty to criminally negligent homicide, a Class E felony. The seven years of probation he was sentenced to were completed without incident; at his request I delayed publication until his rehabilitation and now withhold both his new name and that of the institution where he has joined the faculty.

Acknowledgments

I owe profound debts of gratitude to the following people: Binnie Kirshenbaum, who was the first to believe in this book and its best friend from the very start; Amanda Urban, without whose marvelously unstinting aid and insight nothing would have been possible; Susan Kamil and Noah Eaker at the Dial Press, the best editors a writer could dream up in her wildest fancies; YiLing Chen-Josephson and Nell Freudenberger, who read the manuscript with kind and clear eyes; and Andrés Colapinto, for services extraordinary that can never be repaid and are appreciated to the depths of my being. It's been a long road, brotha. I'd also like to thank my family; all of the Colapintos; Nora von Hagen and Herr Prof. Arne Blum; and Irene Cheng and Nikki Columbus, who taught me a great deal about friendship. The songs of Stephin Merritt sustained and delighted me during the writing of this book. In memoriam Carlo Martino, 1972–2003.

About the Author

Monica Ferrell's poems have appeared in the *New York Review of Books, Paris Review,* and other magazines, and her first collection, *Beasts for the Chase,* will be published in autumn 2008. A former "Discovery"/*The Nation* winner and Wallace Stegner Fellow at Stanford University, she lives in Brooklyn. This is her first novel.